It was an almost subliminal playing across her skin. It might well have brought another man to his feet in an instant, eyes wide, mouth agape, hands clenched, and, perhaps, a faint stirring of nauseous panic beginning to roil in the pit of his stomach at this sudden bit of Hollywood special effects turned real.

TK, though, did not react as another man might. Had he done so, he would have died in a street rumble in Chicago, or a Vietcong tunnel, or in an Iraqi bunker ... or on a sidewalk outside a crack house. He rose, yes, but slowly, and the vision continued. He saw the light in Ash's eyes then, much more light than any human being ought to have had, a light that spoke of years, of ages, of magic. . . .

STRANDS OF SUNLIGHT

by

Gael Baudino

A ROC BOOK

ROC
Published by the Penguin Group
Penguin Books USA Inc., 375 Hudson Street,
New York, New York 10014, U.S.A.
Penguin Books Ltd, 27 Wrights Lane,
London W8 5TZ, England
Penguin Books Australia Ltd, Ringwood,
Victoria, Australia
Penguin Books Canada Ltd, 10 Alcorn Avenue,
Toronto, Ontario, Canada M4V 3B2
Penguin Books (N.Z.) Ltd, 182–190 Wairau Road,
Auckland 10, New Zealand

Penguin Books Ltd, Registered Offices:
Harmondsworth, Middlesex, England

First published by Roc, an imprint of Dutton Signet,
a division of Penguin Books USA Inc.

First Printing, July, 1994
10 9 8 7 6 5 4 3 2 1

Copyright © Gael Baudino, 1994
All rights reserved

Roc REGISTERED TRADEMARK—MARCA REGISTRADA

Printed in the United States of America

Once again, for Mirya

"I will not let you go until you bless me."
—Jacob ben Isaac

ACKNOWLEDGMENTS

Believe me, I didn't make this entire mess by myself. I had help.

Ron Flanagan, my neighbor, came over one evening and gave me the skinny on surveying as a profession and as a business. He kept me from making an utter fool of myself in the TreeStar sections of this book, though I had to take a few liberties with the information he gave me. *Mea culpa*.

My dear friend and fellow Morris dancer, Dr. Dennis Barrett, explained to me the ins and outs of academic hierarchy and protocol while wondering what on earth Gael was up to now. Again, any inaccuracies in the descriptions are my fault, not his.

Mike "Gunner" Thompson, a friend on CompuServe, answered a last minute question about the potency of C-4 explosive, assuring me that two pounds would be sufficient to take out a house.

Mirya Rule, my mate, got me through another one. She put up with my tears and my whining, and she held me through innumerable nights while I thrashed, shook, and behaved like an idiot until exhaustion and tincture of valerian took over. I can't sufficiently express my gratitude to her: bare words on a printed page will, I hope, count for something, though I sincerely believe that flowers, expensive cars, and a Gates Learjet would be more appropriate.

On the receiving end of all this was Christopher Schelling, my editor. He approved without a moment's hesitation the original idea for this conclusion to the *Strands of Starlight* books, and in the course of several phone calls, very patiently listened to me while I described my latest bout of wrestling with my angel. Sometimes I think the angel won. Or maybe it wasn't an angel. Is it possible to wrestle with a myxomycete?

Those of you who have examined the corpus of writings on Christian Hermeticism will recognize something of the writings of Valentine Thomberg—the Unknown Friend—in the ravings of Terry Angel. I offer my apologies and regrets to this honorable man for having so brutally broken his butterfly upon my wheel. We all do the best we can, but after struggling through as much of *Meditations on the Tarot* as I could bear, I figured that *someone* had to say it.

To all of you who have struggled through this series of books, my deepest thanks. I hope that I have repaid you for your loyalty, and I am still infinitely grateful that anyone is willing to sit down and plod through what I write.

PART ONE

PLANH

CHAPTER 1

Sun.

It glared off the narrow band of asphalt that was Interstate 15, sending up heat shimmers that turned the distant mountains into the reflections of a troubled pond. But there was no water here in the Mojave Desert, only sun . . . and sand . . . and Joshua trees . . . and the ovenlike heat of a Toyota Celica that had possessed no air conditioning to speak of for the last ten years.

Sandy Joy shoved her sunglasses back on her head, rubbed at her good eye, wiped sweat out of her bad eye, and shifted her dripping back against the vinyl seat. The wind that blasted in through the open windows brought not a trace of coolness, and though she dropped her sunglasses into place and sucked at a can of cola grown warm with the unremitting heat, the liquid neither quenched her thirst nor eased the ache in her stomach. In fact, prompted by the reality of this journey—the sand, the scrub and trees, the road stretching off toward the mountains and then beyond into who-knew-what—the ache had redoubled, and the soft drink only gave her gut something about which to clench more tightly.

"I'll tell you, Little Sandy," she said to the doll that was seatbelted beside her, "you don't want to worry too much about what happens in Denver, because it sure can't be any worse than what we left in LA."

She glanced at the doll. Little Sandy's cloth face wore, as usual, an expression that lay midway between the winsome and the pathetic, but it seemed today to be touched with something akin to absurd confidence.

Sandy put her good eye back on the road. Little Sandy was confident. Well, that was to be expected: Little Sandy had Big Sandy to look out for her, and that was the way it was supposed to be. But Big Sandy had no one. That was, she supposed, the way it was supposed to be also; but how did one parent oneself when one's only role models were a mother who had committed suicide and a father who had—?

"That's enough," she said quickly. "In the name of the Goddess, that's enough."

But though she spoke the words solemnly, trying yet again to erect between herself and the past a barrier of the sacred and the numinous, her voice was tight, and another swig of warm cola did nothing to loosen it.

The Celica continued on, the road continued to rise to meet it. Joshua trees and scrub flicked by at half a hundred miles an hour, but the distances were such that, in the larger view, nothing changed. The same stretches of sand and waste unrolled to left and to right, and the same mountains—bleached and gray—shimmered in the distance. Sandy seemed to be getting nowhere.

As usual.

She frowned, grappled with the thought, tried to shove it away. But there it was, right outside her windshield: an emblem, symbolic as all hell, of her life.

Ladies and gentlemen, presented for your entertainment and delectation, an iconographic reification of symbological excellence. A summation, in short, of the puerile existence of one Sandy Joy, refugee from the lye-buckets and semen-stained cribs of the City of the Angels, dupe of her own hidden and unacknowledged optimism. Step right this way! Come inside, come inside!

And, indeed, the phantom barker (who, fittingly, spoke with the voice of her dead father) might well have been right. Twenty-five years old, and she had nothing to show for her life save blindness, a scarred face, and a personality that hobbled about like an amputee. This journey to Denver, she admitted, was quite possibly a grasping at a very thin straw ... and a waterlogged one at that.

See the drowning girl in action. See her struggle. See her writhe and wriggle as she swims like a ...

She drained the last of the cola, tossed the can onto the back seat. "Shaddup," she said aloud. "I'm over it."

The voice faded, and as though seeking a talisman to ward off its return, she reached back to the canvas instrument case that lay on the floor behind her seat. For a moment, she felt through layers of nylon and padding to the

slender contours of a small harp, then, still looking for
the charm, unzipped the wide pocket and withdrew a bundle of papers.

With her good eye flicking back and forth between the
road and the topmost letter, she sought the words that
could hold back the barker. She had read them often. She
had them memorized.

"... *pleased to inform you of your acceptance into the
Hands of Grace program. We at Kingsley College are
proud to be the facilitator of Professor Angel's innovative
work, and consider it to be an invaluable asset to the academic, religious, and medical communities. We look forward to your arrival ...*"

The letter was signed by the dean, Maxwell Delmari,
and two pages down was the letter from the financial aid
department about her fellowship. Then came the rudely-
typed article by Terry Angel himself and the correspondence she had received from him over the last two years.
Futility? No: she had been accepted at Kingsley, had been
given a fellowship, actually had the personal interest of
Terry Angel.

She put the papers away with a sense of satisfaction,
and she gave the harp a comradely squeeze. There was a
place for her at Kingsley. There was a place for her in the
Hands of Grace program. Terry Angel was going to teach
her the ancient secrets of the harp so that she could help
people. She might even be able to help herself.

She thought of the encouragement Terry had given her,
his cautions and stern warnings about making a full commitment to his program. *Commitment and authenticity,* he
had written, *are our armor against those in the academic
world who will try to discredit what we do. Our byword,
therefore, is research. Research, research, research!*

Yes, she was ready to commit. After twenty-five years,
she was ready to commit herself to anybody who showed
her the slightest consideration, ready to pledge herself to
anything that offered an end to the futility and the pain.
Terry had been willing to accept her, to make her a part
of the Hands of Grace, and at the thought of his
unlooked-for generosity, her eyes—blind and sighted
both—were suddenly too full of tears for her to continue
to drive.

She pulled off the highway, stopped, leaned her head against the steering wheel. She tried to forget about the past, to think instead about the letters and the encouragement, but the barker began to natter again, a needless and redundant reminder that the past was still with her, that the past was always with her, that no amount of wishing, fantasizing, therapy, or even the spells and ritual of modern Witchcraft would keep it away. It was just there: the irrefutable artifact of an incarnation gone wrong, that had, so far, stubbornly refused any effort to alter it in the slightest.

She pulled Little Sandy into her lap and held her, trying to find in the doll's soft body a sense of her own childhood self, trying to instill into it some feeling of safety and comfort.

"Oh, Goddess," she whispered. "I wish you could hold me like this."

But the arms of the Goddess lay in the future, at the end of a wretched life; and so, after a time, Sandy put the doll back into its seat, restarted the car, and continued across the desert. If she kept moving, she could make Saint George by nightfall, check into a motel, and find, in sleep, at least the end of this particular wretched day.

"Marsh? TK."

"Hey, dude." Marsh Blues covered the phone receiver with his free hand and smiled at the middle-aged woman who was sitting on the other side of his desk. "Hang on," he said. "This'll just take a minute."

He noticed her short nod, the slump to her shoulders. She was used to waiting. With an instinct that he still at times found unsettling, he had known from the moment she had shuffled into Buckland Employment that she had, in the course of her life, waited for everything. For a man. For marriage. For children. For children to grow up.

Now, the man and the children were gone, as was the insurance money. And she was still waiting.

Marsh felt the pang; but TK was talking, his chocolate voice turned metallic and compressed by the phone line. "Man, the guy in Operations done it to me again. I got to work tonight. I got to leave now."

Marsh made a small, impatient noise. "Again?"

A dark chuckle, darker than the voice. "Got me a

southern boy here, Marsh. Tells darky jokes by the coffee machine, but oh! how he is the open-minded one when it comes to working them."

"It's been every night this week, hasn't it, TK?"

"You got it, man. Every day, too. Been working double shifts. The money's good, but who cares when you're too tired to enjoy it?"

The woman across the desk had sunk down into the chair like a bag of flour, and Marsh had been examining her. Resigned. Resigned to waiting. Resigned to failing. TK was resigned, too. It was that way with most people. *Things happen,* they said, *it's just that way,* and the utter tragedy of it all was that the sentiment was accepted as valid currency everywhere. And here was Marsh Blues sitting in an employment agency thinking that he was going to change everything ... why, he ought to have his head examined.

Forever was a long time to see things happen ... just that way. Marsh tried not to think about forever. He failed. "OK," he said, thinking longingly of the slow, sexy notes that TK could draw out of a tenor sax, "I'll call the guys and cancel. They won't like it."

"Come on, man. I feel lousy enough. I got a cracker who wants me to quit, I been up all night, and my leg's hurting."

"That leg of yours again! Have you gone to the VA?"

"Yeah. They want me to pose for Desert Storm promo pix."

"Is that all?"

"Nothing much else they can do. Called *phantom limb syndrome.* Hurts like hell some days, but they have to start cutting my brain to get rid of it."

There were better ways. There *had* to be better ways. Ash had, after all, once cured leukemia, and had actually managed to heal Hadden of a gunshot wound. Self-conscious, rather shaken by the enormity of the experiences, she had never been able to do anything of the sort again, but, well, there had to be more of that somewhere. Maybe Natil knew something.

"Marsh?"

Maybe. But if she did, she was not talking about it. Marsh suddenly wondered—

"Marsh? You there?"

"Huh?" Coming out of his thoughts too quickly to keep them. "Uh, yeah." No music tonight. "Shit."

"No, man. Sheeee-it. Get it right. You want to play blues guitar, you got to get some color in you."

Marsh laughed. "OK. I admit it. I'm vanilla. But let us know how your schedule turns out. Maybe we can get together next week. We all miss the sax."

And, for a moment, from behind TK's habitual mask, a real face peeped out. "You don't think I do?"

"TK?" But TK had hung up. Marsh set the handset back in its cradle. It was just that way. It was just going to be that way. Forever.

It would not be so bad, he thought, had he some place he could go. It was not a question of a vacation, or an easy chair, or a warm bed in which he and Heather could hide in one another's arms. It was not a question even of the gatherings up at the Home, when they all, in one way or another, hid in one another's arms. It was . . .

He was not sure what it was, save that it seemed to be a longing both unspecified and unfulfilled, one that possessed him frequently, that, he guessed, possessed all the others who thought, with involuntary dismay, of forever.

He glanced across the big room. Two desks away, Wheat was talking to a shabby young man in overalls, her cornflower blue eyes big and sympathetic and filled with starlight. *It has to do with love,* she had said at a staff meeting long ago, and everyone, Marsh included, had fallen into stunned silence. *You have to look at the clients that come to you and love them, because they're people and they deserve it. You have to feel them, what they've been through, why they've come to you.*

No one had understood then. No one at the agency save Marsh, Ash, and Wheat herself understood now.

Love. That was it. And if it had to be forever, then it was going to be forever. And so Marsh turned back to the middle-aged woman—still waiting without a word of complaint, without a flicker of annoyance—and picked up her application form. "All right, ma'am," he said, "Sorry about the delay. There's an occasional wetware problem on this side of the desk."

She did not understand the joke. " 'S okay," she said. Her voice was barely a whisper.

"You've . . ." Marsh ran his eyes down the application.

It has to do with love. "You've been with a few other agencies, I see." *Forever.*

"Yeah," she said. "They said they couldn't help me."

Marsh looked at her, held her image in his thoughts the way he might have held an apple in his hand, allowed the starlight in his mind to wash over it. Yes, he loved her. He could not but love her. "We'll help you, ma'am. We've got this attitude problem around here: you see, at Buckland Employment, we do things right or we don't do them at all."

She nodded, looked unconvinced. Marsh knew that she had heard only the second half of the Buckland aphorism.

He grinned. "So we'll do it," he said, holding the woman, the starlight, and the love in balance. But words and balancings were easy. Trying to find an adequate job for someone who had no work history, no skills, and an abysmal attitude promised to be considerably more difficult.

"Can you?" The woman looked almost eager.

That was good. Eagerness was good. Marsh nodded. It would be difficult, but not impossible. And as for the work history and the skills ... well, Elves, as he had heard Natil say often, were known for being ingenious.

But, ingenious or not, it was always going to be like this. Despite the love, the work—and the sorrow—would go on and on. Forever. Elves were immortal: what would get them through?

Heather knew that Kelly was upset even before she walked into the day care center, and when she stepped through the door, she found her blond, blue-eyed daughter reading a book over by the west window, her face mirroring a sadness that seemed terribly out of place on features that had known but five summers.

And Kelly's teacher was beckoning.

Heather ignored the woman, went directly to Kelly, bent down and put her arms about her. "Hi, sweetheart," she said. "Ready to go home?"

Kelly looked up with large eyes—large, sad eyes—and nodded solemnly.

In the glance that passed between them were wordless thoughts that flitted through Heather's mind with the softness of dove wings. "Bad day?"

Kelly shook her head. "Not bad," she said slowly. Her voice was quiet, steady, even, without a trace of childish lisp. "Just . . . sad I guess."

Kelly's teacher was still beckoning. "Hang on, love," said Heather, giving her daughter a hug. "I have to talk to Susie."

"She's very sad."

"I know," said Heather. "They're all sad. You're sad, too."

Kelly nodded, went back to her book. Heather glanced at it. *The Jungle Book?* At five years old? Well, that was Kelly.

Susie took Heather into the corridor. "Kelly is a wonderful child, Ms. Blues," she said. There was a veneer in her voice, though Heather doubted that a human being would have noticed it. "It's so wonderful to have her with us."

"But . . ." said Heather.

Susie blinked. "But what?"

"My question exactly. Kelly is a wonderful child, *but* . . ." Heather tipped her head to one side inquiringly. It was an infantile habit, one she thought she had broken years ago, one that had, for some reason, returned with the awakening of the ancient blood in her veins.

Oh, well: Wheat always cried when she listened to old Judy Collins records, and Tristan doted on his wild birds and animals, and Dell and Fox hugged trees. They all had their excesses. Were they supposed to be perfect as well as immortal?

Heather winced inwardly. She was still not sure why the thought hurt so much.

"Uh," said Susie, "well, now that you mention it . . . she's been . . . uh . . . disruptive."

Heather stared at her. "Disruptive? *Kelly?*"

Susie waved her hands. "Not exactly disruptive, Ms. Blues. I mean, not in an acting-up way . . ." Smiling a little crookedly, she fell silent and nodded to a mother who was just then racing up the hallway. High heels clicking on the linoleum, the woman dived into the classroom and came up with a child like a heron pulling a fish out of a lake.

"See you tomorrow, Ms. Walters," said Susie.

"Right." And the high heels clicked away.

Through the open door, Heather could see Kelly. Still reading. Still sad. "You were saying."

"Well, you see ..." Sally had caught a loose strand of her red hair and was twirling it around and around her finger as though it were a weed she were about to uproot. "... like the kids were all supposed to bring in poems today to read."

Heather nodded. "Kelly had a very nice poem. It was by Dylan Thomas."

"Yeah. Well, Dylan Thomas—whoever he is—isn't someone I'd recite to five- and six-year-olds."

Heather could not suppress a look of annoyance. "It certainly isn't as though Kelly brought in *Do Not Go Gentle Into That Good Night* or something like that. She learned *Poem in October.* It's lovely. Did you actually listen to it?"

Susie was still twisting the hair. "Yes, yes, it was very nice ... but ..."

Yes, yes, thought Heather, *but he's sad. It's all sad. And she didn't understand a word of the poem, and she doesn't understand a thing about Kelly ... which isn't surprising.*

Susie, she supposed, was doing her best. Day care at minimum wage was probably all that she had been able to find, and, in these days of recession, she was probably fortunate to have it. But Heather could not help but sense (her instincts reaching out to examine Kelly's teacher with a compassion that was, nonetheless, impotent) that Susie had hoped for more out of life than day care at minimum wage. With the fleeting awareness of old powers long faded, Heather saw wings, blue skies. Susie had wanted to fly. She had wanted to be a pilot. But the money (it was the old story) was not there, and there had been a child, and the father was not paying any support.

"... but the other kids didn't know what to make of it ..."

But Susie, Heather reflected, at least had a job. There were dozens of men up at the shelter who had none, who would have given much for a chance at what Susie had.

She passed a hand across her forehead. And dozens more who would have given much for a ham sandwich and a place to sleep that was more secure than a cardboard box.

"... and it made a lot of them feel bad."

Caught between anger, pity, and sorrow for all that she could not do, Heather looked up, met Susie's eyes. Wings. Blue skies. And here she was. "Bad?"

"Well, you know, like ... stupid."

A human mother, perhaps, might have thrown the stupidity back into Susie's face. But Heather was not a human mother. "Susie," she said slowly, softly, "Kelly brought that poem in as an act of love, and I'm sure that the other children appreciated it as such ... as much as they could. Someday, they might remember that poem, and someday, one of them might become a poet, or ... or maybe a holy person or something like that ... because they heard Kelly recite *Poem in October* today."

Susie's expression had turned perplexed. Love? Holy person? What did all that have to do with it? Her finger twisted the lock of hair all the faster. "Well," she said, "I understand ..."

Futility. Impotence. *You don't understand at all.*

"... but ... well ... like ... could you make sure that Kelly acts just a little bit more normal?"

Heather transfixed her with a look, wondering whether Susie might be one of those few humans who could see the flash of starlight in an elven eye. But no, Susie only stared back without comprehension.

"I'm sorry," said Heather. "I don't know what normal is."

And, wearing the uniform of normalcy—heels, skirt, silk blouse, conservative jacket—Heather turned and re-entered the classroom. It was a quarter to six: the sun was westering, but the sky had clouded over, and rain was coming down. Kelly had put her book aside and was watching the falling drops, but she looked up at Heather's approach and smiled as her mother scooped her up in her arms.

"She's sad, isn't she?" said Kelly. Her smile turned shadowed, and there was a glistening of something more than starlight in her eyes.

"Yes." Heather's whisper was fierce with both a mother's love for her child and an elven love—no matter how senseless—for all. "Yes, honey. She's sad."

But she was thinking about day care, and about the future. This was not the first time that Kelly's differences had discomfited her teachers, nor would it be the last. She could, she supposed, quit her job with the state, stay home, and shield her daughter from such things. But next year there would be school, and then the years ahead stretched off beyond that, through school and into . . . forever.

She could not shield Kelly forever. And, in any case, Elves were not supposed to hide from the world: they were supposed to work within it, to help and heal.

"Why?" A huskiness had crept into Kelly's voice.

Heather bent her head until their foreheads touched. "That's just the way it is in this place, Elfling," she whispered.

"Can we go see Natil?"

"We'll be going up to the Home tomorrow night. Everyone will be there."

Kelly nodded. "I want to hear Natil play the harp."

"I'm sure she'll play the harp tomorrow night. And sing, too."

"I want to play the harp like that someday."

Heather nodded as she carried Kelly out to the car. "It takes time," she said. "There is time."

Yes, there was time. Time for everything. But what would get them through all that time?

She buckled Kelly into her seat, slid behind the wheel. The streets of Denver suddenly looked alien, strange. *Dear God,* she thought, *this will go on* forever*! What will get us through*?

But as she pulled out of the lot, she could not but wonder whether the God she had known all her life heard the prayers of Elves . . . or cared.

CHAPTER 2

Natil was planting marigolds.

The freshly-tilled flower beds swept in wide, semicircular arcs to either side of the entrance to Aylesberg Hall, and this double row of marigolds would be but the first stroke of color in them. Natil was a careful groundskeeper, frugal and imaginative both, and she had planned for the beds a fantasy of golds and reds and blues and whites that would both contrast with and complement the pedestrian nature of the large brick building known to all the students of Kingsley College as the Pink Palace.

Down on her knees, her long hair pulled back in a single braid and her head covered with a floppy straw hat, she worked her way along the row—scooping holes with a trowel, placing flowers, packing the warm, heavy earth about their roots—her face damp not with sweat (though the day was indeed warm, and growing warmer) but with the rising moisture of the soil. Even now, at the Summer Solstice, the earth was still quite sodden with the heavy rains of an unseasonably wet June, and Natil knew with the instincts of one who had seen weather patterns of various kinds for four and a half billion years that more rain was on the way. She had, in fact, delayed planting until now for fear that rototilled flower beds would, with another downpour, quickly turn into a sea of mud; but the summer session was going to start next week, and the administrators of the college wanted the campus to look attractive when the students arrived. Rain or no rain, therefore, Natil and her crew were putting in flowers.

The dark brown smell of turned earth was about her, and she smiled as she worked, still a little embarrassed by her temerity: it had been Talla who had been the gardener, who had not only brought human infants into the world but had also coaxed the buds of Malvern Forest into a chorus of spring color. Natil's considered opinion was that she herself had not a tenth of Talla's skill, but, then, Talla was gone. They were all gone: Natil would have to fill in as best she could.

"Boss?"

She pushed back her hat and looked up at the stocky man standing beside her. "Carlos?"

His dark face was somber, had been so, in fact, all week. It was a change for Carlos, who usually bubbled and joked, switching between Spanish and English in accordance with the demands of his humor. His humor, though, was gone now. Natil had wondered about the grief that she had been seeing in the man since Monday, and had instinctively wanted to help; but this was America. This was 1991. People kept their pains to themselves, resented, in fact, the prying of others. The wisps of sorrow that she saw among her inner stars would therefore have to remain, for now, unexplained, and elven instinct would remain unfulfilled.

"It's lunchtime, boss," Carlos continued. "Could I use the telephone in the office? I have to call my sister."

"Lunchtime? Oh, dear, it seems to have gotten away from me again." Natil smiled. Because it was her nature. Because she hoped to cheer Carlos. "Of course you may use the telephone. Thank you for asking, but you know that I have never made any rules about such things."

Unaffected by her smile, he shrugged, shifted. "Now's not a time when I want to get into trouble." He started to turn away, but then he stopped and turned back. "You take the bus home alone, don't you, boss?"

"I do most evenings," Natil replied. "West. Out I-70."

Carlos had pulled off his hat, and Natil noticed that his fingers were clenched on the brim as though he would have liked to have ripped it in two. "You be careful, boss. It's not a good world out there."

Elven instinct won out. "Carlos, what happened?"

He shook his head and walked away quickly in the direction of the groundskeeper's shed.

She stood up, looking after him as she brushed dirt from the knees of her jeans. This was America. This was 1991. He was a man, and she, to outward appearance, was a woman. He was an employee, she was his supervisor. Instinct or not, some things were not allowed.

Sorrow was painful enough. Sorrow denied even a chance of healing was a deeper ache. She had to do something. She could do nothing. That was the way it was in this place.

Under the pretense of checking on the progress of the planting, she wandered over to the rest of her crew. "It looks very good," she said in Spanish. "Carlos tells me that it is lunch time. You gentlemen should eat."

She saw their smiles. Whether it was because she was a woman who was willing to grub in the dirt like a navvy, or because she was so invariably polite to those she supervised, or because her Spanish was essentially flawless—save for a persistent trace of an odd little accent that colored even her English—they always smiled when she spoke to them. But perhaps for one or all of those same reasons, they also always listened to her and had never hinted that they were anything less than perfectly willing to work at her side.

Now they put down their tools and rose; but as they left, Natil beckoned to her assistant. "Raoul, after lunch, could you make some telephone calls and see if there is a recycler out there who will take these plastic flats? We are going to have a great many of them by the time we are through with the beds, and I cannot find a recycling number on them anywhere."

"I'll do that, Miss Summerson."

"Thank you." But her expression must have told him that she wanted to ask something else. He waited, and she finally spoke. "What happened to Carlos?"

A shadow crossed Raoul's face. "That bank shooting last Sunday? Those four dead guards?"

"I saw the paper."

"One of them was Carlos' cousin." Raoul shrugged, his dark eyes expressionless . . . and all the more eloquent for that.

Natil nodded slowly. She had read about it in the paper. She had read also about the child who had been beaten to death by her father. And about the despairing man who had killed his wife, then himself. And about the youth who had been gunned down because he had been wearing a baseball cap of the wrong color.

That was the way it was in this place.

"I understand," she said, though all that she really understood was the sorrow and the pain and her inability to alleviate either. "Thank you, Raoul. Please let Carlos know that if there is anything I can do . . ." But there was nothing she could do, and she knew it. ". . . he has but to ask."

Raoul nodded. "What did he say to you, Miss Summerson?"

Natil shoved her hat back until it slid off her head and dangled by its chin strap. The sun was warm on her dark, silver-streaked hair. "He said that it is not a good world."

"Yes, that's true." Raoul looked up at the sky. Clouds were building up above the Rocky Mountains. Rain coming. More rain. Maybe hail. "We have to wait for the good one. But it helps to know that the good one's there, doesn't it?"

Natil smiled politely, nodded, turned to go back to work. "You'd better eat, too, Miss Summerson."

Carlos had sorrows that he wished to keep private, and so did Natil. "Thank you, Raoul, but I think I will finish this row first."

Raoul nodded and departed. Natil knelt down among her marigolds, bent her head, considered Carlos, the Elves, the world into which she had come.

Somehow, centuries and millennia ago, it had all seemed more manageable. Perhaps it had been simply a matter of limited knowledge, but she doubted it. The patterns of reality had always held a full measure of tragedy at all levels, personal to global, and back when the Elves could actually look into the intricate movements of the Dance that was everything and sort potential and probability until all of existence lay open to them, they had seen it all.

Perhaps that was why they had faded: they had seen too much, they had seen the futility. The time had been wrong, the world had been wrong, but the wrongness had proceeded not just from the encroachments of human beings, not simply from the cut forests, the polluted streams, the beings of fur and scale and feather who had been or would be driven to extinction as if in prophesy of the eventual fate of Immortals; it was also that the cutting, the pollution, the extinctions had all been so unstoppable, so inevitable. The Elves, impelled by their nature to help and heal, had been, in the end, unable to do either.

And they had seen, and they had known. And, with the exception of Natil herself, they had faded.

Perhaps that was it. Perhaps that explained it. But now, after five hundred years of absence, the Elves were back, the old blood stirring in a scattering of people here in Denver, awakening and transforming them. And though, in accordance with the age and its customs, their lives were very different from what Natil had known in the past, they still tried to help, to heal, to look at pain and sorrow and do . . . something.

Do something? Do what? Natil saw the limitations and impotence every day, and she knew that the newly-awakened Elves of Denver saw them too. It was a wearisome, frustrating task to which their natures dedicated them, one that stretched off into an infinite future, a chore without comfort, without respite, without satisfaction or completion. And even five-year-old Kelly was beginning to feel the sadness of continuing futility.

It was as hopeless as before. And yet they were all here, come back against all hope or belief. But how much disappointment could they bear? And how were they supposed to bear it when it would never end? Had they returned only to fade again?

What gets us through? She whispered the words as she had whispered them long ago, as she had whispered them often since she had come to Colorado. But she knew exactly what would get them through. Indeed, she was in Denver, in 1991, because she knew, because she, alone now among all the Elves, had once seen it, had once participated in it.

Once. Once, but no more. The vision of the Lady, *Elthia,* the starlit, nurturing wonder of elven existence, remained apart, elusive, ungrasped not only by the those whose blood had newly awakened, but also by Natil herself. But even had Natil still possessed that perfect link with immanent divinity, she could think of no way in which she could have communicated it to her people. In any case, she could not help but believe that revealing its existence to those who needed it—but who could not have it—would, under the circumstances, only deepen their sorrow.

The problem seemed insoluble, seemed, in fact, the stuff of despair. Natil, though, would not despair. Having despaired once, having had her hope restored by unutterable grace, she would not give up again. There was a way back to the Lady. There was a door back to vision and elven mystery. She believed it. She felt it. She knew it.

Darkness roiled in the west, caught her eye, and she looked off toward the mountains. Another afternoon of rain was on its way. She sighed. Bad timing: she was as poor a gardener as she was a teacher.

Bending, she picked up another marigold and put it in the earth. One step at a time. And perhaps one of these days she would find out what the steps were.

From a bed of ratty towels in a corner of a small apartment two miles from where the steel and glass towers of downtown Denver pointed at the sullen sky, a half-feral Yorkshire terrier started up snarling, snapping in blind fear at the burst of ringing from the telephone, and the urgent sound propelled TK Winters up out of dreams that he did not want to remember. He grabbed the K-Bar beside his bed and slashed out blindly at the face (Iraqi or Vietnamese, he was not sure) that was coming toward him, and the knife hit the telephone and sent it clattering to the floor. TK shook off the dreams, groped for the receiver. His hands were shaking.

"Shut up, Rags," he shouted at the dog. "I can't hear this dude if you don't shut up." Even as fuzzy-brained as he was, he knew who was on the other end of the connection, knew also what he wanted. Rags might well have had the right idea. "Rags, dammit, shut up."

Ears flat back, eyes narrowed, teeth bared, the tiny terrier stopped barking and confined himself to snarls and growls, pacing back and forth along the wall as though it wanted to kill something. TK's face creased into as much of a smile as he ever allowed himself. *That makes two of us.*

He set the knife aside, sat up, put the handset to his ear. "Yeah," he said.

"Winters?" said a voice with a honey-thick drawl, "I got a no-show at the Kaiser Center. Downtown. You need to fill it."

Just as he had expected. "Come on, man," said TK. "I just got to sleep."

"You've been off-duty for sixteen hours. You've had plenty of time for sleep."

TK had, in fact, just gotten off five hours before, after

an all night shift, but Hansen, the operations manager, kept such notoriously bad records that the true number of TK's work hours would not be known until the poor, harried timekeeper at the security company sorted through the scraps of paper, backs of envelopes, and sticky-pad notes that were as much of an account of the week's activities as Hansen ever left. If he left any at all.

"Man," said TK, "I'm tired."

"Y'all refusing an assignment?"

No, you motherfucker, because you'd like that too much. TK's eye fell on the M16 that stood in the corner within easy reach. Sometimes he wished—

"No," he said. "I ain't."

"Be up at Franklin and 20th in half an hour," said Hansen. "You know what to do."

TK's grip tightened on the handset. *Yassuh, yassuh, I know 'xactly what to do. I'm gonna take this M16 and put five rounds rapid right up your cracker ass. It was good enough for that lieutenant that kept riding the brothers, and it sure as hell be good enough for you.*

But the connection had been broken. TK tossed the handset back into its cradle. Swinging one and one half legs over the edge of the bed, he bent down to the floor to retrieve the plastic apparatus that allowed him to walk. As he fastened it on, he noticed that Rags was watching him balefully. A sound made of equal parts pleading whine and threatening snarl was coming from the tiny throat.

"Come on," said TK. "I feed you when I feed me. Don't give me no bullshit."

Rags only sneezed once and growled again. Growls, snarls, nips, bared teeth: as much affection as TK had ever gotten out of the dog in the three months since he had taken him in. Another man, disgusted with such a poor showing of gratitude, might have put him right back out onto the street, but not TK. Street wise and survival oriented, even after frostbite, near starvation, and (apparently) a previous owner more interested in a whipping boy than a pet, Rags reminded TK too much of himself.

Well, could've been worse, I guess. Bess only left me. I could've wound up gunned down like that dude in Detroit . . .

She had been gone when he had returned after having

been discharged from the hospital in Georgia. She had taken their newborn daughter, taken everything. The apartment, untenanted since January, had been rented to someone else.

TK stretched out his left leg, wincing, trying to ease the pain that, now that he was fully awake, was building quickly. It was a habitual action, habitually useless, for the muscles he was attempting to flex had not existed for months. Yet he persisted, for though his eyes told him that there was nothing below his knee save plastic, his brain persisted in recreating the feelings of flesh and blood, and the phantom limb burned like cold fire.

He whacked at the prosthesis a few times with a large hand as though to wake up long-vanished nerves, but the pain continued. He supposed that he was lucky he could get to sleep. There were a few old guys up at the VA who were not so fortunate, and years of semi-addiction to pain killers had left them seamed and pallid, like bean plants forced to grow in darkness.

While Rags growled and uttered an occasional bark, TK put his weight on his legs of flesh and plastic, crossed to the window of the apartment, and pushed aside the rude drape that he had made out of an old tablecloth. Afternoon. The sky had clouded up again, and it looked like another evening of rain, if not hail. But no rain was falling yet. There was only a sense of tension in the air, an oppression that descended from the soft, shrouded sun like an invisible fog. Voices carried unnaturally. Sounds—the snapping of twigs, the chirping of unenthusiastic birds—seemed magnified. There would be thunder soon.

The skies had been much like this when he had been pulled off his Patriot radar screen and ordered into a Humvee, the clouds pressing down like a leaden thumb as he had been driven at fifty miles an hour across Saudi desert and Kuwaiti desert, driven to a maze of wadis, gullies, pits, escarpments, and jagged outcroppings. There was a deep bunker ahead, the lieutenant from the intelligence unit explained, and its entrance dropped almost straight down, like a mine shaft, and Specialist Theodore Karlington Winters—it was in his records—had experience in the tunnels of Cu Chi Province, Republic of South Vietnam.

There was an Iraqi officer in the bunker. Someone valuable. Specialist Theodore Karlington Winters was supposed to get him out. Specialist Theodore Karlington Winters was not supposed to ask questions. The cease fire had taken effect twenty-four hours before (the coalition mech units fuming as the Republican Guard gave them the collective finger and retreated to the north for a little Kurd bashing), and twenty years after the claustrophobic and subterranean fighting in Cu Chi had shattered what nerves he had left after endless search and destroy patrols, Specialist Theodore Karlington Winters was supposed to get a man out of a bunker.

Yeah . . . and lose my fucking leg doing it.

Below, in the street, up near the corner, a Jeep Cherokee was pulling up to the curb, and TK, from his second floor window, could just see the pale blur of wadded bills lying on the seat beside the driver. A hand covered the wad just as a young man with an LA Raiders cap sauntered out of a house a few doors down the way, his hands in the pockets of his low-slung pants. TK did not hear the exchange—perhaps, by now, there was nothing to hear, perhaps it had all become wordless—but he saw the bills pass from the driver to the Raiders fan, and he saw something else pass from the Raiders fan to the driver. And then the Cherokee pulled away, and the young man stood alone at the curb, rocking back and forth on his heels, his hands thrust deep into his pockets.

TK let the curtain fall, hating Hansen, hating the lieutenant from intelligence, hating the piece of plastic that throbbed like living flesh but felt nothing beyond pain, hating the inhabitants of the crack house who did a thriving business in genocide and rationalized it all as a means of getting ahead.

He turned away from the window. There were children playing in the fenced yard next to the crack house: two little girls with faces the color of copper and hair carefully arranged in falls of braids and bright beads. They had seen it all. Everyone in the neighborhood had seen it all: it was always there to be seen. But there seemed to be little that anyone could do about it. The cops would not go in without a warrant, and oddly enough (TK smiled as much as he ever did) it was very hard to find a cop or a warrant when you needed one.

A dull rumble of thunder in the distance: the oppression

of the impending storm was like the heat of a furnace as TK went into the corner of the apartment that served as his kitchen. There, from a battered metal cabinet, he produced a box of breakfast cereal, and from a tiny cube of a refrigerator, milk that had not quite gone sour. Rags prowled, now and then snapping at him, but TK was agile even on his artificial leg, and the terrier's teeth met nothing more yielding than plastic.

"Don't give me no shit," said TK. "I feed you. You forgetting who's in charge here."

But Rags looked convinced of neither the availability of food nor the local chain of command until his master pulled out a sack of dog food, filled a bowl, and put it in front of him. Even then, the yorkie snapped at TK's hand . . . and received a cuff in return that sent the four-pound dog tumbling head over heels.

"Eat, you dumb motherfucker," said TK. Again, the smile that was not much of a smile.

Rags staggered to his feet, advanced, plunged his teeth into the kibble. TK filled a chipped soup bowl with cereal and milk, glancing at the clock as he poured. He would have to eat fast if he expected to make it to the Kaiser Center in time.

He shoveled food into his mouth, mentally looking ahead, planning his movements. Eat breakfast, shave, get dressed, call Marsh and let him know that (yes, again) practice would have to be scrubbed. No time for coffee: he would grab some in the guard shack at the Center.

Looking ahead. It was like the tunnels in Nam, or the radar screens in Dhahran, or, at times, the streets of Denver: looking ahead, looking . . . to see the thing that might kill you.

He told himself that there was nothing that was going to kill him on his way to the Kaiser Center, but the K-Bar remained a reassuring presence on the table by the bed, and the loaded and very illegal M16 stood ready in the corner. It had been the tunnels in Vietnam that had put them where they were, a tunnel in Iraq that had brought them back after Bess had made them go away for a time. Now there was no one to make them go away again.

And, as though to belie his assurances to himself that the trip from his breakfast table to his job would be made in perfect safety—save, perhaps, for the attacks of a feral terrier—a screech of tires and a thump brought him to his feet and took him to the window.

He tore the curtain aside. A dark Coupe de Ville had rounded the corner, and the Raiders fan with deep pockets had turned to run back into the house. The driver, though, was already in the process of cutting off the fan's retreat by pulling the big car directly up onto the weed infested lawn between him and the door.

Blocked by the car, the fan vaulted the fence that surrounded the yard where the children were playing. But now the Coupe de Ville's windows had slid down, and the muzzle of an automatic rifle had emerged.

TK saw it coming. Not just the shooting. He saw *more*. He had seen it in the Nam when a girl no older than those upon whom the Raiders fan was advancing had suddenly produced a satchel charge and jumped into a loaded personnel carrier. He had seen it in an Iraqi tunnel when a young man half out of his mind with fear and hashish had dived straight for him with a fragmentation grenade, ignoring the slugs from the .45 that were smacking into his chest like so many blows from a wrecking bar.

And, as before, seeing, knowing the inevitable, he could do nothing. No shout would avert what was coming. No blind run toward the children or the young man would accomplish anything. As had been the case when the child had leaped into the truck, as had been the case when the panicked Iraqi had dived toward him, TK knew himself to be helpless.

Now the young man in the Raiders cap scrambled for the children, and just as the rifle spat out a spray of slugs, he caught up the bigger of the two and held her up in front of him while she shrieked—first with surprise and fear, and then with the impact of the nine-millimeter bullets that ended her cries forever.

The Coupe de Ville pulled back out onto the street with a squeal of rubber and left dark marks on the dark asphalt as it sped off. The young man dropped the remains of the child and bolted between the houses, making for the alley.

Silence. Terrible silence. And then a woman began to scream.

CHAPTER 3

On Friday, Natil stayed late at the college, taking care of paperwork in her tiny office in the groundskeeper's shed. Rain was falling hard, drumming on the roof, and then, near six-thirty, the dark sky darkened even more, and the drumming turned into a dinning rattle for several minutes. Hail.

Going over the records of the cost of the marigolds, the columbines, the snapdragons and violas and pansies that she and her crew had just planted—that were now being cut to ribbons by bullets of ice—Natil sighed. She had delayed as long as she could, and it had accomplished nothing. But there was little she could do now. Tomorrow, she supposed, she could look over what was left of the beds, and on Monday, she and her crew could begin repairs.

She totaled figures, checked time sheets, and signed her name at the bottom of the forms, smiling fondly as her hand guided the ball point pen in even, half-uncial letters: *Natil Summerson*. Summerson. Heather Blues had come up with that. She had used her supervisory position at the Colorado Vital Records Bureau to fabricate an identity and a birth certificate for Natil, but, nervous and frightened at the technical felony she had been committing, she had gone completely blank when the computer had queried her for a last name. After what had seemed to her to be an eternity of dithering, Heather—who had just finished re-reading her favorite Dickens novel—had impulsively named her after Esther, the sweet, nurturing narrator of *Bleak House*.

Natil stacked the papers, clipped them together, dropped them into the basket on the corner of her desk. Nurturing. That was it. She was here to nurture. And so far she had done a wretched job of it.

Time, she thought. *It takes time. There is time.* But she knew that it also took tools, and though when it came to planting flowers, cutting lawns, and building berms, she had tools a-plenty, she found her hands empty when faced with the task of revealing to the Elves of Denver the reality and the immanence of *Elthia Calasiuove.*

A rumble of an engine, a hiss of tires on the wet parking lot. Natil rose and peered through the window and the falling water. A red-and-white Bronco was pulling into a space close to the door, and there was a flutter of waves from within it.

Natil waved back, pulled on her raincoat, locked up. When she had climbed into the truck and buckled her seat belt, though, she noticed that despite the cheerful waves she had seen, Lauri's eyes were puffy and red from crying, and Bright was huddled in the back seat as though she had been beaten.

"Sorry we're late." Lauri's voice half broke. "We got . . . tied up at the Center."

The starlight they all shared was but a shadow of the deep intimacy of the Firstborn. Nevertheless, though Natil could not read the events of the past, she could sense the emotions of the present. "What happened?"

Lauri shut her eyes, shook her head. "It's a rotten world. The scenery's great. The people are fucked."

"Lauri . . . what happened?"

"We . . ." Lauri took a deep breath. "You know I've been working the hot line at the Gay and Lesbian Center most evenings."

"I know." Working hot lines, volunteering at homeless shelters and safe houses, peer counseling: thus did the modern Elves attempt to fulfill their instincts.

"Well, we went up there to pick up some fliers for the Kay Gardener concert." Lauri was looking straight ahead through the rain-spattered windshield. "They called me into the office. There was someone on the line who was trying to find me. Little baby dyke who needed help. Cute kid, I guess: I never actually met her. But she'd called in when I was on one evening, and I helped her come out, held her hand, gave her references, places to go for help, people to see . . . and things to watch out for. I guess she kinda liked me. She'd call and ask for me when she ran into trouble." Lauri lifted her arm, blotted at her eyes with a sleeve. "That's what we're here for, isn't it?" For a moment, she stared out at the rain, then, as though with an effort, she released the parking brake and started across the parking lot.

"It is so," said Natil.

"Well, I hadn't heard from her in a while, but apparently everything had blown up for her. She called the Community Center, and I happened to be there." She waited silently for a gap in the traffic, pulled out onto the street, headed for the freeway. "It always works out that way, doesn't it?"

"Everything that happens, happens as it should."

Lauri's eyes narrowed as though in pain. "I hope so."

For some time, she drove in silence. She merged onto I-70 westbound.

"Bright," she said suddenly, "don't get messed up in this business. There's a bunch of sharks out there. It's no better than with the straights. Worse, I think."

Bright was young and pretty, so much so that her attempt to conceal her attractiveness by dressing mannishly had just the opposite effect. For a moment, she was silent, solemn. Then: "And what about you, Lauri?"

"I'll be all right."

Bright's voice was gentle. "You've got a heart like butter and you know it."

In the gleam of oncoming headlights, Lauri's eyes were troubled pools. "Bright, you can't fix my heart. You're not gay. Don't mess yourself up like that. I'll be all right."

"Lauri." Natil put a hand on her shoulder. "Tell me."

Lauri glanced at Natil. Natil met her grief with starlight. Elves, all of them. Elves taking care of one another, lightening for one another the burden of immortality, the burden of compassion. "Well, she'd gotten herself pretty messed up. She'd come out, and her family had tossed her. Threw her out. Catholic girl: her Church didn't want anything to do with her, and some idiot priest told her that her God didn't either. She believed them. She was eighteen, and she couldn't quite figure out how to make it on her own, so she got involved with . . ."

Lauri's hands tightened on the steering wheel.

"I know who it was," she said. "Hangs around bookstores and all the discussion groups, wants to get her fin-

gers into every little teen-age pussy that comes along.
Used her, threw her away. The baby-dyke was out on the
street with the clothes on her back and no place to go.
Completely messed up, and a broken heart on top of it.
She was . . ."

Lauri held the truck dead center in the freeway lane,
staring fixedly.

"The stars, Lauri," said Natil. "Find your stars."

Lauri tried to hold her voice as steady as the truck.
"She'd just overdosed. She wouldn't tell me where she
was. She just wanted to say good-bye."

Natil felt her sorrow like a wave. All the starlight in
the world, she knew, could not help. "And—?"

"So she said good-bye. I did what I was there to do. I
couldn't hold her hand while she died, so I held the
phone."

In the back seat, Bright was sobbing.

"We tried to trace the call, we called the cops." Lauri
made the transition from I-70 to Highway 6, continued
west. The mountains began to enfold them. Clear Creek
foamed at the side of the road. "Couldn't trace it. But the
cops wanted a statement. They took their time coming for
it. So we were late."

"Oh, Lauri . . ."

"It's what we're here for, isn't it? To help people?"
Lauri sighed. The highway—dark, rainy—stretched off
into the distance. "What a rotten job."

And Natil remembered Omelda, and she remembered
Charity, and she remembered many others: the hope, the
trust . . . the failure. But failure was inevitable. This was,
after all, the world of human beings. "We cannot save everyone," she said, and her voice was barely audible over
the drumming of the rain and the hissing of the tires on
the wet asphalt. "We can try, but some do not want to be
saved, and some do not care whether they are saved or
not. Some are beyond saving, and we can only comfort
them as they leave us."

Tears were running down Lauri's face.

"As you did tonight, Lauri."

Bright spoke softly from the back seat. "You have to
do one thing at a time. It's like I tell the girls at the safe
house. If you try to concentrate on everything, you just
get overwhelmed. So you just do one thing at a time."

"But it's not getting any better," said Lauri. "It's not gonna *get* any better." She bit her lip to stifle her tears. "Was it always this way, Natil?"

Natil could not meet her eyes, could not meet what she saw in them. Only *Elthia* could meet that bleakness, that hollowness, and fill it with something that was beyond love. And *Elthia* was ... was ...

Natil did not know where She was.

"We ... saw many things that made us grieve," she said.

Lauri passed a hand over her face. "I'm sorry, Natil. You gotta cut me some slack. I don't know what the hell I'm doing. I'm ashamed that you had to wait around so long just to meet people like me." She shook her head. "Five hundred years. Jeez."

Natil looked away. She had never told Lauri or the other Elves that, in a blinding instant of grace, she had stepped directly from Renaissance Adria to modern Colorado, for to do so would have required that she explain the source of that grace, and that, in turn, would have required explaining about the Lady. And she could not explain.

But Lauri needed *Elthia* right now. The kind of pain she was experiencing was the entire reason for that immanent, comforting vision. But the vision was gone, and Natil did not know how to bring it back.

She took Lauri's hand. "There is no blame in being what you are," she said. "There is no blame in feeling, or in sorrow." Helping and healing: they could hardly help and heal one another—how, then, were they supposed to take care of the entire world? "And do not worry about slack. You have all made me very welcome, and my only sorrow is that I cannot ... repay you all as I would wish."

Lauri and Bright, she knew, heard only the courtesy in her words. They did not know the misery that lay beneath them.

A bright green sign heralded the return of I-70. Lauri checked her watch. "Elvenhome coming up," she said. "I'll tell you: I'm ready."

Glenwood Springs came up out of the rain like a handful of stars. The mountains were lost in the darkness and cloud, but Sandy knew that they were there. The mountains, then, had not been unreachable: she had reached them—first the Sierras, then the Rockies—had disproved the mocking voice of the past. Tomorrow, she would reach Denver.

Tired and aching after a second day of continuous driving, she pulled into a TraveLodge parking lot and checked into a room. Later, much later, when the restaurant was almost deserted, when there were fewer people, less of a chance someone might see the scars on her face, the frightened hunch to her shoulders, or simply the wrongness of her existence, she went down to dinner and stammered out her order to a waitress who seemed uninterested in her past, her present, or her fears. She ate quickly, signed her room number on the check, and ran back upstairs to put a locked door between herself and the world.

But she did not go to bed. No. Today was the Solstice. Tired though she was, she did not go to bed.

She bathed instead, and donned a necklace, and set candles to the four cardinal points of the tiny space between the double bed and the wall. Then, taking up her ritual knife, she cast a Circle, temporarily consecrating one small section of a mundane motel room to the worship of a Deity that the Christian church had, for two thousand years, declared dead.

It was Wicca—Witchcraft, the worship of the Goddess—that had given Sandy hope when, her father newly dead and her mother, as she had finally discovered, a suicide years before, she had contemplated her future with a will and personality that a lifetime of abuse had reduced to ash. It was faith in recurrent and endless change that had allowed her to look ahead and hope for healing ... or at least for the oblivion of death and a fresh start with a new incarnation. It was feminine Divinity that had offered a return of the sanctity and holiness of her own, violated body, and if she could not yet grasp those precious gifts, she at least knew that they were there, and that they would wait until her hands were strong enough to reach out and take them.

And so Sandy kept the Solstice in a motel in Glenwood Springs. She had not wanted to be on the road for such a holy day, but, standing in Circle, contemplating this turning point in the seasons—spring and awakening had passed, and summer, the time of sunlight and growth, was ahead—she decided that perhaps it was fitting that she celebrate such a transition while being herself in transition. The seasons mirrored the lessons of life, after all, and so she embraced the crossing of this threshold, coupled to it her wishes and desires, and solemnly affirmed between the Worlds and in the immanent, almost tactile presence of her Goddess that the past was behind her, that in Denver and in the months ahead, she would find sunlight and the growth of her hopes.

And, afterward, her harp at her side and Little Sandy in her lap, she sat in the candle lit darkness, meditating. And if magic were the deliberate willing of a future, the substitution of brightness and innocence for all the black sorrow that had gone before, then, yes, she worked magic.

Once, there had been a time when she had seen the brightness, felt the innocence. Oh, she had never lived them. She had never had the chance. But she remembered clearly the glimpses she had been given long ago of a realm of soft mountains and trees, of a blue lake and a warm sun and the white spray of a fountain against an azure sky: a safe place, a new, unspoiled creation that knew no threat or fear, but was, rather, held and protected by its own innate illumination and color.

Other children had watched cartoons. Sandy had looked at backgrounds. The puerile antics of animated bullies and heroes had held little interest for her; rather it had been the environment in which they had moved, acted, and battled that had captured her infant attention, revealing itself to her as though through a closed but infinitely transparent window: mountains sketched in with the ephemerality of the airbrush and the detail of the pen, trees—just a hint of green, really, but clear and precise for all that—shrouding the lower slopes in fluffy mystery, a fountain more hinted at than drawn, a lake of deepest sapphire. And all in the background. No one save a child who knew too much of a paternal penis would have noticed, no one save Sandy would have looked to such a colored, celluloid world as a possible habitation. She had not cared what Mickey or Donald or Popeye had done in such a place. Instead, she had wondered what kind of a life—surely better than what she had, even now as an adult—she might have made there for herself.

Tonight, then, working magic, she was again a child, and in her mind's eye Little Sandy came to life, assumed the dark hair and blue eyes and dimples of a girl long dead of growth and incest, and ran among the soft hills and fresh meads of a land she had in life never been able to find. Fantasy? Perhaps. But for a short time this Solstice evening, it was real, and in it, through a childhood self that she had carefully nurtured for the last five years (ever since, by her father's death, Little Sandy had been safe from discovery and destruction), she allowed herself the rare pleasure of brightness, the warmth of innocence.

Her eyes were wet when she opened them, and her arms, in token of other Arms that she wished that she herself could feel, were wrapped snugly about her doll. She thought about harping a hymn, but it was late, and she did not want to chance disturbing one of the other motel guests, and so she simply thanked the Goddess, dismissed the Elements, and opened the Circle.

As she brushed her teeth, she stared at the face in the mirror. Had a shred of innocence clung to her features, a tiny token of her mental journey into a gentler, safer place? She could not tell. She saw the scars on the side of her jaw, saw the cast in one eye that witnessed sightlessness, the narrowness in the other that witnessed fear.

Mercifully, the closet was about the right size. She spread blankets on the floor, and, with Little Sandy tucked under her arm, turned off the lights, crawled in, and wedged the door shut. Now she was safe. Now she could sleep.

Rain sodden, hail damaged, the morning struggled up along with the sun. The air was heavy with water and humid heat, musty with the odor of wet curtains and damp floors.

TK had not slept. At times, he could deal with things in no other way than by beating them with consciousness until they surrendered. He had simmered in just this way alongside the tunnels in Vietnam, over the radar screens at the Patriot installations in Dhahran, on the edge of his bed in the military hospital in Georgia, outside the apartment in which he and Bess had once lived. But, in truth, he had accomplished nothing on any of those previous occasions, just as he accomplished nothing now. This sit-

uation, like the others, wou
how long he brooded in a da
cup of coffee in his hand, n
as the windows grew pale

The police had shown up
had been killed. The ambu
that. Statements and body
representatives of the au
left. And that was all. Ju

The Chicago police had had a
orderly. It had covered everything from a ba
between husband and wife to an all-out homicidal rum
TK did not wonder what the Denver cops called it. He assumed that they had some appropriate term.

And now, dawn coming up in earnest, the tablecloth
over the window beginning to glow like stained glass, he
heard a car coming down the street. He did not have to
look to see what it was. He knew what it was. He did not
have to see it pull over to the curb, did not have to see
money exchanged for merchandise, did not have to see a
young man with deep pockets standing at the curbside as
the car pulled away. He did not have to see any of it.
Life—and profit—went on.

He stood up, his left leg—flesh and plastic both—
aching. On his pile of towels in the corner, Rags stirred,
jumped up, uttered a growl and a sharp yip.

"Shut up," said TK.

The yorkie thought about the admonition, read the look
in TK's eye, the tone of his voice. He lay back down.

TK went into the kitchen, looked for something to put
into a stomach grown sour with caffeine. Scuffling. That
was what they called it in the projects. Picking up a job
here, a job there, making just enough money to get by,
with never anything left over at the end of the week. It
was a miserable, soul-killing existence, guaranteed to foster resentment toward the white society that lived out
there beyond the freeway interchange, the white society
that had laid out the boundaries of life so thoroughly and
patrolled them with such relentless efficiency that such
marginal survival was the only legal option open.

No wonder, then, that the kids were dropping out of
school, staking out their turf, flaggin', saggin', and
braggin' their way into dollars and death. They had a hi-

uniforms, they had money, they had a
among the Man's offered pittances could
that?

ugh, was scuffling. When the police had ar-
had stayed to give a statement. He had also
to plead with the uniformed men to do something
the crack house, to protect the neighborhood. But
police were only interested in glamorous drug crimes
other—nonspecified—neighborhoods), and that was
all. And so TK had accomplished nothing.

And then Hansen had been at the Kaiser Center, waiting for him to be late. And he had been late. Gloriously
late. Two hours late. It did not matter to Hansen that a
five year old girl had been reduced to bloody pulp two
doors down from TK's apartment building. TK was late.

"I'm going to have to write you up, Winters," Hansen
had said.

TK had felt the cold wrath building. "You do that," he
said. "You write something else up, too."

Hansen was bending over his notepad. "What's that,
boy?"

And TK waited until the silence made Hansen look up,
and then he took the fat, middle-aged man by the front of
his shirt and lifted—slowly, carefully, relentlessly—until Hansen's feet were off the floor and Hansen's face was inches from his own. "You write it up that
this *boy* didn't make ground meat out of you. You write
it up that this *boy* has quit."

Hansen's face was white, streaked with lines.
"You're . . ."

"Quitting." And then TK had let him drop like a sack
of custard. "I be in on Monday to turn in my uniform.
Have my check ready." He had turned toward the door.

"Winters . . ."

"What you want, motherfucker?"

The front of Hansen's pants was wet. "Uh . . ."

"I be in on Monday."

And he had left.

Scuffling.

But, then, that was the way it was supposed to be, was
it not? Bess, black and now technically single, was supposed to have a daughter who did not know her father,
was supposed to go on welfare; and TK was supposed to

prowl around the corners of the world, shacking up with one woman after another until the inner city violence—guns, knives, alcohol, drugs, or some combination of the four—finally caught up with him and turned him into a statistic.

It had been going on that way for years. The demographics were iron-clad, the stereotypes so deeply ingrained that they had staked out their own turf in the racial and social unconscious; and, like the gangs that roamed the deeply urban streets, they were an almost irresistible magnet to those who dwelt within sight of them, a teeming sump, the lowest common denominator that stagnated and bubbled at the bottom of all dreams and aspirations, always on the lookout for a new member to jump in.

TK remembered a time, though (and it had been, perhaps, that memory that had gotten him through the projects, through the tunnels, through the Iraqi bunker and even through the hospital in Georgia ... though with this last he had needed, and had been graced with—help), when, through adolescent bravado or perhaps merely childish naivete, he had not thought of the world outside the projects as something forbidden, something unconquerable, something that would take his life and grind it between the twin stones of race and denial. He remembered a time when he had thought he might, someday, be able to do ... something. Oh, nothing that involved fame or notoriety or money. Just ... something. Something that would make a difference, something that did not even have to change the world, so long as it changed even one life for the better.

But here he was, scuffling, and all he had to show for himself was a missing leg, and a trail of dead men that he and his uniform had left behind him, and now a child whose face had been so mangled by bullets that she had not had enough of her eyes left to stare sightlessly at the Denver sky.

Another car was coming up the street. TK slammed a cabinet door closed and brooded, his stomach roiling from too much coffee and too little sleep, his mouth rebellious at the thought of food. Beating circumstance with consciousness was achieving nothing. He had to do something.

Rags was on his feet again, whining. A glance told TK that the dog food dish was empty.

Well, everything was going to be empty in a few days if he did not earn some money. Demographics or not, stereotypes or not, he was not going to be a statistic. He could scuffle with the best of them. His father had scuffled. His grandfather had scuffled.

But as he fished the sack of kibble out from beneath the sink, TK found himself thinking that although he was a jobless black man in a white man's world, he was not quite bereft of opportunity. No, there was something he could do before he had to scuffle. If that failed, then he would scuffle. For now, though . . .

He picked up the telephone and called Marsh Blues.

CHAPTER 4

Morning at Elvenhome.

For immortals who knew nothing more of nightly repose than what came to them in the course of an hour or two of pondering among the stars that shone serenely within their minds, the little commonplace gestures of awakening human beings—yawning and stretching, shaking off the dullness of sleep—had no meaning or use. But regardless of sleeping or not sleeping, morning was a beginning, and even Elves required some marking of the passage of time, and so, when the sky began to lighten, those who had gathered at Elvenhome assembled at the edge of Natil's vegetable garden to watch the sun rise.

They had spent the night talking, laughing, and, frequently, crying. Finally able to weep openly, Lauri had sobbed out her tale of a young woman's death. Kelly had shyly expressed her young bewilderment at the actions of her teachers and classmates at day care, and Heather had told of her fears for her daughter's future. Marsh had echoed Lauri's intimations of futility, and Dell and Fox had recounted seeing their *pro bono* plantings at an inner city park torn up and trampled.

Every one of them had something to say, every one of them needed someone to listen. But that was the reason for Elvenhome: it was a place where human concerns did not come, where immortals could abandon themselves to their immortal griefs and turn to one another for sympathy and solace. Nestled into a hollow of the Rocky Mountains like a warm fledgling held in cupped hands, the big house was a gathering place and a shelter, designed by mutual consent, built by shared labor and pooled funds, cared for by all.

The clouds had departed in the course of the night, the morning was clear, and the Elves stood together and watched the dawn. A diamond glitter on the horizon, a flash, and suddenly a spreading arc of brilliance sent the shadows flying before it, banished the blues and lavenders of elven night-vision, wakened the clear colors of day.

And when the sun at last lifted clear of the horizon, there were sighs, smiles. As though remembering their fled humanity, the Elves of Denver shook hands, embraced, wished one another a good morning and a good day. Here was a beginning, here was a new chance, here was a daily renewal blazoned across the blue skies of Colorado.

"It's nice up here," said Lauri. Eyes closed, her mop of black hair sparkling in the sunlight, she was breathing deeply of the soft air. "It's nice. I kind of wish there were more of us to share it."

Heather was holding Kelly, and she had shed her business clothes for a warm robe the color of a hazelnut. "There will be more. Almost everyone has the blood to some degree. And if they have it, there's always the chance that it will wake up."

Kelly nodded with large blue eyes. "And then my classmates won't tell me about hell?"

Heather hugged her. "There will always be some, Elfling."

Lauri seemed to be turning pensive again. "Yeah. Always."

Natil took her arm. "Come," she said. "Wheat insists that she will have breakfast prepared by the time we return, and we are all determined to prove her wrong."

Lauri gave a sad laugh. "Oh, we are *so* bad, aren't we?"

Wheat had, in fact, run back to the big kitchen as soon as the sun had cleared the horizon, and now her voice carried throughout the hollow: "Breakfast is ready!"

"I guess we lose," said Lauri. But she turned and, almost impulsively, hugged Natil. "Thanks," she said.

"Thanks?"

Lauri's dark eyes were serious. "For being there for us. For taking care of the Home when we're not here. For harping for us until we stop thinking about all the problems. For . . ." She blushed. ". . . for showing us how to be Elves."

Natil shook her head. "You all knew how to be Elves long before I found you. You had one another, and you had the earth and the stars. You had everything you needed. You still do." But her words had a bitter aftertaste, for she knew well what the Elves lacked.

Lauri's blush deepened. "Awww . . ."

From ahead came a squawk. "She's made *blueberry muffins,*" Raven shouted as she cleared a ditch with a bound. "They're mine! All mine!"

Natil pulled Lauri toward the Home. "I think we had better hurry, or we may get nothing but grass and rain water."

They joined Hadden and Ash who, hand in hand, were strolling toward breakfast, apparently unconcerned about Raven's potential depredations. Ash reached her free hand to Natil, and Hadden put his arm about Lauri's shoulders. "Ash told me about what happened," he said. "I'm sorry."

Lauri shrugged. "I guess I'll have to get used to it. I guess I'll have plenty of time to get used to it. But, dammit, I don't want to get used to it."

Hadden shook his head. He was, arguably, the first of the reawakened Elves, and he had already had plenty of time, in human terms, to get used to it. "Don't worry, Lauri. You won't. No one ever does."

His assurance, true as it was, was either harsh comfort or sympathetic doom, and not even Natil could decide which to call it. Lauri appeared unwilling to try: she changed the subject. "You got in pretty late last night. Problem?"

Hadden shook his head. "Nothing big. The new computer system is driving me mildly insane. The EDMs and the electronic transits were about as much as I ever wanted to deal with. The Total Station is nice, but the software . . ." He shook his head. "I wish I could avoid it. Web insists that he's a pencil and paper kind of guy . . . uh . . . I mean Elf." He grinned. "Bright's in school half the day, you're in charge of the field teams . . . so that leaves me stuck in the office looking at a monitor." His sea gray eyes twinkled. "Unless Natil wants to get involved, of course."

Natil laughed. "I think not. When I left Europe, they had only just discovered Am—" But she caught herself.

If she wanted to avoid uncomfortable explanations, there were certain things that she could not say. "I . . . believe I will stay with my gardening."

"We're doing fairly well at TreeStar," said Lauri. "If we can afford to blow the bucks on the Total Station, we should probably scrape together enough to hire someone who knows what the hell they're doing with the PC software."

Hadden considered, looking off across the trees to the curved eaves and blue slate roof of Elvenhome. The silver filigree around the tower sparkled in the new light. "We could. We can afford it. But it will be hard to find someone who will fit in. The office is so full of Elves that . . . well, you remember what happened to you and Bright. It really comes down to a question of who."

Lauri shook her head. "A question of who, as in: *who wants to live forever?*"

"It's hard sometimes," he agreed. "But would you give it up?"

Natil saw doubt cross Lauri's mind. But she saw also firelit evenings, eyes filled with starlight, immortal hands offered and clasped . . .

"No," said Lauri at last. "No. Never. I just . . ." She tipped her head back. A hawk was aloft, catching the sunlight and the first stirrings of the thermals. "I just wish to hell it could be a little easier."

Natil spoke softly, with a reassurance meant as much for herself as for Lauri. "Everything that happens, happens exactly as it should, happens exactly when it should, because that is the way it happens."

"Yeah. You said that last night. You really believe that?"

Natil smiled. She had had her doubts. "Well?"

Lauri sighed. "I guess, under the circumstances, I have to believe it or go crazy." She shrugged, tried for a laugh. "I'll tell you, Natil: sometimes you remind me of those crazy witches at the Center. They're always saying weird shit like that."

Natil blinked. "Witches?"

"Yeah. Well, they call themselves witches. I don't know much about it, really. Sometimes they act kind of flaky."

"Elves, of course, never act flaky," said Ash. "Especially the ones who run employment agencies."

"That's true," said Hadden. "And surveying companies. Epitomes of middle-class respectability, all of them."

"Except when it comes to blueberry muffins."

"Absolutely. There's no telling what might happen, then. Raven has even threatened to take scalps when it comes to blueberry muffins." He mused for a moment. "But I don't really know anything about witches myself. Just what you read about in stories."

"Oh," said Lauri. "They're not like that. It's all that women's spirituality stuff. They worship a Goddess, dance around on the solstices, stuff like that."

Natil's heart was suddenly pounding. Witches? In Denver? And they worshiped a Goddess? What if . . .

"Worship a Goddess," said Ash as though struck by the idea. Her voice turned wistful. "Would a Goddess want anything to do with Elves, I wonder?"

Silence. Hadden looked off at the mountains. Lauri examined the toes of her sneakers. Ash seemed a little taken aback by her own question. Religion was not something that they customarily talked about, for as there was no place for Elves in any of the currently available dispensations—as there was, in fact, no place for immortality—it seemed a particularly fruitless and depressing subject to pursue.

"I . . . don't know," said Lauri after a time. "Do you want me to ask them?"

"I am . . . am very sure," said Natil through lips that had, with a sudden upsurge of hope, turned uncooperative, "that . . . that She would love Elves." Her heart was still pounding. Witches! "As Her own children."

They had just reached the kitchen door when the telephone rang. Inside, Wheat, who stood nearest to it, had several plates of muffins and pancakes and eggs balanced on each arm, and she looked pleadingly at the new arrivals. But Marsh came dashing in from the dining room. "My fault! My fault!" he called as he grabbed the receiver. "I've got some clients who are worrying me sick, and I had my calls forwarded."

Raven's voice drifted in from the dining room. "Your

blueberry muffin allowance is hereby reduced by one. I guess I'll have to eat it. It's a big sacrifice, I know but—"

But Marsh had the handset to his ear. "Hello? TK! Hey, dude, what's happening?" His eyebrows lifted. "You didn't! You did! Yeah? Hang on a sec." He put his hand over the mouthpiece, turned to Hadden. "Hadden, this is the guy I was telling you about last night. The one who knows about computers. He's good: he helped track down that Patriot failure during Desert Storm. He's a great guy. He just quit his job. He's looking for work."

Lauri, who had moved to help Wheat—and who was receiving a very warm smile in return—paused thoughtfully, almost as though she were stricken. Natil saw the futility rising again. "Lauri . . ."

"Does he want to live forever?" Lauri asked of no one in particular.

The buses ran fitfully on weekends, and so Natil drove herself into town later that morning, taking the old battered van that had once transported Hadden and Wheat across the tortured landscapes of southeast Utah and the green mountains of Colorado. She had intended to make this trip ever since the hailstorm the previous evening, for she had wanted to see what was left of the flower beds. But since Lauri's remark about witches, the journey had assumed at once more impetus and more hope.

Once, Natil had known witches, had befriended them, had, in fact, shared with two of them the intimate secrets of elvenhood. In Roxanne and Charity of Saint Brigid, the Elves had known human sisters, for the two women had worshiped their Goddess with the same love and intensity with which Natil and her people had honored *Elthia*. Indeed, they had, over time, absorbed so much imagery and attitude and practice from their immortal friends that they had eventually found their way into the same direct and immanent vision of divinity with which the Elves were privileged.

Those times, like that vision, lay far in the past, and up until this morning, Natil had assumed that the religion of the Goddess had died out during the centuries of persecutions. But Lauri had said that she knew witches, and she had said also that she thought them, in some ways, similar to elves. Maybe . . .

Immanent religion, immediate and personal experience of the Goddess: that was what Roxanne and Charity had practiced. Their ways were human, decidedly more in tune with the transience and decay of mortal flesh than with the starlit eternity of the Firstborn, but Natil could not help but wonder whether the practices of the simple, honest witch-folk she had known might prove helpful to an immortal cousin who had lost her Divine Friend. Armed, then, with two names that Lauri had given her and three references that she had gleaned from the pages of the telephone directory, she had set off toward Denver.

As she had feared, the flower beds at Kingsley were a disaster. The hail had mutilated blossoms, shredded leaves, and smeared what was left with a thick layer of mud. Natil spent a few minutes straightening the plants that seemed the least damaged, packing the earth loosely enough to allow air to reach their half-drowned roots, but she knew that a complete repair would have to wait until Monday, when she had work crews and flats of replacement plants available.

Wiping her hands as she walked, she returned to her van, her thoughts heavy with the symbolism of the beds. Flowers, Elves: both of her charges were half drowned and muddy.

She tried to be hopeful as she pulled out the names that Lauri had given her, but though she admitted that many facets of modern life mystified her, she could guess with reasonable certainty that such appellatives as *Willow Mountainwoman* and *Crystal SunPhoenix* were either self-chosen in a fit of nominative pique or deliberately assumed to keep the bearer's true identity secret. In neither case had Lauri been able to supply an address or a phone number; and upon making inquiries at the Gay and Lesbian Center, Natil was informed that she could, if she wished, leave a message at the desk. Someone would get back to her. Maybe.

She left her name and her work number—reflecting that the latter action doubtless cheated Raven out of a blueberry muffin or two—and set off in her van once again, looking this time for addresses.

There were several shops in Denver that offered a mix of wares usually lumped together under the hazy designation *occult* or the even hazier *new age*. Neither category, in Natil's opinion, was liable to produce any better results than Willow Mountainwoman or Crystal SunPhoenix, but one or two of the display ads in the metro Yellow Pages had made veiled but obviously deliberate references to Witchcraft, and it was toward the first of these that she now drove. She could only look. She could only hope.

After pulling off the freeway and picking her way through the warren of alleys and one-way streets that lay to the southeast of the city center, she parked and walked to a small, narrow storefront. A bell jingled with a desultory clank when she took hold of the knob, and the door, warped from years of hot summers and cold winters, at first stuck, and then gave way suddenly, almost pitching her onto the floor of a dark interior that reeked of incense.

The door swung to behind her, and her sight shifted partially into blues and lavenders. She saw dirt and candy wrappers on the floor, cobwebs in the corners, a miserable, caged owl that huddled behind steel bars up near the ceiling. The rickety shelves were empty save for a tumbled collection of pots of incense and a thin spattering of books.

She glanced over them. Ceremonial magic. Tarot. A shopworn copy of something called *The Satanic Bible*. A series of meditations designed to bring the practitioner various unspecified but most assuredly worthwhile abilities. Beneath the cash register, the display case held a number of gaudy pendants, some tarnished silver rings, and a motley assortment of knives with the handles made of everything from the amputated feet of deer to (as indicated by a paper sign) "real human shinbone."

Natil looked, felt the sadness. Roxanne and Charity. Was this all that was left of Roxanne and Charity?

She lifted her eyes to the thin, bearded man behind the counter. As slender as his assortment of wares and as dusty as his shop, he wore a threadbare gray robe that Natil doubted had seen the inside of a washer since it had been made.

"C'n I help you?" he said.

His eyes were narrow, bright, and her first instinct was to decline politely and withdraw, but the thought of the ruined flower beds returned to her. Muddy and ruined . . .

because she had waited. She could wait no longer. She had to try.

"I am . . ." She looked into his face, examining him. This, too, she had come to help and heal. "I am looking for information about the practice of the Old Ways."

"Huh?"

"Witchcraft."

"Oh . . ." He shrugged his shoulders into alertness. "Oh . . ." he said again. "Well, you're in the right place. We got classes here all the time. I teach. I'm a warlock. Qualified, you know. In fact . . ."

He eyed her. Natil knew what he was seeing.

". . . our coven is looking for a new member. We want a woman. Gender balance, you know." His voice had turned as narrow as his eyes.

Sadness . . . and a terrible emptiness. Had it all, then, come to this? "And abundant sex, I imagine."

"Huh?"

"Thank you." She turned to the door, mouth clenched with the memory of Roxanne's love and Charity's bright laugh. "I suggest that you use condoms: AIDS is, after all, a concern."

"Huh?"

"Good day."

"Huh?"

When she had climbed back behind the wheel of the old van, she discovered that she was shaking. "Warlock," she murmured, closing her eyes and breathing the starlight. "It is so: traitor."

But though the second shop she tried was different in a few respects—a fat woman instead of an emaciated man, a dyspeptic fern instead of a miserable owl, a plethora of wind chimes instead of a pervasive darkness—the shelves were still relatively bare, the atmosphere still oppressive.

"My . . . partner . . . can probably help you," said the woman in response to Natil's question. She rested a black-draped elbow on the counter, sizing up her customer from behind dark glasses as she chain lit her third cigarette in as many minutes. "She's giving a reading right now. She's a professional, you know."

Natil smiled graciously . . . and slipped out the door and into the pure air. "Well," she said, trying to stare down the growing disappointment. "I suppose that it would be too much to ask that this be easy."

The third address led her to a stretch of west Alameda, where French restaurants stood alongside gay nightclubs, and adult booksellers vied for prominence with hardware stores. There, on a corner, was her goal, its windows tall and wide, its sign proclaiming in two foot, blue plastic letters:

WATTERSON'S NEW AGE EMPORIUM

Natil parked, got out . . . and stared. There might well have been an exclamation point after each word.

She entered through a plate glass door to find a large room that was dominated by a long counter with an enormous cash register sitting on top of it. At present, the register, as though impelled by its very size, was totaling up three-figure purchases for a milling crowd of women clad in various combinations of fringes, shawls, bead work, turquoise, silver plated tin, and imitation eagle feathers.

Natil, perplexed, hung back by the door. She could not help but notice that at least three shelves of the bookcase next to the entrance were crammed with books on "Iridiology."

She peered at them. Iridiology?

Racks and shelves of books, in fact, filled every free section of wall and spilled out into the middle of the room in double-sided displays, but as Natil strolled through the store, narrowly avoiding collisions with the milling customers, their fringes, and their imitation eagle feathers, she saw that Watterson's New Age Emporium offered much more than books. In fact, it seemed to have one, if not several, of everything.

The selection was overwhelming. Scented oils with astrological correspondence. Tiny suede sacks adorned with iron-on Nordic runes. Aluminum cards that attracted "pyramid power." Crystal pendants. Feathered sticks. Little chrome balls that jingled mysteriously when shaken. Bags of incense specially blended to mediate the energies of the Solstice (now one day out of date and therefore on sale). Dark mirrors. Pseudo Native American shields, pipes, head dresses, and amulets. Talismans of Mercury, Mars, Ariel, Uriel, Jupiter, and several planetary and angelic powers that Natil did not recognize at all. Baskets of landscaping rocks. Lumps of clay. Boxes of glass marbles. Large arrangements of copper wire and iron ingots that appeared to have something to do with "channeling energy." Egyptian necklaces. Oriental earrings. Celtic bracelets. Museum replicas of ancient statuary. Mass produced replicas of modern kitsch. Alabaster eggs. Teakwood boxes. Color-coded zafus. Little pewter figurines of sorcerers and mermaids. Large plaster images of satyrs and nymphs. Chalices of stainless steel, brass, bronze, and copper. Wands of wood, stone, and plastic. Gourd rattles. Staves with carvings . . . and without. Bowls. Incense burners. Crude paintings of Goddesses (breasts and hips prominent) and Gods (penises and horns prominent). Muslin robes. Colored cords. Quantities of quartz crystals, geodes, apache tears, jasper pebbles, moonstone beads, and . . .

Natil, having wandered up to the display in the long counter, bent closer. What . . . ?

"Boji stones," said the frowzy woman behind the counter. She had blue eyes, and her round cheeks almost matched her red hair. "They balance your energy. You should try them." She examined Natil vaguely. "I can tell your energy needs balancing."

Natil inspected the dull black stones that looked like nothing so much as charcoal briquettes, then looked up. The women who had crowded the store with shawls and imitation eagle feathers had vanished, and a murmur of voices was drifting out of a closed door toward the back of the shop. She was alone with the clerk. "It is true," she said, "I cannot but say that I feel rather. . . unbalanced at present."

"Oh! Here!" The woman swooped into the display case, pulled out two of the briquettes. "You see, here's a male stone and a female stone . . ."

They looked exactly alike to Natil.

". . . and you hold each of them in your contrasexual hand."

She had already plopped one stone into each of Natil's hands. The Elf examined them. They appeared to be metallic, obviously some sort of semi-oxidized pyrite. "And then?" she inquired politely.

"Then they balance you." The red-haired woman nodded her head vigorously. "It's automatic. Feeling better?"

Natil looked at her for a long moment, then smiled softly. "Why," she said, "I am indeed. My thanks."

"There you are. Some people come in and just buy one, but you really have to have two to get the full effect. It's like a great big battery. Everything is. Positive and negative. Male and female. Just like the God and the Goddess."

Natil had never heard divine energy described in quite that way, but she had noticed that each age had its preferred metaphors. "Of . . . course . . ." She handed the stones back, noting as she did so that the clerk was wearing a ring shaped like a crescent moon and a five pointed star. A silver chain about her neck bore a pentagram. "I am sure that I feel much better."

"Can I help you with anything?" The clerk was a little fuzzy around the edges, Natil decided, but she obviously had a good heart. She really wanted to help.

And Natil needed help. "Well . . ." She weighed the possibilities, decided, despite her previous failures, to come straight to the point. "I am looking for information about practitioners of the Old Ways."

To her relief, the woman knew what she meant and nodded seriously. "Are you looking for training?"

"That . . ." Natil almost laughed. To such an end had the Elves come! "That might be a possibility. I do not appear to be doing overly well on my own."

The woman came up with a clipboard. "The first thing to do is put your name on our mailing list," she said. "And then . . . let's see . . . Her red cheeks got even redder as she thought. "I've got those booklists around here somewhere, and Lady Sammi is starting her Introduction to Wicca course in another two weeks—that's thirty-five dollars . . . for her time, you know—and then the local Pagan network is doing their usual Wicca 101 series . . . I can get you into that. That's starting this Monday night, and it covers all the basics in six weeks. Melissa Green is doing the first class on astrology."

"Astrology?" Natil was puzzled. What did astrology have to do with the Old Ways? For that matter, what did teaching for a fee have to do with the Old Ways?

The clerk was hunting behind the counter, shifting stacks of paper back and forth. "Melissa's very good. She has her own line of planetary oils and incenses—right over here, you see, on the display: we've got some on sale—and she does custom blends, too. (Where are those dratted booklists?) She does everything right. And then (where was I? . . . oh yes:) numerology the next week, polarity, ethics, divination, magick, the usual. It's very complete."

Natil had heard nothing in the syllabus that would help her. "Just . . . so . . ."

From behind the closed door at the rear of the shop, the sudden thudding of a drum made the crystals in the displays clink against one another, the shelves rattle, the chrome balls jingle. The clerk straightened up, listened, closed her eyes, and sighed. "They're starting again. That's so good to hear. The native ways of this country have been so desecrated."

A moment later, a chorus of women's voices took up something like a chant.

"That's a genuine Apache spirit chant," said the clerk. "Do you feel the power?"

Natil frowned. She knew Apache, and all of the other Native American languages as well. The chant was not Apache. It was, in fact, not anything at all. "What are they doing?" she asked politely.

"Deena Anthony is taking a group of women through shaman training."

The thudding continued. So did the chanting.

"I am afraid that I am not familiar with Ms. Anthony," said Natil, raising her voice a little so as to be heard.

"You aren't? Oh, my. Come over here, then." The clerk pulled Natil over to a table near the front of the shop. On it lay stacks of books, all of which bore Deena Anthony's byline. Deena Anthony herself—in buckskin dress, beaded headband, and feathered necklace—smiled from the cover of one. "She's a shaman," the clerk explained. "An Apache medicine woman trained her and passed her medicine bundle to her when she died."

The thudding became louder. So did the chanting.

Natil stared. "But . . . medicine women do not train white people, or give away their medicine bundles when they die. They take apprentices from among their own kind, and their bundles are . . ."

The clerk seemed disinclined to argue with someone who could not possibly know anything about Deena Anthony, Native American practices, or medicine bundles. "Deena—she lets us call her Deena, even though her Indian name is White Star Woman—is in town on a book tour. She's doing a signing and a workshop with us today. All those women back there are going to be shamans."

Natil nodded slowly.

The clerk was staring off toward the closed door. A sigh. "I wish I could do that."

At the sound of the genuine regret in her voice, Natil pulled herself out of her bewilderment. "It is a great and terrible calling," she offered, instinctively trying to help. "There are very few who can—"

"But I just can't afford the three hundred dollars." The clerk shook her head as the drum continued to thud, the crystals to clink, the shelves to rattle, the chrome balls to jingle. Above it all screeched the nonsense chant. "Oh, well: better luck next lifetime." She turned back to Natil. "Lady Sammi's class is filled, so I'll sign you up for the Wicca 101. You'll still get all the basics. There's a pot luck at the end of the series, and so you can meet some of the people in the community who are taking students."

Natil could, for some reason, think of nothing but the ruined flower beds.

The clerk was heading back to the counter. "And did you want those boji stones? They're sixty dollars apiece, but we've got some smaller ones for thirty . . ."

CHAPTER 5

Dear Nora,

So sorry I haven't written to you before. Shawna is determined that she's going to show me absolutely everything, and she seems to want to do it all *now,* so I've been rather on the run . . .

Paris is delightful, though crowded. (It *is* summer, isn't it?) Everyone at the Académie sends their very best, and they've been reading your columns with green-eyed jealousy. You have a knack for putting everything so succinctly! But you always did that. Anyway, Shawna dragged me off to the Louvre for the required visit, and I quickly got so muddled with old masters that I couldn't tell one from another. I still can't!

I haven't had much of a chance to do any in-depth searching for those articles you asked about, though I've made some efforts. Estie and the rest at the Académie have never heard of Terry Angel, and Estie adds that no one of that name ever had any kind of a fellowship with them. She's head of the department, so she should know. They don't have a fellowship program, as a matter of fact. Maybe he was referring to some other school?

I looked around for *Initiations* and *Prana,* and Shawna actually gave me a chance to catch my breath long enough to ask about them at the Académie library. You can imagine what they thought of my French there! We wound up speaking English! But Mme. Bleuet, the head librarian, is unfamiliar with those publications, and my efforts at translating titles like "An Eloquent Ecstasy" into French (from which, if I understood you rightly, they'd already been translated into English) turned the whole thing into a frightful game of Chinese whispers. Mme. Bluette said she'd look, but she squinted at me through her glasses with a look that said *Crazy Americans*!

Sorry about my dismal failures. Here is Terry Angel with a bibliography as long as my arm, and I can't seem to track it down!

Give my love to Rick, and tell him not to worry: Shawna is keeping me from shrinking quite away. And if you see that sweet little gardener wandering around Kingsley, give her my best, and tell her that Chalice Well was everything she said it would be.

Love,

Georgina

Sandy came down out of mist and cloud, crossing over the last rise of the mountains and coming into sight of a Denver that shimmered in the afternoon sunlight, its office buildings freshly washed by yet another evening of rain, its urban sprawl of asphalt and concrete and snarled interchanges gentled by her uninitiated gaze, turned by her unfamiliarity to a vision of hope and opportunity.

And there she goes again, looking ahead for something that's not there, that silly grin on her face, those clumsy little steps that she takes just before she falls—

"Shaddup," she said to the inner barker. "It's going to be better." She reached back and patted her harp. "I'm going to make it better."

And you'd think she'd know by now that it never gets any better . . .

"It can. It will. So . . . *shaddup*."

Following the directions that Terry Angel had given her, she stayed on I-70 until the Federal off ramp, and then she turned north into a genial residential neighborhood: bungalow houses and vinyl siding, old elm and cottonwood trees, sturdy rose gardens and clumps of daylilies in full bloom despite the batterings they had received from yesterday's hail.

Terry's directions took her up one street, down another, and finally led her to a small apartment building that surrounded a central court. She parked in front of it, and, giving Little Sandy a kiss on the head to let her know that she would be safe—a small, feeble attempt to convince Big Sandy of the same thing—she got out, went up the walk, and rang the manager's bell.

The door opened a crack, and an eye peered out at her from behind a perfectly round lens. "Whaddaya want?" It was a demand, not a question.

She took a step back. "I . . ."

"Who are you?"

"I'm . . ." She glanced back at her car, suddenly realizing that she did not have her letters with her. They did not apply to this situation, but maybe . . .

"Don't look at the god-damn street, look at me. You one of them god-damn college kids?"

"I'm Sandy Joy," she said, freeing her tongue at last. "I'm here to see about an apartment."

"You want it for the summer?"

"Yes. And for the . . ." But she could not help but wonder now whether she would want it even for five minutes. ". . . the school year."

The eye glared out at her from behind its shield of glass.

"I'm Sandy Joy," she tried again. "Terry Angel said that he'd reserved an apartment for me. Here I am."

"Angel . . . Angel . . ." The eye squinted, rolled itself up in its socket as though attempting to look at itself, then settled down once again on Sandy. "Don't know anyone like that. You tell me he came, he didn't come. What the hell am I supposed to do about it?"

"But he told me he'd done it months ago," said Sandy. "It was . . . all arranged."

The owner of the baleful eye did not appear to have heard her. "And if people like you show up just when they god-damn feel like it, they can't expect me to have things ready for them. You remember that. You just god-damn remember that. Hang on."

The door closed. There was a rattle of a chain. The door swung open again. The owner of the eye was a stunted little man with a face that was shiny with the handling of years. He squinted at her from behind circular spectacles, from beneath the brim of a canvas cap, from above a stained undershirt through which poked the stiff gray hairs of his chest.

"You god-damn kids always want it right now," he complained. He started out into the courtyard, motioning impatiently for her to follow him. "You never tell me ahead of time. You just want it right now. Well, you'll just have to take it like it is."

"But Professor Angel told you months ago—"

"Expects me to have it cleaned up and ready just like that, and after those god-damn kids just moved out and left it." He glared at Sandy, this time with two eyes behind two lenses. "God-damn kids."

Effectively silenced, Sandy followed him upstairs to a door that looked as though someone had tried to kick it in.

"Here it is," he said. "It's not clean. You'll have to clean it. I'll knock twenty-five dollars off your first month's rent. Want it?"

He swung the door open and beckoned her in.

Sandy entered, felt the helpless nausea. The apartment 'was a wreck. Carpets were threadbare where they had not been slashed into tatters. A stained sofa was tipped forward on two broken legs as though making an introductory bow. The kitchen table was covered with paper plates and wrappers from fast food hamburgers, and it was not hard to guess why the previous occupants had given up preparing their own food, for the stove top was caked with crumbs, burnt spaghetti sauce, and what looked like melted plastic. The inside of the oven was thick with black grease.

Elsewhere, it was much the same. The bedroom was littered, and heaps of dog-eared newspapers choked the corners. The odor of cat urine was strong, mixed with the acrid smell of stale cigarette smoke.

"God-damn kids just moved out. And you just waltz in and expect me to have this cleaned up for you?" He goggled at her from behind his thick lenses. "You want it?"

"Isn't . . ." Sandy tried to imagine herself living here, found that an ache of terrified insomnia was already forming behind her eyes. "Uh . . ." She opened the bedroom closet. It was large, not too messy. Maybe . . .

"Twenty-five dollars off your first month's rent," said the manager. "Deposit'll be the same, though. You kids are always running off on me." When she still hesitated.

He stared at her, chest hair bristling. "Didn't your daddy give you enough money?"

She flinched. "I'm here on my own," she said.

"Well, it's a nice safe place, and like I said, I'll knock twenty-five dollars off your first month's rent. Deposit'll be the same, though. And you don't pay, I throw you out. You got it?"

Sandy looked around the room as though seeking an escape. Tainted air, clutter, a stove and an oven that would need a more than liberal application of caustic cleaner . . . she did not even want to think about what the bathroom looked like. But Terry Angel had arranged for this place, and Terry Angel was going to teach her how to heal. She would give him no excuse for not liking her, for not accepting her, for not leading her out of the past and into a new life.

"I'll take it," she said.

When she returned to her car to fetch her suitcase, her harp, and her doll, the barker was back, and she did not have the heart to tell him to shut up.

The fire on the Elvenhome hearth burned low. The evening had faded long before, night had fallen firmly, and in the darkness that was not dark to immortal eyes, the Elves dreamed their waking dreams of starlight.

Natil's harp was silent, and Kelly was cuddling up on her lap. Web, who had practiced Zen long before the awakening of ancient blood had removed the last shred of illusion from his world, sat quietly in a lotus position, his eyes open, gleaming. Lauri was sprawled full length on the thick carpet, staring into the fire. Raven sat with her back against the wall, smiling as softly as Tristan, who mirrored both her pose and her expression on the other side of the room. Allesandro had closed his eyes, but his occasional sigh of contentment said that he was not anywhere near human sleep.

Others lay or sat elsewhere, finding in silence and the stars a shadow of the peace for which they unconsciously and instinctively yearned, to which they could put no name. Marsh. Heather. Wheat. Dell. Fox. All of them. The Elves of Denver were gathered here, in Elvenhome, sheltered from the world.

The fire crackled, throwing up a sudden brightness that

momentarily shaded the blues and lavenders of Hadden's vision back into yellows and russets. Beside him, Ash lifted her head, then returned it to his shoulder. "Let's go outside," she said.

He smiled. "It's raining outside."

"I could care." She smiled in return, rose. Her bare feet noiseless on carpet, parquetry, stone, and earth, she led Hadden to the door, out into the trees, and the chill of the evening and the rain appeared not to touch her. Her flesh shone with a lambent radiance as of silver, and Hadden could not help but consider what a holy thing it was to be an Elf, to be among the trees, and to see so plainly that there was, in fact, no separation between himself and Ash, nor between the two of them and the forest and the mountains and all that lay beyond.

They made love on the soft bed of pine needles beneath a tall tree. It was a little house of living branches that they shared, and the shimmer of their naked bodies played among the sheltering limbs as the raindrops rustled down and the night birds fluttered and called in the echoing distance. They had been lovers for a long time, but though their hands and their lips knew the intricacies of one another's bodies with a surety that was the product of custom, still this act of love, like all the others they had consummated in the months and years since they had first taken one another's hands, was new, fresh, as redolent of the beginning of the world as a sunrise, and like a sunrise it swept out and away from the beginning, mingling their spirits first with one another, and then with the land, and then . . . beyond into infinity and silence.

The rain pattered down. It was very still. Spent, they lay curled together like foxes in a den.

"It's so beautiful," whispered Ash, and her voice was as the sound of the rain in the pine needles. "It's so beautiful and so . . . so . . ."

Hadden touched her cheek. "Terrible?"

"Yes. Terrible. How . . ." Her eyes glistened, sought his. "How did you and Wheat manage? I mean, at the beginning. You were all alone, and you had to think of . . . forever . . ."

Hadden thought back to a man named George Morrison. He might as well have been trying to remember another incarnation. "We got through as we get through now, Ash. You said it yourself: it's beautiful."

"It is." She shut her eyes as though in pain. "But . . . dear God . . ."

Hadden was silent. Beautiful, yes. But terrible, too.

Ash's eyes were still closed. The rain fell. The tree was a living temple. "What do you think of God, Hadden?"

Hadden heard the weight in her words. "How so?"

"Lauri was talking about witches this morning. They worship a Goddess, she said. And . . ." Now her eyes were open again, looking up at the undark canopy of pine boughs. ". . . and I started to think about God. Again. About . . ." She groped for words. "Who cares about Elves?"

"We care about each other." It was a beautiful thing to say, it was a terrible thing to say.

"Is that enough? We're trying to take care of the world, and the world's so big . . ." For an instant, as though the globe and all its people and hates and sorrows had fallen into her consciousness like a stone into her belly, Ash seemed close to tears. "Who takes care of us?"

Hadden felt the old heaviness. The answer—that there was nothing and no one—was unthinkable, and so they did not think about it. They had one another, and they had the world. That was, apparently, all that they could expect. But: "Natil seemed to think that the Goddess would take us in."

"What do you know about the Goddess?"

"Nothing."

"Do you think Natil knows?"

He rolled over on his back, put his head against hers, found her hand and linked their fingers together. Together, they stared up at the branches and needles. Elves and trees: Natil had told them about the old forests. Elves and trees were as one. But then, Elves and everything were as one. That was the beauty of it. And that was the terror of it. "I think," he said, "that Natil knows a lot of things that she's not telling us. I also think that she doesn't realize that a few of us have picked up on that."

"What are you talking about?"

"You weren't at the Home when she first showed up. Lauri and I were the only ones. We were doing a traverse—control for the water lines—but we'd taken a break for lunch. Lauri was the one to answer the door, and . . . well, there was Natil." He chuckled. "Lauri almost had heart failure. It was an absolutely instinctive recognition."

He breathed. Pine and rain were in the air. And silence. And night. Beautiful. And terrible. "But Lauri and I both realized something when we talked about it later: there wasn't a cloud in the sky that day, but Natil was soaked to the skin and muddy from head to toe. She would have had to have taken a header into a swamp to do that."

Ash understood. "And there aren't any swamps around the Home."

His eyes were still on the branches. Spreading, branching into fractal randomness, they nonetheless formed a network, a consistent and comprehensible pattern. What was Natil's pattern? What was the Elves' pattern? "Nope."

"So where did she come from?"

"I don't know, beloved. But she's been so good to us all, so determined to be . . ." He chuckled again, felt the softness of elven emotion, relished it. *You're not a man anymore,* Wheat had said long ago. And it was true. And it was wonderful. ". . . one of the gang, that I haven't had the heart to ask her."

"Do you think . . ." Ash spoke almost timidly. "Do you think that Natil can tell us about God?"

Hadden did not speak for a long time. The rain fell, rustling. The forest seemed frozen, held in stasis, its breath caught . . . waiting.

"I fear so," he said at last.

Beautiful . . . and terrible. They lay together until morning, until the rain stopped, and then they put on their clothes and went out to watch the sunrise.

Normally, Natil took the bus to work, hiking two miles over the rolling mountains to the park-and-ride station, arriving at Kingsley just in time to greet her crew as they showed up at eight o'clock. But she had things to do this morning—very early this morning—and so once again she was in the old, battered van, rolling down Sixth Avenue as the sky paled and the lights of the city center vanished slowly into the rising day.

Just at dawn, she pulled into the lot beside the groundskeeper's shed. Noting with satisfaction that hers was the only vehicle there, she parked, got out, and, swinging the passenger door open, took out her old harp.

She smiled fondly at the feel of the cherry wood. Climbing about on the outside of medieval castles, performing *chansons de geste* for despairing noblemen, easing the pain of an attempted rape—or successful revenge—this harp had been a part of her for a long time. Now she tucked it under her arm, pocketed its tuning key, and started off for the ruined flower beds. She had something else to do with her harp this morning, and she needed to do it before anyone else showed up.

It was her search for witches on Saturday that had goaded her to an action that was, as she freely admitted, not only an attempt to heal but also something of a defiant shake of the fist at the modern perversions of the religion and life of her old friends. There was little enough magic left in the world, but there was some, and it was real, and it was untainted by commerce and exploitation. Though splendid alterations of natural law were now well beyond Natil, she thought that a little help for some battered flowers might, perhaps, be within her abilities.

The sun was not far from the horizon when she sat down on a stone bench beside the beds and put her harp on her lap, but her thoughts of the past had brought an emptiness to her heart, an aching hollow of silence and void that had nothing to do with peace, but only with longing: longing for the Lady, for faces she would never see again, for the life she had once known. Here, Elf though she was, she might as well have been mortal. She cared for flowers while rain forests were cut down. She pulled weeds while deserts spread and nuclear power plants churned out waste that would not be safe for half a million years. She spoke courteously to all while children were shot to death in their front yards and pesticides gathered in the food chain and contrived famines killed millions.

For a moment, overcome, she wept, one hand holding her harp, the other covering her eyes as though in an attempt to shield herself from the knowledge that came from within, from that hollow place in her heart, from that void.

But voids and hollows could be passages. Empty as

they were, there was nothing within them to impede or obstruct. And so, putting her fingers to the strings despite her tears, she started with that. With emptiness. There was no music in emptiness, to be sure, but there was potential. Potential for music, potential for life, potential for the Lady. Anything was possible: there were only differing degrees of probability.

The first sounds she made, then, were but single notes, a whisper of melody that, like an inhalation, filled the void, flowed and swirled through the hollowness. It strained at the confines that gave it shape and volume, widened them, filled them, and then, giving way in exhalation, it flowed back out into the world, spreading out over her sorrow, over the flowers, touching both as though with balm.

In her mind, in her heart that was now filling once again, she reached out to the flowers with melody, wrapped them suddenly in the warmth of harmony. Lost in the fullness of the passage that had turned abruptly from hollow to flow, Natil allowed herself to become a clear channel for what came from within her, the music that—as she herself was rooted in the workings of the universe, as she herself had knowledge of the earth and of the life that made it and nurtured it—could not but express as perfectly as material existence allowed all those workings, all that knowledge, all that life, all that nurture.

Yielding to herself and to her memory of what she had once been, she felt something change. It was like a wind. It was like a tide. It was like a season that passed quickly over her, and the melody and harmony that chimed from her bronze strings beat like a heart, like her heart, like the Lady's immanent, nourishing heart . . .

. . . and when she opened her eyes and let her strings ring into silence, the flowers were alive, and upright, and the blooms were open and wide to the sun.

She wept still, but as she hugged her harp, resting her shimmering cheek against the smooth wood, she thought that perhaps a small portion of her emptiness had remained filled. The breath, the music, the magic had stirred: it could stir again.

"Lovely," said a voice. "Exquisite. The still place within oneself reflecting the divine mystery. Perfect gnosis."

The speaker was a small man, very fair of face, with blond hair that gave the impression of a charming and absent-minded disarray. His clothing, in contrast, possessed a kind of dapper artlessness that was, perhaps, most noticeable in the care with which the sleeves of his unseasonably long-sleeved shirt were drawn down to his wrists. His very blue eyes harbored a certain sense of the beyond, though, as if he were seeing not what lay before him, but rather something much more important and splendid, something quite sufficient to make a man forget such paltry things as material existence and instead stand in simple awe of the Invisible.

He appeared not to have noticed the flowers.

"Heart," he continued to himself, though his words were loud enough—seemingly, intentionally loud enough—to carry clearly to Natil. "Such heart. Such a perfect expression of heart and holiness." He blinked at her with vague eyes. "Have we met?"

Natil blotted her tears. "Natil Summerson," she said, offering her hand. "I am your groundskeeper here at Kingsley."

"My pleasure," said the man. "My very great pleasure. I'm Terry Angel." He smiled, obviously expecting a response.

Natil heard the plea behind his words. "I have heard of your program, Professor Angel."

Terry smiled, an expression absolutely without guile. "It's so gratifying to hear that from someone like yourself. There are . . ." He sat down on the bench beside her, folded his hands simply in his lap, and looked out over the bright flower beds as though his glance contained a benediction for everything except the common fact of flowers and dirt and sunlight. ". . . so many who would like *not* to have heard of it. There is always opposition in the world. After all, we live within the closed circle of the Serpent—but I cannot judge! I cannot judge!" He sighed. "I'm very fortunate to have found such a shelter as Kingsley. It's like wings here, sheltering wings. There has been a sense of gnosis in everything about it. Dean Delmari and I, in fact, discussed the formation of the Hands of Grace program throughout the course of the twelve holy nights of Christmas . . . in the silence. It was

. . . gnosis . . ." He scattered his benediction again. "Gnosis. Have you heard the term?"

"I . . ." Natil glanced at the sun. Her crew would be arriving soon, and she wanted to get her harp into a safe place. "I have heard of it."

"Oh, but you *live* it, Natil. You *live* it!"

"Thank you," she said. "I . . . try."

"It was prayer," said Terry. His voice had dropped again into a magnified whisper. "I have never before witnessed such a perfect expression of a natural interior practice." He squirmed on the stone bench, his hands clenching with pent emotion, his eyes full of a lambent fire that glowed with the fitful radiance of will-o'-the-wisps—far away and beckoning into the unknown. "Oh, I can't help but believe that we were meant to meet this way. Tradition is so alive! It quivers with life! And there are powers that work through it, that arrange meetings like ours, that Tradition might continue to grow and live!"

Natil knew only one tradition, and it lay in the stones of the earth, the growth of trees, the slow tides of oceans. She had seen it in the plodding but graceful tread of the dinosaurs, in the skittering of trilobites in the warm shallows of Cambrian seas, in the flutter of ancient birds too new to their wings to even dream of flight. She had coaxed it up out of seething pits of slime and onto dry land. She had taken it by the hand when it had groped its way out of the trees and looked for a future on two feet. "Tradition," she said softly, "is life."

And something about her words, perhaps, carried to Terry a sense of what she actually meant, for the vagueness suddenly went out of his eyes, to be replaced by something akin to fright. "Yes," he said quickly. "Yes, it is. And life is . . ."

Staring out past the flowers as though he did not see them, his fists clenched tightly, he groped for words. Words, however, failed him, and there was a long silence. Thoughtfully, Natil ran a hand along the forepillar of her harp. The bronze strings glinted in the light of the rising sun, and the flowers waved in blinding ripples of color. There was magic in the world, and she had, once again, taken a handful of it and healed. It gave her hope.

She touched Terry lightly on the arm in the same fashion as she had, three million years before, offered reassurance to one of his ancestors on a dark night of rain. "Life simply is," she said.

But at her words, he rose—quickly, nervously—and took his leave, shaking her hand as one might shake the hand of an apostate bound for the stake, going his way down the walk, up the stairs, and into the rambling, pink mundanity of Aylesberg Hall.

Natil sighed. She bent down, touched an unmarred bloom. "Thank you, my brothers and sisters," she said softly. "The Hand of the Lady be on you."

CHAPTER 6

The click of the car door lock reminded TK too much of the brief, metallic warning given by a booby-trap an instant before its detonation. As it was, the simple, mundane sound—a little too loud, it seemed, amid the quiet of a suburban parking lot—was, just like the booby trap, an incontrovertible sign that he had entered a realm hostile to him, one in which his enemy had not only made all the rules, but was unwilling to tell him just what the rules were.

Car locks clicking, middle-aged women clutching their purses, young white men falling silent—with such spoor did one of TK's sex and skin color mark his trail through America. He should, he thought, have been used to it by now. But no one ever really got used to it. One buried it beneath layers of fundamentalist piety, poisoned it with unfocused anger, wrapped the sharp edges in simple hopelessness, or . . . reached an accommodation with things as they were. TK had reached an accommodation. Had he not, he would long ago have gone mad or gone to drugs.

To his right was a silver-gray BMW, the source of the click of the lock, and its driver was now staring casually (a little too casually) ahead as he tried to fit his key into the ignition without looking at it. He was not looking at it, TK knew, because to do that, he would have had to have moved, and if he had moved, he might have given that black man out there some reason to notice him.

That's right. You be cool, white boy. 'Cause if you ain't cool, this nigger here's going to take off this fake leg, smash his way in through your windshield, and cut your throat with the machete he got hidden in his inside coat pocket. Then he gonna drive to your house, rape your pretty little wife, sell your kids into slavery, loot your fur-

niture, and . . . yeah, burn the place down and sow the ground with salt. Happens all the time, don't it?

The driver of the BMW managed to get his vehicle started, into gear, and out of the parking lot.

TK shook his head. *You lucky, white boy. Another two seconds and you been dead meat.*

Standing at the door of the office building, wearing an old blue suit that was neither comfortable nor in character, TK watched the departing car speed down the long, curving driveway of the business park. In Vietnam, they had called it *Indian Country*: areas that the VC controlled without question. But here, Indian Country, despite the irony, was white man's country, and white man's country was everywhere.

From the beginning, the signs had been clear. The projects in Chicago had been effectively walled off from the centers of commerce by freeway interchanges, ill-kept streets, blocks of run-down storefronts and clutter-choked alleyways that had, seemingly, held as many junkies as tin cans. The scanty bus service that led nowhere save back to the inner city told the residents that they had best keep to their own turf; and as though to add one last sign, a lifted finger of warning that, like the pernicious labor laws of years past that closed profitable doors to women while herding them into sweat shops and abusive marriages, that professed fairness and aid while in reality tightening yet another set of social restrictions, the open balconies of the complexes were screened in with chain link mesh, ostensibly to prevent children from falling. But those who lived in Trey-Nine—and Trey-Eight, and Trey-Seven, and on and on through the Treys, and the Deuces, and all the other shorthand and familiar terms designed to give a sense of home and belonging to the intolerable—those who lived there had another, much different interpretation of the wire and bolts that confronted them when they sought to look beyond their poverty and isolation, for the lattice of unyielding metal fell across their view of the city like the bars of a prison.

TK climbed the steps of the office building and pushed in through the heavy glass door, feeling the almost subliminal snick of his prosthesis with each step, the there/ not-there sensation of a phantom limb moving in perfect accord with its plastic replacement. It was not hurting

much today. That was good: he did not want to have to
sweat his way through this interview. If he had to shuffle
and smile and do his best Stepin Fetchit for the white
man, he ought at least to be comfortable.

The offices of TreeStar Surveying lay just up the corridor, and TK opened the door to find a large, pleasant
room that was heavy on the potted plants. Moss green
carpet. Light wood paneling that reflected the brightness
of the sunlight pouring in through one wall of solid windows. The furniture was simple, echoing the paneling,
and someone had obviously arranged everything with an
eye toward the homelike and the comfortable that dove-
tailed neatly—and inexplicably—with the sylvan. TK
would not have been particularly surprised had there been
a stream running through the middle of the place.

The woman at the front desk looked up. "Yes, sir?"

TK saw it in her eyes. No matter how liberal the individual, no matter how open-minded, the cultural stereotypes were there, and he knew that she was seeing a black
man, someone who had no business being in this safe,
suburban white world, someone who was—oh, God, here
it was again—maybe even a little *dangerous*.

*Right. And I'm going to unscrew this leg in a minute,
honey chile, and then . . .*

But: "Theodore Winters," he said. "Here to see Hadden
Morrison."

She brightened. "Oh! They said you'd be in . . ."

*Oh! A tame nigger. Oh! He's not dangerous after all.
Oh! Some of my best friends . . .*

". . . this morning. Just a moment." She picked up her
desk phone, punched in a number. "Mr. Morrison . . ."
She colored. "I mean, Hadden. Mr. Winters is here."

Hadden arrived in the outer office in a moment. TK
was not entirely sure what he had been expecting, but he
decided that, whatever it was, Hadden was not it. But that
seemed to be the way the day was going. Buckland Employment had not been what he had been expecting, either, had, in fact, turned out to be something of a foretaste
of TreeStar Surveying; and Wheat Hennock, the counselor to whom Marsh had given TK's application because
of conflict-of-interest considerations, had been . . .

. . . well, was turning out to have been something of a
set up for Hadden Morrison.

TK looked him over: the instinctive act of a street fighter. Casual clothes. An easy grace that bespoke either years of martial arts training or an uncanny comfort with his own skin. Hadden's hair was cut on the long side of conservative—long enough to cover the tips of his ears—but though his sea gray eyes seemed to reflect just a little more light than TK might have expected, there was not a trace of a flicker in them as he returned the examination.

Wheat had been like that too, he recalled. She might have been perfectly, unnaturally colorblind. Smiling graciously, she had offered her hand, and, when TK had taken it, he had discovered her grip to be firm, direct, and possessed of something TK could only call *precision.*

Just as was the case now with Hadden's.

Colorblind. Sincere. Both of them.

They made the usual greeting noises, but TK found it a little unnerving that Hadden (again like Wheat) actually seemed to mean what he said. He *was* very glad to meet TK. It *was* a good afternoon. There was no artificiality in Hadden's voice, no pressure, no sense of anything forced or hidden: just solid sentiments, solidly and precisely expressed.

Hadden gestured TK back toward his office. "Come on back. We're going to have to talk a bit: we might as well sit down and take it easy."

The receptionist lifted her head. "Mr. Morrison?"

Hadden smiled. "Yes, Sheila?"

"Will Bright be coming in this afternoon? I've lost track of her schedule."

"This afternoon?" Hadden closed his eyes, considered. "Let's see ... it's Monday. Yes, she'll be here." He turned and escorted TK into his office. "Sheila," he explained, "is with us courtesy of a temp service. Bright is usually at the front desk, but with her being in school, sometimes we can't stay ahead of her."

"She in college?" TK tried to sound interested, was finding that, in the face of Hadden's impeccable courtesy, it was a little hard not to.

Hadden laughed. "Bright's going to be a surveyor. In another six months or so, she'll be joining a field team. I suppose we'll have to find another receptionist then."

TK recalled the flicker in Sheila's eyes, compared it with what he saw in Hadden's, what he had seen in

Wheat's. Bright's eyes, he found himself thinking, would not have flickered. He just *knew* they would not have flickered. "You ... promote from inside, then?"

Hadden pulled up a chair for TK. "A good question. I think I'd have to say yes, but I've found that people usually wind up ... well ... promoting themselves."

It was not quite an understandable answer, but TK decided that it would have to do.

They talked about his background, about Vietnam, the reserves, the Patriot station in Iraq, the work he had done to help find the software bug that had allowed a Scud missile to take twenty-eight lives. He tried to tell Hadden about his jobs in security, about the scuffling, but Hadden was not interested in either security or scuffling.

"Do you mean to say that with all this work with computers, you've just been working security?"

TK had been warming up to Hadden, but reality was reality. "What else?"

"TK ..." They had fallen into familiarity within the first two minutes. "... you've got skills. Why haven't you been using them?"

TK wanted to tell Hadden about the difficulties inherent in being black, from the projects, and one-legged. He wanted to tell him that quotas, while assisting some, could also hinder others. *Well*, it was easy to say, *we've got enough blacks, and enough cripples, and enough vets. Send me something else, will ya?*

He shifted uneasily. "Was all military stuff. You know: mainframe. You use a PC here, right?"

Hadden laughed. "I'd hardly call it *using* at this point, since I can't use it. But software is software. Bugs are bugs. You helped track down that problem with the Patriot programs ..." For a moment, his gaze turned shadowed as though at the thought of the reason for Patriots and programs for Patriots.

"Why did you leave your last job?" he asked suddenly.

It was the usual sort of question a prospective employer asked. "Got ..." TK looked at Hadden, met his eyes. There was frankness there, and TK decided to be honest. "Got called boy once too often."

To his surprise, his reply was met not by a liberal declaration that TreeStar was not at all like that—Sheila, temp though she was, had proved that much—or by a thinly veiled (and equally liberal) condemnation of the bigots and racists in the world. Instead, Hadden's face turned troubled. "Yes," he said softly. "That's still happening, isn't it?"

And it sounded to TK as though the fact that it was still happening was, to Hadden, some kind of personal failing, as though the owner of a small surveying firm in a Denver suburb really should have been able to do something that would prevent its happening ever again, but could not.

He rose, and TK was sure that the interview was over, that he would now be told *We'll call you* or *I need to talk to some other people.* But instead, Hadden gave him another one of those shining, open, perfectly frank smiles. "Let's take a look at this equipment that's been giving me such hell, shall we? I want to see what you think of it."

As they were crossing through the front office, a tall woman with a mop of black hair was just coming in. Her face was tanned as though from long hours spent outdoors, and TK might have called her rangy had her movements not exhibited the same grace and comfort he had seen in Hadden. "All done, chief," she called out to Hadden as she waved a notebook in the air. "Did I set a record?"

Her arms were lean and well muscled: martial arts training there for sure. And something about her demeanor made TK suspect that she was gay. Regardless, he had the feeling that he had seen her before, though he could not recall where.

Hadden glanced at the clock, then at the notebook. "I think you set several records," he said. "Am I going to have to check your figures?"

"Nah," she said. "I'm perfect." She approached TK, stuck out her hand. "Hi. I'm also Lauri. You must be TK."

TK took her hand and doled out a carefully measured smile as he reflected that it was easy for one to be cheerful when one never came within arm's reach of violence . . . or watched a child die before one's eyes.

Hadden smiled wryly. "I'm just taking TK to look at the . . . uh . . . monster."

There was light in Lauri's eyes. "The one that ate New York? Or just all your spare time? Good luck." She gave TK a wink.

But Hadden stood his ground. "Marsh says TK's a computer genius, Wheat says TK's a computer genius, and now I've talked to him, and I say TK's a computer genius, too."

TK, embarrassed by undeserved praise that, coming from other lips, would have sounded hideously artificial, nonetheless found that his memory had been jogged. "Oh," he said to Lauri, "you're the woman in the picture on Wheat's desk."

Dead silence. TK felt his face grow warm. Despite his precautions, he had inadvertently dropped his guard. Bad move. He was forgetting the tunnels, forgetting the dead center concentration required by the Patriot screens, forgetting the day to day caution that circumscribed a black life . . .

Indian Country.

"A picture of me?" said Lauri. "On Wheat's desk?"

"It . . . uh . . ." TK tried to cover for himself. "She . . . looked . . . like you. She was about your build. Leaning against a red and white truck." He doled out another smile, embarrassed now. "I guess I'm mistaken. Sorry."

"Not at all," said Hadden. "That sounds very much like Lauri."

Lauri was obviously puzzled, but also obviously determined to put TK perfectly at ease. "I guess when you do ILCs for a living, you get popular. I do a mean backsight, you know?" Another wink, a slightly bewildered smile, and she turned back to Hadden. "It's all in the book," she said. "A full day ahead of schedule. Web can have it by morning, and he can draw it up."

For a moment, Hadden glanced at TK. "All right," he said to Lauri, but TK suddenly knew that it would not be Web who would receive the raw data in the morning, but rather himself. Just something simple and useful with which to start off, to familiarize him with his new job.

Colorblind. Sincere. Precise. *These people are out of their minds,* he thought. But an instant later, it occurred to him that it certainly seemed to be a pleasant enough insanity.

The day was warm and muggy, but Sandy's hands were cold as she parked in the north lot at Kingsley. She took out her harp, and after peering with her good eye at the map that Terry had sent to her, started off across the campus.

Monday. The college had opened for the summer session, registration had begun, and she was on her way to meet Terry Angel for the first time. Even her inner barker appeared to be rather struck by the occasion, for he had fallen into a befuddled silence broken only by occasional mutterings that Sandy found easy enough to ignore. But even had he been pouring out full-throated abuse, Sandy would not have heard, for her tension and fear left no room for him this morning. She had worked for two years to come to Kingsley for the Hands of Grace program, and what would happen in the next hour would determine her final success or failure.

Her entire life had been traced out with just such pressured determinings, from her father's first entering of her body to her horrified mother's desperate flight with her from city to city, to the lengthy and vicious custody hearings, to the crushing verdict. And yet here was what Sandy hoped was the final crisis: her first meeting with Terry. After that would be, she prayed, a straight path. A smooth path. A healing path. The Hands of Grace was, according to Terry's letters, a large, interdisciplinary program at Kingsley, well-funded, well-supported by the schools of medicine, philosophy, and music. Staff translators were delving into the mysteries of ancient monastic customaries, extracting words and melodies that had once been used to cure and to comfort. Technicians at local hospitals were monitoring life-support systems, recording the sometimes dramatic changes—all positive—that occurred when one of Terry's contemplative musicians played for the sick and the dying. Philanthropists in the area were planning to fund a hospice based around Terry's techniques. Surely in all that grace and graciousness there was room for one young, abused woman who was looking for shelter and a little healing for herself.

She was mildly surprised when she realized that Terry's map was directing her to a basement room of the main administration building, but perhaps it was Terry's intention to keep his office humble, and out of the way. That would be very like him: monkish, simple in his wants, almost fanatically self-effacing. He was not the sort, Sandy guessed, to demand grand towers of steel and glass for his holy work.

The map he had given her, though, was thoroughly

muddled. Kingsley College was not large, but Sandy found herself wandering off onto the athletic fields, stumbling into the back door of the gymnasium and the library, turning the same corner not less than three times to find that she had come yet again upon the student union and the bookstore. The day was hot, the closet of her filthy apartment had been stifling and damp, and she was still exhausted from a day of cleaning that had stretched off late into the night without any sign of real progress.

. . . and she can't even find the administration building, and now look at her, she's starting to cry . . .

The barker's voice arose with her increasing confusion—Terry would think her stupid, she would arrive late, she might not arrive at all—and she did not have the strength to banish him. Sitting down heavily on a bench outside the student union, she laid her harp across her knees and put her shaking hands to her face. "Goddess," she murmured, "you know where I'm supposed to be going. I could use some help with this."

She heard nothing, but she sensed movement, and when she looked up, she found that a slender woman in a big, floppy straw hat was standing before her. She was holding a shovel in one gloved hand, and her t-shirt and overalls were stained with mud and grass, but her face was sweet, her eyes were a soft blue, and her expression . . .

Sandy had never seen such a concerned look.

"A harper," the woman said, and her voice was as soft as her eyes and sweet as her face. "Unless I am very mistaken." There was a touch of water in her accent, an accent that Sandy could not place. "Blessings upon you this day."

Her words, quaint and old fashioned, echoing the old witch greeting—*Blessed Be!*—made Sandy feel hopeful. "Not a very good harper," she said. "I can't even find the administration building."

The gardener pointed to her right. "Down this walk," she said, "and then turn left at the fountain. Aylesberg Hall will be straight ahead. You cannot miss it." The soft blue eyes twinkled with a shimmer as of starlight. "It is pink."

"Pink?"

"Pink." Again a twinkle. "I will take you there if you wish."

It suddenly occurred to Sandy that she was talking to a

perfect stranger. Instinctively, her stomach clenched. "No . . . uh . . . thanks. I'll . . . I'll . . . I'll find it." She got up hurriedly, tucked her harp under her arm. "Thanks."

The gardener touched her forehead with her free hand, bowed slightly. "It is what I am here for."

True to the gardener's words, Sandy came within sight of the pink building within a minute, and, since Terry's map had already proved deficient, she asked directions at the information desk just within the front door.

"Hands of Grace?" The secretary frowned. "I'm not sure . . ." She frowned again as she looked through a tattered directory. "Is that in Comparative Religion?"

"No . . ." Sandy was suddenly afraid that the receptionist was going to shout at her. "It's . . . it's a separate . . . uh . . . group. Terry Angel . . ."

"Oh, Terry Angel. All right, then."

"Is he here today?" Sandy asked. "Is he at the hospitals or the hospice?"

"Hospitals? Hospice?" Another frown.

"Well . . ." Sandy was again afraid. "I mean, he's working closely with the medical department."

"Kingsley is a liberal arts college," said the woman. "It doesn't have a medical school. Are you sure you've come to the right place?"

Sandy felt the flush of mortification rising. "Terry Angel . . ." she managed, using the name like a charm.

"Well, Professor Angel is downstairs, in room 1A."

"I don't want to interrupt him. Does he have students with him?"

The secretary was now plainly puzzled. "Students? Professor Angel doesn't have any students. He's on a research fellowship."

"But . . . the Hands of Grace program . . ."

Faced with an obviously deranged young woman who was clutching at the oddly shaped case under her arm as though it were a life preserver, the secretary turned conciliatory. "I don't know anything about any Hands of Grace program," she said, "but if you want to talk to Professor Angel, he's down in room 1A."

Sick with fear, Sandy nodded and made for the stairwell. Halfway down, though, she stopped on a landing and pulled out her bundle of letters and papers. Yes, they were still there. Yes, they were still real. Yes—she read them over, skimming page after page—they still described the Hands of Grace program, the fellowship offered to Serena Kathryn Joy that would cover lodging, texts, and tuition for a full year at Kingsley beginning with the summer session of 1991. Acceptance letter, registration forms, photocopies of Sandy's school transcripts . . .

It's not real, said the barker, suddenly turning insinuating. *How can you say that it's real? That woman didn't know a thing about it. There you go again, right back to the lye buckets. Didn't you get enough from old dad?*

Her hand flew to her face. The scars on her jaw were rough, ichthyic.

Nausea was gripping her as she seized her harp and stumbled down the stairs, and she reached the basement level in a blind haze of panic. The door ahead of her said 1A. It might as well have said *Courtroom, County of Los Angeles,* with a custody dispute on the docket that day between Frederick and Gloria Joy. Shaking, sick, Sandy knocked.

"Hello! Come in!"

Was that *him*? Astounded by her temerity, Sandy actually took hold of the knob, turned it, pushed.

It was an old classroom: wooden floors, windows that looked out and up deep wells toward ground level, smooth slate blackboards. A disordered scattering of tables and chairs faced front like tired soldiers. The teacher's desk was a ruin of old wood, burns that had obviously been acquired in a chemistry lab specializing in Gothic reanimation, varnish that had flaked like a leper's skin.

Sandy hardly saw the desk, for a man was just then standing up from the chair behind it. He was but a few years older than Sandy, but he was blond where she was dark, sighted where she was blind, and there was an expression of holy peace in his bright eyes.

Her mouth was dry, her throat tight. "Professor Angel?"

"Sandy!" And his beatific smile banished her nausea, sent the barker flying out the door. It was a smile that made Sandy feel as though she were the most important person in the world, an absolutely essential individual upon whose presence depended the entire Hands of Grace program. "I'm delighted to see you. Did you have any trouble finding me?"

"Uh . . . no . . . no . . ." She was important. She had to remain important. "I . . . I . . . didn't have any trouble at all."

"Wonderful." Terry's smile was dazzling, and Sandy felt almost giddy with relief. She was, she was sure, accepted. Paperwork was a formality. The fellowship moneys would arrive without interference or delay. Everything would be all right: Terry Angel had accepted her.

"I was just kind of surprised . . . that they've got you down here," she said as she set her harp down and took the chair that he offered her.

"Down here?"

The question in his voice was a little more than a question. Sandy immediately felt uncomfortable. "Well, I'd expected that you'd have an office . . ."

Terry looked at her. There was a great deal in that look.

"I mean . . ." What did she mean? Was she questioning Terry? And after he had accepted her without question? "I mean . . . with the hospitals and the hospice and all the . . . other students . . ." Her voice trailed off.

She looked around. There was not a sign that there were any other students. She sensed that, indeed, there were no other students. Worse, though, Terry's smile was gone. To be sure, it had not been replaced by a frown, but after such a dazzling and palpable presence, its simple absence was something terrifying.

Sandy, of a sudden, did not feel important or accepted.

"My mistake, I'm sure," she said quickly. "It's wonderful to meet you at last. See, I've brought my harp. I'm ready to get to work."

"Good, good." Terry's smile was back, and he took her hands in his as though in so doing he were touching something precious. "There's lots of work to be done. This program is just beginning, and we're both in a very fortunate position, because we can decide just how it's all going to go together."

It was an odd thing for him to say about a course of study that was receiving so much funding, had the interest of several hospitals, and was about to receive its own hospice. But Terry was still smiling, and Sandy pushed her doubts away, for already she was feeling better, feeling accepted . . .

. . . feeling important.

CHAPTER 7

From *The Front Range Metaphysical Journal,* June 1991:

The man whom many call "the Saint of Denver" has finally been given the academic backing he needs to heal the world.

However, if Terry Angel actually heard anyone referring to him or his work as a saint, he would be the first to protest.

"Tradition, and by that I mean the great spiritual Tradition of the Christian world, is something that is so big that there is no room for personal concerns," he says. "What I offer is something that serves every single person as a spiritual brother or sister, and that service is essentially anonymous. You might call me a mid-wife, a sacramental midwife, of Tradition."

Terry Angel practices his work at Kingsley College. But though he holds the title there of professor of music, his real work is healing. Since 1981, he has created an academic and practical program of ministry for the sick based upon the mystical use of Roman Catholic plainchant.

"It's really fascinating," he says. "The holy monastics of Europe chanted their office hours eight times a day, immersing themselves in music so much that their physical beings eventually came to be in perfect accord with the notes that they sang. Gradually, they developed a method of using their music to banish disease and illness [discord] from themselves and those who came to them for help."

It was in 1981 that Professor Angel first stumbled over the clues that subsidiarily led him to obscure monasteries and libraries of Europe to seek out the renmants of a forgotten spiritual practice. He was a graduate student at a local university at the time, specializing in medieval harp studies. As he tells it:

"I received a telephone call from a classmate. His father was dying. It was a difficult death. The old man had lived in pain so long that he had become embittered. Practically the only thing that my classmate could suggest that caught his interest was some live music."

"You can imagine how I felt! But at the time I was working with a lot of plainchant. I've always been drawn to monody, which was a natural outgrowth of my expertise in ancient harps, and when I got to the bedside, I couldn't think of anything to play for the old man except some chants. The *Adoro te devote,* the *Ubi caritas,* the *Salve Regina.* To my complete surprise, as soon as I started, the old man's breathing and heartbeat became more stable. There were monitors hooked up, and you could see it on the dials. I felt, unaccountably, as though I were folding him within spiritual wings, and I let that loving feeling penetrate me and surrendered myself to it."

Though his classmate's father died soon after, Doctor Angel decided that he had hit upon something wonderful. He was an already attending national and international conferences on ancient medieval music, and he started to ask some of the lecturers. Eventually, he attended a lecture by noted researcher David Parnassus on an obscure monastic customary that referred to a tradition involving chant and healing. Soon after, Terry received a fellowship at the Academy de San Lucy in Paris, where he spent several years tracking that tradition down to its source. When he was in the vaults of the Trinity College Library in Dublin, he had been granted a stipend for research on monastic singing techniques, and he found several medieval writings that confirmed his carefully formulated hypothesis.

"There was a whole alchemical tradition of inner practice with the medieval harp. The harp is a frame, like a cross, upon which the soul of the harper, like the strings, is crucified. In an alchemical sense, you see, that's exactly what happens when you take up the harp. You're always being stretched, stretched. The monks would use it that way, though, of course, they were forbidden by Canon Law to actually perform on instruments. But they used their voices in the same way, because the metaphor was the same. Medieval life swam in a sea of metaphor that gave meaning to every phase of existence."

When he returned to Denver, though, Angel found his research efforts interfered with by simple economics. Teaching harp to a small group of devoted students did not give him either the time or the money he needed, and only with difficulty he managed to write a number of articles that later appeared in several major European journals of religion and historic music.

But, fate again smoothed his path. A telephone call requested that he lecture on his work at the yearly medieval conference held annually in Kalamazoo, Michigan. Reports of his findings eventually reached Kingsley College, who offered him a teaching position.

Terry is working closely with two Denver hospitals who want him to add his "contemptlative musicianship" to their staffs, and with a number of charitable organizations who are planning a hospice based upon his work, which he calls the "Hands of Grace."

"It's a continuing series of miracles," he says. "People seem to have an instinctive recognition of the goodness and rightness of this work, and they really want to help further it. It really demonstrates the living quality of tradition, that a branch of knowledge that had appeared dead for so long has suddenly come back to life."

"You have to do one thing at a time."

Evening was falling over Denver, its shadows softened into misty grayness by the clouds that had again gathered to bring rain, and in the dim living room of the battered women's shelter, Bright knelt beside a woman in a rocking chair. "You have to do one thing at a time," she said again, and the woman, whose name was Suzy, and who was not really listening, nodded.

"There's just so much to do," she said, half to Bright, half to the other women who sat in the room, who had wrapped silence about themselves like a sheath of bandages. "Mick would take care of everything. He'd take care of me. I just don't know what to do now."

"You can learn," said Bright, and she could not help thinking of Rob, who, long ago, had also taken care of everything—from gutting her paycheck to blacking her eyes. "It's not so much to learn."

"I think he still really loves me," said Suzy.

Bright could not but wonder what kind of love could include guns and broken bones; but searching back into a life so remote from her present existence that it seemed truly to belong to someone else, she remembered that when she had been Amy, she herself, against all reason or rationality, had held to a similar belief.

She closed her eyes, felt the starlight, breathed it. Its shimmer mingled with the growing patter of rain on the roof. "Okay," she said softly, noncommittally. She was not a psychologist, she was just a volunteer. She was not allowed to counsel the residents. She could only listen.

"I think I still love him." Suzy lifted her head. Across the room, a woman with a broken arm was attempting to nurse her infant. The baby fussed at the harsh presence of the fiberglass cast, and the woman, whose face and breasts were bruised, was having difficulty letting down.

"One thing at a time." Bright patted Suzy's shoulder. "You don't have to make any decisions now. You just stay with us as long as you need to. Take your time."

"Yeah, thanks," said Suzy, but Bright sensed with a flicker of hopelessness that she would be returning to Mick within the week, to face again his threats, his intoxication and his fists.

Would she eventually come back to the safe house? Perhaps. Sometimes a woman needed two or three tries before she could find the strength necessary to leave an abusive mate. But even then, after she had freed herself, after counseling and state aid had set her up with a job and a place to live, she all too often would find another man who would treat her in exactly the same fashion as had the first.

Bright got up to go to the woman with the fussy baby, but Monique, the counselor on duty that night, was beckoning to her from the door to the office. Bright gave the struggling mother a quick smile and a gesture that told her to wait for a moment. When she entered the office, though, Monique shut the door.

"Is Suzy okay?" she asked in a low voice. Her manner, though, told Bright that Suzy was most assuredly not the subject at hand.

"She's still sorting herself out."

Monique stared off at the curtained windows. "That's . . . to be expected . . . I guess."

"What happened?"

Bright's question seemed to take all the strength out of Monique. She sagged, half sobbed, then sat down hard in the chair in front of the computer. "I just got a call. You remember Vicki?"

"She . . . left last week, didn't she?"

Monique had covered her face with her hands. "She went back to her man."

Bright nodded slowly. It happened. If it worked out, if the court-ordered counseling broke the cycle of anger and abuse, then that was fine. But that did not happen very often. She sensed that it had not happened in Vicki's case.

"They had another fight," said Monique. "A big one. He was drunk, and he had a gun."

"He shot her?"

Monique shook her head. "She got it away from him. She shot *him*. He's dead."

Bright slumped. No, it had not happened in Vicki's case.

"She's been arrested."

Bright lifted her head. "But it was self-defense."

"The police don't see it that way," said Monique, her face still in her hands. "As far as they're concerned, it's murder. Maybe first degree murder."

"But he was beating her up!"

"She had the gun." Monique shrugged helplessly. "That's all that counts." She dropped her hands, sat back with closed eyes. A tear found its way down her cheek. "You get beat up, and beat up, and beat up, and no one pays any attention. And then one day you break, and you do something, and then *you're* the one who's wrong."

Suddenly, she rose, crossed the room, jerked open the drapes, stared out into the backyard where jungle-gyms and see-saws glistened in the rainy darkness against a backdrop of six-foot privacy fence. "And it just keeps happening." Her fists clenched. "Dammit," she said, "what's the use?"

Bright thought back to her own abuse, her own tragedy. Had it not been for elven blood, had it not been for Elves, her fate might well have been one with Vicki's.

Grace. She had been graced. And Elves were here to grace others. But Monique had said it perfectly: it just kept happening.

She went to Monique, laid a hand on her shoulder. "You just have to do one thing at a time," she said softly. "Just one thing at a time."

But her words seemed hollow even to herself. One thing at a time . . . forever. *Forever.* What did that really mean? How did one cope with it? What got one through eternity?

Monique was still staring into the night, looking as though she herself wanted a gun. Bright stood for another minute, and then she went out into the living room and talked soothingly to the woman and her baby. The milk eventually let down, and the child nursed and fell asleep. There was gratitude in the eyes of the mother as Bright kissed her on the head and gave her a *God bless*.

God bless. Sure. And one thing at a time.

Natil floated among the stars.

They burned in the velvet blackness of her inner firmament, but though they were immanent, close, even comforting, they were also distant and cold, for Natil remembered how, once, the limits of the universe had been as much within the reach of her mind as the earth was within the grasp of her physical fingers. Then, like all the Firstborn, she had held the sun as though it were an apple, cupped the world in tender hands, felt the life and the energies flow, whispering through darkness, whispering through light.

No more. She had the stars, and that was all. And where, in the dungeons of the Inquisition of Furze, the stars had perhaps been enough, now they were terribly, terribly insufficient.

Below, in the city of Denver and in its scattering of suburbs, Heather was ladling stew into the tin cups of men whose faces were seamed with poverty. Bright was trying to be a comforting presence for women who knew too much of habitual battering. Web and Ash peer-counseled at a community mental health facility. Lauri, a telephone receiver pressed to her ear, strained to capture the emotions and the fears of yet another caller. Hadden and Raven were at a city council meeting, trying to ar-range financial assistance so that people could buy the houses that Marsh, come the weekend, would be helping to build. And throughout the long summer evenings, while Dell and Fox landscaped low income homes for free, Allesandro and Wheat heroically planted trees in park and forest alike.

And on and on. Seventeen Elves in Denver. Seventeen attempts to bring a little compassion and a little grace to a world that seemed at times to have none of either. Seventeen untiring efforts to help and heal. No one com-plained. Helping and healing were what Elves were for, were the reasons for their existence. No one doubted it. It had been that way from the beginning.

But despite their similarities to the Firstborn, the Elves of Denver were profoundly different; for, having once been human, they would never find in their new status any refuge from the mingled terror and tragedy of mortal life. If there had been a joining of the elven and the hu-man, it had come not only from the awakening in mortal bodies of immortal blood, but also from the persistence in immortal minds of a very mortal care and immediacy. If elven grace had returned to the world, it had come not to dwell apart, but to live next door; not to be dispensed with divine impartiality, but bestowed compulsively; not to be passed from the above to the below, but from hand to equal hand, with, at times, an almost clumsy naiveté.

There was for these modern Elves no buffering sense of separation, no emotional isolation into which to with-draw. And yet, at the same time, there was for them still no vision of the Lady to make up for the pain and the lacks that, as a result of their naked and immortal con-frontation with everything that had to be done—everything that could not be done—was beginning to assume a poignancy and a heartbreak far beyond what any soul, elven or not, could contemplate enduring for all eternity.

Starlight.

The stars were all about her, but none called to her

save in her memory of the distant past. And so, as she had done countless times since she had come to Colorado, she chose one, moved toward it, threw herself into the blinding incandescence.

But when her vision cleared and she opened her eyes, she saw no grassy plain, no skyful of stars, no Woman, robed in blue and silver, whose eyes mirrored divine compassion and love. Natil saw only Elvenhome, the lands about it, the glow of city lights upon the low gray clouds.

The rain was a warm, soft drizzle, but her back was against the trunk of a pine tree, and the thick canopy of needles had kept her dry. Her eyes, though, were wet. Again she had tried, again she had failed. And if she had garnered from her harping at Kingsley any sense of elven magic and power, it was gone now, and the futility had returned. The Elves were without the Lady; the Goddess whom Roxanne and Charity had worshiped and loved had been reduced to a matter of superstition and outright profit. Once again, Natil was groping with her memories.

The night turned slowly, the rain dwindled, diminished, ended. Natil stood up, brushed needles from her overalls, and made her way back toward the big house. Tonight, she was alone, for the others did not usually come up to Elvenhome save on the weekends: human griefs and human sorrows were in the city, and so in the city they stayed.

Only Natil lived full time at Elvenhome. By a consensus that had been arrived at within days of her appearance in Colorado, she had been given a room of her own on the second floor, and no one would have questioned her had she decided to remain there always, to be caretaker of Elvenhome, keeper of its gardens, incarnate spirit of the holy place. Indeed, after a hundred years of wandering and eons of concern and interaction, she had found the idea tempting, but instinct had told her that she could not so withdraw, and therefore, like the Elves into whose welcoming arms she had come, she had left her isolation behind. Equipped with a social security number and a driver's license, she had found a gardening position at Kingsley that had quickly grown into the responsibilities of head groundskeeper, and she had tried—as she continued to try, as they all continued to try—to help and heal.

In the darkness that held for her eyes the transparency of clear water, she entered the Home, passed through the kitchen that had been, but a day ago, filled with laughter and starlight, climbed the stairs to her room. She was still the keeper of Elvenhome, but, unlike her people, she knew that her task involved far more than the maintenance of a house, more than the balancing of its accounts or the management of its gardens. Natil kept a physical home, true, but she also kept the memory of the elven spirit, a spirit that had, somewhere in the past, faded along with the Firstborn. Like the gardener she had become, though, she was concerned not with static preservation, but rather with growth and the sudden blooming of life where once had been only the terrible color of barren fields.

But it was an unknown field that she tilled, and so far her efforts had proved fruitless.

She opened a door of dark wood that Wheat had set with an elaborate panel of stained glass and grisaille: trees, flowers, birds, mountains. Within, though, the room was quite spartan. A desk, a chair, a mirror, a dresser full of human costume, a bookcase full of her current reading—she needed no more, for she had the earth and her inner stars and the love of her people. And, in any case, after the deprivations and hatreds of the cities of men, and after a hundred years of wandering, she considered even so barren a personal space to be a sign of great wealth indeed.

But in the closet, carefully cleaned and hung with reverence, were her old clothes of green and gray. And on a table, in a place of honor, stood her old harp. She left the clothes where they were, for it was not time for her to wear them again—perhaps it would never be time—but she took up her harp, threw the windows wide, and with the night air pouring in, bringing with it the odor of past rain and the calls of mockingbirds and owls, spent the rest of the dark hours adding to the music of mortality her immortal song . . . and sorrow.

"What you want?"

The eye, black as the maw of a VC tunnel, peered out of the aperture left by a door that had been opened no more than a finger's breadth. TK could see only the eye—young, narrow, hostile—but he knew without a shred of doubt that there was an AK or a 'gauge or something even worse leveled at him from the darkness within the crack house.

"I want to talk to you," he said. The matter of guns did not bother him, nor did the prospect of an inherently useless death. No, if anything about this interview disturbed him, it was the utter youth of the individual on the far side of the door.

" 'Bout what?"

He was talking to a Tiny. He did not want to talk to a Tiny. "Who's in charge here? Where's an OG?"

A rasp of laughter. The young eye vanished, was replaced by an older eye, and then the door was abruptly jerked open. The question was repeated, this time in a voice that rang like iron.

"What you want?"

The man was only a shade shorter than TK. From his ear dangled an earring in the form of a Cadillac emblem. His eyes held . . . nothing.

Black. Flat black. The color of numbness. The color of a renunciation of pain so permanent and irrevocable that it precluded forever the recurrence of anything as paltry as emotion. Was there any need for AKs or 'gauges or Uzis when such eyes, by their very negation of life, held within themselves the pure essence of lethality?

TK was not sure what idiocy had brought him to this door. He had just gotten a good job, he had just taken his first step away from scuffling, he had much to anticipate. Someday, he might be able to move away from this neighborhood and get something where the streets were wider and the houses did not jostle against one another like a band of drunkards, where crack houses existed . . . somewhere else, where the idea of children being pulped by bullets was only a bad dream that did not partake of waking life in the slightest.

But no one ever really left the 'hood. TK himself carried the projects with him like a slab of ice in his heart, as integral a part of his makeup as the pigmentation of his skin, the tunnels in the Nam, the bunker in Iraq, or any one of the countless things that had shaped his being. But maybe that was why he was here: because months ago, in a hospital in Georgia, as he had lain despairing over the loss of his leg and the news of his wife's desertion, someone had done something for him that was as unself-conscious as breathing, as homely as a plate of beans, as nurturing as the milk of a mother's breast. And that something was a part of him, too.

"You in charge?" he said levelly. One did not show fear. One simply did not. Whether cut, stabbed, shot, or beaten, one simply did not react. Even the gangs of TK's youth had held to that vicious code which had taken the adversarial bedrock of society for a beginning and there-after distilled it into a life of constant, unremitting, and universal enmity.

The flat black eyes did not even flicker. Again, the voice like iron: "What you want?"

TK was calm. He could not be otherwise if he expected to survive. "I want to tell you to get out of this 'hood."

The eyes narrowed. The man was large, his muscles taut. TK could easily envision those arms rhythmically beating someone to death, or those hands holding an au-tomatic pistol at the ready while the electric windows of a stolen car whined down. "You dis'n me, nigger?"

"I ain't dis'n you, man. One of your homeboys got a kid hit the other day, and I don't want no more kids hit."

There was still nothing in the eyes. "He was a buster. Been a buster for a long time. Off brands come in here fixing to splash on him, he cut and run. Took our money with him. I don't know where he is. None of us know where he is. He try to claim with us anymore, we gonna take care of him."

"I don't give a damn about him," said TK. It was a lie: he cared very much, for he wanted to see him in jail, or bloody and face-down on the sidewalk. "I care about the kids."

"We'll watch the kids."

TK persisted. "You gonna get them all killed. You gonna get them killed with bullets, or you gonna get them killed with crack. You want that little girl's sister to grow up and be a cluckhead?"

There kindled within the flat black of nothing a spark of something that was much like flame, save that it burned without light, without heat, without anything save the destruction of what it fed upon. And TK knew what it was, and he knew what it fed upon. "This be our 'hood, nigger," said the man, and the iron was still in his voice. "You want anyone to move, you go move yourself."

"So you won't quit."

The man reached for TK, grabbed the front of his shirt. TK just stood where he was, let his weight sink down.

The man pulled. TK did not move.

TK met the coldly burning eyes. This was no mad dogging going on here, no visual challenge that played along with the current gang etiquette, no excuse for the homeboys to open up with the artillery. TK just looked, and in his eyes, he knew, were the projects, and the tunnels, and the bunker, and the absolute impossibility of ever moving him.

And, slowly, the man let go of his shirt.

"Nigger," said TK softly, "you be killing your own people." And if there was iron in the voice of the earringed man at the door, there was steel in his own. "I am asking you to wake up."

And then, knowing full well that if he betrayed even the slightest uncertainty in his glance, in his gestures, in his gait, he would at that very moment feel the bullets smack into his spine, he turned, descended the steps, and walked slowly down the sidewalk toward his apartment building.

The hospital in Georgia. And that little girl. He had to *try*.

There were no bullets. But, behind him, he heard a car pulling up to the curb, and he thought that if he strained his ears, he could hear the rustle of bills.

CHAPTER 8

Research.

Terry had said it, written it, reiterated it. Research was the foundation upon which the Hands of Grace program rested, the armor that would protect it from the brickbats hurled by those who would see in its simple ministry of the heart a threat to their administrative power, the key that would unlock the doors of scientific materialism and allow contemplative musicians unimpeded entry into hospital and hospice alike.

Sandy had understood, had embraced the idea of the Hands of Grace. To her, the program was no mere academic exercise, but rather an effort to bring something of divinity into the world; and whether, like herself, one believed in an immanent Goddess who poured Her love out upon the earth without condition and without reserve, or, like Terry, viewed the universe as a corrupt and transient state that could upon occasion be graced by the otherwise miserly good will of a transcendent Supreme Being, the worthiness of the endeavor was beyond questioning.

But, despite her enthusiasm and willingness, Sandy found herself unprepared for the immense amount of reading, note taking, and preparation with which she was faced, not only as an ordinary student in the program, but as Terry's assistant, a position to which he elevated her within a week. Assistant! To the director of the Hands of Grace!

But now she found herself caught between the honor of her position—an assistant to work that she perceived as at once holy and important—and the tacit deception that had brought her to Kingsley. She had expected, given the content of Terry's letters and self-published brochures, to find a thriving program with many students and full facilities. There were, however, no other students. There would, it appeared, be no other students, even when the regular semester started in the fall. And the facilities for the program—the money, the hospitals, the hospice—remained ephemeral: Terry referred to them, but they never seemed to make any kind of inroad into Sandy's direct experience.

Indeed, direct experience told Sandy that she was alone with Terry in a wretched little classroom and dependent upon him not only for her status, but also for her livelihood. She had sold everything in Los Angeles, she had spent everything in order to come to Denver, she was living on a Hands of Grace fellowship. She had burned her bridges. There was no going back.

In truth, though, she did not want to go back. There was nothing for her in Los Angeles, and here in Denver was a door she hoped would take her beyond even the memories of the ghosts she had left behind. Indeed, as both abuse victim and as witch, she had always habitually searched for such doors, such escapes. Sandy the battered child had looked to the backgrounds of cartoons for solace, had yearned to enter those soft green fields of sunlight, comfort, and plenty. Sandy the witch wanted to heal, to make of the physical world, if not an absolute reification of divine love, then at least an echo of it, to touch pain and sickness with a hand that was at once her own and that of her Goddess, manifesting divinity with word and with music.

But there was no music in the work that Terry set before her. There were words, to be sure—articles, books, doctoral theses, dissertations—but nothing else. Terry, in fact, consistently avoided any mention of music. Research was what he wanted. Research and information.

She wondered, though, whether research pertinent to a hospital and hospice ministry could possibly consist of a lengthy table of correspondences between the old duration letters of Gregorian chant and the symbols of the ancient Russian *znamenny* notation. Or of summaries of countless articles from early music periodicals that argued relentlessly over the proper execution of admittedly hypothetical medieval ornaments. Or of repeated viewings and summaries of video tapes produced by an obscure British pseudo-scientific organization dedicated to advancing the theory that everything in the universe was made up of sound waves ... and never mind what medium those waves might be propagating in.

For all its incomprehensibility, though, the work was involved and meticulous, requiring long hours. Very quickly, Sandy found herself spending almost all her time in the library or in the shabby classroom that doubled as Terry's office. She had given up trying to finish cleaning her apartment—bottles of cleansers and a can of spray-on oven cleaner still sat unused in the cupboard beneath her dirty kitchen sink—but since she only went home to eat a bowlful of cold cereal for dinner and crawl into her bedroom closet for a few hours' sleep with Little Sandy held tightly in her arms, it hardly mattered.

What did matter, though (and as the weeks went on and a scorching July turned into a sullenly hot August it mattered more and more), was the lack of music. Sandy never failed to take her little harp to school with her, but Terry never gave it more than a glance. He had, in fact, never asked to see it or to hear her play it. He was far more concerned with such things as how many times and with what complete acceptance, devotion, and belief she had read an abstruse and rather senseless article on the chastity of plainchant melodies.

"You have to read material like this at least three times," he informed her. "Once for the sense, once for the emotion, and then, after you've meditated on every unfamiliar word so that you've attained complete submission to the author's will, once for the hidden meaning. This is a matter of heart. This is gnosis, and it can only be understood as gnosis, and by complete ..."

His blue eyes fastened upon her, and Sandy was shaken by their intensity.

"... submission. It is through powerlessness that true authority is attained. The Son of Man was crucified. That was the ultimate affirmation of powerlessness. And so you can see that abject helplessness is divinity made manifest."

Sandy's instinctive revulsion to Terry's comments was something that she could not deny, for, paralleling as they did her father's constant demands for her submission to his abuse, they produced an almost physical dizziness and nausea that made her at once frightened and ashamed. In the past, she had found refuge from such conflicts in her harp; now, though, there was no time for her harp. There was no time for anything. If she needed a refuge, she apparently would have to find it in work, in research, in the furtherance of a project that was beginning to usurp all of her waking hours just as it had apparently usurped Terry's entire life.

He himself worked tirelessly, traveling, as he told her, from hospital to hospital, from sickbed to sickbed, bringing his musical ministry to those who were ill or dying while hospital technicians took notes on the efficacy of this particular melody, or that particular mode. Harp music, he declared, was wonderfully effective against the torments of AIDS, some patients even receiving the music he played in the form of an immediate relief of physical pain. Others, he went on, had more of a multidimensional experience of body, soul, and spirit.

The prospect of one day participating in such work captivated Sandy. Yes, she wanted to help. Yes, she wanted to do that. But as the summer passed, as her work load increased, and as her harp remained unplayed, she began to sense a faint, desperate fluttering in her mind, as though a caged bird were battering itself against the iron grillwork of its prison. She wanted music. She wanted harp music.

"Is there a chance that . . . like . . . I could play for someone?" she asked late in August when Terry was patiently explaining how she had missed the entire point of a book about the philosophical meanings of the ecclesiastical modes. "I'd really like to play."

And Terry sighed. The look (she had come to know it well) that was not so much disapproval as a withholding of complete acceptance passed across his face as he slowly and unconsciously straightened the cuffs of his long-sleeved shirt. "When you first wrote to me," he said, shifting his gaze as though into a spiritual world that only he could perceive, "I could tell from your letter and from the tape that you sent that your playing was a perfect expression of a natural interior practice. I'd never before heard anyone with such an affinity for plucked strings. But you, Sandy, have to strive for simplicity in your playing. You have to empty yourself of your Self and become merely one who keeps vigil beside the bed of the sick, a chalice, as it were, of healing sound."

When he said such things to her—and he said them often, as often, in fact, as Sandy found the courage to ask questions—his eyes would grow brighter, his smile more intense; and though he had not answered her, had, in fact, obliquely told her that it was impertinent of her to have asked, Sandy inevitably felt her self-worth expanding beyond the disfigurements and blindness of a victim of childhood abuse and incest, felt herself growing into a young woman who, with her harp, might someday actually be able to do something for someone else . . . as well as for herself.

It could happen. It *was* happening. And all it would take was work. Research.

But near the beginning of September, when she had half convinced herself that now, with the beginning of the regular school session, she would actually get her fingers on harpstrings and begin to learn some of the actual Hands of Grace material, Terry presented her with an even more extensive project.

The *Liber Usualis,* which had, before the second Vatican Council, been the primary book of the Roman Catholic liturgy, contained an immense amount of plainchant. In over two thousand closely printed pages, it managed to include all the festal days, the Hours of the monastic Office, the complex and elaborate rites once performed between Holy Thursday and Easter Sunday, the psalms and their intonations, a wealth of antiphons, Glorias, Credos, Introits, Graduals, smatterings of Ambrosian and even Gallican chant, and much more. The problem, Terry explained, his eyes bright, was that all the texts were in Latin, and therefore relatively inaccessible to the layman. "The Hands of Grace serves everyone," he said, "as a sister or brother. Even if we're singing in Latin, or harping Latin melodies, we ourselves must know the meaning of the words so that the membrane of light that is taking shape in the sickroom can be properly received by the patient. That's the whole point: we receive God, and the patient receives the music of God."

"But are the texts really important?" Even through her increasing discomfort with Terry's Christian mode of expression, Sandy was already suspecting what he wanted . . . and was dismayed by the prospect. She could not help but recall, in any case, that he had frequently told her that the program had access to a large staff of Latinists and translators, as well as to complete copies of all the ancient manuscripts, customaries, and chant books. "And, anyway, I thought—"

Terry was looking at her.

"I mean, we're eventually going to be playing for people who might not be Catholic, who might, like, have some bad associations with Latin." She was, she reflected, really only thinking of herself, for her family had been Catholic, and her father's prominence in the Knights of Columbus had effectively ensured that any revelations Sandy had made—to the priest in the confessional, to the nuns who taught her—went unheard, unheeded. "Shouldn't we just concentrate on melody?"

And Terry smiled. "Sandy," he said patiently, "you must recall that, in plainchant, the melody merely compliments the text. All the meaning is contained in the text. The text informs and shapes the melody, and the melody submits without reservation to the precepts of its guide. You understand, of course, that I'm not arguing with you: I'm only presenting this to your inner forum of consciousness, for your consideration and final discovery of truth."

"But melody is universal." Sandy felt the ache: Terry's esteem for her was withering before her eyes. But though her instinctive belief in the universality of melody and harmony had convinced her that a devout witch could find a place in a program that used as its source material the monodic compositions of the Catholic Church, she simply could not see herself singing the praises of a God whose Church had, in the course of three or four centuries, overseen the slaughter of nine million of her kind.

Terry looked at her again.

"I mean . . ." Helpless. Useless. Caught. She had never told Terry about her religious affiliations. She would not tell him now. To do so would, she was sure, slam closed a door through which she desperately wanted to pass. But she was a witch, a priestess of her Goddess, and that which was divine could no more be force fitted into a narrow definition of acceptability than could music. "Someone might have a vision . . . like from God . . . that isn't something that the Church would have approved of. We can't just . . . uh . . . like . . . discount that."

"Only true visions come from God," said Terry. He was still looking at her.

"Yeah, well, say that I had a vision . . . I mean, I remember I had one when I was a kid . . . uh . . ." She was thinking of the cartoons, of the backgrounds, the escape forever barred to her.

A flicker came into Terry's eyes. "You . . . had a vision?"

"Well . . . I guess you could call it that." Green fields, soft grass, fresh meads . . . what else could it have been to a five year old with a bloody vulva except a vision?

But Terry suddenly turned away, turned to the window. Sandy saw his fists clenching, shaking, but: "I think," he said softly, kindly, but with a weight of disinterest behind his words, "that we had best end for today."

"I . . ." Sandy fought for words, the sick fear in her belly redoubling. She wanted to heal. She wanted to *be* healed.

Terry said nothing.

"You wanted all this . . ." She looked at the thick book. Two thousand pages of chants and their corresponding rubrics. ". . . translated?"

Terry said nothing. He was looking out the window, his eyes wide as though he were seeing something . . . wonderful.

Sandy did not know Latin, and her memory still stubbornly insisted that the staff translators were supposed to take care of things like this; but she was dizzy with the threat of sudden invalidation that now lay over everything for which she had come to Denver. If she left the Hands of Grace, she would have nothing.

And there she goes again, came the voice of the barker. *Now she'll probably start telling everyone that Terry Angel is abusing her, just like the lies she told about her father . . .*

With a violent wrench, she pulled her thoughts back to the book. "I'll do it," she said. "I'll do it. Is . . ."

Terry said nothing.

". . . is that okay?"

Terry said nothing.

———

AUGUST 13, 1991

NORA JERUSALEM, PH.D.
DEPT. OF CMPRTV. RLGN.

KINGSLEY CLG.
DENVER, CO 80221

Dear BOOKLOOKER customer:
We are sorry to inform you that *INITIATIONS / PRANA / CLUNIAC DEATH PRACTICES (T. ANGEL)*

( ) is out of print.
( ) is unavailable at this time.
( ) is available only in a French, German, Spanish, Arabic,_____, edition
(X) other: *UNABLE TO FIND ANY RECRD OF PBLCNS*

If there is any way that BOOKLOOKER can help you with your book and periodical needs in the future, please do not hesitate to call us.

The same thing happened every morning.

TK arrived at TreeStar Surveying fifteen minutes early, a practice that was as much a reaction to years of hearing about black folks who spent their lives on welfare as it was an expression of an innate desire to do something more than minimal work. He had been given his own key to the office at the end of his very first week—a fact which still amazed him—and so he let himself in, booted the computer, and called up the Lietz software. The evening before, Lauri and Raven had left the RAM cards from their Total Stations beside his CPU, and so, by eight o'clock, TK had already loaded the previous day's coordinates and was busy manipulating plots and numbers.

Hadden invariably arrived just then, pulling the light blue company van into a parking space right outside the office window. Lauri was always about ten seconds behind him in her red and white Bronco, followed by Bright (current receptionist, future surveyor) in a pink Volkswagen. Through his window, TK watched them say hello to one another (not unusual), hug (a little peculiar, but still acceptable), and then greet the sparrows, finches, grackles, jays, squirrels, and even an occasional butterfly that would flutter, swoop, and run to fawn over them like children meeting a beloved grandparent (completely bizarre). By the time Web and Raven pulled up, a small crowd of animals, fairly dancing with excitement, was quite ready to pounce on the newcomers with chitters and chirps and clucks and boinks of joy.

Every morning.

They were not after food: of that TK was sure. In fact, he never saw any of his TreeStar co-workers feed any of the birds or beasts directly, though Hadden had placed a feeder near the building and kept it stocked with shelled peanuts and sunflower seeds. No, it was not food that was the attraction. It was, rather (and TK could not understand at all why such an idea came to him), a matter of friendship. The animals appeared to recognize Hadden and the others as comrades, fellow travelers in the world to whom it was only fitting that they offer good will and love; and as far as TK could tell, the good will and love were returned a hundredfold.

But he wondered sometimes as his co-workers entered, greeted him, and set about the day's work: had he not himself experienced much the same thing? The people of TreeStar Surveying had looked at him and, far from seeing black or danger or any of the other nightmares of middle-class, white mentality, had accepted him as something identical to themselves. Not white. Not at all. Colored, to be sure, but colored . . . just like they themselves were colored. TK was a comrade, a fellow traveler in the world. Even Bright, as pretty, blond, and blue-eyed as a Cherry Creek prom queen, obviously saw in him only a reflection of herself . . . and, just as obviously, thought this not at all unusual.

It made no sense. These people were white. But these people did not appear to consider themselves white. And it was such an unselfconscious, natural act that TK could only accept it as genuine, could only offer back to them a kind of bewildered good will. He could not love them: there was too much distrust in the world in general, and between the races in particular, for love to be given so easily. But as the wet summer passed, he allowed himself to see them as friends, as comrades, as fellow travelers.

He was, though, floundering, for nothing in his life had prepared him for such unconditional acceptance. In the projects, good will was but a gossamer web of belief that could be possessed only by those who succumbed to the pious rantings of ecstatic preachers . . . and then only for the duration of a church service. And acceptance, when it existed at all, was inevitably flavored with the rank taste of resignation, for, like abused children, like condemned prisoners, like slaves, the residents of the brick and steel-mesh towers had to accept: there was no other option available.

And it was much the same in TK's present neighbor-hood, for since the death of the child, a dullness that had nothing to do with the enduring heat and uncharacteristic humidity of this Denver summer had settled in. Children no longer played in their yards. Pedestrians kept their time on the street to a minimum. Cars were no longer parked at curbside with any assurance that morning—or even the passage of an hour—would find them in driv-able condition. Exposed walls filled up with daubings, drawings, names written by one hand and crossed off by another in wishful obituary.

Throughout the day would come the sound of automo-bile engines and the flash of chrome. Money and drugs changed hands. Tinies went on missions, jacked the occa-sional and unwary passerby, splashed on rival gang mem-bers (Crip or Blood it did not matter: hostility was merely a matter of a tribal mentality so old that it was one with the slaughter of the Great War . . . or the invasion of Ca-naan). OGs took care of their Tinies and their sales, and they watched TK (he knew they were watching) from be-hind curtained windows, from within the tinted glass of automobiles, from sunlit positions on street corners or be-side fragrant dumpsters.

Like all black men in America, TK was living two lives. But the utter dichotomy of existence that he expe-rienced as he shuttled from his neighborhood to the sub-urbs and back again was such that it made all the other such polarizations of his life seem trivial. At TreeStar, he smiled and he joked with his co-workers, fairly wallow-ing in a warm bath of camaraderie and mutual trust; and at times he even felt a sudden loosening in his chest that he finally recognized as the slacking of a knot of defense and wariness that had more than likely been present since he had drawn his first breath and had heard the doctor say—in words that he could at the time not understand but which he would come to know too well—*well, here's one more nigger.*

At home, though, the knot returned, was, in fact, necessary. The M16 and the K-Bar seemed fitting emblems of that place, even more now than when, freshly returned from Vietnam and with a headful of memories that he could not shake, he had taken them for his bedside companions. The slow and scattered procession of cars, the slouching figures in baseball caps, baggy pants, and t-shirts, the lurching and uncertain gait of the wandering crack addicts: all these and more were reminders, echoes, and, yes, amplifications of his origins, of the pervasive hopelessness and violence of an environment that had for centuries been an unwilling repository for all the dark suspicions and nightmare fantasies of a society unwilling to acknowledge its intrinsic bigotry and hate.

And so, just as he had once crawled through dark tunnels, wary to the point of vomiting that the next turning could put him face to face with a frightened man and an automatic rifle or, worse, a pound of plastic explosive and enough shrapnel to render his body unrecognizable, TK, come evening, would plod up and down his neighborhood street, watching the shadows, listening for sounds, the defensive knot in his chest expanding into a tumor of inferred danger as the stump of his leg ached with an immediacy that only an amputee could know. He would knock on doors, would talk to people about their fears, about the crack house, about just how many petitions, letters, and telephone calls it would take to prod an overworked police force into action.

There was distrust of the gangs among TK's neighbors, but, perhaps even more deeply ingrained, there was also a distrust of the police. From the deep South sheriff who watched with folded arms while men were lynched and burned to the more recent and well-known officers in Los Angeles who had beaten a motorist nearly to death in full view of a video camera, the agents of law enforcement had never been kind to TK's people, and among the latter he found—as he had expected to find—an inertia that bordered on petrification.

"What the hell do I wanna be doing getting the cops in here?" said one. The day had been long and hot: he stood behind his barred security door in a tank top and shorts.

" 'Cause the only other thing do to is blow 'em away ourselves," said TK. "And I don't particularly feel like getting sent up because of a bunch of punks. We paying taxes: the cops supposed to do it."

"Supposed to? *Supposed* to? Where you been living the last century, TK?"

Was he losing his touch? Was his daily interaction with people who petted birds and chucked squirrels under the chin and hugged one another (and Bright, one morning, with one of her brilliant smiles, had even hugged *him*!) causing him to lose his connection with the way things were, the way things had always been? Some evenings, with his feral Yorkshire terrier prowling and snarling in the kitchen, TK would lean his elbows on the sill of his window, look out at the silent, deserted, deadly street, and wonder: what did he think he was doing, anyway? Did he think he was going to change the world? What the hell had gotten into him?

But he knew what had gotten into him. It was not the dichotomy, not the surveying office and its people, not even the senseless death of a five-year-old girl. No, all these had merely spurred into continuity something that had first awakened in a hospital in Georgia, when an old janitor with a face the color of burnt leather and hands so worn and callused that they might have been gloves had sat down beside the bed of a man who had lost his leg, his wife, and any inclination toward living that he might have possessed—and had offered to him the only nurture that was his to give.

TK had accepted that nurture, and now, in his own clumsy and blind fashion, he was trying to pass it on. Rags had, perhaps, been his first attempt, and had TK been cynical, he might have taken the dog's continuing ferocity as an omen. But TK was not cynical: like many men of his race, he was simply without hope. And so his failure to turn Rags into anything more than a tiny, snapping embodiment of distrust did not discourage him. He merely kept on trying to get it right, expanding his efforts from a single dog to an entire neighborhood (and never considering for a moment where such expansion might eventually lead him), assuming that his current lack of success was simply another example of the way things were, the way they had always been.

But the going was slow (perhaps it was imperceptible, perhaps nonexistent), and if he needed immediate gratfication, it appeared that he would have to find it in the successful manipulation of figures and lines on a video display terminal; and though at night and on weekends he prodded his neighbors and dodged the bites of his pet, weekdays would find him at TreeStar, smiling, succumbing further to the infectious good will that dwelt within the office like a resident spirit, holding to a split existence that neatly summarized—and compartmentalized—two entirely opposite aspects of humanity.

CHAPTER 9

Near the end of September, the weather turned cold, bringing out overcoats and glazing the streets with wet snow. Marsh had to turn on his windshield wipers when he went to pick up Kelly, and, shortly after they had reached their small house, sleet, driven by a north wind, began spattering the kitchen windows.

Kelly was looking out into the wet, lingering light. "Will mommy be home soon?"

"Your mother's at the shelter tonight," said Marsh. He tried to keep the unease out of his voice. The shelter was in a dangerous part of town, and, on top of that, Colorado weather was nothing if not unpredictable. This minor storm could remain minor ... or it could wind up dumping ten inches of snow on an unprepared city. "She'll be late." He opened a cupboard. "How do you feel about macaroni and cheese?"

"I like macaroni and cheese better than tofu enchiladas," said Kelly with great seriousness. "And mommy will be all right."

Marsh trusted Kelly's instincts, for as the only modern Elf who had actually been born that way, she seemed more at one with her status than even Hadden and Wheat. But still he fretted about Heather, and he wished again and again that he and his people possessed something of the easy psychic communication he sensed had been the birthright of the Firstborn.

On evenings like this, when daylight savings time still stretched the light toward eight and even nine o'clock, Heather usually arrived home just at dusk, after she had helped the shelter staff serve supper and clean up. The storm and its inevitable traffic delays made Marsh expect her somewhat later, but it was nearly ten o'clock when her headlights finally swept across the front windows.

Kelly, who needed sleep no more than any other Elf, was sitting on Marsh's lap as he read her a story by the light of a lamp that he had switched on more out of old human habit than from any real need. That the story happened to be the Odyssey and that Kelly already could have read it herself—though not yet, perhaps, in the original Greek—were factors that would, perhaps, have been a little odd for a human child, but not for Kelly.

But when the front door opened, Kelly bounced up from Marsh's lap (and he reflected that only Kelly could find a way to bounce up with such seriousness) and ran to meet her mother. Heather had already kicked off her heels, and she dropped down on one knee. "How was day care, Elfling?" she said, filling her arms with her daughter.

Kelly pursed her lips, considered. "Fine," she said at last. "This time. A man brought rabbits for us to play with."

"Did you like the rabbits?"

Kelly smiled brightly. "They liked me. A lot."

Marsh came up, hugged Heather, exchanged a kiss. "She had them all on her lap at one point," he said. "She had to tell them to go visit with the other kids."

Heather shook her head. "Elves."

Marsh kissed her again. "Ain't it the truth."

They laughed, but he caught in her voice a tightness that did not go away even after he had poured her a glass of wine, put dinner before her, and rubbed her feet.

"Have you talked to TK?" she asked as, afterwards, he settled her onto the sofa and sat down beside her.

The lights were off, and the blues and lavenders of his night vision lent a softness to her face that was one with the gentle shimmer of her flesh. Elves. Elves here, now, in Denver. It was a strange, magic thought, and if immortality had consisted of nothing more than the closeness that he felt to his beloved, his joy at the sight and touch of his child, the confidences exchanged with full knowledge and wakefulness while the world of mortals slept, then Marsh could have faced that immortality without a shred of fear or regret.

"This morning," he said. "We're going to practice Friday night. The summer's winding down . . ." He looked at the window, laughed at the streaks of water that clung to the glass. ". . . and people aren't thinking so much about building, so the work crush is over at TreeStar."

"He offered to help me take supplies up to the shelter if we needed someone who could lift," said Heather. "Such a good man." There was a flicker in her eyes that was a little more than starlight. "How is he . . . doing?"

He caught her meaning. "No stars yet. At least none that he's mentioned." He wondered again whether he deserved praise or condemnation for steering his bandmate into a job at TreeStar. "But you never know: he might not have to worry about the blood."

Heather shifted uneasily. "We can't worry about the blood either," she said. "If we did, we'd never stop to help anyone. We'd just be hermits, and live up at the Home all the time and eat . . . and eat . . ."

Marsh grinned. "Pine cones."

She shrugged with a sense of unease: they were all a little uncomfortable about inadvertently triggering off the blood in someone. It could happen. It had happened. "Pine cones."

But Marsh was nodding. "Regardless, he's happy . . . as far as TK ever lets anyone know whether he's happy or not. You should hear him play the sax these days."

"He was always a good sax player." Again, the tightness in her voice.

"The best."

Kelly had been coloring with her usual uncanny precision, but now she put her crayons aside and approached Heather and Marsh with outstretched arms. Hugs. Kisses. Heather took her into her lap.

"You were late, Mommy," said Kelly, voicing Marsh's thought, Marsh's worry.

"I stopped somewhere . . ." Heather looked at the window. The sleet had ended, but there was a heaviness to the night that spoke of cold and cloud. "A bridge on Speer . . . over Cherry Creek . . ."

"And a man?" said Kelly.

"Crossing the road, yes," said Heather. "He lived, I think, under the bridge. It's cold out there, and I pulled over to see if he was going to be all right."

Marsh said nothing, hid his worry. Heather, alone and in the night, stopping to see if a complete stranger needed help. But that was just like her. And that was, he knew, just like all the Elves. He would have done it himself. He would have given the man his overcoat, or the canned food and blankets he kept in his trunk for just such occasions. "What happened?"

Heather closed her eyes, seemed torn between laughter and tears. "He told me, in no uncertain terms, to get back into my car and stop talking to strangers. His language, though, was considerably more coarse." She shook her head, still torn. "He asked me who I thought was going to take care of me if I did stupid things like that. He seemed more worried about me than I was about him."

"*I'm* a little worried, too, darling."

Heather shrugged. "I told him that I had to stop. I told him that God would take care of me." But Marsh saw a shadow cross her face.

They were silent for some time. Outside, the city was falling into sleep. But there was no sleep in this house, only starlight.

"Kelly," said Heather softly, "I think you should lie down and find your stars for a while. You're growing, and Dr. Spock doesn't say anything about raising Elflings, but I assume you need a little more than we do."

"All right, mommy." Kelly never quarreled. She would discuss, would, in fact, occasionally argue with persuasive and unnerving logic; but the obstinacy and contrariness that characterized most children her age was entirely absent. She went to her room as though she knew better than Heather—or Dr. Spock—what Elflings needed.

Heather looked after her. "She's so beautiful," she whispered.

"And so elven."

Heather nodded.

"What's wrong, love?"

"God . . ." She bent her head, covered her eyes. "It was so automatic. I told that man that God would take care of me. I didn't even think. I just said it. Just like I would have said it years ago. But . . ." Her shoulders shook, and the tears came then, streaking her face as the sleet had streaked the windows. "But I started thinking about it on the way home. I'd thought about it before, sure, but it didn't really hit me—I mean, really hit me—until tonight."

"Heather?"

She sobbed, her voice dropping to a hoarse whisper. "I don't know anything about a God who takes care of Elves," she said. "I don't know anything about anybody who takes care of people who are immortal. I mean, angels are immortal, but they see God all the time. It's just their nature. But here we are . . . and we don't . . . we don't see anything. Except the stars."

Marsh folded her in his arms, held her. "Somebody's taking care of us," he said softly. "It's like when the blood wakes up. It only seems to wake up in people who need it, or who can handle it, or who can find someone else with the blood who can help them. Somebody obviously takes care of that."

She looked up, her face damp. "But who?"

"I don't know." Despite his reassuring words, he felt the ache. Like everyone else, Elves worked in the dark.

"Do you think Natil might know?"

"She's never said anything about it." But it suddenly struck him that Natil had been silent about a great many things. What had the Firstborn believed in, anyway? What had gotten them through age after wearying age of persecution and loss? What was getting Natil through after four and a half billion years?

Heather bent her head. She had always been religious, having in her adolescence struck a compromise between the precepts of the Church and the demands of her own conscience. But after her transformation, the admonitions of her priests—geared as they were toward the salvation of mortals, reflecting an increasing reactionism—had alienated her beyond any possibility of accommodation, and she had turned away from what had been up until then her spiritual foundation. But she missed it, missed it terribly, and sometimes Marsh would see tears come into her eyes at the sight of Easter decorations, or the smudge of ash on a believer's forehead at the beginning of Lent, or, at night, the faint glow of stained glass windows lit from within by candlelight and devout worship.

"Keep holding me, Marsh," she said. "I feel . . . so lonely."

"Do you want to go up to the Home? Natil is always willing to harp."

She shook her head. "Just hold me."

And so he held her, and when Kelly arose from her bed

a few hours later, her eyes gleaming with the light of the
stars among which she had been drifting, she found her
father and her mother curled up together on the sofa,
wandering down paths of ineffable radiance that held, for
now, as much of assurance and nurture as Immortals
could ever know.

One season prepared the way for the next, and in much
the same fashion, Natil had spent the summer readying
the campus for the beginning of winter. That winter had
sent out scouts a little early this year was of little consequence, for if the trees, shrubs, flowers, and lawns were
strong enough to withstand an unusually hot and wet
summer—and Natil had made sure that they were—then
they were strong enough to take a little premature cold.

Her floppy straw hat exchanged for a warm knit cap
and her t-shirt put aside in favor of flannel, Natil swept
slush off early-morning sidewalks just as cheerfully and
efficiently as she had, the week before, mowed lawns and
weeded flower beds. Teachers who knew her—and most
of them did—stopped to exchange words and jokes about
the Colorado weather; and even Nora Jerusalem, the
stocky head of the Comparative Religion department, actually came up with a *Cold enough for ya?* that made
Natil smile as much for the jest as for the usually grave
professor's attempt at humor.

But though she sensed that warm weather would return
within the week, she could not help but be dismayed.
Here was winter again, the third since she had come to
Colorado, and she had accomplished little beyond keeping the grounds of a private college green and attractive
for the benefit of people who rarely noticed such things.
To be sure, taking care of plants was a good thing to do,
and though Natil could no longer see any way in which
it contributed actively to the Elves' spiritual welfare, she
nonetheless held to the belief that it did indeed contribute. Still, that leap of faith represented yet another failing,
another loss, for she remembered a time when the Elves
possessed not faith, but certainty, a certainty founded
upon exact, elven knowledge.

It was with such thoughts that, at the end of the week,
with the weather finally warming back toward what she
sensed would be a prolonged Indian summer, she put

aside her tools, washed her hands, and set off toward the
cafeteria at the student union. Normally, she brought her
own lunch to work, but the Elves had gathered in the har-
vest from the Elvenhome gardens just before the cold
front had struck, and Natil, concerned that the fruits and
vegetables might spoil, had devoted so much of her free
time to canning, pickling, preserving, and wrapping for
storage that, come that morning, she had not even had a
chance to throw together a sandwich before she had been
forced to leave for Kingsley.

Even Elves can run out of time, she thought as she
pushed in through the glass doors of the cafeteria. And
the pang made her stop right there, brow furrowed, hand
pressed to her lips. Long ago, the Elves had indeed run
out of time, and now they seemed on the verge of running
out of time again. At the gathering at the Home that
weekend, Heather had talked about God. She had not
wept: her weeping was, apparently, over. But what had
taken its place was a quiet sort of resignation that was far
worse than tears, for she had concluded that whatever divine agency considered the Elves its special concern had
decided to give them over to an abusive uncertainty and
abandonment. And Natil had been unable to say anything
against her conclusion.

How long would it be before Heather found her tears
again? How long would it be before those tears turned to
despair? How long would it be before the others joined
her, falling into a loss of hope that could not but be one
with the quiet longing and regret that had, ages ago,
leached the presence of the Firstborn from the world?

And as she stood gripped in the pain of the past and a
fear for the future, the clatter of silverware and plates and
the sound of a hundred conversations lapping about her
like a cacophonous sea, her eye fell upon a woman at a
nearby table. Hunched, pale, her dark hair shoulder-
length and haphazard, she was bent over a tumble of
books and a stack of legal pads. She was writing furiously, pausing only long enough to thumb frantically
through something that looked like a dictionary before returning to write again.

She could well have been any overworked student, and
indeed, there was something plain about her overall appearance, as though one could look at her and forget her

in an instant. But Natil, who looked beyond overall appearance, remembered her as the student who, months before, had been sitting on a bench in front of the student union, close to tears because she could not find Aylesberg Hall.

Sure enough, the canvas case that could only have held a small harp was on the floor beside her; and Natil noticed again both the cast to her left eye and the scars along her jaw. But she noticed something else, too: the young harper was again close to tears.

Natil watched for a minute. Scribble, thumb, weep, scribble again. The woman was keeping her tears under control, but they forced themselves out anyway, squeezing from her eyes like coins from a miser's purse.

"Hey, do you mind?"

Natil discovered that her steps had taken her into the food line and that she was consequently blocking the path of a beefy individual who appeared to have placed all of his aspirations in athletics. "Not at all," she said, giving him a smile and moving out of his way. "God bless you."

He stared at her, then grabbed a plastic tray, stocked it with silverware, and hurried off toward the steam table as though he had encountered a madwoman.

Natil sighed, collected her own tray and utensils, and in a few minutes was at the register with a hamburger and a salad.

"Four-fifty," said the cashier without looking at her.

Natil counted out her money and accepted her change as though she had been doing such things all her life—or at least for the last two years—and then, picking up her tray, she looked for a place to sit. But it was lunchtime, the cafeteria had filled up, and all the available tables were occupied. She was considering taking her food outside and confirming the beefy individual's opinion of her by eating beneath the trees when she again found herself staring at the miserable harper. The chair across from her was unoccupied.

Well, here was certainly someone who appeared to need help and healing, and Natil decided that if she could not assist her people, she could, at the very least attempt to do something for a single human being. With a shrug and an attempt at optimism, therefore, she wandered over to where the woman scribbled, thumbed, and wept.

"Hello," she said. "Do you remember me?"

The woman looked up, and there was a flash of fear in her eyes as though the appearance of anyone, even this innocuous and friendly gardener, constituted a threat. "Uh . . . yeah, I remember you."

"Would I be troubling you if I joined you?" Natil was uneasy about the reaction she was producing, almost wished that she had opted for the trees. "The room is full."

"Uh . . ."

Natil fully expected her to say that she was busy, that she had work to do, that she needed the table all to herself. But, with a kind of a frightened shuffling of papers and a clearing of space:

". . . okay. Yeah. Come on," she said.

There was a quaver in her voice that was audible even by through noise of the busy lunchroom, and Natil guessed that she was consenting only because appeasement and compromise had become instinctive to her.

A memory nibbled at the back of the Elf's mind. An unpleasant memory. Unable for the moment to place it, though, she set her tray down across from the woman and took the vacant chair. "I should introduce myself," she said. "My name is Natil Summerson. I'm the groundskeeper here at Kingsley."

The woman stared for a moment, then appeared to shake herself out of her thoughts and fears enough to respond. "Sandy," she said. "Sandy Joy."

The unpleasant memory nibbled again. Natil was annoyed that she could not place it, for it seemed suddenly very important. "I am very happy to meet you, Sandy." She peeled the cover from her cup of green-goddess dressing, dumped the concoction on her salad, instinctively looked for a recycling symbol on the empty container. She did not see one. With a sigh, she set it down on her tray.

Sandy was watching. Fear. "What's . . . the matter?"

Natil hastened to reassure her. "Oh . . . I just wanted to recycle this. The manufacturer, though, does not appear to be interested in telling me what kind of plastic it is made of."

Suddenly, abruptly, nervously, Sandy managed a smile. "That's really nice of you."

"I should think that it would be expected," said Natil. She was relieved to see the smile, but she still wondered whether the trees would have been the more compassionate decision after all.

Sandy shrugged. "Lots of people don't even think about things like that."

"We do." Natil blushed. "I mean, I do."

Sandy smiled again. "I do, too."

It was as if the question of what to do with an unrecyclable plastic cup had punctured Sandy's fear, for she seemed suddenly to consider her unexpected visitor something of a comrade, and she responded warmly as Natil, between bites of salad and hamburger, described her occasionally hilarious efforts toward convincing the college administration to start a waste-management program.

She had, in fact, met with some success: the copy center now had a barrel for waste paper; the aluminum cans, glass bottles, plastic jugs, and styrofoam cups collected by the grounds crew were now sent to collection centers instead of landfills; and a large compost pile took care of the assorted leaves, grass clippings, and plant litter produced by the campus. Her efforts, though, had apparently fallen short of salad dressing cups.

Smiling wryly, Natil picked up the offending container. "Next year, perhaps, we will cross that threshold," she said, but her humor could not but be tempered by her knowledge that she would be around to see the ultimate fate of everything that had been, was, or would be discarded, cast aside, ignored, buried, or left to rot . . . or not rot. Including salad dressing cups.

Yet one more elven responsibility.

But she looked down at the case at Sandy's feet. "How is your harping going?"

Sandy's warmth evaporated, and her furtiveness returned. "Well . . . uh . . ." She shrugged uncomfortably, shrugged again. "It's not."

"I am very sorry to hear that."

Sandy touched the case as though, more than anything else, she wanted to unzip it, take out her instrument, and make music. "Do you . . . uh . . . play?"

"I have, at times, been seen with a harp in my hands."

"Pedal harp?"

"Not at all," said Natil. "I play a harp that is no bigger than yours. It is of ancient design, and is strung with bronze."

"Really?" Sandy suddenly warmed up again. "I didn't think anyone in town worked with the old harps except for me and Terry."

"There are a few," said Natil. "I must say that I felt rather as though I had discovered a kindred spirit when I saw you last June. But I think I understand now: you are in the Hands of Grace program."

"Yeah . . . well . . . yeah."

The memory that Natil could not quite place came again, but this time she saw a face. Though unscarred and sighted, it was, nonetheless, disturbingly similar to Sandy's, and its bearer had plodded through her life until . . .

Omelda. Not, though, Omelda as she had been when Natil had first met her. Rather, Sandy partook of the acquiescence and resignation that had come to the runaway nun only after weeks of abuse had—

And then Natil understood.

Sandy was still talking. "Yeah . . . I kind of *am* the Hands of Grace program. There's no one in it but me."

Natil nodded, swallowed a bit of now-tasteless hamburger. "That must be somewhat advantageous." She kept her voice light to mask her dismay. Omelda's torments had lasted for a few weeks, and had ended with her death in the prison of the Inquisition; Sandy's, she sensed, had gone on and on without any such horrific but merciful release.

"Advantageous?" said Sandy.

"Having an instructor like Terry Angel all to yourself."

Sandy seemed even more uncomfortable. "I . . . guess so," she said, in a voice that indicated that she did not guess so at all.

Natil gave up on the hamburger, put it down. "I do not understand."

"I just do research for Terry." Another shrug, another gesture of resignation. Did Sandy wonder about God? About what would get her through? "I've been doing nothing but research for the last three months. I haven't been able to play a note since I came to Denver."

Clatter and crash, shout and giggle: the lunchroom commotion lapped about them. Sandy, sitting in the middle of it, seemed a still point of misery at the eye of an unselfconscious storm. Natil just stared. "You have not . . . ?"

"Haven't had time." Sandy gestured at the pads and books with a sense of defeat.

Natil looked at her work. "What is it that you are doing?"

"Translating the *Liber Usualis*."

"Trans . . ." Natil blinked. "But . . . but why?"

"Well, all the musicians in the program—whenever we get some—are going to have to know what the chants say in order to play them right." Sandy looked down at the pads, sighed. "It's just such slow going. I don't know Latin, and so I've just got to kind of pick out the meanings from the dictionary."

"I still do not understand," said Natil. "There are several translations available for most of the material in the *Liber*, perhaps for all of it. Why are you starting from scratch?" She turned one of the legal pads around, examined the antiphon that Sandy was currently deciphering. "And you not even knowing Latin . . ."

Sandy sat as though stunned. "Translations? There are translations?"

"To be sure," said Natil. "If the college library does not have one, then I am certain that interlibrary loan can supply something."

"There are . . ." Sandy stared at Natil, then at the pads that were covered with weeks of smudged and smeared handwriting, then at Natil once again. And then she began to cry. "Oh, Goddess, there's *translations* of all of this? Oh, dear Lady, I've been so stupid." Half blind, scarred, she clenched her fists with a mixture of sorrow, fury, and despair. "But why didn't Terry tell me about them?"

CHAPTER 10

Maxwell remembered that Audrey had always liked these October days of sunlight and warmth, the brief return to summer that came after the initial stirrings of autumnal cold and before the first hard freeze. She had always been one to dwell between, to look into the interstices of the world, whether to discover an Indian summer or a humble but opportunistic violet.

She had been much like her mother in that. Indeed, Greta had inevitably perceived her life not as a series of events, but as a sequence of transitions; not as goals, but as journeys. Maxwell himself, plodding along in his clumsy male fashion, his eyes fixed on his objective, had always missed it, but Greta and Audrey had always seen.

Now, he too was seeing it, but it was too late. Greta was dead, and Audrey was no longer quite alive, and so Maxwell, in a way, had been entirely subsumed by betweens. With Audrey neither gone nor present, Maxwell could not really grieve for either his wife or his daughter. And if he visited a grave at a local cemetery or a young woman's life-supported body at a local hospital, it was without any sense of change or futurity. No, Maxwell would be between. Now and forever.

His office at Kingsley looked out over the flower beds that, still abloom in spite of the lateness of the season, lay before Aylesberg Hall. He did not know—and no one, whether they wore the black suit of a priest or the white smock of a physician, could tell him—whether Audrey knew that it was autumn, that it was warm, that the flowers were still blooming. To be sure, he told her all these things and more when he sat by her bed each evening, but her half-closed eyes remained half closed, the fluttering of their lids and the intermittent stirring of her arms and hands indicating, so the doctors insisted, nothing but random nerve firings, Brownian motion *in vivo,* the vagaries of a uncontrolled limbic system.

But maybe she heard. Maybe she heard everything. The doctors admitted that they knew no more than the brute facts of blood circulation, breathing, elimination. They knew nothing of souls, or of consciousness, or of psyches. And so, Audrey *could* be there, *could* be thinking, *could* be feeling, *could* be hearing, her existence defined as much by the between and the liminal as Maxwell's own.

A buzz from the intercom on his desk. His secretary's voice. "Dr. Delmari, Professor Angel is here to see you."

"Send him in, please, Sherri."

And the door opened, and Terry Angel entered.

The doctors saw only sinew and bone, only flesh and breathing and circulation. Terry saw much more. The doctors spoke in terms of life support systems. Terry spoke of soul and spirit, of psyche and the numinosity of divine manifestation. Medicine could not help Audrey. But music . . .

"Good morning," said Terry, and he smiled, and Maxwell felt better. Yes, there was hope—for Audrey, for everyone—and transitions and liminal states were but transitions and liminal states. Necessary, perhaps, but not eternal. There was healing in the world. There was help.

"Good morning, Terry," he said, rising, and the two men shook hands in the brown office as the sunlight and the chirping of birds and the distant singing of the woman who took care of the landscaping stood as witnesses to their greeting. "Have you seen Audrey today?"

"I've just come from the hospital," said Terry. "I played for her this morning."

It had been a needless question, an expected answer. Terry played for Audrey every morning. Every morning. "Wonderful . . . wonderful. . . . How is she?"

Terry's eyes were radiant. "I think we have improvement. I could feel Audrey's spirit in the room—"

Maxwell grasped at the hope. "Then she's coming back?"

"Oh, yes! She has always been coming back." Terry's eyes were still radiant, but there was a hint as of disappointment in his voice, as though he were chagrined that Maxwell had, even for a moment, doubted him. "Ever since I started to play for her." A look. "But you know that."

Maxwell Delmari, dean of Kingsley College, sat down behind his desk, folded his hands. His fingers, he discovered, were like ice. Had he ever doubted Terry? He hoped that he had not. "I do," he said. "You can see her trying to ... to ..."

"To wake up."

"Yes." Terry's prompt crystallized Maxwell's surety. "Yes, that's it."

"And indeed she is," said Terry. He pulled up another chair, sat down, and Maxwell mentally kicked himself for not having brought the chair himself. Making Terry Angel carry his own furniture! And not even asking him to sit down!

But Terry, a holy man, did not appear to notice the unintentional rudeness, or, if he did, it was only with the faintest look of sadness. "The bond between soul and spirit," he said, "has been torn, but not sundered. Death, you see—"

He broke off, for Maxwell had started at the use of that terribly final word. "Death ..."

"Is merely an act of forgetting," said Terry. "Spiritual forgetting. This is a matter of fact. Of history. Of Tradition." And he nodded. "From body to soul to spirit the Self forgets what is below in order to embrace what is above."

Maxwell nodded. Whenever Terry spoke of the above—and of embracing it—he could not but feel petty and unclean for desiring that Audrey should embrace anything else ... himself, for instance.

"But Audrey has not forgotten," Terry continued, "because, you see, a recall to God is a natural process, an ascent—a forgetting first of the natural world, then of the astral world, and then of the etheric world. Death itself, though, is never a natural process, and Audrey's death in particular was a violation of nature—"

Maxwell clenched his hands. Again, that word. "But she's not dead!"

"No," said Terry quickly, "not at all. Not the ... final death. But sleep is a kind of death. Forgetting is a kind of a death. And so death is also a forgetting, and a kind of a sleep. But Audrey is not dead. Nor has she forgotten."

Maxwell was nodding again.

"What I am doing," said Terry, drawing his chair closer, gripping the edge of Maxwell's desk as though his hands were nailed to it, "is helping Audrey to remember. It is a kind of birth here, a birth of which the old monastics were very well aware . . ."

"As your research has demonstrated."

"Oh my, yes," said Terry, his hands still gripping the desk. "Over and over again. At Trinity College in Dublin. At the Académie de Sainte Luci. Only a few . . ." He looked toward the door, and his voice darkened a shade. "Only a few deny it."

"You mean . . . Nora Jerusalem."

Terry kept his eyes on the door. "It is easy for all of us to fall into materialism and error. Teresa Neumann of Bavaria lived for forty years on nothing but the Host she received every Sunday, and though that fact was established over and over again even according to the most stringent requirements of science—"

Maxwell understood. But: "I can't do anything about Dr. Jerusalem."

"Please, don't give it another thought," said Terry. "You don't have to do . . . anything." But the hesitation in his voice was, to Maxwell, something akin to a slap.

"Has she been interfering?"

Terry shook his head, the shadows vanishing from his voice in an instant. "Not at all. It's been wonderful. It must be a manifestation of the all-pervasive gnosis of which this world is only a small part. You and I . . ." And his hands trembled on the wood. ". . . are like midwives, birthing this new program."

Maxwell thought of Audrey, pale and bloated in her hospital bed . . . twitching, twitching, but nonetheless drawing closer to the rebirth that Terry was offering her, nonetheless trying to remember life. "Any trouble with funds? Anything?"

"Oh, no!" said Terry. "And as a matter of fact, I have a team of Latinists working on an entirely new translation of the corpus of chants from the *Liber Usualis*. They're wonderful people: they're donating their time because they recognize what a unique opportunity this is."

"Good . . ." From the beginning, Maxwell had determined to give Terry complete academic freedom.

Through his own spiritual disciplines, Terry understood what had to be achieved. Through a worldwide network of like-minded scholars, Terry had access to research materials both at home and abroad. Through his unique position as both an academic and a healer, Terry saw a little bit farther than people like Maxwell Delmari . . . and considerably farther than people like Nora Jerusalem.

Maxwell's hands clenched. That woman! But Jerusalem was not doing anything overtly improper. Her sole offense, as far as Maxwell could tell, was doubt.

But she doubted very well. And she the head of the Comparative Religion department!

He saw Terry to the door, received assurances that Audrey would continue to hear music of healing and rebirth every morning, and went so far—Terry's openness and cheer infecting Maxwell with a lighthearted camaraderie—as to remind the slender professor to eat enough so that a strong breeze would not blow him away.

Terry nodded in response to the admonition, but Maxwell noticed that a shade crossed his face, and he felt suddenly uneasy. Had he been too friendly? Terry was . . . someone different. Someone holy. Someone so gentle that he made the clumsy graspings of men, no matter how well-intentioned, seem hurtful things. That shade that had crossed his face . . . Disapproval? Pain?

But Terry would play for Audrey, and so she would hear the strains of ancient music calling to her, summoning her back to life, to remembrance, to the arms of her father, who waited . . . between . . .

Ash Buckland was one of those women who appeared to have everything . . . and then some. She had independence, a fair amount of money, a good car, and a splendid man by the name of Hadden Morrison. She was thirty-five, looked ten years younger than that, and had a figure and a face that were perfect by any contemporary standards. Under normal circumstances, TK would have expected her to wander through her days contemplating her own satisfaction, with no time to spare for such things as courtesy or sincerity, but normal circumstances did not appear to exist among the TreeStar folk or their friends, and so, when Ash breezed into the offices to meet Hadden for a lunch date (her customary form of locomotion

appearing to have more to do with dance and flight than
with mere walking), and when she had an absolutely sincere and bright smile for everyone—including TK—and
when accompanying her like a subtle perfume was a
sense of youth and love and something that TK could
only describe as *rightness,* he thought no more about it
than he did about any of the other bizarre happenings that
he saw every day, that he had been seeing ever since he
had stepped through the door of Ash's employment
agency.

But had he not been seeing something similar even before that? He had met Marsh at a music store back in
April, when, just returned from an Iraqi bunker via Georgia, with a fake leg and a shattered marriage, he had managed to scrape together enough of a willingness to vent
his sorrow in the blues to look around for musicians with
similar desires . . . if not backgrounds. He had not paid
too much attention to his bandmate and his family at the
time, but familiarity had lent him perspective, and now he
began to realize that Marsh and Heather and Kelly
shared—had always shared—something of the lightness
and demeanor that he had come to perceive as an inseparable part of Ash and Hadden and Lauri and Web and
Wheat . . . and of all the others he had met through them.

But today, with his thoughts drifting for the moment
back to Marsh and his family, with the sun warm on the
potted plants, with the birds singing in yet another absolutely, positively, final performance *(don't miss it!)* before
winter hushed their voices in a blanket of snow, and with
the only discord in the otherwise universal pleasantness
the fact that the pain in his phantom leg had decided to
grow from a dull ache into a white hot lance of agony,
circumstances abruptly turned even more bizarre than
usual, for when Ash entered and TK looked up from his
computer terminal to smile hello through the open door of
his office, he noticed that . . .

He rubbed his eyes, looked again.

. . . Ash was glowing.

It was an almost subliminal shimmer that he saw playing across her skin, one that had absolutely nothing to do
with subjective perceptions of youth, health, demeanor, or
personality; and the brute violation of common sense with
which it confronted him was such that it might well have

brought another man to his feet in an instant, eyes wide, mouth agape, hands clenched, and, perhaps, a faint stirring of nauseous panic beginning to roil in the pit of his stomach at this sudden bit of Hollywood special effects turned real, immediate, tactile.

TK, though, did not react as another man might have. Had he done so, he would have died in a street rumble in Chicago, or in a Vietcong tunnel, or in an Iraqi bunker . . . or on the sidewalk outside a crack house. Yes, he rose, but he rose slowly, and he said hello to Ash as much from courtesy as from an instinctive need to conceal the motives for even his most mundane actions.

But the vision continued: yes, Ash's flesh was suffused with the softest of shimmers, and when she turned to acknowledge his greeting, he saw light in her eyes, much more light than any human being ought to have had, a light that spoke of years, of ages, of power.

The pain in his leg came again, then, and he sat down hard. For an instant, he clenched his eyes, fighting down the anguished protestations of a limb that no longer existed, but when he opened them, he found that Ash had entered his office and was looking into his face.

"TK," she said softly. "You're not well."

The shimmer was gone. The light in her eyes was gone, too. Ash looked much as Ash always looked. "Sorry," he said, still trying to cover himself. "Just my leg. Hurts sometimes. Caught me off guard."

"Your leg?"

"Phantom limb syndrome."

"Oh . . ." And, dammit, Ash's sincerity and concern did not waver, did not shade even in the slightest toward a nice white, liberal, guilt-ridden empathy for this black boy with a blown-off leg. Instead, she nodded slowly. Her expression was concerned, sympathetic, as though it stemmed from much more than TK's personal pain. "I've read about that. Does it bother you often?"

"Uh . . . not . . ." But he looked up into Ash's blue eyes and discovered that the untruth died on his lips. "All the time," he said.

Their conversation had been quiet—a woman and a man speaking in the softest of tones. But Hadden came through TK's door just then as though he knew exactly what had happened. Which, given the way TreeStar seemed to work, he probably did.

"TK?" he said. "What can we do?"

TK shook his head. "I be fine."

But that was a lie, too, for the pain was, if anything, getting worse. Hadden and Ash exchanged glances. A barely perceptible lifted eyebrow from the woman. An equally faint nod from the man.

"Would you . . ." Ash actually seemed a little embarrassed. "Would you mind if I touched your leg, TK?"

It was such an outlandish question that at first TK could only stare at her. Despite civil rights and open-mindedness, there were as many connotations inherent in a touch between a white woman and a black man in 1991 as there had been in 1865. Very similar connotations. Perhaps miscegenation was a term that had been coined during the Civil War, but it had spliced itself thoroughly into the genome of the American mindset, never to be completely extirpated.

But Ash's face was serious, and while the determination in her eyes appeared not quite identical to the stellar brilliance TK had seen a minute ago, it, too, projected a sense of inherent power. And TK assented to her request.

Ash's hands came down precisely at the juncture of prosthesis and flesh, and through his trousers her fingers probed for a moment at the faint seam of union, at the straps, the buckles. Ash's smooth, perfect face was inches from his own, the scent of her blond hair a presence like a forest meadow . . . and, just for a moment, TK caught another gleam of radiance, felt a sudden warmth in a leg that was no more.

And then Ash straightened. "Thank you, TK."

"Uh . . . sure." He had no idea what to make of it.

"TK," said Hadden suddenly, "you know, I entirely forgot: we're having a cookout up in the mountains next Saturday. Everyone from TreeStar, Marsh and Heather and Kelly, and some other people we know. You're one of the crew now, and . . . well . . ." He laughed. "I must be losing my mind. I forgot to tell you. Would you like to come?"

A cookout? With a bunch of—?

But this was TreeStar Surveying. This was a place that was different, that ran by rules that had nothing to do with the world of lynchings, housing projects, and crack houses. Ash was looking at him with calm blue eyes. Hadden's face was straightforward, honest. And TK recalled that he had not only already come to be a participant in the genial community that was TreeStar, but had also been assisting Heather with her work at the homeless shelter, and had even helped Wheat muscle a two hundred pound tree out of a pickup truck and into the ground. It was, apparently, time to go even farther. It could not last—he was black and they were white: of course it could not last—but for now, "Yeah," he said, a little shaken. "Yeah. I'd like that."

And it was not until after Hadden and Ash had left for lunch that he realized that his leg had stopped hurting.

Lauri worked late that night. The season of frenzied construction had ended, her shift at the Center would not start for several hours, and she had paperwork to take care of. Actually, she wanted time to be alone. Time in which to think.

She shuffled through file folders; stacked and stapled maps, charts, drawings, notes; even consulted the screen of the computer that Bright used for all the TreeStar correspondence and reports . . . and occasionally, her homework. She made notes, cleaned up field book entries, sorted through her life.

Eight years ago, she had been human, and she had come to Denver in search of stability and a fresh start after a Los Angeles love affair had self-destructed. Whether blame could be assigned in that destruction, Lauri no longer knew. It had been eight years. Matters of blame and responsibility had become blurred, even trivial.

But eight years ago, she had supposed that a fresh start would include a fresh relationship, that she would eventually find herself in bed with a woman, that there would eventually be fresh discoveries, fresh joys, and (probably) fresh heartbreaks. But she had not found a fresh start. She had, instead, found a completely new existence, one that had nothing in common with her past save, perhaps, her name and the color of her hair. Everything was different now. Even the shape of her face had changed. Oh, she was recognizable enough, and her parents, when she had visited them, had known her for their daughter, but such appearances were deceptive, for Lauri Tonso, like Hadden Morrison and Ash Buckland and Wheat Hennock and a baker's dozen others, was not human. And as though such a profound alteration were not enough, she was also (again like the others) a kind of vector within her society, one that carried not disease, but rather a kind of irresistible comfort and enlightenment, for as her own blood had been triggered off by her elven co-workers, so she herself—willingly or not, knowingly or not—could work the same kind of transformation on those with whom she came into contact.

And Lauri, the sole homosexual among the Elves, had guessed the implications: could she, knowing as she did that even a single night of deep intimacy could lead to irrevocable and eternal alterations in the body and spirit of another, ethically seek among human women for a mate?

Bright had offered herself. But though, consummated, the liaison would have been loving enough, it would also have been dishonest . . . and therefore tragic. Bright would have been sacrificing her own preferences in order to take care of Lauri, and beings who contemplated immortality had, above all, to live honestly, for the future held for them no termination of existence that would wipe away the accumulated lies of their lives or render those lies meaningless. And so, regretfully, Lauri had declined.

But now something had happened . . . or, rather, Lauri had now discovered that something had happened. Or might have happened. She was not sure. True, her picture had come to occupy a corner of Wheat's desk, and she thought that, over the last months, she had perhaps noticed a change in the Wheat's behavior toward her: a warming of an already warm smile, a shining of already bright eyes. But as yet, Wheat had said nothing to Lauri, and Lauri, reflecting that forever was a long time to regret over-eager assumptions, had said nothing to Wheat. Having become used to her celibate life, Lauri was not inclined to push matters. She had, to be sure, no clear idea that there were any matters to push. There was simply a photograph, a smile or two, and a vague but very understandable ache that had been with her since she had realized that physical love would more than likely not be hers for a long time.

So how do I feel about Wheat?

She did not know. She had, perhaps, so submerged her feelings beneath a sea of responsibility that she could now only peer down into an obscurity of troubled waters, but Elves did not lie, even to themselves, and so Lauri admitted that she simply did not know. It could be. It was possible. And then again . . .

She looked at her watch. Time to leave for the Center, to counsel others about matters from which she herself had been sundered for years. And yet she could not help but consider—honesty again—what it would be like to be able to think of Wheat as a lover. No guilt, no frantic worry. Wheat's blood had awakened already, awakened long before Lauri had even contemplated coming to Colorado.

She finished up, locked up, started down the hallway for the outer doors and the parking lot. And now TK had seen something in Ash, and Ash had healed him. How long would it be before something else happened? What people—black or white, mortal or immortal—would he call his own? Where was the plan? What logic, natural or otherwise, determined this slow progression of immortal transformation—?

She stopped with her hand on the push bar of the outer doors.

She was not sure why she had stopped, but she had the distinct impression that someone had called her name. A woman's voice. And a flash of blue and silver among her inner stars. But though she dismissed the impressions as imagination, she followed an insistent prompt from within herself and, retreating back up the hall, let herself into the office again.

She left the lights off, lifted a blind to look out the window. This late, the parking lot was almost invariably empty. Lauri saw her own Bronco, to be sure, but she expected that. What she did not expect to see, though, was another vehicle, a small, imported truck. It was parked near the building entrance, half hidden from the bright sodium lights by the shadow of the ornamental pear trees, and its tinted windows plunged its interior into a darkness that not even elven eyes could penetrate.

On the surface, this meant nothing: someone else was working late, that was all. But, for some reason, the presence of this particular vehicle chilled Lauri, for it seemed (though she could not say why, no more than she could say what had prompted her to stop at the plate glass doors and return to the office) a violation, something hideously out of place.

Again, following the inner prompt that she could neither understand nor place, she waited, watched.

Minutes went by. Half an hour. The truck finally flicked on its headlights and drove off. Only then did Lauri, inexplicably shaking, leave the building, and climb behind the wheel of her Bronco. She was a little late when she arrived at the Center, and she was still shaking. It was as though she had looked out of the office window to see a face pressed against the glass, a face that somehow summed up all the terrible things in the world that the Elves were required to mend, that refused to be mended, that would kill anyone who tried.

PART TWO

Tenso

CHAPTER 11

Sandy had time on her hands.

Terry had sent her off to translate the *Liber Usualis,* and was, apparently, disinclined to work any further with her until she could show him some definite progress. But, in truth, any concept of *working with* Terry that Sandy might have possessed had evaporated months ago. One did not work with Terry Angel. One did as he said. And so, like the saints of whom he was so fond of talking, the saints who had been forced to abandon themselves to helplessness and submission when gripped by the overpowering hand of God, she had allowed her interests, her needs, her harping—her life, in fact—to languish.

But she was no longer translating now, no longer spending hours fretting over dictionaries and passages of archaic liturgy, no longer, in a way, submitting to Terry: she was simply waiting for a book to arrive.

She had discovered that the library at Kingsley was not as well stocked with books relating to medieval music and religion as Natil had expected . . . or as Terry had, in his letters, intimated. The exhaustive overview by Gustave Reese had been on the shelf, likewise the study of Gregorian Chant by Willi Apel, but little else. Certainly there had been no translation of the *Liber Usualis.*

Interlibrary loan, though, had turned up several pertinent volumes at the University of New Mexico, and, still wondering why Terry had not known of the existence of the books, or, if he had known, why he had not told her of them, Sandy filled out the request forms. Could it be that he had wanted a fresh translation? But he had known that Sandy was ignorant of Latin. Surely, given the resources of his program, he could have found an experienced Latinist to do the work.

But since Sandy had come to Kingsley, she had been

systematically stripped of her illusions about the resources of the Hands of Grace. She had expected other students. There were no other students. She had expected a decent classroom. She had discovered shabby hand-me-down facilities that had not seen maintenance in twenty-five years. She had expected to learn about healing. She had learned nothing.

Still, though, as she waited for the books, as, finally, she found time to eat, to sleep, to shop, and, perhaps most important, put her hands to the strings of her beloved harp and, nearly weeping with relief, falteringly pick out the few tunes she knew, she clung to her hopes. Whether Terry had unwittingly exaggerated, whether she herself had naively read more into his statements than he had actually intended to convey, the program at Kingsley yet offered a bright, beckoning light in the darkness of her life.

. . . and there she goes again. See her delude herself. See her throw away what sight she has left with the most outrageous of imaginings. Yes, ladies and gentlemen, step right up to witness the incredible . . .

She wanted to scream. Had she been safe within her apartment, she might have crawled into the closet that held her bedding, buried her face in a pillow, and done just that. But here in her car, driving down Alameda Avenue, she had to content herself with a shake of her head and a mental *shaddup*.

The barker fell into a mumble, but she knew that he would be back. And now his words were even more telling, more wounding, more penetrating, for Sandy, despite the hopes and beliefs that she continued to foster in herself by dint of pure, frantic willpower, had begun to suspect that the program for which she had sold all her possessions and left behind an entire life was not itself an illusion.

With angry tears in her eyes, she pulled to a stop in front of Watterson's New Age Emporium. Even the journey she was making today was an emblem of her failing hopes. Once, she had submerged her religion for the sake of continuing her work with Terry, but since it appeared that, for now, she would most assuredly not be allowed to work with him, all her efforts had acquired a sense of the pointless, the useless. Terry, to whom she had turned for both instruction and support, had abandoned her, and so she had decided to seek out her own people.

Up until now, she had always been a solitary witch. Her training had come from books and from work. Once she had discovered that there was a name for what she had come instinctually to believe in, she had located and studied carefully every text that was available. True, some of what she found was wishful thinking, and a great deal of it bordered on ignorant and abject superstition, but Sandy, as though impelled by a vision—whether founded upon memories of a previous life or the cartoon backgrounds of her childhood—had formulated out of the few scraps of goodness that she had found a spiritual practice that revolved about an immanent, loving Goddess and the certainty that strength, sincerity, and devotion could not but lead her into psychological health, into a place from which she could eventually dispense to others, freely and unconditionally, some of the love with which she herself had been graced.

It was rather novel—and exceedingly terrifying—for her to consider breaching her customary isolation, but to her relief, Watterson's was not at all like the dim and seedy shops she had encountered—and run away from—in Los Angeles. Brightly lit by both fluorescents and huge plate glass windows, it was stocked with a staggering amount of merchandise of all sorts, and, in fact, bore no little resemblance to a supermarket or a department store.

The openness and familiarity was both comforting and unsettling, and Sandy hesitated, hanging back from the long counter and the red-haired clerk even after the brisk lunchtime business in incenses and oils and Anna Riva artificial voodoo books had settled down and left the store essentially vacant.

Finally, though: "Excuse me," she said, approaching. Her hands were cold, her heart aching with stress.

"Hi there!" said the clerk. She peered at Sandy, broke out in a smile. "I haven't seen you here before."

Mortification set in. Sandy wanted to hide, but she pushed on. "I'm new in town," she said. "I'm a . . ."

The clerk waited, her blue eyes bright but a little vacant. Sandy wondered whether she were actually hearing anything she said, decided not to make a complete hash of everything by revealing herself.

"... I'm looking for some ... uh ... witches. Is there a community or something here? Some ... uh ... others?"

Others. Sandy blushed, realizing that she had indeed revealed herself, but the clerk, having missed Sandy's telltale choice of words, was nodding. "We've got a mailing list," she said cheerfully. "It's right around here ... somewhere." She pawed through stacks of papers, receipts, checked under the cash drawer. "Oh, it's around here. I'll find it. Are you looking for a teacher?"

"Uh ..." Sandy felt very much on the spot. There was no way out. "... no. I'm ..."

The clerk finally appeared to understand. She stopped looking for the mailing list, and, leaning forward and propping her elbows on the counter so that her face was inches from Sandy's, asked in a very serious undertone: "Have you been initiated?"

There was no way out now. "Self-initiated," Sandy faltered, realizing that an initiation one performed for oneself was doubtless worth little among strangers.

And, true, for all the change in the clerk's expression, Sandy might well have expressed no more than an affinity for a particular flavor of Jell-O. "What tradition?"

"Uh ... I guess you'd have to say ... uh ... kind of ... Dianic."

A long pause. Pineapple? Sandy liked *pineapple*? The vague blue eyes turned suddenly distant.

"I ... I mean, the Goddess ..." But how could Sandy tell this stranger that what had brought her to the Craft was the Goddess, that despite the orthodox conventions of Wicca—conventions mandating a divine polarity symbolized by a Goddess and a God—she had always turned to the Mother without a spouse, the primal, original Creatrix.

The clerk straightened, stood back. It was not quite a dismissive gesture, not quite an *I think that we had best end for today,* but it was close. "Well, we don't really have any Dianic teachers. I know some women down in Englewood who don't work in a gender balanced tradition, and they might take you on, but I'd have to talk to them." She peered at Sandy. "Are you sure you want

Dianic? We have a Wicca 101 course starting up on Monday night. I can still get you in. You might find a real teacher there. You know: mainstream."

"Yes . . . I mean . . . no . . . I mean . . ." Sandy wanted to run. "I mean I'm not looking for a teacher. I'm just looking for some other witches."

The clerk looked at her for several moments. "You just want . . ."

"Well . . ." Sandy struggled, squirmed, managed to get the words out as a question. ". . . maybe some friends?"

The clerk abandoned Sandy to her ignorance. "There's a local pagan network. They're very open-minded, even with . . . uh . . ." She peered at Sandy again. *I think that we had best end for today.* ". . . eclectic traditions."

Sandy flushed, but she discovered that she was a little angry, too. She knew what she believed in.

"They're having a Samhain party next month." She pronounced it *sow'n,* slurring expertly but inaccurately through the modern Irish word for the month of November. "You could go, I guess. You might meet someone there."

Sandy felt a sudden upwelling of panic. She did not go to parties. There was too much noise at such gatherings, too much confusion, too many strangers. And a Samhain party could not but exhibit overtones of Halloween: costumes, makeup, masks . . .

Her father had liked masks. He had made her wear masks and makeup upon occasion. *Pig,* he had said even when cancer had turned his voice into a ragged whisper of phlegm and sputum. *Pig. I'm going to fuck you, pig.*

The clerk supplied Sandy with both a number she could call and a vague but gratuitous reminder that the people involved were *very* open minded. Sandy gritted her teeth with mixed terror and rage, thanked her, and then, shaking, moved away from the counter and pretended to look at book titles, though in reality she was too distraught to see anything.

It would have been easier, she thought, had she remained a Catholic. Everything would have been simple. Her community of co-religionists would have been open, respected, easily found. The priest, the bishop, and the pope would have been there to tell her what to do, and, with the exception of the most outré of fundamentalists, the general public would have had no question about the basic wholesomeness of her religious practice. Everyone knew what Catholics did. Everyone knew what Christians did.

Easier, yes. Just as it would have been easier to accept without question the dogmas that Terry Angel had forced upon her with a determination not dissimilar to that with which her father had pushed his penis into her infant body. But Freddy Joy had at least been at variance with the accepted norm and would have been immediately and universally condemned ... had the word of his daughter been accepted as truth. Terry, in contrast, worked with an acceptable, mundane, and well-understood Christian piety that had solidified over the last two thousand years into a foundation so taken for granted by believer and non-believer alike that it could no longer be perceived as a discrete and arbitrary entity.

But as Sandy still clung to Wicca despite its inherent problems—*and bigotries,* she thought as she glanced at the red-haired clerk—so she still believed in the Hands of Grace, but the sudden and unlooked-for juxtaposition of Terry Angel and Freddy Joy struck her suddenly with a rash of parallels and gripped her already panicked belly with a hand so tight that it made her dizzy. She almost fell, steadied herself against a rack of self-help videos, and finally sat down on a stack of cushions and tried to gasp herself back into control, back into belief.

And when she opened her eyes, she saw Natil entering the store. Wearing jeans and a t-shirt instead of overalls, and with the strap of a purse on her shoulder instead of a shovel, she nonetheless looked as confident and as comfortable with herself within the precincts of Watterson's New Age Emporium as she did among her flower beds.

Sandy's sickness was abruptly augmented by a fresh wave of panic. She had not told the groundskeeper about her religion. Natil had seemed to her to be a perfectly respectable woman, kind and rather sweet, but her familiarity with the *Liber Usualis* had pointed to a deeper than usual Christian background, and Sandy had assumed that Wicca was not something about which she could be expected to be understanding or accepting.

But Natil, Sandy considered, did not seem the sort to indulge in uninformed opinion. In fact, had Sandy been forced to sum up the groundskeeper in one word, she would have instinctively and unflinchingly said *grace,* for Natil moved, spoke, and acted with an almost unnerving elegance that seemed to have nothing to do with haste or prejudice. Even in the course of their single, brief lunch together, Sandy had found herself wishing that she could have gotten to know Natil a little better. At the same time, though, she had understood—and she still understood— that someone like Natil could have little in common with an abused little witch from California.

But here was Natil, striding gracefully up to the counter of Watterson's New Age Emporium and asking politely where the books on contemporary witchcraft were located.

"Are you on our mailing list?" asked the clerk.

"Please," said Natil, "the books."

"Here's our schedule of classes."

"Thank you, no."

"I've still got a few openings."

Natil only looked at her.

"Oh . . . over there," said the clerk, pointing, "by the video rack."

Natil gave the clerk one of those smiles that had so dazzled Sandy—albeit tinged with a faint weariness— turned away from the counter, stepped around a pile of multi-colored zafus, half-circled a table laden with plaster museum replicas and small suede bags, and stopped dead at the sight of the young woman who was sitting on a stack of cushions with her arms folded around her churning belly.

"Sandy!" she said. "Hello! How wonderful to see you!"

"Uh . . . hi . . ."

"Has your book come in at the library yet?"

"Uh . . ." Frightened, sure that something terrible was going to happen to her as a result of her coming to Watterson's today, of her attempting to do anything at all for herself, Sandy floundered at the simple question. "Uh . . ."

Natil knelt beside her. "Be at peace," she said. "I am here to do some research."

"On . . . Wicca . . . ?"

"You overheard? Just so."

Sandy did not know what to say, and Natil appeared to notice that she was distressed. "Beloved," she said softly, "is there anything that I can do?"

From someone else, the question would have evinced nothing more than empty politeness. But Natil's concern, Sandy knew, was genuine. "I'm just ... uh ... scared."

Natil watched her for a moment. "Scared?" she said, her voice still so soft so that only Sandy could hear. "Of what are you scared?"

The only honest answer to the question, though, was *of everything,* and Sandy was not willing to admit that to someone she hardly knew, even if that someone were Natil. "I'm ..." But as though she saw for a moment with another's eyes, she suddenly had a vision of herself as she was—crouched, frightened, almost craven—and she did not like it. And so she took Natil's offered hand and forced herself to stand up. "I know a little bit about Wicca," she said when she was on her feet. "Can I help you?"

Natil did not force her previous question, but now her eyes held another, held also, as far as Sandy could tell, absolute acceptance.

Sandy swallowed. "I'm a witch," she said. Natil's gaze did not falter. "I ... hope you know what that means."

And as though Natil had seen both the depth of the damage within Sandy and the height of the goal for which she was striving, she smiled. "I do indeed know what that means," she said. "Though ..." She glanced at the store, at the laden tables and shelves. The cash register rang, and she almost winced. "I am not certain that most of the witches in Denver do."

Sandy did not speak of boji stones, nor was she concerned with amulets or astrology or tarot or profit or any of the other diversions that, seemingly, had come to occupy modern witches. Coming to the Craft on her own, without the benefit of a teacher, and forced, therefore, to acquire her knowledge and practice from books, she had nonetheless managed to strike to the heart of the religion that Natil so fondly remembered from the days of Roxanne and Charity.

And so, when Sandy talked about Wicca, she spoke of the Goddess, and of the deep, personal union with Her that the witch sought in order to manifest divinity both in Circle and in day to day life. She spoke of robes and incense and other accouterments not as ends in themselves or opportunities for profit, but as symbols—toys, she called them—that helped one to transcend mundane reality. Sandy knew theory, to be sure, but she also knew practice, and it was not a dry practice of custom and rote work, but rather a living, vibrant spirituality. Sandy loved the Goddess because she knew the Goddess, and she knew the Goddess because, in an admittedly limited way, she had *been* Her.

Natil listened, and with Sandy's help she collected a stack of books that she would purchase; but all the while, her eyes were tearing. Once, the Elves had known Elthia in something of the same way. They had, in effect, been *Elthia* from moment to moment, from microsecond to microsecond, their very beings a constant, physical manifestation of the Dance that was everything, the Dance that was the Lady; and the direct, face-to-face vision that was a natural consequence of that existence had sustained them throughout the ages of the earth.

What had happened? Here was Sandy, who, though she could not say that she had ever seen her Goddess face to face or been held in Her arms, nonetheless knew of Her presence with a surety born of inner recognition, while Natil, an Elf. . . .

"It's like, you just can't talk about it, Natil. You have to—Oh, man . . ." Sandy pulled out another book. "Here. *The Spiral Dance*. You've just got to have this one. This, an athame, a little chutzpah, and you can put together your own coven—" She broke off, blushing, the caustic scars white against the rose of her face. "I mean, if that's what you want to do."

Despite her damp eyes, Natil felt a smile rise up from deep within her. "I really do not know what I want to do at this time, Sandy," she said. "I do know, however, that I need to know more."

Sandy nodded.

Natil was holding her stack of books with both hands, and she tapped the topmost volume with her chin. "*The Spiral Dance*, Sandy. Pile it on." Sandy added the book to the stack. "But you were saying about not just talking about it . . . ?"

"Uh ... oh, yeah. Well ..." Sandy went back to searching through the shelf of books, found a large paperback. "Oh, jeez ... *Real Magic*. Cute, but garbage. This guy's so full of himself—"

Natil smiled. "Sandy ..."

Sandy shoved *Real Magic* back onto the shelf. "Well, it's like we *are* the Goddess. All the time. But we just don't usually realize it until we stop and think about it. Sometimes we need a bunch of stuff to help us, like robes and ritual knives and incense and oils and candles ... that kind of stuff. But the real point of Wicca ..." She pulled out another book. "Oh, good. *Drawing Down the Moon*. Revised edition. Margot Adler is just great. You can learn all about the crazies you've gotten involved with."

"Crazies?" Natil kept her smile bright.

"Well ..." Sandy glanced at the room, at the overpriced merchandise, the cheap statues, the mass-produced mysticism. "... you've seen it."

"I have," said Natil. "But I have also seen you. And I know a true witch when I see one."

Sandy blushed again. "Aww ... Natil ..."

"I am serious. But what is the real point of Wicca?" Natil knew, to be sure, but she wanted to hear it from Sandy's lips.

"Well ... it's to be the Goddess. All the time." Sandy still looked ready to cry, but now it might well have been because she realized how terribly, terribly distant that goal remained for all that was human. "It's to give the way She gives. It's to love the way She loves. All the time. And you can't just talk about it. You have to do it." She saw then that Natil was weeping, the tears running down her face and beading the cover of *Drawing Down the Moon*. "Natil?"

The Elf managed to set down the stack of books without toppling it, and she fished a handkerchief out of her purse and wiped her damp face. "Thank you, Sandy."

Sandy looked a little frightened. "For what?"

"For giving me back my confidence."

Sandy still looked frightened. "I don't understand."

Natil shook her head. "Someday, maybe, I will be able to explain it to you. For now, though ..." She blotted her eyes once more, smiled at Sandy through continuing tears. "... thank you."

Confused, wide-eyed, Sandy nodded. "Okay."

Natil glanced at her watch. "Oh, dear. I am on my lunch hour, and I have just missed my bus. Could I possibly beg a ride back to Kingsley from you?"

Sandy forced a laugh. "Natil, you're so neat that I'd drive you out to Idaho Springs if you asked."

Natil examined Sandy for a moment. *Everything that happens,* she found herself thinking, *happens exactly as it should, happens exactly when it should, because that is the way it happens.*

Everything. Even this chance meeting at a metaphysical supermarket.

Hadden and the others had planned a cookout for the coming Saturday, and Natil, her tears still bright in her eyes, was now of a mind to make sure that there would be yet one more human who would that day eat and drink among the trees of Elvenhome. Sandy's religion was her own business, and Natil would not betray her confidences, but . . .

"Well," she said, "not, perhaps, as far as Idaho Springs, but a good distance. Are you busy Saturday?"

CHAPTER 12

Ash had put her hands on TK's leg on Monday, and the pain of the phantom limb had abruptly ceased. On Friday, he found that someone had put a bullet through his front window.

When he opened the door of his apartment, Rags was cowering in the corner, his growling and snarling now interspersed with piteous whines and whimpers. The yorkie's pads had been lacerated by the widely scattered shards of glass, and both the kitchen linoleum and the threadbare carpet were dotted with bloody paw prints that witnessed his panicked scrambles for safety.

TK reached for the light switch, instinctively thought better of it: he knew who had fired the bullet, and why. He therefore left the switch alone, locked the door behind him, and crouched down in the spill of soft, autumnal light that found its way in through the shattered window. "C'mere, Rags. Come on, boy."

Rags snarled and whimpered and would not come. Well, TK considered, the dog had never demonstrated the slightest sign of affection before. It was ridiculous to expect him to change now.

"OK, man," he said. "You just stay there. You let Uncle TK take care of things, and we see about getting you to a vet tomorrow."

He loosened his tie and stayed low as he eased around the perimeter of the apartment to the M16 that rested in the corner by his bed. He picked it up, felt the familiar heft of metal and fiberglass, knew without looking, knew without having to remember, knew from the *feel* of the weapon that the clip was full and engaged. Lock and load. Just like old times. No radar screens here, no Patriot missiles, no sanitized TV war: this was jungle fighting. The crack house homies had just resurrected the past.

Outside, he could hear crickets, and a mockingbird warbled and twittered from somewhere up the street as Rags whined and growled in the kitchen. Staying far enough away from the window to be well out of the light, his shoes crunching through glistening splinters and the rifle ready in his hand, TK moved slowly from left to right, examining the street below.

Nothing. Only a warm Friday afternoon in Denver. No one was out on the street (no one was out on the street much at all these days, because the local drug economy insisted upon counting casual passers-by as infrastructure and income both), and there was no movement in any of the parked cars, except for—

His eyes narrowed at the sight of the small, imported truck across the way. There was movement inside, the grotesque excrescence of a high top, a white t-shirt.

The rifle seemed to quiver in his hands like a live thing, a fish pulled from a cold river throwing itself to his shoulder, straining, as his hand found the trigger ...

But the present came back to him. This was Denver. Someone had put a bullet through his window, true, but could he kill a man on the basis of a supposition?

The rifle was cold, eager. So was his heart. But he put the weapon down.

He had decided that he could not.

Sizing up the truck, weighing the rifle, he walked to the light switch and snapped it on. The broken glass glittered like a field of stars. Rags prowled and whimpered and dotted the floor with blood. The truck whirred, pulled away from the curb, vanished around the corner. The warning had been given. TK was mildly surprised: warnings were an oddity, or, rather, warnings usually took the form of five or six small caliber bullets inserted into one's chest.

The telephone rang abruptly, and he nearly shot it.

Forcing himself to throw the safety on the rifle, he picked up the receiver. "Winters," he said.

"TK? Marsh here. Listen, the cookout's tomorrow, and I forgot to ask you if you needed a ride. We can pick you up any time you want."

TK's eyes were on the window, on the street. "Sure, man," he said. "Sure. You pick me up." He tensed the muscles of his stump, felt the prosthesis snap to attention.

Ash had done . . . something. And TK Winters had almost done . . . something else. "Tell you what: I meet you over on Broadway. Far side of the street. By the ice cream store. I be inside watching for you. 'Bout nine. OK?"

"Sure. Nine it is." A pause. Rags prowled and whined. "TK, is something wrong?"

"No, man," said TK. " 'S all right. Rags . . . just hurt himself."

"Do you need to get him to the vet? I'll give you a lift."

"I . . ." That was just like Marsh. That was just like all of them. Any one of them would have gone out in the middle of a snowstorm to save a cockroach. Crazy. "He's a tough little guy. I'll see how he is in the morning."

"OK. You be sure to call if you need help."

"Sure." TK hung up, stood with one hand on the cradled handset, the other wrapped around the rifle. "Sure," he said to the room. "Sure I'll call. But all the help in the world ain't gonna fix what's ailing this place." He set the rifle aside. "C'mere, Rags," he said to the whimpering, snarling yorkie. "Let's take a look at those paws. And you bite me, I swear I use you for target practice."

Sandy saw Natil often that week, both at school and at her apartment, but while she was very glad of the continuing chance to talk about what had been, for months, a forbidden subject, she was still rather puzzled by the esteem in which the groundskeeper obviously held her.

Natil was eager to know about Wicca, and during the long evenings of this unusually warm October, they would sit on old kitchen chairs in the dirty living room of Sandy's apartment and talk about such things as Circle casting, the four elements and their symbolic tools, guided and unguided meditations. But what appeared to interest Natil the most, and what she returned to constantly, were the methods witches used in order to invoke the presence of the Goddess.

Sandy answered as best she could, but there were some things that words simply could not express. "I keep telling you, Natil," she said that Friday night, "it's no good just to talk about it. You really have to *do* it to make any sense out of it."

Natil fell silent, looked as though she were struggling

with an uncooperative memory. "You are right, of course," she said finally. "I suspect that pride is my problem."

Sandy blinked. "But you're not proud, Natil!"

Natil smiled softly. "There are all kinds of pride, beloved. I, perhaps, have found the most insidious of them all." But she laughed lightly of a sudden, tossed off her gravity with a shrug. "I need to mention something, though. The cookout is tomorrow, and it is rather difficult to give you directions as to how to find the place yourself. I would suggest that you come up now. With me. You can spend the night at Elv—" She caught herself. "—at the house."

Sandy shuddered, still regretting the burst of infatuated gratitude that had caused her to accept the invitation. But accepting was one thing, sleeping elsewhere was another. "I . . ."

Natil appeared to fathom her distress. "You will be safe," she said. "Indeed, you will be safer there than you have ever been in your life."

Sandy shuddered again, looked away. "That . . . wouldn't be too hard, Natil."

Natil nodded. "I know."

And Sandy knew that she did indeed know. "I'm afraid, Natil," she said. "I don't want to be a bother to you . . . I don't know if I should even come up at all."

Natil's voice was gentle, without a shred of accusation. "Are you so afraid of friendship?"

"Natil . . . I'm so messed up. I don't know . . . I guess I'm afraid of everything."

A long pause. Then, very softly: "I understand."

"You don't even know me."

Natil shook her head, her long braid rustling across her back. "Not so, Sandy. I know you well enough. I know that you have been hurt, and that you are still being hurt. I know also that you are a witch, the first true witch I have met in a long time." The groundskeeper's blue eyes were filled with a kind of light. "Months ago," she said, "I went to Watterson's looking for someone who could tell me what I need to know. I went away from it because I found no such person there and no hope that I ever would. I returned last Monday because I thought that I might find in books what I had not found in people. And

I found you." She smiled fondly at Sandy, a gesture that had nothing in common with Terry's oblique compliments. It was something else, something (and Sandy almost hated to use the word, so damning it was to all the hopes that had led her to Denver) genuine.

Sandy looked away, torn between pride and embarrassment.

"You need to be safe," Natil went on. "Very well: I think that for tonight you should come and be safe with me. I think that it will be good for you." There was a flash as of starlight in her eyes . . . or maybe it was a twinkle. "And, as a good witch, you should appreciate the chance to save gasoline."

"Huh?" Sandy lifted her head.

Natil had stood up. "I promised Wheat that I would help her make pumpkin pies in the morning, so, there being no time for me to take the bus, I would have to drive into Denver in order to pick you up. Much better you come tonight. What say you?"

Her quaint manner of speech made Sandy smile. "And what if I say no, Natil?"

Natil shrugged. "Whatever comes is acceptable."

And maybe it was that perfect expression of openness and willingness to accommodate her needs and her fears that quelled Sandy's doubts. Her father, as addicted to control as a crack addict to refined cocaine, had always been determined to have his own way, whether with her body or her life, and he had bullied, threatened, battered, and even splashed her with lye in order to get it. Natil, though, was different. *Whatever comes is acceptable.*

Sandy found herself smiling. "Okay, Natil," she said. "I'll come. Just . . . don't laugh at me, will you?"

Natil shook her head. "Never."

And as Sandy had realized by now that Natil spoke only the truth, she was not surprised when the groundskeeper, presented with a closet, a futon, and a rag doll, did nothing to indicate that she thought Sandy's sleeping habits anything but ordinary. In fact, when introduced to Little Sandy, Natil took the doll into her arms and hugged her with the blissful expression of a woman who had just discovered her favorite daughter hiding behind a stand of wildflowers.

"It's . . ." Sandy fumbled for words. "It's like she's me.

I try to take care of her as though she were me back ...
back when. I hold her like I want to be held."

Her voice trailed off, and her good eye was suddenly
blind with tears.

Natil put her arm about Sandy's shoulders. "That is a
good thing," she said. "And she is beautiful. As are you."

Sandy blushed, for she knew what she looked like. But
it occurred to her that perhaps Natil was not speaking in
terms of outward appearance.

A few minutes later, with Little Sandy sitting in Natil's
lap, Sandy's small harp on the floor, and the futon and a
change of clothes on the back seat, they were in the
Celica, driving toward the mountains. And when they
reached the turnoff, Sandy admitted that Natil had been
perfectly right: by herself, she would have missed the
strange little byway that appeared suddenly from around
a bend in Highway 6 and then wandered up into the surrounding hills.

It was dark when Natil told Sandy to park in a small
widening of the road. "We must go the rest of the way on
foot," she said.

Sandy nodded. It made sense. She could not have
imagined Natil living anywhere else but in the mountains,
among the trees, at the end of a walk beneath darkling
pines and aspens.

And so, carrying Sandy's things, they walked. The sky
was clear, and mingled starlight and moonlight filtered
down through the interlacing branches. At times, the foli-
age became so dense that Sandy was plunged into darkness, but Natil took her arm and guided her without
hesitation.

"Here," she said at last, and, in the moonlight, Sandy
could see a building standing whitely in the middle of a
large clearing. A tower rose from one wing, and a silver
filigree glistened just beneath the curved eaves. Everything gleamed: the walls, the slate roof, the windows ...

Sandy had expected a small cottage or a timbered
lodge. Instead: "It's like a fairy castle," she said aloud,
and then she blushed.

Natil, though, was smiling. "In a way," she said, and,
leading Sandy to a side door, she opened it (it was unlocked). As though struck by a sudden thought, she
snapped on the light switch.

The kitchen was large and bright and outfitted with cheerful copper pots and pans, a modern stove and oven (which were so clean that they made Sandy blush with embarrassment), a big refrigerator, gleaming counters, and burnished cabinets. Beyond, down the hall and deeper in, were dark wood paneling, precise parquetry, and carpets thick as meadow grass. There were snug rooms with cushions and plants, and a small fountain filled the air with silver presence. Wide, double-insulated windows looked out onto moonlit trees and mountains, a courtyard, gardens . . .

Sandy was staring. "This is . . . all yours?"

"Oh, by no means." Natil led her up the stairs and along a hallway. "A number of us are co-owners. I am . . ." She stopped before a door. ". . . a caretaker, in many ways."

And as though she had guessed that anything of any size would have aroused Sandy's fears, Natil opened the door to reveal a cozy nook of a bedroom, its wooden paneling figured with carvings of leaves and birds. The bed was on a shelf so carefully fitted to the wall that it might well have grown out of it, and, from behind an amber shade, an incandescent lamp provided illumination with the softness of candlelight.

"Is this acceptable?" said Natil.

"It's . . ." Sandy stared, touched the paneling. Gently, she turned and set Little Sandy down on the bed. The doll looked at home. Indeed, Sandy felt at home. No, *home* was not quite the right word. Rather, she felt safe. Very safe. She had exposed herself, and she had not been hurt. So far.

So far. She almost wept. "It's . . . wonderful," she managed.

Natil smiled. "The bathroom and shower are just down the hall. I will have towels out for you come morning."

Sandy still stared. "Why . . ?" She shrugged, trying to put all her bewilderment into the gesture.

Natil looked sad. "Is it so strange?"

Sandy nodded. "Yeah."

"Can you not simply accept this for what it is?"

"Nothing's ever been what it is . . . or what it looked like." Sandy sat down on the bed, took Little Sandy into her arms, pressed her face against the yarn hair. "It was never that way with my . . ." She swallowed, staggered on. ". . . with my father. It doesn't seem to be that way with—" Her throat slammed shut of its own volition.

Natil was standing by the door. "With Terry?"

Sandy, nodded, eyes clenched. "Yeah."

"Have you spoken with Terry concerning this?"

"I can't talk to him."

A silence. Then: "I understand," Natil said. But she waited until Sandy looked up, and then she stretched out a hand to her. "Come, though. You can leave that behind for now. You are here, and this place is safe. Let me fix you something to eat, and then you can go to bed."

And later, after grilled-cheese sandwiches and hot chocolate, Sandy curled up beneath a soft comforter in the quiet bedroom. The door was not locked. She did not care. Her closet was miles away. No matter. Her futon lay rolled up on the other side of the room. That did not bother her in the slightest.

With Little Sandy in her arms, she looked up at the shadowed ceiling where beams and plaster glimmered in the soft moonlight from the window. She heard the distant fountain. She heard the whisper of pines, the flutter of aspen leaves golden with autumn.

Safe. She was safe. She knew it. She felt it. It was not a question of *so far.* Not here. And though she cried for a time—cried for all the places she had known that had not been safe—it was not long before sleep came to her as softly as a Mother Goddess, held her in Her arms, and took her off to see the starlight that played upon the mountains of gentle dream.

Pride.

Natil admitted it: she had been proud. Perhaps her pride had lain more in thoughtlessness and omission than in direct, stiff-necked refusal, but pride was pride. As Elf, as Firstborn, she had held herself away from the gritty, fleshly, mortal practices of the witches. She had sought among the occult stores of Denver for old, human wisdom, true, but she had sought as an outsider. Once again, an Elf, starlit and semi-divine, had descended from her mountain solitude to grant human beings the privilege of her wondrous presence.

That morning, with the kitchen of Elvenhome warm

with the heat of the oven and the odor of baking pies, with her hands thick with dough and her apron splashed a hundred times with flour, Natil could not but laugh at herself. Here was a fine Firstborn Elf, clattering in the kitchen like a *hausfrau,* her face smeared with pie filling. Such a demigod! Such a perfect embodiment of the eternal Dance!

Wheat, as floured and spattered as Natil, brushed back a tendril of hair and managed to put a distinct streak of butter across her cheek. "How many of these were we going to make, anyway?" Her cornflower blue eyes were bright, laughing.

"Seventeen Elves and two humans," said Natil, "and that means five pies."

Wheat frowned. "Raven."

"All right, then: six. And some blueberry muffins."

They laughed and went back to work, Wheat singing a Judy Collins song to which Natil added her own voice on the choruses.

Warm humanity. Natil had seen it countless times, but somehow, she had never thought about what it meant until now. Yes, in this kitchen, making pumpkin pies, she was indeed a perfect embodiment of the Dance. The isolation was over: Firstborn or not, she would, like the rest of her people, make pies, or plant flowers, or vacuum carpets, or take care of abused young women who wanted desperately to be whole.

A step on the stairs to the second floor made her lift her head. "Hi," said Sandy, looking timidly around the corner. "Am I intruding?"

"No one ever intrudes here," said Wheat. "You must be Sandy. I'm Wheat. Welcome to Elvenhome."

Natil, working butter into flour for yet another crust, bit her lip at Wheat's revelation. But Sandy laughed. "That's a good name for this place," she said. "I feel as though I've walked into a Tolkien book."

Natil cleared her throat gently. "We ... ah ... try," she said, glancing at Wheat. Wheat saw the glance, raised her a smile.

It was a good day. The weather remained unnervingly warm, and toward mid-morning, as the pies came out of the oven, the rest of the Elves and their guests carpooled in. Raven was mollified by the provisions made for dessert, particularly since she was supplying a chocolate cake and a dozen muffins of her own. Dell and Fox had come with trees to plant after lunch, and Hadden (who had brought steaks and hamburgers) and Web (who had brought tofu and tempe) made everyone laugh by sneering at one another with a mock hostility that was interspersed with comments about "people who eat dead animals" and "new-age fungus munchers."

TK, though, had also brought something.

Natil had met the big man several times since he had started work at TreeStar, and his habitual reserve had invested him with an air of somber, almost brooding menace. But today, as he descended into the small valley that cupped Elvenhome, he held cradled in his arms a tiny dog. The animal's feet were bandaged, and the big man was murmuring comfortingly to it despite the fact that it snarled and growled at him as much as it whined and whimpered.

"And who have we here?" said Natil, giving TK's hand a squeeze that he, doubtless, hardly felt.

"This's Rags, Natil," he said. "He got into some broken glass yesterday."

"The poor thing." She held out her arms. "May I?"

TK looked doubtful. "He's not very friendly, Natil. I'm surprised he didn't bite the hell out of me on the way up here. Vet can't see him until Monday, and I didn't feel right about leaving him alone. Maybe he hurts too bad to bite." He put his hand on Rags' head, jerked it away as the dog lunged at it with bared teeth. "Then again . . ."

Natil kept her arms out. "Allow me."

With doubt still plain on his face, TK handed the dog over. After examining Natil out of suspicious eyes for a moment, Rags stopped growling, snuggled down into her arms, and went to sleep with a soft *grrf*.

"I don't believe that," said TK.

Natil kissed Rags on the head. "It is well," she said. "I will be harping later. Perhaps I can do something for him."

TK looked even more doubtful; but throughout the day, as he was passed from one pair of elven arms to another, Rags remained placid, happy. Even when Sandy took him after lunch, he only gave her a slightly puzzled look, then settled down again with the canine equivalent of a shrug.

"He don't do that at home," said TK.

Kelly ran to TK and jumped into his lap, then threw her arms about his neck and kissed his dark cheek. "This is a good place, TK."

TK's eyes turned suddenly far away, as though he were seeing places that were anything but good, and he suddenly hugged Kelly tightly, even protectively. "Yeah," he mumbled into her blond hair. "It's a good place all right."

And after lunch there was music. Marsh and TK played a set of acoustic blues that brought Web to his feet and to a dance with Kelly as TK's sax floated bittersweet and human among the branches of trees that usually witnessed only the emotions of Immortals. Wheat sang Judy Collins songs to Raven's accompaniment on guitar, thereafter settling down—quite by accident—beside Lauri, who looked nervous, pleased, and bewildered all at the same time.

And then Natil took up her harp. "Sandy?" she said. "Would you bring Rags over here? Just sit down beside me. I am going to play a bit, and we shall see if it helps his feet at all."

Sandy, singled out, and asked to sit in plain view of everyone, did as Natil asked, but she hung her head. Her dark hair fell forward but did not quite cover the scars along her jaw.

Would that I could do something for you also, beloved, Natil thought, but the old powers were no more, and she would count herself lucky if she could even partly mend the feet of a Yorkshire terrier.

"You brought your harp, did you not, Sandy?" she said suddenly. "We will have to play together later on."

Sandy nodded, still with her head down. "I'm not very good."

"Good is a relative term." Natil touched Rags on the head. "Listen, little one," she said, and, with a quick ripple of bronze strings, she went off into a song that she had composed long ago, ages ago. It was, in fact, the first melody she had made, and she had played it at the beginning of the world. Then, she had sat upon stone instead of grass, for there had been no life to soften the land and make it green. The air had been black and turgid, corrupt with the belchings of volcanism, and blue skies had lain far in the future.

But even then the promise of blue skies had been present, and the potential for life—life that would eventually come and make such things as grass and trees and people who would grow up and find starlight in the Colorado mountains—had been present, too. And Natil found that her old song came to her effortlessly today, as was, she thought, entirely fitting, for as blue skies and life had been promised back then, now the Lady was promised, promised by the appearance of a young woman who worshiped her Goddess with all the love and devotion that a human being could offer to Someone she had never seen.

Natil let her music become the future, casting it around the clearing like a web, catching her listeners and drawing them together in hope, in healing. Deprived though they were of *Elthia,* they could at least participate in the promise, learn to recognize it, accept it, and so be ready for the reality that was to come, that had to come.

She must have played for an hour or more. She could not have said. But the sun was dropping toward the western ridges by the time she lifted her hands and allowed the strings to fall silent, and the air was beginning to cool with the approach of evening.

The silence grew, continued. There were tears on the faces of Elf and human alike, and Lauri had not yet noticed that she was holding a sobbing Wheat in her arms.

But beside her, Sandy, her eyes brimming, was removing the bandages from Rags' feet as the dog struggled to free himself from the unfamiliar cloth. The wrappings came off layer by layer and finally fell to the ground in a clump.

"Oh ... dear Goddess." Sandy's voice was a hoarse whisper. "They're perfect.

Natil leaned over and looked. There was not a trace of a wound on any of Rags' pads.

Rags struggled. Sandy let him go. Yipping shrilly, the terrier bounded about the clearing, throwing himself into laps, licking faces, rolling on the ground and pawing the air. He bolted up slopes and down slopes, disappearing into the trees, reappearing, like a comet in an irregular orbit, as he streaked through the clearing with his long fur flying and flared for a moment into a bright burst of barking and excited wiggles, then vanishing again.

A hand touched Natil's arm. Sandy's face was streaked with tears, and though she again manifested the fear that seemed such an intimate and chronic part of her makeup, there was, beneath it, bubbling up like a spring, thrusting up like a determined flower, a sense of eagerness, a desire, a longing. "Please, Natil," she said. "I didn't realize that you . . ."

Natil shook her head. "I am a harper. It is the reason I am here."

But Sandy was struggling, fighting the fear. There was something, something she wanted, something that was bigger than the fear, that could split it asunder as the roots of trees could rive rock. "Please, Natil . . . can you . . ."

Natil felt the question before Sandy uttered it, knew it for what it was. *Whatever happens*, she thought, *happens exactly as it should.*

The fear gave way. "Can you . . . can you teach me how to do that?"

Natil closed her eyes and let the relief wash over her like a warm wave. It could happen. It would happen. Gritty humanity . . . and witchcraft. "I will teach you," she managed. The stars blazed at her, their light washing through her, promising blue skies, promising grass, promising life. "I will teach you," she said, "if you will teach me."

CHAPTER 13

Jesus was pleased to show Terry His hands this morning.

They appeared on his kitchen table, just out of the corner of his eye: a pallid whirl as of the wings of a seraphim, a quivering movement, and then a presence unspeakably bright to his mind. He knew Who had come, and the surety of the visitation brought his reason and his will to their knees, bound them, and bent their foreheads to the floor in mute acknowledgment of the miracle.

But Terry could not look directly (that was forbidden), and therefore he made it his act of faith this morning that he *would* not look. But he at least allowed himself to imagine the Hands as he might have seen them had he actually turned aside from his breakfast bread and water, turned to face the vision. The pale, lovely flesh lying limply on the Formica, the wounds left by the iron nails seeping with sweet blood (and Terry knew that it was sweet, for he had once been allowed to taste it, drawing it up through the quivering stiffness of a golden tube that had been placed in his mouth as omnipotent hands had guided him—there was no possibility of resisting—to the place where he should suck) as the skin that rimmed them, tattered a little where the rough metal had passed, gaped open like dead lips, a faint white shadow of bone peeking out from the dribbling crimson . . .

But there: he had almost looked, almost violated the divine trust. Taking up his bread, therefore, he tore it in two and threw half of it on the floor to punish himself for his momentary yielding to temptation. Then, quickly, he twisted his trunk to one side, letting the sharp points of the barbed wire he wore beneath his clothing cut in deeply, drawing forth a blood that was most certainly not sweet, but which was, in its own way, blessed.

Afterwards, he finished his bread, chewing morsels and

crumbs that had abruptly turned tasteless, for the Hands were gone, the breakfast table achingly bare where, a moment ago, the attraction of the celestial realms had so caught his thoughts and feelings that he had, for a moment, *seen*.

Now, nothing. The soul, suspended between heaven and earth, its arms bound, its senses and powers riven and wounded, could only long for the pleasures of God. There was no comfort for Terry from earth, and heaven had spurned him. He would, then, hang, his heart an inward desert, until he was mastered again, penetrated by divine urgency.

He gave the barbed wire another jerk, and the pain ran like a lance from his groin to the small of his back. But the Hands did not return, and Terry remained panting for the touch of divinity, willing and open to that imperious thrust.

It was always that way, though. His visions of the divine were invariably limited. He was allowed to see Hands, but only when he did not look directly at them. He was given blood to drink, but only when he was blindfolded, bound, helpless. He was caught up in rapture, but it was a lightless place to which he was taken, one in which he lay, trembling, submissive, waiting for something to be done to him. He did not complain, however, for he knew that his own inherent weakness was the reason for these deprivations. Try as he might, though, he could not correct his error, could not make the suspension of his will perfect, could not yield completely to his seducer, could not give over, even for an instant, every shred of himself to the desires of another.

But that was a lie. He could. He had. That he had not yielded to God was an error for which he was justly and divinely spurned. But he could not deny that once, months ago, he had stood in the morning and sunlit quadrangle of Kingsley College, his being sundered from itself, brought low, captured and enslaved by the music of the dark-haired groundskeeper as she had played melody after melody upon a strange wire-strung harp. He did not know how she had done it, knew only that on that day he had been destroyed, for it had been not to God but to a woman that he had given himself as completely as if she had drawn him into bed and lapped him in the musky sinfulness of her body.

Since then, though, he had avoided her scrupulously. He had ignored her flower beds, her trees, her lawns, had not even looked at her. She had become for him an occasion of sin, monstrous sin, for in debauching not just his ears but also his very soul, she had turned his own playing into a shadow of itself. Worse, a shadow of a shadow, for music was a shadow to begin with, a crude depiction of the spiritual world, and he could not but suspect that, having once heard and yielded to Natil, he would be forever mirroring a more earthly music.

Natil had as much as admitted that her music was earthly. *Life simply is,* she had said, and in those three words she had denied any connection between herself and anything save the enclosed world of evolution, death, and the Serpent. *Life simply is.* What a terrible fate! And he had fallen under the spell of her denial!

Sandy, he was sure, was different. Sandy had spoken to him of a vision, and she had spoken so offhandedly, as though such things happened to her every day, that Terry sensed that they did indeed happen to her every day. Walking beside him, placidly and submissively recounting the results of the researches and tasks to which he had set her, even complaining about her work with childish and unrepentant pride (but he would attend to that), she was seeing—seeing constantly—beyond the confines of the world, straight into divine mystery.

She had said it so casually! What had happened that had so forcefully fixed her upon the remote heavens, solarized her thought, zodiacalized her will, selenized her imagination, and opened her to revelations and sights from which he himself was barred? He could not think of what might have happened. Was she a messenger? No, that could not be. Could it be that, like himself . . .

. . . bonds—

He jerked away from the upwelling memory, and, impelled by disgust, lifted his right arm and brought it down on the corner of the table, wincing with the pain but also exulting in it. He lifted it again, smashed it down again. And four. Three, four, five . . .

When he was done, his arm was bruised, gashed by the sharp edge, the livid white of the impacts shading quickly first into pink, then into the red of outraged blood vessels that blended with the dark bruises left over from days and weeks before: a motley patchwork of self-abuse. The pain, though, had cleared his head, redirected his meditations, transfixed the five dark currents of his being with holy wounds. He would submit only to God. His work would demonstrate that. And if people like Natil wished to live solely in the unnatural world of death and enfoldment—the world of the Serpent—he could do nothing to help them save work and pray. *Ora et labora.*

Pushing aside the remainder of his breakfast—he would not eat today—he rose from the table, and then he rolled down the long sleeves of his shirt, hiding the stigmata that he had, in abject devotion and willing submission, inflicted upon himself.

Dear Dr. Jerusalem:

I regret taking so long to reply to your letter. Denver General Hospital does not have any music therapy program for IC patients. I am not sure what to make of your questions about the spiritual nature of such programs, but I can assure you that our chaplain, Father Frank Baldwin, is perfectly capable of handling that side of our patients' well being. He will be more than happy to answer any questions you might have, and so I refer you to him.

Very sincerely yours,

Thomas H. E. Ghato
Director

"Mr. Winters—"

"Lieutenant, you got a problem right in your back yard, and I'm asking you what the hell you doing about it."

TK had given up being subtle. He had tried petitions, he had tried letters, he had tried confrontation. Nothing had worked. The crack house was still in operation, and his neighborhood was still afraid. He had therefore been forced into simple harassment . . . of the Denver police department.

"That's just what I'm trying to tell you, Mr. Winters." Lieutenant Brown's voice, in contrast to his name, was very white: a pinched little whine of a tenor. "There's a drug problem throughout Denver, and we just don't have the manpower to do everything instantly. We just have to take things one at a time. Mr. Early is being pretty aggressive about prosecuting these crack house people, but we just have to make arrests first, and investigations just take time. It's no good if we bring them in and then just have to let them go again."

TK drummed his long fingers on his desktop. He had closed his office door for this call, half because he had thought that he might lose his temper, half because he did not want his coworkers to know that he came from a neighborhood in which existed anything so totally antithetical to their world as a crack house. They were sweet people: they had made him feel welcome, had ignored his color—or, rather, accepted it as their own—had even ... well ...

... no, he did not want to think about those other things.

"Man," he said into the phone, "these guys are aggressive. Got a bunch of Tinies trying to make OG overnight. No one even goes out for the paper until the sun's all the way up, and even then it's chancy. Old lady got her social security check jacked last week—"

"Like I just said, Mr. Winters ..."

TK's temper finally gave way. "Lieutenant, a kid got killed in her own yard a few months back. You guys give a shit about that?"

Silence. Brown was, doubtless, angry. Well, TK considered, that made two of them. That little girl had been a sprite of a child, her face a precious mixture of innocence, knowledge, and deviltry. But she had been black, and so, after the papers had finished deploring the killing, after a few well-meaning and well-off citizens groups— all white—had held meetings, created task forces and investigative committees, and delivered an impressive bouquet of flowers to the grieving mother, everything had settled down; and the crack house, like everyone else, had gone back to business as usual.

Brown, though, did not react. "We're just doing everything we can, Mr. Winters," he said.

"You realize that I'm going to keep calling you, Lieutenant."

"That's just fine, Mr. Winters. The Denver police department believes in being pro-active. We're just always glad to know that there are citizens out there who are trying to clean up their neighborhoods . . ."

Yeah. So long as they do it by themselves.

". . . and you have a nice day."

Brown hung up without waiting for a reply. TK sat with the receiver against his ear for the better part of a minute, held back from a scream of rage not only by propriety, but also by an instinctive wish to protect the people he had come to love—*And it's love now? Oh, Lord!*—from the horrors of the world. They were not like the other white people he had known. They were not, in fact, like anyone.

The thought of them—of Hadden with his sea gray eyes, Bright with her perpetual smile, Lauri with her raunchy good humor, Natil with that damned incredible harp of hers . . . of all of them, in fact—eased the anger that was pounding against the front of his skull and allowed him to end his half of the phone connection with no more than a slamming down of the receiver.

But that action, he thought, summarized the difference between himself and his new friends, for not one of those with whom, for the last several months, he had eaten, laughed, played music, and . . .

. . . no, better not think about that part . . .

. . . not one of them would have felt a need for anger or violence. Of any sort. TK felt accepted, befriended, loved . . . and terribly, terribly different. They were all something more than what could be attributed to mere white skin and opportunity, something that, yes, appeared to desire to transcend questions of color and lifestyle and, seemingly without reason, transform itself into a living embodiment of help, whether that help involved referring TK Winters to a job opening at TreeStar, dragging a dishwater little thing like Sandy Joy up to a mountain cookout, or even taking a little dog with cut up paws and . . .

. . . and there it was again. TK found that his fingers were unconsciously probing at the juncture of his leg and his prosthesis. His pain had disappeared. Rags' paws had been healed.

Miracles. Some kind of miracles. He had told himself a hundred times that he should have been afraid, but he was, in fact, not afraid. Instead, he wanted to draw closer.

The old janitor in Georgia had offered him help, and he had accepted it, and in that accepting he had pledged himself to help others. And now, here were folk who helped, who seemed to have no other purpose than to help, and who, unlike himself, actually seemed to succeed sometimes.

He wanted to be like them.

He got up to open the door of his office, but stood for a moment beside his desk with his head bowed, his hand to his face. He could not be like them. Was it that he was black? Yes . . . and a hundred other things. But he could not help but wonder how so many people had come to be so wonderful. How had they arrived at their present state? What had they been like before?

Whatever they had been, though, TK guessed that it could have had no experience whatsoever with projects, gangs, poverty, or prejudice; and when he opened the door to the sylvan decor of the outer office, and when Bright looked up from her receptionist's desk with a smile that seemed to convey, visually, the essence of a hug, and when Lauri, just entering, gave him a wave and a "How ya doin', TK?" he was absolutely sure of that. He would, in fact, have staked his life upon it.

Maxwell,

   Could we get together for lunch sometime this week? Any time after Tuesday is good for me.

Nora

Had Natil wanted to laugh at herself, she had hit upon a course of action that allowed her plenty of opportunities to do so. Here was an Elf, an Immortal who had spoken with Divinity, who had been held in Her arms, who knew Her by name . . . learning how to be a witch.

Sandy took her task seriously but humbly. She had at first claimed that she knew nothing about teaching Wicca, that, self-initiated as she was, she was not even vaguely qualified. "You need a High Priestess for teaching, Natil," she had said.

And Natil had nodded. "I have found one." And Sandy had first blushed, then protested, then, finally, given in. She would teach Natil about Wicca, and Natil would teach her about harp.

And so Sandy started with the basics of her version of witchcraft, introducing Natil to the meditations from *The Spiral Dance,* acquainting her with the feel of the energy of the four Elements, preparing her for experiencing the divine energy that came from the invocation of the Goddess in Circle.

"We work in Circle," Sandy explained. "It's a safe place for us. Ceremonial magicians get all hung up on the awful critters out there that are going to get you if you don't protect yourself, but for us, a Circle is a place where things are holy because you *make* them holy, where you don't have to be afraid of each other because you all love each other."

They were in Sandy's apartment, talking quietly into the evening as the furnace rattled and clanked with the demands made upon it by a sudden cold snap, as snow, driven by a stiff wind from the north, fluffed against the windows. The season had abruptly shifted from autumn to winter, but that, Natil thought, was appropriate: winter was a time of rest and introspection, of preparation for spring. And so Natil was turning inward, hoping as she did so that spring would bring much more than the unfolding of leaf and flower, that it would bring, in fact, the blossoming of the Elves.

"That is the way it should be," she said.

"I think so," said Sandy, but a shade crossed her face. "Some don't." She was silent for some time. Then: "Anyway, let's try some of this stuff. Like I keep saying: you really have to do it."

Natil nodded. "And it is to do it that I have come to you."

Compared with the instinctive effortlessness of starlight, the meditations and energy workings of Wicca were crude and unreliable things. Crosslegged on the floor, eyes shut, Natil had to consciously ignore the stellar energies and instead concentrate on something human, homely, transient. But regardless of any inadequacies inherent in Sandy's religion, Natil could not but feel that she had entered a warm place, a sanctuary of maternal nurture that she had not known since, coming for the first time into consciousness, she had felt the Lady's loving and starlit hand smoothing her face into its final shape . . . four and one half billion years ago.

And Wicca was indeed warm. Born as it was of the hopes and fears and loves of farmers and herders, shaped by the cycles of environment and season, it tasted and smelled of rich grass and earth, of animals warm in a winter barn, of foals and calves rising with trembling legs from the straw onto which they had been birthed, of human mothers and babies and all the importance and tragedy of fleeting, mortal life.

And so Natil put aside her starlight and concentrated instead on the world of humanity. She fumbled her way through the unfamiliar exercises that Sandy gave her, feeling out the nature of Earth, Air, Fire, and Water. She examined how they fit together, blended into one another and into her own personal energy, and she looked consciously at connections that she had, throughout her long existence, taken for granted.

And on other nights, she guided Sandy up to Elvenhome, and in the warm room of cushions and paneling and carpet where the Elves, come the weekend, would cling to one another and weep over the vastness of the wrongs that they had set themselves to putting right, she listened while her young student struggled with the strings of her harp. Gently, patiently, she guided Sandy's hands into easier positions, helped her to relax, listened approvingly as the flow of notes smoothed out.

Sandy had talent. Even within the course of a week, the clumsiness left her hands, and the flow of her music began to break loose from the shackles of abuse and fear. Sandy's harp was small and upright, with a slenderness that was enhanced and complimented by a narrow sound box: a Gothic harp, built to resemble as closely as possible the instruments played in the early Renaissance. Its voice was, therefore, soft, hardly able to carry to the hallway outside the room, but that was perfectly all right, for to accomplish Sandy's desires, its voice had only to carry to the ears of someone who was in need, and the quiet gentleness of its gut strings suited well the touch of the incest victim's hands.

It was only Natil's second attempt to teach a human being the elven way with music, and as her first had ended in failure, she was, in the beginning, apprehensive. Sandy, though, was determined, and although her fingers were untrained, she loved the harp not only as an instrument by which she could express herself, not only as a potential vehicle for the healing of others, but also as an icon of another world, a better world, a world in which all who looked for safety might find refuge, all who hungered for love might be fed, all who thirsted for help and healing might find themselves offered a brimming chalice.

Such immense tasks to give over to such a fragile instrument! But Natil knew what things harps could do, for she had done many of them. And Sandy guessed what things harps could do, for she had dreamed them all.

"Sit up straight, Sandy," said Natil at the end of a two hour lesson. "You must not slouch like a human."

Sandy blinked at her. "Like a *what*?" But she sat up.

Natil cleared her throat. "A . . . figure of speech. Sit straight, though. It lets the . . . energy flow better."

Sandy nodded. She understood energy.

"I'm going to give you an old melody to work with," said the Elf. "Very old." She took out a sheet of music paper, and in a fine hand, wrote out notes, slurs, suggested ornaments.

Sandy was peering over her shoulder. "No harmony?"

"I want you to supply the harmony," said Natil, finishing up the last lines and dots. "This must grow like a living thing, and therefore I do not want you to hold slavishly to my recommendations. I have played this hymn many times, and each time, I play it differently. I would like you to do the same."

"Jeez . . ." Sandy took the page, examined the notes. "That's different. Terry always—" She caught herself, blushed. "Well . . ."

Natil was almost angry with Terry. What had he been doing with Sandy? What had he been doing with the trust that others had placed in him? But she kept every trace of harsh emotion out of her voice. "Terry always . . . what?"

"Well . . . for him there's always just one way of playing anything." Sandy did not sound quite comfortable with the admission. "He says he has all the right ways worked out." Her brow furrowed. "Not that he's ever showed me any of them."

Natil nodded. But: "There is no right way."

Sandy looked uncomfortable. "Okay."

Natil smiled. "Be at peace. Let us listen to this." And, taking Sandy's harp, she played the melody through.

"But that's *Ave, maris stella*," said Sandy.

"From the *Liber*?" Natil shook her head. "Not so. This was the tune before one of the old Church fathers heard it sung from far away in an ancient forest. It struck him—it does that—and he took it back to his monastery and offered it to his own God. But in doing so, he altered it."

"It sounds the same."

"Ah, but that is because I did not add the harmony, and you are used to hearing it in only one way." *Terry's way,* she thought with another upwelling of annoyance. "*Ave, maris stella* is in the dorian mode—Mode One in the old Church usage—but the original hymn was in the plagal form of the mixolydian mode. Mode Eight, that is, though those from whom it was taken it did not call it so."

Sandy examined the written music. "Okay. I see that there's nothing in the melody that makes it go one way or the other. It depends on what harmony you put to it." She nodded for a moment at her discovery, then: "What's this called, anyway? You said it's a hymn."

"I did." Natil examined Sandy. How much, she wondered, would it be wise to say? Probably very little. Even if Sandy had the blood, it was much too early to speak of it. "It is called *Ele, asta a mirurore.*"

"What language is that? Italian?"

"It is an . . . old dialect," said Natil. She blushed at her equivocation, and, to settle herself, struck a chord on Sandy's harp and sang:

"Ele, asta a mirurore,
Cira a ciraie,
Elthia Calasiuove,
Marithae dia."

And when she looked up, Sandy was sitting back, her hands gripping her knees, her eyes clenched tight as though the sudden beauty of the music was painful. Not until the harpstrings finally fell into complete silence did she sigh and open her eyes. "That was . . . beautiful. I want . . ." She drooped as though it were an impertinence for her to want anything. "I want to be able to play like that someday. What do the words mean?"

"Essentially," said Natil, "much the same as those of the *Ave* that you already know: *Hail, star of the sea; enfoldment of all enfoldments; bright Lady shining with clear radiance, divine friend of my heart.*"

"It's a hymn to the Goddess, then."

Natil nodded. "It is so."

Sandy sagged suddenly, put her hands to her face, shook her head. "I don't know why the hell you're bothering with me, Natil. For Wicca, I mean. What do you need a teacher for? You're already there. There are a lot of witches out there who'd give their eyeteeth to be where you are."

Natil lifted an eyebrow, smiled wryly. "And give up their stores and their congregations?"

"No, really. You know what I mean." Sandy spread her hands. "What are you wasting your time for?"

Natil handed the harp back to Sandy. "I want to learn how to be the Goddess."

"Natil," said Sandy, "you're the most Goddess-like person I've ever met. You should be teaching me!"

Feeling helpless, Natil shook her head. She had to explain. She could not explain. "I cannot teach you. You must teach me."

"Natil, you're *already* the Goddess."

"I know, Sandy."

"Right. And you act like you know it, too. What the hell more do you want?"

Feeling the sudden return of a familiar emptiness, the Elf passed a hand over her face. Already? And, being Her, she could nonetheless not find Her? Was there no hope, then?

"Natil?"

Natil dropped her hand, mustered a calm smile. There was nothing to do but continue. She had tried other paths, and they had led her nowhere. "I . . . suspect, then, that I have not got it quite right."

Sandy shrugged, nodded. "All right, Natil. You know what you want. I'll do my best."

Natil dipped her head, grateful for Sandy's patience. "Thank you," she said. "That is all I can ask."

But worry gnawed at her. If not Sandy's way, then how?

CHAPTER 14

"Dr. Jerusalem? This is Sherri, Dr. Delmari's secretary. Hi. Fine. I'm calling for Max today. He wanted to let you know that he got your very kind luncheon invitation last week, but he's been in and out of the office so much that he hasn't had a chance to accept it. He's sorry. Oh, he doesn't think he'll have any time next week, either. He's ... uh ... well ..."

West of Denver, well into the Rocky Mountains, Interstate 70 rises in soft, almost feminine sweeps. For a time, there are signs that nearby cities and towns hide among the alternately rugged and rolling slopes—Evergreen, El Rancho, Georgetown, Idaho Springs—but then the off ramps become fewer, smaller, and they lead not into clusters of houses or little shopping centers, but rather into small roads that seem to have nowhere to go save into the trees and around curves that draw and then confound the eye, or through quaintly decrepit gates whose signs— Lazy Bee, Rocking S—attempt a feeble echo of wide-open ranch living amid peaks and ridges that preclude herds of anything save bighorn sheep.

Up past the Continental Divide, though, just after the Eisenhower Tunnel, a paved highway intersects I-70. It runs north and south, the trees pressing up against it amorously and throwing branches across it like possessive arms, and it was onto this road that Hadden turned the TreeStar Surveying van. The blast of cold weather had come and gone, the snow had turned to puddles even at this altitude, and the skies were blue. For now.

TK shifted in the passenger seat. It had been a long drive, with more still lying ahead, and he still could not comprehend why Hadden had asked him to come along. Oh, on the surface, the premise was credible enough. A

bid on a subdivision job that would take months of work
would require input both from the field team members
who would collect the raw data and the office staff who
would process it. But, somehow, that explanation did not
quite satisfy TK. It was as though he sensed that the
question of the subdivision bid was merely an excuse for
something else: an opportunity, perhaps, to take a long
drive into the mountains with a certain member of the
TreeStar staff who still seemed in some way to be different from everyone else at the surveying firm ... for reasons that had nothing whatsoever to do with the color of
his skin.

But if TK knew what the differences were not, he still
had not the faintest idea of what they actually were. To be
sure, the people of TreeStar and their friends all shared
something in common, something that he himself lacked,
but, paradoxically, their manner implicitly acknowledged
that TK not only was accepted whether he had it (whatever it was) or not, but also stood every chance of getting
it (whatever it was) at some time in the future.

It. He could only call it by the vague appellation usually reserved for grade B movie monsters. But it was not
monstrous. It was, rather, something good. Very good. In
fact, riding in the van and looking out at the mountain
meadows and rocky slopes that flicked by as the van followed the cracked pavement, TK was staggered by how
good it felt.

These honkeys are fucking up my mind.

But they were not honkeys. They were not white. And
that was yet another problem.

Hadden spoke suddenly. "I've got some doubts about
this job, TK."

TK looked up, caught his breath. Hadden was driving
with an expression of alertness on his face that appeared
to go beyond matters of road or scenery. He seemed to be
seeing more, much more, and to take from it a certain
mixed pleasure and pain. But this was nothing new: Hadden was always like that. No, what had startled TK was
the faint sheen that he was seeing about Hadden, the
same soft shimmer, as of starlight, that he had seen about
Ash.

He caught himself stealing a glance at his own hands.
No, nothing. Just good, black skin. Black. The color of

night. The color of rich earth. Some of those reverse-racist preachers made much of that. Europeans: ice people. Cold minds, cold hearts. Africans: sun people. Warm, fertile. Even James Baldwin had shied a few bricks at whites, likening them to bloodless things with nothing but a deep freeze in their sexless little voices.

He smiled involuntarily. James Baldwin had never heard Natil sing. But: "What about the job, Hadden?"

Hadden sighed. "I did some research before we came up here. I think we're going to find some fairly unspoiled land ahead. Mr. Parker has a thousand acres of it, and now he wants to subdivide it so that he can sell it off."

TK shrugged, tried to ignore the gleam of Hadden's skin. "It's progress."

"Do you really think so?"

"No."

Hadden nodded, drove in silence for a while. The road was paved, but little else, and it bounced the van around and rumbled beneath its wheels as though to protest the passage of a vehicle. And then Hadden turned off on a dirt road, and the way became worse.

But Hadden still drove with that same expression of seeing more than what was actually there. Or rather (the thought coming to TK involuntarily) of seeing what was really there.

And still that gleam. TK could see it plainly now. He had seen it in Ash. He had caught frequent glimpses of it up at the cookout . . . and had done his best to ignore it. Only Sandy—mousy, ill-at-ease, a little scared—had lacked it.

He gave an inward shake of his head at the recollection. Sandy had looked so frightened! And he had taken pity on her and had given her his phone number and address, forgetting for the moment that he was black and she was white (and everybody knew about black men: it was a stereotype as persistent as violence, drugs, or absent fathers), desiring only to help a frightened woman who had obviously felt as out of place as he. And to his surprise, she had taken his offering in the spirit in which it had been tendered, and had thanked him. Doubtless he would not see her again, but he still felt good about what he had done, for not only was it one with the mantle of responsibility and caring that had been bequeathed to him in the Georgia hospital, but it seemed also to be concomitant with the aura of help and healing that surrounded those who had that day brought him away from the crack house and up into the mountains.

After a long time: "Neither do I," said Hadden.

"Huh?"

"I don't think it's progress, either." Hadden shifted uneasily in his seat. "I sometimes wonder what I'm doing in this business. After all, I'm helping people build buildings that other people don't really need."

TK shrugged. "People need houses."

"At a million and a half dollars a throw? And this job in particular . . ."

In another hour, Hadden guided the van down an incline and brought it to a halt. The road had ended. Ahead was a shallow ditch, and then trees.

"Looks like we walk," said TK.

"Is that leg of yours up to it?"

"Shit, Hadden, some guys run *races* in these things."

He caught Hadden's pleased smile, remembered Ash laying her hands on his stump. "Uh . . . man . . ." he said, the words worming free of his mouth, "I been wanting to ask you . . ."

Hadden was unperturbed. It was as though on this day, in this place, he had expected the question. "About Ash? She can do things like that sometimes."

"Yeah . . ." TK found himself hesitating. Did he really want to know? ". . . but what the hell'd she do?" He apparently did.

Hadden considered. Then: "Come on," he said. "Let's take a look around. There are supposed to be some old monuments out here from the survey back in 1895. I want to see if I can find them."

TK knew Hadden. Having asked a question, he knew that he would eventually be answered.

They got out of the van. Hadden consulted a compass and a USGS map and pointed straight into the trees. TK shrugged, closed another snap on his down vest, pulled his gimme cap a little lower. His leg did not hurt, and he was with Hadden: he figured that he was ready for almost anything.

He followed Hadden across the ditch, and in a minute, pine needles were crunching beneath his sneakers. This was Colorado forest: pines, dark and straight, aspens (leafless now after the arctic blast that had come down of a sudden the last week in October), slender and waving. A few had burst with the cold, and when Hadden came upon one of these, he would stop and lay his hand for a moment upon the pale trunk as though to ease the tree's passage into death.

The trees were thick about them, and TK was surprised that the instincts of a jungle fighter—instincts etched deeply into his unconscious by four years of service in Vietnam—did not arise, seize him, bend his legs into a crouch, narrow his eyes and set them to scanning the shadows for hostile movement. Something about being with Hadden, apparently, lulled him into an acceptance of the forest as its own entity, its own fastness. There was nothing hostile here because, with Hadden walking beneath their branches, the trees kept themselves, husbanded themselves, would have turned away anything that even remotely constituted a threat.

And he noticed then that Hadden's feet made no sound on the forest floor.

In another minute, the ground sloped down steeply, the trees angling upward in precise verticals. Hadden tapped the map. "I think we're on the right track. There should be something up ahead."

"Think so?" The trees were thick, and no landmarks were visible: Hadden could only have been navigating by dead reckoning.

"I'm . . . pretty sure." But a bright smile told TK that Hadden was more than just pretty sure.

And in another minute they stepped out into sunlight. Fifty feet away across a meadow was a pile of stones about five feet high. Though it was tumbled down and overgrown with opportunistic grasses, it was obviously one of the monuments from the survey of 1895.

"Good," said Hadden. "Mr. Parker's land lies just up there." He pointed to the north, and TK caught a twinkle in his sea gray eyes. "I'd say it starts just about where the topsoil is replaced by rock and the slopes go to 45 degrees."

TK frowned at the tumbled ridges of granite, sandstone, and shale. The cold sun glowed on mineral veins, turned patches of lichen into flares of pale green and yellow, warmed the branches of gnarled pines that had some-how managed to find a place to put a root down amid so much harshness. "Ain't no one going to build anything up there."

"You're absolutely right. But what about the software? Can it handle that?"

"Oh ..." TK estimated. "... it'll eat processor time, but we got eight megabytes running at 33 meg, and Lietz has a damned good triangulation subroutine. It can handle it."

"Will it be slow?"

TK shrugged. "'Longest part be plugging in all the fig-ures. For horizontal control in something like *that* ..." He pointed up the rocky slopes. "... you need five times the usual control points." He parceled out a smile. "And a field team of mountain goats."

Hadden nodded. "I suspect that, if anything, we'll have to establish *diagonal* control."

They looked at one another for a moment, then laughed at the joke. TK felt something loosen within him despite the persistent shimmer of Hadden's skin.

"Let's go on a little farther," said Hadden.

"You going to answer my question, Hadden?"

"Yes ..." Hadden, though, folded his arms and stood in silence, looking away and off up the barren slope whose few plants could best be spoken of not as growing but as merely enduring.

And as Hadden's silence lengthened, TK found himself wondering whether he himself had not been merely en-during. Enduring since he had come home to find Bess and their child gone. Enduring since he had been dis-charged from the hospital in Georgia. Enduring since the explosion in the Iraqi bunker. Enduring since the tunnels of Cu Chi. Enduring ...

Well, enduring since his birth. It was the lot of black men. They endured. There was no grace to their harsh ex-istence, no more grace than in this slope of rock upon which a white fellow with a lot of money wanted to build a community of mansions.

Hadden was still standing, arms folded, looking at the slope. And maybe it was simply the way in which he was looking at it—a mixture of awe, love, and acceptance—that made TK himself take another look and realize that its harshness was illusory, or, rather, that though it was harsh, it was certainly not without grace. It was, in fact, redolent of grace. It shed grace the way a mountain spring shed water: ceaselessly, freely. It flooded the world with grace.

It was itself. And then, when TK looked at Hadden, he understood what it was that had so puzzled him. Hadden and his friends were themselves. Simply, unassumingly, unselfconsciously. If they acted, they acted from the heart. If they puzzled over something, then it was an honest puzzlement. If they accepted someone, then the acceptance was absolute. No wonder they were colorblind! No wonder they acted as though they themselves were colored!

"There's some old blood in the world, TK," Hadden said at last. He did not turn around. He might have been looking to the desolate, graceful slope for strength. "Ash has it."

"You got it, too, don't you, Hadden?"

"Yes."

"And the others . . ."

"Yes."

TK stood silently. They had it. He did not. He wondered whether he were yet another black man facing a sign that said *colored entrance at rear*. "So what'd she do?"

Hadden shrugged. "We can do things sometimes. Ash can do more than almost any of us." He dropped his eyes. "She healed you, TK. She healed you as much as she could."

TK was silent. Was he a monkey? A pet? Someone they kept around for entertainment? But then he recalled Bright's smile, Ash's expression as she had probed at his leg . . .

"Can you accept that?"

. . . Natil's face when she had held out her arms to a vicious little dog.

"What about Rags?" said TK.

"That was Natil's work."

TK pulled off his cap, threw it on the ground. "You telling me that you people just . . . just go around . . . *healing* everything?"

"Yes. When we can. We can't do much, but we do

what we can. I hope . . ." Hadden almost looked embarrassed, and uncharacteristically, he fumbled for words. ". . . I hope that's all right with you."

TK stared. "What the hell you asking *me* for?"

Hadden turned to him. "I'm asking . . . that is, we're all asking . . . because we like you, TK. Because we care about you. We consider you a friend. We hope . . ."

Monkey? Entertainment? No. Never.

"We hope that you feel the same way about us."

Colored. Yes, they were colored. Every single blessed one of them. As out of place in a grasping, covetous, bigoted white man's world as the blackest, soul-jiving nigger out of Bedford-Sty. Healing? Who the hell did they think they were? They had to be crazy!

TK envied them.

But he returned to his reserve, the reserve that had preserved him in the projects, in the streets, in Vietnam, in Iraq, and even on the front porch of a crack house. "That why you brought me up here today?"

Hadden shook his head. "I had a legitimate reason, if that's what you mean. This will be a big job, big enough to keep us all jumping for a year if we get it. The general operations buck stops with me, but you're in charge of the computer work. I wanted us both to see this before we sat down to do the paperwork and the proposal."

"You ain't even sure you want the bid, Hadden."

Hadden shoved his hands into the pockets of his jacket. And then he laughed. "Oh, we can do the subdivision work, all right. Mr. Parker will get someone to do it, I'm sure, so it might as well be TreeStar. But Mr. Parker is forgetting that he's going to need EPA reports, impact statements, permits . . . and then he's going to need a road up here, and he's going to have to convince some people to buy the houses that he wants to build, and convince other people to open the restaurants and the stores and the gas stations that the people who buy the houses will need." He looked again at the architect's nightmare of cliffs and steep slopes. "If he can get anything built in the first place, that is."

"You going to screw the bastard." TK laughed.

Hadden shook his head. "No. We don't operate that way at TreeStar. I intend to put in an honest bid, and when I do, I'll remind Mr. Parker about the EPA and all the rest. And he'll take me seriously: after all, this is a state that's willing to put half a billion dollars into the Glenwood Canyon project . . . just to keep everything looking pretty. And if Mr. Parker doesn't care and tells us to shut up and do our work, then we'll shut up and do our work, and we'll set monuments and record them with the state, just like we're supposed to, so that eventually, when people care a little more, we'll have something to go by when it comes down to taking care of places like this."

"You talk like you expect to see the day."

Hadden smiled. "Maybe."

They walked back to the van and spent the rest of the morning navigating overgrown roads to other parts of the property. Again and again they found that Mr. Parker's land consisted of a great deal of bare rock, a great many steep slopes . . . and little else.

"It's going to cost the man," said TK.

"It is." They were back in the van now, rumbling and bouncing back toward I-70. They stopped in Dillon for lunch, were stared at while they ate (*Yes,* Hadden had said softly, as though it were a personal failing, *that's still happening, isn't it?*), and then headed for Denver. Maybe they could salvage a few hours of office work out of the day.

But as they came over the last rise to find Denver lying spread out on the plain before them, as glittering and hazy as an image out of a dream, TK could not but consider how easily distance and imagination could conceal a reality too harsh to be touched by any grace or self-possession, no matter how limitless. The crack house was waiting for him in Denver, along with the phone calls to the police department and the shadows that seemed always to be slipping around a corner just before he could turn and see for sure . . .

Waiting. All waiting. And it occurred to him then that he was glad that he knew people like Hadden and the others, that it was good to have friends . . . whoever they were, whatever they could do. And it occurred to him also that he had not answered Hadden's questions.

And so he turned to his friend and answered.

Classes were in session this morning, and the corridors of Aylesberg Hall were therefore silent save for the whir and clack of an IBM Selectric in somebody's office, muffled conversations, the rise and fall of distant pedagogy.

Sandy made her way down the hall, the translation of the *Liber Usualis* in her hand, her footsteps sounding too loud in the silence because of her worry. Terry had asked for a translation, and she had procured a translation. But perhaps the assignment she had been given was personal rather than utilitarian, perhaps it was not so much a translation that Terry had wanted from her as a commitment to spiritual discipline, perhaps in simply acquiring a ready-made translation, she had somehow failed a test.

No matter: she was here, and she had the book. She would deliver it to Terry and await the consequences.

She descended the stairs. Maybe he would not be there. He spent a great deal of time playing for sick people in the local hospitals, lecturing to charitable groups about his work, and singing at the bedside of the dying; and so there was a good chance that she would not find him in the classroom. She had, in fact, not seen or heard from Terry for several weeks. She had called him, left messages on his answering machine, had even introduced herself after the beep and waited for the better part of a minute in the hope that he was merely screening his calls and would, upon recognizing her voice, answer. But it was as though Terry had sent her off to translate the *Liber* and did not want to see or talk to her at all until she was finished. That the translation of over two thousand pages of small print would take many months even for an accomplished Latinist had apparently not occurred to him. He had simply told her to translate.

She shook her head, feeling a familiar ache in her belly. It had been a test. It had most surely been a test. And she had failed. Maybe Terry would not be there, and she could simply leave the book and depart. She could wait for him to call her then.

And how long would she have to wait? She already knew.

Shaking, feeling sick, she tried to remember the hymn to the Goddess that Natil had taught her. She was new to the language—whatever it was—but somehow she understood its meaning instinctively, and from her first hearing of the words, they had become a part of her.

Now, frightened, her belly roiling, she sang softly in the echoing stairwell:

> *"Ele, asta a mirurore,*
> *Cira a ciraie,*
> *Elthia Calasiuove,*
> *Marithae dia."*

The hymn steadied her, and at the bottom of the stairs, she leaned against the banister for a moment and wiped her forehead with her sleeve. Healing. The hymn was redolent of healing. Natil was teaching her healing. And not only was that healing possessed of an immediate sense of rightness and comfort, it was also couched in terms shared by Sandy's own religion, for Natil spoke of cycles, of seasons, of interlocking webs of cause and effect, of simple being at the heart of which lay the certitude of divinity, of the Goddess.

What had Natil called Her? *Elthia?* An odd name, but a pretty one. It made Sandy think of the lands that she had seen but had never been able to enter, the sunlit lands that lay, all overlooked by most, in the background.

Sandy took another swipe at her forehead. "Be with me, *Elthia*," she said, and then she went toward Terry's classroom.

She knocked on the door tentatively, and felt almost as though she wanted to run away when a gentle voice from the other side called out, "Come in!"

Trapped. Her father had called her, and she had been forced to obey. Now Terry's voice was exerting the same hold over her. With another soft invocation to her Goddess, she turned the knob and entered the room.

Terry's eyes turned toward her as though drawn away just this moment from visions of other, more spiritual worlds. "Sandy." He smiled at her as he tugged down the cuffs of his long sleeves, but his tone was noncommittal. Was Sandy good today? Or was Sandy bad?

She shoved the thought aside. Sandy had been forced to be good to Freddy Joy, because when she had not been good—

Shaddup. Finding that her mouth had suddenly turned dry, metallic, she offered the book to Terry. "I found this," she said simply. "I hope it'll work."

Puzzled, Terry took the book, opened it, glanced at the title page. He frowned, but he leafed slowly through the pages, examining the closely spaced print as he mumbled softly to himself over the passages of plainchant and their interlinear translations.

Sandy read disapproval on his face, and she thought that perhaps it might be best if she sidled gently to the door, slipped out, and left all thoughts of the Hands of Grace behind. Natil was teaching her healing—though Sandy doubted that any healing unsupported by academic research would ever be accepted by the hospitals in which she had hoped to practice one day—and if she wanted friends, why, there were other witches in Denver: surely some of them could be her friends.

But, in fact, she had discovered that she already had friends. The people of Elvenhome had made her as welcome as if she had been family. Even TK, who had seemed just as out of place at the cookout as herself, had treated her like a sister, and, as though on an impulse, had given her his address and phone number.

"OK," Sandy had said, taking the paper from his hand. "Thanks."

And her puzzlement must have been apparent, for TK had nodded with a thin smile. "It's OK, girl," he had said. "You look like you need someone to talk to now and then."

The memory was a warmth in her heart, and though the withdrawal from the Hands of Grace could not but be both a confirmation of her father's curses and a personal defeat, she was nonetheless almost smiling as she started toward the door of the classroom.

But Terry, with an apparent effort, wrenched his eyes away from the book, and to Sandy's near shock, smiled at her. "This is very good, Sandy," he said. "This will . . ." He seemed to strain at something, then relaxed. ". . . help the program immensely."

"You didn't know—" But Sandy caught herself. She had gambled and won. She did not want to push her luck.

"I think," said Terry, "that it's time for us to do some musical work." He blinked at her. "Why don't you have your harp with you?"

Sandy was torn between anger and embarrassment. Terry had not bothered to teach her anything for four months: by what right did he assume that she would remain patiently in readiness for lessons that were never given? But, then again, here was a chance to learn something of the ancient arts, and she had fumbled it. It was her own fault.

... and there she goes again ...

"That's all right," said Terry quickly. "We'll do something else today. Here ..." He cast about, then started to riffle through the translation of the *Liber.* "There's something in here for you. We can sing it. Singing is important in this tradition. Instruments, you know, were forbidden by canon law." He fumbled through the pages. "It's here." He strained against something again, his eyes fixed on the wall, his fingers tight on the pages. "I know it. We'll do some work today, Sandy."

But he suddenly stopped, turned, looked at her with his blue eyes. "Have you ... seen anything?"

Sandy was both bewildered and frightened. "Seen?"

"You said that you have ... visions ..."

Sandy shrugged nervously. "Well, you know. They come when they're good and ready."

"Yes ... yes ..." Terry's eyes held her for a moment more, then flicked back down to the page. "We'll do some work here today. Musical work." He weighed the book in his hands. "Very good," he said. "Very good, indeed. This is very helpful."

MEMORANDUM

DATE: November 8, 1991

TO: Maxwell Delmari, Office of the Dean
FROM: Marian Westover, Administrative Finance Office

re: Hands of Grace program

In response to a request from Dr. Nora Jerusalem, I am forwarding to you this cost analysis of the Hands of Grace program ...

CHAPTER 15

The winter evening crept over Denver, turning to ice the melt that had puddled the sunlit ground. It was after hours, and the campus was quiet, and Natil, meditating, sat in her small groundskeeper's office, her hands clasped loosely on the desk before her.

It was a witch's exercise she performed, an imaginary and interior journey through time and through seasons, a mental search for the Goddess who was all, whose body was the universe, the rhythms of whose life were the changes of the earth. This was no elvish wandering through memories so vivid that they bordered upon reality, no starlight plunge into the waters of life that flowed abundantly through the interstices of existence. No, this was a very human attempt to find, beyond the mundanity and tragedy of the mortal allotment of life, something that might give meaning and context to a struggle that ended only with a last exhalation and a sleep that teetered upon the brink of hope.

Natil held to the discipline that Sandy had taught her, ignoring the stars, turning instead to the cold earth and the sleeping trees. Although she knew better, she told herself that she was for now but a human woman who had gone into the inner worlds of imagination and dream to look for the Goddess of whom she was an incarnation. Brow knit, eyes closed, hands clasped, she plodded inwardly through the winter, following a trail of footprints that led across the white snow, following it through the cold season and then into spring. The land greened, the arc of the sun in the sky rose higher and higher, and it was summer. And now the trail was strewn with apple blossoms, and it led across meadows and fields of warm wheat, led off and away into the mountains and into the autumnal clouds beyond.

In her mind, Natil paused, looked at her hands. Human flesh. But divine nonetheless. She was, she reminded herself, the Goddess, and yet she was human, too, and the years would therefore take the softness from her face and death would eventually claim her and there would be rest for her in the Summerland and then rebirth into a new life.

But despite her efforts, the starlight shone through. She could not lie. She was an Elf. She was immortal. She could not be otherwise.

And again in her mind, still keeping for the moment to the world of her meditation—the world that had suddenly turned false with her rejection of falsehood—she dropped to one knee, examining the blossoms and the footprints with the dispassionate gaze of the Firstborn. Who, really, was she following? What lay ahead of her? She, Natil, had felt unalloyed divinity shape her hands and then take them in friendship, had heard that same divinity call her by name, had seen *Elthia* with her own eyes. There had been no veil of imagination or wishful thinking between the Elves and the Lady. They were, and She was, and with perfect knowledge they existed in perfect consubstantiality.

Whose feet had left this trail that led from winter to summer and then back? Were they Elthia's? Or were they merely those of a fleeting hope that human ways could become elven ways?

With a sigh, Natil opened her eyes to her small office, saw the lamp, felt the desk, smelled the faint odor of gasoline and oil from the snowblowers stored in the adjacent room.

And she noticed that headlights were illuminating the frosted windows, casting indistinct patches of brightness on the opposite wall. She rose, peered out, waved. But when she had donned her down jacket, locked up, and gone out to the little Celica, she discovered that the young woman who was both her teacher and her student was subdued, tense. There was a shadow on her face, and she beckoned Natil in, drove silently down Lowell Boulevard, and took the on-ramp to westbound I-70 without saying anything behind "Hi."

Clouds. Shadows. For a while, Natil rode in silence, but then, softly, she laid a hand on Sandy's arm. A touch of comfort: she and Sandy had become friends. "Tell me," she said.

Sandy shrugged. "I had a bad dream last night. It's been bugging me all day."

"It was more than a bad dream."

"You're reading me again, Natil."

The Elf sighed. "I do not need telepathy: your demeanor tells me everything. By the way, there is an icy patch coming up."

Sandy slowed, and in another thirty seconds, her tires lost traction. But the patch passed, and the Celica sped on. "How did you know that?"

"Ah . . ."

Sandy tried for a smile. "Talent, right?"

"You could say that."

Sandy nodded, stared gloomily at the road. "I'll be glad when we get up to Elvenhome."

"Tell me about the dream," said Natil.

"Oh . . . it's crazy."

Natil, who had left her hand on Sandy's arm, tightened her fingers for a moment. Friends, yes. Since they had accepted one another as teachers, Sandy had spent at least one night a week up at the Home, tucked safely beneath blankets and comforters in the little bedroom. And while the Elves struggled to bring healing to all, they struggle all the more mightily to bring healing to their own. "It most assuredly is not crazy. If it has troubled you throughout the day and into another night, then it is very real."

Sandy was plainly uncomfortable.

Natil understood. "My telephone rang at three in the morning, but when I answered, there was no one there. Was that you?"

It was obvious that, had Sandy not been driving, she would have hung her head. "It . . . uh . . . yeah, it was me." Her jaw tightened. "I didn't know what else to do. I couldn't seem to wake up . . . it was just so *real*. But then I got embarrassed and hung up." She glanced at Natil. "I'm sorry I woke you."

"It was not a problem, Sandy. I was not asleep."

Sandy looked at her, puzzled. "Don't you *ever* sleep, Natil?"

Natil smiled. Friends noticed things that mere acquaintances did not. "Not if I can help it. But . . . your dream."

Sandy tensed again. "It was about Terry."

Natil nodded. She had guessed as much.

They drove on into the night, the winter darkness compounded by clouds. Clouds, too, darkened Sandy's eyes. "I dreamed that I'd gone to see him at his house. No one knew where I was. I wasn't there for anything in particular, but, then again, maybe I was. I'm not sure. But Terry was trying to keep me there. It's all jumbled up. It was jumbled up in the dream, too. But Dad . . . I mean . . . Terry kept finding reasons for me to stay in the house. Where no one could find me. And he . . ." A tremor had entered her voice. ". . . he kept trying to steer me onto his bed. I mean, I think it was a bed. It was all greasy rags and dirt. Tatters, like."

"And so you woke up, and you were afraid. And you called me."

Sandy shook her head, her eyes clouding even more. "No. It wasn't until I started finding pieces of Little Sandy lying around that it really got . . . bad. . . ."

Natil glanced into the back seat. Smiling placidly, Little Sandy was snugly strapped in beside Sandy's overnight case and harp. "Little Sandy . . ."

"Yeah . . . it's . . ." Sandy's voice caught. She choked. "I'm sorry, Natil. She was all over the house. I found her arms in one place. And her legs had been torn off and tossed into a corner. And then . . . and then I found her eyes. They were lying on the floor. They'd been cut out and safety-pinned together."

Natil's hand had gone to her mouth.

"And then I got scared, and I ran out of the house to my car." The words were suddenly tumbling out as though Sandy were afraid that if she stopped she would never speak again. "And I knew there was a bomb in my car. But I got in anyway and started it up. And then something started pounding underneath the street, like . . . it was trying to tunnel its way up through the pavement." She choked again. "And that's when I woke up. I was screaming my head off, and I couldn't figure out how to get out of the closet."

The Celica splashed through puddles of slush. Ahead, the mountains began to take on shape and mass among the clouds. Natil thought of Sandy in the stuffy little closet, screaming, battering on a door turned strange with nightmare.

Helping and healing, and Sandy was her friend. She should have been there. She wished that she had been there. Now she could only nod understandingly. "The closet has always been a refuge for you," she said

Sandy nodded tensely. She had not looked for help and healing. She had, in fact, guiltily turned away from both when she had hung up. "Yeah. I hide. I'm afraid. But last night . . ." Her hands clenched on the wheel. ". . . last night I couldn't hide."

"It was . . . but a dream, beloved." It was all Natil could say. Could she still heal? Did immortal blood mean anything at all in this place?

But Sandy shook her head. "Sometimes I wonder. Terry's giving me pieces to play now, and he's talking to me about healing, but it's . . . like he's trying to bribe me. Like he doesn't really want to teach me anything. He just wants to keep me in the program."

"How do you feel about that?"

"I don't know." Sandy stared at the road as though it went on forever. "I don't know what to feel. He keeps on with his preaching at me about Christianity, and . . . and he just assumes that I agree with everything he's saying. And I haven't told him about Wicca, and I haven't told him about you and me. I'm, like, lying all the time." The clouds in her eyes grew darker, more turbulent. "Just like when I was in grade school. Mommies and daddies and nice little families, and girls who got all the way to eighth grade without knowing what a penis was. And I had to pretend . . . to pretend that . . ."

Natil, in reply, reached back to Little Sandy, lifted her out of the seat belt, and set her on her lap. "You are safe, little one," she said, wrapping her arms about the doll. "You need not fear."

Looking as though she wanted to find Natil's words believable, Sandy took the transition to Highway 6, and a little while later—with Natil still having to prompt her to turn—she was guiding the Celica up the sloping dirt road.

But when Sandy had parked and, carrying her bag, her harp, and her small alter-ego, had walked to within sight of the lights of Elvenhome that Natil had left on for the benefit of her human friend, her emotions finally got the better of her, and, slowly, she sank to her knees. Her eyes were clenched, her face contorted with the sudden rush of tears.

"Beloved?" Natil knelt beside her, held her as she had, a short time ago, held Little Sandy.

"It's too nice here, Natil," said Sandy. "It's just too nice. I feel safe here. I don't think I've ever felt safe before it in my life." And she laid her head on Natil's shoulder and sobbed.

Natil pressed her cheek against Sandy's dark hair. *It always hurts,* she thought. *It always hurts when they find peace. Dear Lady, why does it hurt them so?*

"I'm sorry, Natil."

"Beloved Sana, there is nothing to be sorry about."

Sandy lifted her head, blinked through her tears. "What did you call me?"

Natil blushed in the darkness that was not dark to her. "Sana. I once knew a witch by that name. It refers to the color of a knife flashing in the moonlight. It . . ." She felt her blush deepen: the name had come out of its own accord. Sana. The Elves had called Roxanne by that name long ago, and Roxanne, human though she was, had eventually stood face to face with the Lady, her Goddess. Maybe, someday, Sandy . . . and maybe, someday, once again, the Elves. "It seemed appropriate."

Sandy did not appear to notice Natil's embarrassment, and the novelty of the name had, for a moment, taken her mind off her sorrow. "Sana." She grinned suddenly. "I like that. I really like that."

"Then Sana it is," said Natil, and she smiled her way out of her discomfiture. "It is comely enough, and many take a new name when they find this place."

Elvenhome beckoned: yellow light, a gleam of good stone and polished wood. "Like in initiation," said Sandy. "A new life. A rebirth. Are you thinking of a name for your initiation, Natil? A good witch name?"

Natil, who in four and a half billion years had never had any name besides Natil, felt the pang. A witch? Could she be a witch?

She hugged Sandy, trying to reassure herself. "I have not as of yet, Sana," she said. "I confess I do not know whether I will make it that far."

Sandy shook her head, sniffled through a nose stuffy with tears. "You'll make it, Natil. You're already there."

"I am rather afraid that I am," said Natil.

December that year was as dry as October and November had been wet. The snow that had fallen sublimed into the cold aridity and left the streets dusty and the lawns brown, and the Christmas decorations looked out of place and just a little tawdry.

TK, though, was feeling good. His job at TreeStar had become something he could count on, and the fact that there were a few oddities about the people with whom he was working no longer made him wonder when the arrangement was going to abruptly explode and blow him out onto the street. No, whether TK were comfortable with Hadden's revelation or not, Hadden and the others were apparently comfortable with TK.

TK might have worried. He might have been afraid. The thought that he was mingling with people who possessed "old blood" was disturbing, for it hearkened back to atavistic fears about strange races that lurked in the dark corners of ancient forests . . . waiting for a chance to take back a world that had once been theirs. But there was nothing dark about Hadden and his people. There was, instead, a sense of sunlight about them, sunlight and gentle power, and that was both TK's belief and his attraction.

True, he might have dismissed Hadden's words as mere ravings and thereafter found some excuse for changing jobs so that he did not come into such intimate and daily contact with people whose grasp on reality had obviously slipped so far into delusion, but he did not, for he had seen that Hadden's words were true. Ash had taken the pain from his phantom leg, and Natil had healed Rags' paws, and in both instances, the giving of health had been instinctive, unconditional, effortless, gracious.

And TK wanted to be able to do the same.

That he could not was a disappointment, a seeming reinforcement of the helplessness that had been bequeathed his race by centuries of discrimination; but TK had decided that if such miraculous powers were beyond him (and, indeed, it appeared that even enlisting the aid of the police department against a crack house was beyond him), then he could at least offer what aid he could to those who possessed them, and so he had let Heather know that he continued to be on call at any time for assistance with her shelter work, he had helped Wheat and Allesandro care for trees that were on the verge of dying from the extremes of weather that had battered them that fall, and he had even helped Marsh raise the walls of a few houses for the city's home-building project.

And if, as a result, he had grown closer to them all, he had most definitely grown closer to Marsh and his family. Where before Marsh had been only an acquaintance in a basement band destined for nothing greater than rehearsals once a week and a case of beer on the porch afterward, now TK saw him and his wife and his daughter as part of something that had, all unlooked-for, grown up in the middle of Denver. Something healing. Something wonderful. Something with a smack of limitless grace to it. Now he was at their dinner table several nights a week. Now he took Kelly to movies, shot baskets with Marsh, participated in the planning of next year's vegetable and flower gardens.

He was not intruding. Indeed, the three of them seemed anxious that he become a member of their family. And if he felt any pangs of conscience about the neighborhood that he had left to shift for itself while he participated in white, suburban life, he could only shrug them off. He had tried. He was, in fact, still trying. Without success. The crack house still thrived, the police were still uncooperative, and his neighbors were unwilling to batter through their walls of inertia and distrust even though the daily hassles and shakedowns had grown intolerable.

But he knew that he was living a dream, knew that, inevitably, the differences of race and culture would rise up and separate him from what he had found, for though the people who had accepted him behaved as though they considered themselves colored in some way, they were, in fact, not colored. No, they were whites, with the privileges of whites. Old blood or not, their ancestors had never been bought and sold, had never been hunted down and killed for sport, had never known anything but perfect acceptance from the society about them.

And so his sense of well-being was tempered this last Sunday before Christmas. It had been a good rehearsal, he had played well, and now, afterward, he was sitting in the Blues' living room with Kelly on his lap and a can of beer in his hand: just one of the family. But for a moment he saw everything as though it were but a reflection on the surface of a still pond, an image, fragile and molecule-thin, that a stray breeze could fragment and banish.

"TK?" Kelly was looking up at him with big blue eyes.

"Huh?" He glanced down at her, felt sheepish. Kelly could never understand the thought that had possessed him for a moment.

But: "I know, TK," said Kelly, "but we'll always be here for you."

He blinked at her. "Always . . ." He did not know what to say. The child might have read his mind. *Old blood*, Hadden had said. And what else could these people do? "Always is a long time, little girl."

"I know." And, to TK's shock, Kelly's expression lay between the puzzled and the tragic. "I know. It's forever."

Marsh was just coming in from the kitchen with another beer. "How are you doing on that one, TK?"

"I got no problems." But he glanced uneasily at the sprite on his lap.

"Heather's just pulling in. You up for supper?"

TK stood, set Kelly gently down. The girl ran to meet her mother. "Man, I got to stop freeloading on you guys. I got to have some self respect." For an instant, he considered trying to repay Heather and Marsh by inviting them and their daughter to his own apartment for dinner. But only for an instant. What did he have to offer them? A run-down neighborhood, a crack house, and a feral Yorkshire terrier?

Marsh shook his head patiently. "It's only freeloading when you're not wanted, dude. And we most definitely want you."

Something about his words made TK a little nervous. "What?" he countered. "You recruiting?"

Marsh shrugged. "Could be. You never know."

TK tried for a laugh to ease the tension, failed. But Heather was coming in just then, and she bent and swept Kelly into her arms with an ease that made TK wonder whether the little girl weighed anything at all.

A kiss for Marsh, a hug for TK. Then: "Can I borrow

you this afternoon, TK?" she said. "One of the department stores just donated a whole truckload of mattresses to the shelter. All we have to do is pick them up. The men will have real beds for Christmas!"

TK grinned. Heather was one of the few people who got more than a rationed smile. "And all *I* got to do is tote them, right?"

"Well . . ."

"No problem," said TK. "No problem at all. You want to go now?" She nodded. "Okay, then. Marsh?"

"I'll look after Kelly . . ." He winked. "And I've got a few presents to wrap. In private."

"We'll be back in a couple of hours," said Heather.

"I'll have dinner ready," Marsh replied. He gave TK a wink. "Freeloading. Sheesh. I ought to make you cook dinner."

"I *have* cooked dinner. A bunch."

"So there. See?"

Laughing as he had not laughed in a long time, his pensiveness banished, TK went out with Heather and fitted himself into the passenger side of her little compact car. Heather took the wheel, pulled out, and headed downtown. "We can pick up the truck the shelter uses," she explained. "The mattresses should just fit."

"In how many loads?"

"Well . . ." Heather blushed again, tipping her head to the side. "Two?"

He smiled. "We'll say three, Heather."

But it was as though, in leaving the house, they had left a sanctuary of sanity behind. Drunks catcalled observations about Heather's body when they picked up the truck at the downtown shelter, and at the department store warehouse, the manager—working on Sunday and all the more surly for that—stared at them with an expression that TK would have understood even had he not overheard the man murmur to Heather: "You gonna be all right with him, ma'am?"

Heather bristled. "He's my brother," she said loudly. "Of course I'm going to be all right with him."

And the manager, in shock, stammered something about a long day and the light not being good . . . and retreated.

But Heather was quiet as TK drove the laden truck toward the tall buildings at the heart of the city. "It's still happening, TK," she said after a time. "It's still happening. And it's going to be happening for a long time."

There was sorrow in her voice, and TK understood, for he felt it himself. What he did not understand, though, was the sense of responsibility that lay beneath the sorrow. Heather, like Hadden, appeared to take the prejudice of others as a personal failing.

He was torn between bewilderment and gratitude. "It ain't your fault, Heather."

Heather shook her head, plainly upset. "It *is* my fault. It's all our faults. We're here to do something about all this. We're here to fix it. But it just doesn't seem like we do anything. I mean . . ." She was looking out the window at the passing cars and buildings, talking as though to herself. ". . . we've got forever, but at this rate even forever isn't going to be long enough."

TK felt uneasy. Forever? And Kelly had said . . .

He dismissed the thought. No. It was crazy. People just didn't . . .

"And I wonder sometimes whether God . . ." But Heather suddenly caught herself, appeared to quickly wipe away tears. "Listen to me, will you? I say all kinds of crazy things. It's always bad for me this time of year."

TK shifted uneasily. "You worried about God, Heather? That ain't crazy. When I was crawling around in the tunnels in Nam, I thought about God a lot."

"What did you think?"

"That the Man didn't give a damn about grunts."

Heather looked stricken. "Oh, TK . . ."

He shrugged. "If it helps, Heather, I think that if He cares about anyone, He cares about people like you."

He took the Auraria Parkway turnoff and descended into the downtown area, skirting Metro State College, approaching Speer and the grid of streets that slanted diagonally through the city center.

Heather was watching him, and when he glanced at her as he waited for a stoplight, he saw starlight—he saw it plainly, he knew it was starlight—in her eyes.

And he suddenly had the eerie feeling that the woman in the passenger seat was not human. "Even if . . ." she started, appearing to search for words. "I mean . . . even if . . ."

But there was movement in the street. A small, imported truck was pulling up next to them, pulling up much closer than the lane markers allowed, pulling up so close that, on Heather's side of the truck, sideview mirror suddenly met sideview mirror with a sharp *clack*.

And then, just a few feet beyond her face, TK was seeing another face, a face with iron in its eyes, a face that had, in its expression, seemingly concentrated every particle of the white man's hatred for the black man, turned in inward, and made it part of itself.

"Heather!" he shouted. "Down!"

He grabbed her shoulder and pulled her sideways, trying to drop her below the level of the window. The action was guaranteed to leave him exposed (and, yes, he was seeing motion in the back seat of the truck: seeing the window coming down, seeing the glint of a blued gun barrel thrusting out, stiff and cold), but he pulled her anyway, trying to help, trying to heal, trying to offer what assistance he could to beings who, starlight or not, powers or not, human or not, seemed possessed of more love and sorrow than he had thought himself capable of imagining.

But Heather's arm caught on the shoulder strap, and so, when the Uzi erupted in a blast of bullets that sounded like a veil of sackcloth being rent from top to bottom, she was sitting up, straight in their path.

The slugs hit her from behind. TK saw her features suddenly go slack, then bloody, felt her shoulder turn in an instant from vibrant to limp.

A roar, a squeal of tires, and the imported truck was gone.

Dear Rick:

Thanks for your help. I hope Nancy and the kids are all right. Here's the breakdown on the Terry Angel bibliography so far.

"An Eloquent Ecstasy", *Prana*, Fall '90. — *Prana* doesn't exist.

"Cluniac Death Practices", *Initiations*, '90 — *Initiations* doesn't exist.

"Servants of God: Meditations on Musicians' Hands", *Initiations*, Easter '91. — See above.

"The Flesh of the Harp Is Jesus: Song, Alchemy,

and Inner Void", *Apollo's Servants,* Vol. 58, Winter 89-90. — Magazine exists. It's a little London periodical. I wrote to them. They've never heard of Terry Angel.

"The Hands of Grace Project: a Musical-Medical Initiative", forthcoming issue of *Mystics Quarterly,* University of Iowa. — They've never heard of him either.

"The Mystic's Bondage: the Quest for Loss of Freedom", *Serpent Fire,* Vol. 57, Winter 90-91. — This article actually exists. *Serpent Fire* is a little metaphysical magazine down in Sedona. The article is fairly strange. Lots of rape and S&M imagery. Gave me the creeps. I'm enclosing a copy. Don't read it at night.

"The Use of Plucked Stringed Instruments in Medieval Christian Mysticism", *Annual Hermeticist Review.* — This one exists, too, but *Annual Hermeticist Review* is completely written and self-published by Terry Angel. Found it up at Watterson's New Age Emporium. Very contradictory article. (Goes along with the store.) Says at first that the monastics used harps. Then says they didn't. Footnotes refer to themselves. No decent biblio. Just his own articles. The ones that don't exist.

I'm tracing down the rest as I have time, but it really looks as though this man is a loon. I've been unable to make any kind of a case to Maxwell. He won't even have lunch with me. It might come down to you bringing it up to the curriculum committee.

Would you be willing? Let me knew what you think.

Yours,

Nora   _____

CHAPTER 16

Wednesday night. Christmas night. The skies over Elvenhome were clear and cold, and, this far into the mountains, there was a smell of frost in the air. Natil, indoors, was sitting by the window, looking out at the upright and staggered rows of tall pines that grew on the hillsides surrounding the house. Her harp was on her lap. She was not playing. She had not played since Sunday.

Near midnight, she saw a flicker of headlights through the trees. She had been expecting it. She had been expecting it since sunset.

Human eyes could not have detected the shimmering form that slipped along the path to the Home, but, save for a few terrible months in 1500, Natil's eyes had never been human, and so she saw. The Elf-lass who had come was slender and blond, and she moved at ease among the trees. Natil, though, felt her emotions. It was easy to feel her emotions, for Natil shared in them.

Ash was crossing the courtyard in another minute. In contrast to her usual, formal business garb, she was clad casually—down jacket, flannel shirt, jeans, sneakers—but there was a focused intent to her demeanor that told Natil that there was nothing casual about this visit, that there was, rather, a terrible immediacy and importance.

And Natil did not know what to say to her.

Ash found her in the upper room by the window. "Natil."

"Ash."

Natil looked out at the trees. The emptiness that had long ago taken up residence in her heart had deepened. Now there seemed to be nothing within her but a pit of darkness unbroken even by stars.

Ash stood in the doorway. She was silent for some time. "Have you eaten?" she said at last.

"I . . ." It was an unexpected question, and it made Natil lift her head, look toward the door. But, no, it was not really unexpected. It was just like Ash to ask something like that. "I have not."

"Since Sunday."

"I believe that is so."

Silence again. Then: "Come down to the kitchen, Natil. Let me fix you something."

"The others . . ."

"Are still at the hospital."

Natil hung her head. "There was nothing more that I could do. It was late."

"I know. They threw us all out at the end of visiting hours anyway. We've taken over the cafeteria." A pause, a soft shake of the head. "Raven nearly brought the police."

"What did she do?"

"She heard one of the orderlies talking about Heather's appearance. She . . . objected. Rather strongly."

Natil nodded. "Indeed, Raven would do that."

"Come have something to eat."

"I should be there."

"Come and eat."

Natil smiled thinly, feeling the ache of muscles that did not want to smile. Emptiness. "Did you come to feed me?"

Ash still stood in the doorway, and there was an intensity about her that reminded Natil of Mirya when she had held a sword in her hand. "I came to ask some questions."

"I understand."

Ash took her down to the kitchen and made soup. She set a hot bowl and a stack of crackers before Natil and told her to eat. For herself, she made coffee and found a package of Keebler cookies that Lauri, with wry humor, had put in the cupboard a week or two before.

Natil ate, spooning up soup that was tasteless with sorrow. Ash drank her coffee and ate a cookie or two while she examined the package with an expression that was at once amused and tragic. "I wish it were that easy," she said.

"Easy?" said Natil.

"I wish we just lived in a hollow tree and made cookies for a living. Then maybe people would leave us alone. Then maybe we wouldn't get—" Ash broke off, shook her head.

"We are here to help," said Natil softly.

"And heal, yes," said Ash. The silence grew uncomfortable again. Finally: "What can we do for Heather?"

Natil set her spoon aside. The soup had abruptly gone beyond tasteless.

Ash was looking at her, the starlight in her eyes as focused and intent as her demeanor. "We're both healers, Natil. And though you haven't said anything about it, I know that you've done things that make anything I've done look sick."

"You have cured leukemia, Ash."

"It was a fluke. I didn't know what I was doing. I've never been able to do it again, anyway. It's like I don't . . ." Ash squirmed with her lack of words. Elvish would have conveyed her meaning without difficulty, but she did not know Elvish. ". . . see enough."

Natil nodded. Vision. The patterns of the Dance. The intersecting strands of starlight. Without the Lady, the knowledge was not there. And therefore the powers were not there. And sometimes she wondered whether she herself remembered Elvish. "I understand."

"What can we do for Heather?"

"How is she?"

"They're still only saying that she's stable. Marsh is the only one they've let in to see her, and he says she's a mess. The doctors are surprised that she's survived at all. They're not giving her much of a chance."

"I know," said Natil. "I was there when they brought her in."

"You knew, didn't you?"

Natil turned her eyes back to the window. The world outside Elvenhome looked cold. Cold and dark. "I knew. I felt the bullets. How is Marsh?"

Ash only looked at her.

"And Kelly?"

Ash said nothing.

Natil nodded.

"Heather isn't getting any worse," said Ash after a time, "but she's not getting any better, either."

"I should be there," said Natil, but the emptiness

within her only grew. She had thought that she had
known helplessness when, for a brief time, she had fallen
into humanity. But human helplessness was a worn and
comfortable thing, its edges blunted by centuries of
missed opportunity and bad judgment. It was as nothing
compared to the aching abyss left behind by abilities that
had evaporated into impotence.

"Natil," said Ash, "we *both* should be there. And we
both should be there to do something. What can we do?"

Natil hung her head. "Very little."

Ash's dissatisfaction was plain. "Natil, I sense what
you've done in the past. I don't know how you did it, but
I know that you did. I haven't asked about it because I
figured that you'd tell us when it was time. All right: I
think it's time. What do you mean we can't do much?"

The question cut too deep, and Natil wanted desperately to avoid it. "Even if we could do something, Ash,"
she said, "would it be wise to have the hospital staff wondering about a miraculous cure? TK accepted his leg, and
he went along with Rags' paws. Whether he has the blood
or not, TK is a good man. He feels, and he is tolerant. I
doubt that the medical establishment would be as tolerant."

"You think they'd . . ."

"I am sure that they would probe at Heather until . . ."
Natil shook her head. "Perhaps they would discover that
she is not human. Perhaps they would only make her life
miserable and put her too much in the public eye."

"I'd rather have her in the public than d—" Ash
choked on the word, but she recovered quickly. "You're
dissembling, Natil."

Natil looked down at her half empty bowl.

"Why don't we have the power?"

Natil did not look up.

"We used to, didn't we?"

Natil still did not look up. But she nodded. "We did."

"What happened? How did we lose it?"

"We faded, Ash."

"You didn't fade, Natil. You're still here. You stayed
around for us."

Natil said nothing. The implicit lie made her feel sick.

Ash shoved her coffee and cookies aside, leaned forward. She was a gentle Elf, blond and quiet, and pressing

for information did not come easily to her. But she pressed. "What happened, Natil? I'm not asking for me. I'm asking for Heather. If there's anything I can do, tell me and I'll do it. For Heather."

Natil surprised herself: she had not expected that her tears would come so readily . . . or so fiercely. But it had been a long time, and she had experienced nothing but false starts, dead ends, and futility. Even her work with Sandy seemed destined to lead nowhere, for though Sandy's ability with the harp had grown quickly, Natil's efforts to learn the Craft lay stunted amid the obvious. She was not a witch. She could not be a witch: she was simply not human.

And so she cried, and so Ash, an Elf who had come to immortality but recently, held in her arms the last surviving Firstborn, trying without understanding, trying instinctively, to offer comfort.

It was dark in the kitchen, for the light of the Elves was within, amid the stars, amid the incandescent swirlings of the universe. But for all that light, Natil wept. Heather hovered near death, a living, perhaps dying symbol of a world that had seemingly grown too corrupt for even the Elves to cure. And the others, Natil was sure, realized that. Who was taking care of Heather? Who looked after Elves? Or were they all, terribly, on their own, left to face an infinite future like children abandoned on the roadside with nothing to see them through but a stuffed animal and a sack of ratty clothes?

Natil's eyes ached with her sobbing. She could talk about *Elthia*, explain Her nature, describe the privileged, face-to-face relationship that the Elves had shared with Her. But it would do no good. Sandy had said it perfectly: it was no use talking about it; one simply had to *do* it.

But Natil could not do it. And so, slowly, sadly, at odds with a frantic urge to just blurt out the whole story and trust that some miracle (there were still a few miracles left in the world, were there not?) would endow her listener with sufficient understanding, she shook her head. "Ash," she said, "there is nothing we can do. It is not time."

"What does time have to do with it?"

"It is not time. I have . . . work to do still."

Ash's eyes were gleaming, starlit. She did not understand. Natil knew that she did not understand. "What about Heather, then?"

Natil lifted her head, considering. "Let us bend all our efforts toward getting her well enough to come home," she said after a time. "After that, perhaps the two of us can ..." Without the Lady? Absurd. "... can do something."

"You think so?"

"I can only pray."

"How do we help her, then? What do we do to get her well enough to come home?"

"We ..." Again Natil looked off toward the window. Outside, the stars shone coldly, distantly. Too distantly. She could find no more comfort in them than in their inner counterparts. "We use the magic of the witches, Ash. We band together. We hold Heather in our thoughts. We see her as alive and well. We attempt to reshape the futures to our will."

Yes, that much they could do. They were not witches—they could not be witches—but they could use the old witch knowledge that was as irrelevant to the true practice of the Old Religion as diamonds were to dogs. Odd: Natil had learned from Sandy nothing but precisely the wrong thing ... the wrong thing that had turned out to be right.

Everything that happens ... But any sense of an inward smile was buried in tears.

Ash nodded. "I'll let the others know."

"And there is something else." Natil reached out, touched the harp that lay on the table beside her. "We will harp for her. Music is healing, and if Marsh specifically requests it, I do not think that the hospital authorities will object to a harper in Heather's room. We can call it ..." She wrinkled her nose. "... music therapy. If Terry Angel can gain admittance to medical institutions, then so can we."

Ash frowned. "We? Do we have another harper in Elvenhome?"

Natil felt a sad smile. "We might someday. But, elven blood or not, there is someone else who can help. I will talk to Sandy. This is what she has always wanted to do, and her hands have grown free over the last month. It is time for her to learn to heal." And, she reflected, the only way to learn to heal . . . was to do it.

Ash was not satisfied: that was easy to see. But she did not complain. "Like I said, then: I'll let the others know." Thoughtful, she washed out her cup and the coffeepot. "Will you be coming back with me tonight?" she asked as she dried them and put them away.

"I will come in the morning with my harp. Please ask Marsh to make his request before then."

"I shall."

Natil felt Ash's eyes on her, felt the question, felt the certainty that she could not answer it. Not now. Perhaps, she feared, not ever.

"Is there . . . is there anything else I can do for you, Natil?"

"I will come in the morning."

"All right, then." Ash turned to go, but she stopped at the door. She seemed on the verge of asking something else, seemed to think better of it, and departed.

Natil's hands were on the table, and she bent until they cupped her face. Eyes closed, she contemplated the stars within her, searching, hoping to catch among them a glimpse of blue and silver.

The world of the Elves lurched to a halt that week. It fell as Heather had fallen: pale and bloody, wheezing out shallow breaths, its eyes—for all their starlight—glassy and fluttering. But if Heather did not grow better as the days passed, neither did she grow worse. Tubed and wired, she lay hovering between life and death in the intensive care unit of the hospital, and as one week led into two and then into the New Year, she continued to do so.

And so the Elves picked up their lives and staggered on. Buckland Employment found jobs for people. TreeStar Surveying established horizontal control and told people where the new carport should go. And, after work, Lauri picked up the receiver at the GLCC hotline, Wheat and Allesandro went out and watered the trees that they had added to the forest the previous fall, Hadden and Raven harassed the city council about housing . . . and on and on. There was no relish in it for any of them: they worked by dull, brute instinct. They were Elves. They were supposed to do things like this. They were supposed to help, to heal. But with one of their own lying riddled by bullets, their questions were rising again, silently and aloud: *What happened? Why can't we do what I know we used to do?*

And Natil had nothing to tell them. She, in fact, did not know.

And Heather lay hovering.

And TK drifted. Away from the rational. Toward violence.

He should have expected it: the dichotomous existence that he had led for months had collapsed, the two extremes of existence encompassed by his life coming together, breaking through the false and artificial barriers that he had—mentally, ignorantly—erected. But where a more optimistic man might have hoped that something of the goodness and healing of his friends would have infected the denizens of the crack house, it had been, predictably, the other way around. Like a vortex of water pouring down a drain, the two halves of his life had collided, swirled, and plunged, carrying with them everything he had come to love.

And now there was nothing.

Oh, he went to work, plugged numbers into databases, generated charts and topographic maps, but it was all theater, even more now than ever, for he saw the care etched into the faces of his friends, and he felt the ache of the certainty that it was because of him that Heather had been shot. To be sure, there was no sign that anyone blamed him, but TK knew with all the instinct of the streets and the projects that Heather had been gunned down because she had been in his company, because, by being so, she had tacitly claimed membership in whatever gang the crack house deemed affiliated with the man who had declared war upon their lifestyle and their profits.

And it occurred to him that, yes, in many ways, he and Heather were members of a gang. But, contrary to the assumptions of the crack house, she had not joined him. He had, rather, joined her . . . joined her and all her friends, allied himself with all their helping and healing, pledged himself to all the old blood in the world that sought to bring together what had been put apart.

Yes, they were white. But that, he now realized, did not matter, for in them TK had found something that transcended matters of race and color, showed them for the trivial things that they were. Heather and her people were not white, or, rather, were white but incidentally, for by their efforts, by their grace, they had essentially sundered themselves from the white society in which they lived; and if some privilege indeed lay within the realm of pale skin, it but afforded them additional means to further those efforts, that grace.

Others, however, thought differently. The press and the police, having dismissed the murder of a black child with infuriating casualness, were not so tolerant of the shooting of a white woman. Heather had made the headlines of both the *News* and the *Post* on the Monday following the shooting, and, within twenty-four hours, the man with the Cadillac earring had been arrested. True, within another twelve he was free on bail, and his attorney had announced that he had an alibi, but notice had most certainly been taken. Now the periodic appearance of police cruisers on TK's street began to cramp the business-as-usual dealings of the crack house. There were rumors, too, of an all-out legal assault on the dealers.

And, in the corner of TK's apartment, the M16 stood, cleaned, oiled, ready, a full clip rammed home. And even before the Crips and the Bloods had elevated to such a fine point of irrational violence matters of gang honor and revenge, Damon's Demons, Satan's Saints, and the Blackstone Rangers had enforced a no less exacting code in the Chicago projects.

And as far as TK was concerned, Heather was one of his.

"Drew! Hey, how's it going man! Been a while, hasn't it? Yeah, lost my leg. Right below the knee. No, not too bad. I get around. Got a job . . . working with computers. Yeah, can't get them out of my system. Listen, Drew: you still at the reserve armory? Yeah? Can you do me a big favor?"

But idle M16s and intermittent police inspections could not achieve everything, and, weekends and mornings, as TK lay in his bed, staring up at the ceiling, trying to forget the sight of Heather's face turning slack and bloody, trying to remove from his fingers' memory the sensation of vibrant flesh turning in a heartbeat to inert meat, he heard the periodic sound of automobile engines advancing, idling, pulling away. Commerce went on.

And Heather lay . . . hovering.

"Yeah, man, I know it's illegal, but hell, that never stopped us in Nam, did it? C'mon, for old times' sake. No one's going to miss a little C-4 and a few detonators. Hey, would I lie to you?"

And TK drifted.

The phone rang. Rags jumped up from sleep with a start and a snap. TK grabbed the handset: "Drew?"

A moment's hesitation. "TK, this is Sandy. Sandy Joy. Do you remember me?"

He dragged himself back into the present. Sandy. Yes, he remembered. Sandy with the scarred face and the sightless eye. Sandy who looked terrified. Sandy to whom, in a moment of peace and generosity that now seemed to lie so far away that he could not even recall its bare outlines, he had offered his address and phone number. "Yeah. Sure I remember. How's it going?"

"Not too good," she said. "I didn't know Heather very well, but . . . well . . ."

Hovering. When was Drew going to call?

". . . anyway, I'm going over to play harp for her tomorrow afternoon. Do you want a ride up so that you can see her?"

He passed a hand over his face. In her own way, Sandy was as sweet as the rest of them; but she possessed in addition a fallible humanity that contrasted oddly and quaintly with the limitless reserves of tolerance and love maintained by the Elvenhome folk, that made her sweetness seem somehow more fragile and, therefore, all the sweeter. Yes, she was just the sort of woman who, shy and terrified, would call an almost-stranger to see if he needed a ride.

It was like a splash of water in a parched mouth, and he hated to spoil the gesture with a refusal. But: "Uh . . . tomorrow's Monday, Sandy," he said. "I be at work."

"Oh . . ."

He heard her embarrassment, heard it go a little too deep. "Hey," he said, "thanks. Maybe we can make it some other time. I'd like to see Heather. If they let me in."

He almost heard her squirm: she was mortified. "Marsh

made up a list," she said with a catch in her voice. "You're on it. They'll let you in."

And that was just like Marsh. That was, in fact, just like all of them. White? Fuck it.

"That's one great bunch of people," he said, wondering whether Sandy had ever heard anything about old blood.

"Yeah. They're . . . just great. They're so nice they scare me sometimes."

He chuckled, doling out the sound with a hand made all the more miserly by the agenda that he had begun to establish with Drew. "That make two of us, girl."

Silence. He wondered for a moment whether he had offended her by calling her *girl*. Liberated women and all that. But he sensed that the origins of her discomfort went back farther than his unwise use of a word, went back all the way, perhaps, to the reasons for her scars and her blindness.

He wondered for a moment whether Sandy belonged to anyone, whether her wounds had been avenged.

"You say you're going to harp for her," he said quickly.

"Yeah. Natil's been teaching me, and she says I can do it." A silence that TK interpreted as an apologetic shrug. "I don't know. I don't know if I'm that good."

"You got to understand, girl . . ." And there he was saying it again. Asshole! ". . . the important thing is that you be playing."

"I'm not that good. I'm . . . afraid that I'm just going to mess her up more."

Help and healing? Was that not what he had wanted to do? Well, here was someone who needed both. And TK, who blew a sax in a weekend hobby band and who knew nothing about harps, was yet in a position to provide them. "Let me tell you something, girl." Damn! He struggled on, chagrined enough at yet another lapse that he did not at first realize what he was saying. "Back when I lost this leg, they put me in a hospital down south. Took it off right below the knee. Bam!"

Why was he telling her this?

"And then I got a letter from my wife, said she leaving me. They had me all doped up, but I knew what she said, and I knew that I lost my leg."

"I'm sorry," said Sandy. "That must have been awful."

"You bet. Was damned near killing myself. But something happened . . ."

Yes, something had happened. And something had happened at the TreeStar office when Ash had laid her hands on his leg. And something had happened up at the cookout when Natil had harped for Rags. And something was happening now that was causing him to reveal himself to a white woman he hardly knew.

The sound of a car engine in the street below. Eight cylinders. Had to be eight. And leather seats. And a burlwood dash. And a fancy hood ornament that went with ninety-five thousand dollars. He stared at the window. Something had happened on the Sunday before Christmas. And something else was going to happen.

"There was this old black man who mopped the floors," he said, hardly aware that he had continued with the story he was half afraid to tell. "No one paid no attention to him. You know: the South and all. He just mopped. Doctors didn't have no time for him. The nurses didn't look like they even saw him. But he saw me one day, and he came in to say that he appreciated what I done over in Iraq and all . . ."

He had said Iraq. It had happened in Iraq. It could have happened in Vietnam. He had seen it happen to others. Vibrant to meat, faces to slack . . . and that young fellow—dark skin, eyes crazed with drugs and fear—coming at him.

". . . and I said *Sure, man* and all that shit. But he meant it. And then one day just before they were fixing to send me home, I sitting on the side of the bed looking at my stump, and he came in with a harmonica."

He remembered. The perpetual summer that was Georgia, the trees green and the skies blue and humid. A brutal stump to which a prothesis fitted only reluctantly. Memories like eyes peering in through an unlocked window.

"And he just sat down and played for me. Must have played for an hour. People coming in to listen, standing out there in the hallway . . . just to listen. And it didn't really matter—you hearing me, girl?"

"Huh? Yeah, TK. I'm hearing."

"It didn't really matter how good he was, or what he played, or anything. The important thing was that he was *there,* and that he *cared.* And that made all the difference in the world."

Silence.

"You understand?"

He sensed Sandy's smile, sensed also her relieved tears. "Yeah, TK. I understand."

"You go and play for Heather, girl. You let her know that we all care."

He said good-bye and hung up. Helping and healing. He felt good. But another car was coming down the street, and just then the phone rang again. He knew the reason for the car, and he knew who was on the other end of the phone, and he knew what he was going to do.

Helping and healing? Who? What?

CHAPTER 17

6 January

David Dickens
Curriculum Committee
Kingsley College
Collegiate Park
Denver, Colorado 80221

Dear Dave:

It has never been my habit to present the Curriculum Committee with questions or problems, and I certainly do not intend ever to make it so, but I hope that you and the other members can find time to examine the documentation attached to this letter. Though my colleagues and I have only collected it with the greatest unwillingness, it appears to bear out our beliefs that there are some inconsistencies in the Hands of Grace program, not the least of which is that Mr. Terence Angel appears to have no academic credentials on record with any of the institutions that he references in his *curriculum vitae*. There is also the question of the quality, lack of peer review, or outright non-existence of the articles that Mr. Angel purports to have written. In addition, the Hands of Grace is receiving substantial support in the form of both maintenance and fellowship moneys, but only one student is enrolled, a Ms. Serena Joy, and we have been unable to discover any actual record of her classwork.

Kingsley College is not a large institution, and though our students frequently complain about the yearly tuition increases, money does not go so far now as it used to, and so the question of misspent funds is an important one. But far more important, we think, are the academic standing of the college and its commitment to learning that our founder, Aylesberg Kingsley, summed up so pungently as: *"Go out there and teach those sons of bitches how to make an honest dollar."*

Very sincerely yours,
Richard P. Harris

———————

Heather was in darkness.

She knew what had happened. She had felt the bullets punching into her back an instant before she heard the sound of the weapon, a moment before the pain gripped her like a fiery hand, a heartbeat before the world turned gray, then black. In the few, fleeting seconds before she had been swept away from everything that she could call familiar and safe, she had seen much of the story and the reason in TK's face.

And now she wandered, though wandering seemed to her to imply too much volition and action to justly apply to this aimless drifting among shadows, this hapless poking into corners of the . . . universe was it? She did not know.

Was she dead? Was this the dim realm to which things that were immortal came when they were stripped of their lives? Surely there was no sense of heaven or hell in this shadowy half-existence. No heaven or hell, no reward or punishment, no . . .

. . . no God.

She had wondered about God ever since the blood had taken her, wondered what divinity cared for Elves. Was this her answer? Did she wander in shadows because there was, in fact, nothing? Were the immortals of the world so completely alone?

She walked—at least she thought she walked—along dusty, unseen roads that stretched into infinite and obscure distances. And in that walking, she thought, she might have been the perfect representative of her people, for Elves had been walking from the beginning of time, walking and walking and walking . . . into darkness. Some had been killed, and some had faded, but not one of them had known any more, it seemed, than this blind walking.

She did not know how long she had walked. There was no time here. There was no light. But after what seemed like weeks or perhaps years she at last fell to her knees, felt the dust that could not have been dust grit beneath her fingernails and sting her legs. She wept, and in the wind that was not a wind her tears were cold on her face.

"Is there anyone out there?" she cried. "Is there anyone there?"

Her voice, unconfined by walls, mountains, trees, anything of substance, faded into the shadows. But despite her seeming loss of everything, there were still stars behind her closed eyes, and the sight of them was a comfort to her in this starless, comfortless place.

She put her hands to her face. "God . . ."

No, she could not call out to God, for God was not here. There was nothing here.

"God!"

She called anyway, for the sight of the stars had reminded her that, though she was not Firstborn herself, she was of that blood and that heritage. Perhaps, she considered, Elves had been walking since the beginning of time, walking into darkness, walking into night and loneliness, but in the course of that walking they had, freely, unstintingly, dispensed such help and healing that perhaps even a jealous God, one who had banished a primal mother and father from Paradise for their faltering grasp at immortality, one who had spurned angels because they would not worship Him—even such a one might turn at least a half-considerate ear toward those who, after having given so much to others, had *nothing*.

She called again, and again. But there was no reply. There was not even the sound of wind. And so, frantically at first, but then with an increasing and deliberate surety, she turned to the only divinity that she could, by right, claim for her own, the more immediate Godhead of her family. Breathing the starlight that continued to shine within her as though it were a beacon lighting her way into unknown passages of mind and spirit, she called up Kelly, called up Marsh, folded their memories in mental arms, clasped them to herself as though in defiance of anything that would ignore such holy things or attempt to render them valueless.

The God she had once known had not answered her,

and so Heather made these her God: the gentle clasp of lovers' hands, the gaze of one who was both husband and friend, the sudden bearing down of life that brought forth a screaming infant, the squirmings of a soft and fragile body against a mother's belly.

These were her God. *These* were her divinity.

And she suddenly realized that she was no longer on a dusty road, that she was no longer on her knees. She was floating in a star-filled darkness. And from somewhere, somewhere so close that it might well have been within her own heart, there was a struggling, a struggling as of something trying desperately to batter its way through paradoxical barriers and distances to her side, something that wanted her as much as she wanted it. Something . . .

She lifted her head, stared out, searching, her heart touched of a sudden with a faint, instinctual fluttering of what she could only call *recognition*.

. . . or Someone.

"Where did you come from, Natil?"

The question—straightforward, direct, brooking no artful change of subject—came from the Elfling who was riding on Natil's lap as she plowed out the north parking lot of the college. Marsh, with misgivings, had gone back to work even though Ash would have granted him an unlimited (and paid) leave of absence; but he had not wanted to leave his daughter to the uncertainties and prejudices of day care. And so Kelly, bundled up in a down snowsuit, went to work with Natil, rode the snowplow with her, waved at the passing students . . .

. . . and asked questions.

Natil spun the plow expertly, dropped the blade, and cut another clear swath through the record January snows: the December drought had ended . . . with a vengeance. But she was considering Kelly's question.

"How do you wish me to answer that, Kelly?" she said.

Kelly tipped her head back and stared straight up into Natil's face, and Natil noticed that the bright starlight in her eyes shone with a firm evenness. Heather's condition had made Kelly even more solemn, and had added a strange sense of purpose and focus to everything she did. It was as though, in Kelly's opinion, her every action bore directly or indirectly upon her mother's welfare.

And, Natil considered, she was perhaps right. Everything was connected. Everything was a part of the Dance, the Dance that was the Lady.

The Lady that the Elves could not see.

"One of the girls at the day care center is a Christian," said Kelly. "And she told me about hell."

"Oh, dear." Natil glanced down as she backed up and positioned the plow for another run. "Did she frighten you?"

"No," said Kelly. "Elves don't go to hell."

Natil nodded. It was so. But she could not help but wonder whether Elves went anywhere anymore. "I . . . I am glad you think that," she said.

"Well, it's true."

"I know."

"But she said that God made her. Mommy and daddy made me, I know. But who made you, Natil? Where did you come from?"

"I was made when the Earth was made," Natil said truthfully. "I was put here to help."

"To help people?"

"To help everything." Natil bent, kissed Kelly's head through the hood of her bright pink snowsuit. "Including Elflings."

"My mommy, too?"

Natil was glad that Kelly could not see the sudden mist in her eyes. "Your mommy, too, pretty lass."

"Do you have a mommy, Natil?"

My Mother brought me forth, Natil had said once as armed and armored guards had stood before her, waiting for her reply, *and I am She.* It had been a perfect expression of the truth, but, somehow, that perfection had cracked. If she were indeed her Mother, then why could she not find Her? "I . . . I do."

"Where is she?"

"She . . ." Again the mist of tears. "I do not know where She is." Another perfect expression of the truth. *Elthia* had sent her to Denver, but five hundred years and several worlds had passed between Natil's leaving of Adria and her coming to Colorado. What if . . .

It was a grievous thought, but Natil faced it. What if Elthia was no more? Oh, the patterns would continue, the Dance would continue, but what if *Elthia,* the visible embodiment of the patterns, was gone, faded along with the Firstborn? It could be. With her last efforts beginning to wilt like flowers in a blast of subzero cold, Natil had to admit that it could be.

She guided the plow once more into position, scraped clear another patch of asphalt. "I do not know," she said again.

But Kelly lifted her head. "Is she the lady in blue and silver?"

Natil's foot went down on the brake so hard that she had to grab Kelly to keep her from sliding off her lap. "The . . . the lady?" she managed. "What . . . lady are you talking about?"

Kelly's cheeks were pink with the cold. "The lady," she said, as if that explained everything. "The pretty lady."

"In . . ." Natil was almost afraid to ask. There had been too many disappointments. ". . . in robes?"

"Blue and silver."

Natil tried very hard to keep her voice steady. "Where . . . did you see this . . . ah . . . lady?"

Kelly frowned. "It's kind of hard to explain."

"Can you try please, Kelly? It is rather important."

Snow sifted down and spangled Kelly's eyelashes. "Mommy sent me to bed early an awful lot," she said. "I didn't really need it, but she sent me."

"That was good of her," said Natil. Her heart was throwing itself against the inside of her chest. Besides herself, Kelly was the only Elf so born. Maybe . . . "I am not sure that you did not need it, though."

"I didn't sleep."

"Well, that is true, Elfling."

Kelly looked at Natil as though suspicious that the grownups—Elves or not—were in collusion. "I just laid there."

"Lay, Elfling."

"Okay, I just lay there, and I looked at the stars an awful lot. And sometimes I saw her."

"Her . . . ?"

"The lady in blue and silver. She was a long way away. I could hardly see her."

"Was her hair dark?" said Natil. "Were her eyes gray?"

"Her hair was dark. I couldn't see her eyes because she was too far away."

"Did she come closer?"

Kelly shook her head. "It was like she wanted to, but she couldn't. Not yet."

Natil felt her eyes tearing again. "Not . . . not yet?"

Kelly nodded. "Not yet. Sometime, though." She examined Natil carefully. "Is she your mommy?"

And Natil folded Kelly in her arms, bent her head until her cheek rested against the child's pale forehead. "It is so," she managed at last. "She is my mother."

Her small harp cased against the cold weather and carefully tucked under her arm, Sandy entered the lobby of First Friends' Hospital and made for the elevators. In the course of the last week, her face and her reason for coming had become familiar to most of the hospital staff, and so no one paid much attention to her save the security guard, and he only nodded.

Sandy hardly noticed, for she was too caught up in what she was doing. In contrast to all the unfulfilled promises that Terry had made—promises that he was continuing to make, promises that remained unfulfilled—she was in a hospital with her harp, and she was playing for the sick. That her presence was not official, and that she was playing for but one person were unimportant details. She was playing, and she was playing for someone. And she even allowed herself to believe—just a little—that she was, perhaps, helping.

She had said nothing to Terry about her work at First Friends', for despite her constant disappointments, she was still clinging to her hopes that the Hands of Grace would yet take her somewhere. Terry's program possessed legitimacy and organization, and it offered a stable and respected environment in which she could eventually pursue her twin vocations of music and healing on a larger scale. She herself was presently playing for one; Terry, though, was constantly playing for many, realizing in his day to day life the dreams that Sandy had always cherished. He had, in fact, mentioned that he played in this very hospital.

Riding up on the elevator, her arms clasped about her harp, she suddenly caught her breath. What if she ran into him? *We have to be very clear,* he had told her during one of her meandering, occasionally pointless lessons, *that we are playing for the sick and not just for our egos.* Would he think that she was here for her ego? What would she say to him if he discovered her?

Her father had discovered her mother when her mother had run away. And her father had—

But another voice rose in her head, and it talked about free passage, about openness and honesty and the need (echoing Sandy's own words) to play in order to learn. And then TK's words about the old janitor and the harmonica came back, too.

Why was she here? She was here because of an urge that was all but physical, an urge to put her fingers to harpstrings and make music for someone who needed it, an urge that was not born of pride or a desire for fame, but which grew straight out of her heart like a tree whose roots lay in the primal desire to bring forth, whose branches waved in the honest air of grace.

To help and to heal. Natil had said that she existed to help and to heal. And now Sandy, who was beginning more and more to think of herself as Sana, the harper, was also beginning to believe that she existed only to help and to heal.

What would she say to Terry? She would figure that out later. At present, someone needed help. Someone needed healing.

With a rumble and a hiss, the elevator doors slid open to reveal the nurses' station, the white walls, the steel tables and instruments, the video screens displaying the vital signs of those who lived, those who faltered, those who wanted to die and could not. The nurse at the desk looked up for a moment and then went back to her paperwork with a frown.

Sandy knew her, but she stopped at the desk anyway. "I'm here to see Heather." She tried hard not to sound proud.

The nurse nodded curtly. "That's fine," she said, hardly looking up. "Room 1058."

"Thanks, " said Sandy. "I know." She started to turn away, turned back. "How is she doing?"

The nurse lifted her head, examined Sandy, examined

her cased harp. She frowned again. "Are you a family member?"

Sandy caught herself before she said *no,* for it occurred to her that perhaps she was indeed a family member. "Heather," she said firmly, "is my sister."

The nurse eyed her. "There's been no change," she said at last.

"None?"

"I said there's been no change."

And Sandy suspected that, even had there been a profound change, the nurse would not have told her of it. "Okay."

But before Sandy had a chance to depart, the nurse frowned again and said: "What do you think you're doing with that thing, anyway?"

Her tone was accusing, derisive, but Sandy found such openness actually refreshing compared to the patronizing attitude of some of the other staff members. *Oh, here's the little half-wit with her harp gonna play some Broadway show-tunes for that pointy-eared girl in 1058.*

She had heard about Raven and the orderly. She wished that Raven were with her. Or, better, Natil. But she was alone, and so she had to make do with herself. "I'm trying to heal," she said.

The nurse's mouth abruptly turned small. "That's Satanism."

Sandy blinked. "Oh, come on."

"Jesus said that only He could heal," the nurse insisted. "Anything else comes from the devil."

Sandy's religious forebears had been put to death because of similar theological niceties, and the instinctive resentment and anger welled up. "Well, I don't see Jesus playing for Heather," she said quietly, mindful that an outburst would give the nurse exactly what she wanted: an excuse to have her barred from the hospital, "so I guess that I'm going to have to do it. Okay?"

And without waiting for a reply, she turned and, mildly surprised that she had kept both her calm and her self-assurance, she went down the corridor to Heather's room.

When she entered, she found a doctor leaning over the still form in the single bed. She looked up at Sandy, straightened, pulled the stethoscope from her ears. "Hello," she said. "You're Sandy, aren't you?"

"Uh . . ." Sandy felt uncertainty welling up. "Yeah. I'm here to play for Heather."

The doctor was tall and horsy, and she ran a hand back through dark blond hair that seemed to go in a great many directions without much apparent concern for uniformity or style. "I think I'm jealous. Heather seems to have some terrific friends."

She smiled, but Sandy nodded tensely. "She's our friend. We want to take care of her."

"You've done a splendid job." The doctor smiled, offered her hand. "I'm Dr. Braun."

Sandy dutifully shook hands.

"Was Phyllis giving you the third degree out there?"

"She wasn't very nice," Sandy admitted.

Braun nodded. "I'll speak to her about that. Don't take it to heart though: she gives *everyone* the third degree."

Representatives of two wildly divergent schools of occult healing, they stood for a moment, facing one another silently over the body of one who had loved . . . and fallen.

"How . . ." Sandy glanced down. Heather's face was pale. The hospital staff had cleaned up most of the blood, but Sandy knew that beneath the deceptively white and even bandages lay a mass of damage. An Uzi was not a precise weapon: it simply directed a fire-hose spray of bullets in the general direction in which it was pointed. Heather had lost a tremendous quantity of blood, and her brain had been penetrated, likewise her lungs. That her aorta had only been grazed was a blessing, but, in view of the rest of her wounds, an ambivalent one. "How . . ." Sandy could not finish the question. She sensed what the answer was.

But Braun surprised her. "You keep playing," she said. "I don't know what music does. To tell you the truth, I've always thought that for sick people it's just something pretty to listen to. But for someone in Heather's condition . . ."

She looked at Heather. Sandy saw doubt in her eyes.

". . . something pretty to listen to just might make all the difference in the world."

"She not getting any better, is she?"

"She's not getting any worse," said Braun. But she shook her head, plainly discouraged.

Sandy nodded.

Braun picked up her clipboard. Before she left, though, she touched Sandy on the shoulder. "You play for her," she said. "Let her know that we're all pulling for her." A trace of a crooked smile. "Even Phyllis is pulling for her."

Sandy felt the weight of responsibility that came with her music and her harp and her desire to heal; and she suddenly understood why Natil was so frequently quiet and sad. "I'll ... I'll do that."

Braun looked at Heather again. "God knows, I wish a few others on this floor had someone to play for them."

"I thought Terry Angel was playing for people here."

"Terry Angel? Who's he?"

Sandy was confused. "He's ..." What? Her teacher? Still? "I thought he had a program. He said he was playing for sick people here at First Friends'."

"Never heard of him," said Braun. "I wish he were, though. There are a few ..." She sighed in resignation. "Like that Delmari girl. She's been in coma for years, and no one ever comes to see her except her dad." She seemed to consider for a moment, then: "He talks about music sometimes, I think. But no one ever plays for Audrey."

Sandy's confusion dropped directly into bewilderment. She was actually dizzy. Terry had said ...

But Terry, she recalled, had said a great many things.

"I'll play for her," she found herself saying. "If you'll give me permission, I'll play for anyone who needs it."

Confused. Dizzy. But Terry had *said* ...

Braun was nodding. "I'll make a list. Thanks. If you can pop in on them even once a week, it would sure be nice. Will you be in tomorrow?"

"Every ... every day."

"I'll look for you and take you around. And I'll give the word to Phyllis and the others to stay out of your way. I don't believe in the mumbo-jumbo that some people try to pull with music—remind me to tell you some day about the woman who was here a few years back with some kind of 'death and dying liturgy': a real screwball— but I believe in taking care of my patients, and if playing music helps, I'm all for it."

Dr. Braun left, and Sandy leaned dizzily against the bed.

Terry had *said* . . .

But she was here for Heather, and so, shaking, she sat down and uncased her harp, searching among Natil's songs for something that would calm her.

Ele, asta a mirurore . . .

She sighed, relaxed. An old melody, Natil had called it, and it had found a place in Sandy's heart from that very day. And so she made that hymn, a song to the Goddess heard long ago by a churchman and altered to fit the needs of a monastic community, her offering to Heather. Putting aside her confusion, opening herself to the music, she lifted her hands to the strings of her harp and played. Simply. Lovingly.

Hail, star of the sea, the words went, *enfoldment of enfoldments, Bright Lady, Divine Friend:* Sandy offered her concern and her healing through the symbol of the only divinity that she could worship. The Father God of the Christians had, through His earthly representatives, abused her too thoroughly; and even the Divine Consort of the witches, the Horned God of the woodlands who had been so perverted by the propaganda of medieval Christianity that his twisted images were still the drug of choice for those addicted to spiritual pathology—even He had been irrecoverably tainted by Sandy's father. All she had left was the Mother, the Mother to whom she had pledged herself, the Mother who she could—upon occasion, in shadowy fashion—become.

Ele, asta a mirurore . . .

As she played, repeating, varying the hymn, her thoughts were on Heather, encouraging whatever pieces of her spirit might still have been inhabiting her shattered body to take heart, to heal, to return to her friends and her family.

And without her being aware of it (for she had left awareness behind with the first ripple of plucked strings), the music took her deeper, far deeper, into a place for which she had no name, a place that seemed to consist solely of a profound and infinitely potent present. And then, faintly, beyond the music that suddenly filled her harp and her being like clear water, she had the impression of a hand being offered. Not to her. Not yet. To

Heather, rather. Offered gently, offered kindly. The hand of a friend. There was no sense of mastery or of dominion in it: it was merely offered, offered as though between equals, offered with the same care and concern and love with which Sandy was offering her music.

And Sandy sensed that, in return, Heather reached out . . .

She opened her eyes, stared at the room, at her harp. It was the better part of a minute before she knew where she was, knew that she was not still floating somewhere, witnessing the offering of a hand and . . .

Hand? What had she seen?

She rose unsteadily, peered into Heather's face, saw no more than she had seen before; and then, shaking, even a little frightened, she sat back down and rubbed her eyes. And there in the darkness behind her closed lids, comfortingly bright, lovingly close, illimitably distant, she saw stars.

CHAPTER 18

The pounding on TK's door was urgent, demanding, and it brought him straight up out of a deep sleep that had been filled with an unaccountable luminescence. Still fuzzy, blinking at the light from the street lamps that seeped in through the makeshift drapes, cursing at Rags to shut up and quit snapping at his good leg while he bent and fumbled with the fastenings of his prosthesis, TK at last stumbled to his feet.

The clock on the stove—about the only thing that still worked on the appliance—said that it was three in the morning. Who the hell could want him at three in the morning? He was half of a mind to go back to bed, but he did not, because the police cruisers had put only a superficial damper on the gang activity: beneath the now deceptively calm surface of the neighborhood was a turmoil of petty theft, nightly muggings, rapes. . . .

TK had intervened in not a few cases, had established himself as someone who would help in time of need, and so, as he approached the door, he wondered who he would find outside. A girl, perhaps, used and dumped and bleeding? Or an old woman who had been stripped of what little money was left to her this late in the welfare month? Or . . .

He paused, started to wonder. Three in the morning. And he, after hassling the crack house for months, was the sole witness to Heather's shooting.

Or . . .

The pounding came again, just as urgent, just as demanding.

In the back of his mind, the faint luminescence that had filtered into his dreams surged forward, roiled lambently, gave him the definite impression that his thoughts were on the right track. TK backed up, therefore, tiptoeing, and took the M16 from its bedside corner. "Hang on," he said, trying to sound sleepy. It was difficult for him to sound sleepy, though, for all his fatigue and fuzziness had abruptly fled, to be replaced by a hammering alertness that made his hand encircle the stock of the rifle as though the fiberglas grip were the waist of a willing woman. "I'm coming."

No answer. Just pounding.

Rags snarled and prowled about his ankles. TK grabbed him and, ignoring a slash to his wrist, tossed him into the closet and kicked the door shut. That done, he crept back across the room, and (the rush of adrenaline clarity giving his fingers a sureness that they had not possessed a minute before), he flicked the chain off, spun the deadbolt free, and yanked open the door.

Light from the hallway spilled in, and he saw the barrel of the Uzi a split second before it swung to line up on his chest. But he was ready for that. Before the man who held the gun had a chance to fire, TK had seized the barrel and jerked both weapon and wielder into the room. A solid smack from the butt of the M16 opened the man's scalp and set him sprawling, and TK was left with the Uzi.

TK gave it a quick glance. Yes, the clip was in, the safety was off, and the first round was chambered. It had not been a courtesy call.

The would-be executioner was frantic. Stripped of his weapon, dizzy with the blow to his skull, his wound sheeting blood down the side of his face, he scrambled to his feet and made for the door. TK thumbed on the M16's safety, tossed it on the bed, and caught him by the collar. The man spun, flailing, but, abruptly and wide-eyed, went limp when TK shoved the barrel of the Uzi into his throat.

TK looked carefully, felt sick. This was no man. This was a boy, a weedy boy. He could not have been older than fourteen, and he was possibly younger than that. His face was that of a baby, or of a woman, and TK could not help but recall the faces—infantile, womanish, youthful— that he had confronted in Vietnam and in Iraq, faces he had fought, faces he had killed.

Then, they had screamed when they had come for him, but his prisoner tonight—a boy sent out to do a man's job, a boy who had failed—said nothing. His glazed eyes, coupled with the blood that covered half his features as though with a red satin drape, gave him the look of the corpses that TK had seen dragged out of Viet Cong tunnels after the explosives had done their work, dragged out and stacked like the discarded limbs of a freshly pruned tree. Eyes glazed just like this, blood-covered just like this, incredibly youthful just like this, they had lain face up, staring blindly at a sky grown gray with heat.

The muzzle of the Uzi had dimpled the youth's throat. TK shoved it in until the glazed eyes clenched in pain. "Don't you never fuck with me again, nigger," he said. "Don't you *never.*"

Despite his words, he felt spineless, weak. Where was all his helping now? His healing? To whom had he pledged his future efforts when, nearly weeping with gratitude and long suppressed grief, he had watched the old hospital janitor depart? From black hand to black hand, grace had flowed in that endless Georgia summer, and now . . .

What color was this boy? What color was the hand that held the Uzi? And what color were the hands that exchanged crack for money, that put poison into the bodies of the poor and the homeless?

Oh, this was fine business indeed!

The child in his grip opened his eyes, stared at the gun that could take his life in a heartbeat, and TK could not help but wonder whether he had been the one who had put the bullets into Heather. This infant? Yes, this infant. It had happened before. It would happen again. These infants . . .

"You understand me?" he said, forcing the words out through a thick and rising wave of nausea, forcing the muzzle of the Uzi deeper into the soft, womanish flesh of the boy's throat. "You understand?"

A flicker of an even deeper terror in the wide eyes, a barely perceptible nod. TK glared at the youthful face, cursing himself for not being able to kill this child, cursing himself even more because he suspected that his qualms this night would, in the end, prove to be no more than a temporary reprieve. Yes, he would let him go. No, he would not call the police, for the police would only want to protect him from further incidents of this kind, and that protection would interfere with his . . . plans.

Plans. A delay in the execution, then. No more than that.

Pivoting, TK jerked on the boy's collar, hurled him out into the hallway. The boy skidded along the cheap carpet, fell part way down the stairs. For an instant, he lay stunned, but then he got up and stumbled down the remaining flight.

TK heard the front door open and then slam closed.

In the semi-darkness of his room, he looked at the Uzi. Small, compact, lethal. And he had the M16 also. And a little over four pounds of C-4 explosive, thanks to his old buddy, Drew.

With a sigh, he closed his door, rechained and rebolted it. The gang was moving. He would have to move, too. Soon.

Terry appeared to have something on his mind when he walked into Maxwell Delmari's office that morning, but Terry shook hands and smiled, and he sat down beside the desk in much the same fashion as he always sat down, and so Maxwell decided that he must have been mistaken.

"I saw Audrey this morning," said Terry. "I saw her in the room."

"Her . . ." Maxwell thought of his daughter, anticipated her return. How dismayed she would be by the changes that three years in coma had wrought in her body! But Audrey was a determined one: she would fight her way back to her athletic litheness, just as, with Terry's help, she was fighting her way back to life. " . . . her soul?"

Terry leaned toward him. "Yes," he said. "Her soul. It's beautiful . . . her soul." But again, Maxwell had the impression that something was on Terry's mind; and with a pang he glanced surreptitiously at the manila folder on his desk, hoping that he had not inadvertently left it open, praying that it bore no external marks to indicate what it contained. Someone like Terry did not need to be troubled by the fact that Jerusalem and Harris were still pursuing their hateful agenda against him. Folder closed? Yes? Good!

"I see her in the room with me," Terry continued, hunching over in a curious way that always made Max-

well think of bindings and shackles. He tugged the long
sleeves of his shirt down toward his wrists. "She remembers now. She wants to come back. And she will come
back, because . . ." The customary light of other worlds
was in his eyes. " . . . because I'm building a bridge of
music for her."

Maxwell closed his eyes, thinking of Audrey. He
would never see Greta again, save in heaven. But he
might yet see—and be seen by—Audrey.

"But I have a request to make of you," Terry went on.
"A simple thing, really. A small matter. I should have
taken care of it months ago."

Maxwell smiled. "Name it, Terry." He suddenly wondered: did Terry resent being called by his first name? He
should have asked. Terry was so . . . different. He reacted
so oddly to some things. Which was not to say that his re-
actions were unjust. "Name it."

"I need a letter from you . . ." Terry seemed to search
for words. Such a careful man. Maxwell was glad that
Audrey was in such good hands. " . . . a letter to First
Friends' Hospital, one that explains the purposes of my
program and tells them that I'm working with the cooperation and permission of Kingsley College."

Maxwell opened his eyes, stared. "But you're already
playing at First Friends', Terry. You have been for years.
Why do you need a letter from me?"

Terry's eyes clouded with the wound. "Well, I suppose
that I can . . . get along without it."

"Terry! Terry!" Maxwell was on his feet in an instant.
"Of course you can have the letter. No question about it!
I was . . . uh . . . only surprised. Is the hospital giving you
problems?"

Terry still appeared wounded, but Maxwell's assurances about the letter had obviously moderated the effects
of the injury. "It is always a trial to have to confront
those who have no belief. There are . . . " He leaned again
toward the dean, his fingers interlaced on the desk, but as
he did so, the sleeve of his shirt drew back a little, and
Maxwell was startled to see on Terry's arm what could
only have been dark bruises, red welts, fissures where
thick scabs had cracked and released a bloody pus.

"My God! Your arm, Terry!"

Terry sat back abruptly, pulled his sleeves down with

an almost brutal haste. His lips were suddenly flat against his teeth, and he hissed in a breath. "An accident. An accident," he muttered. "Only a blessed accident."

Maxwell sat down, wondering, almost shaking at the frightful incongruity of Terry's wounds. "Uh . . . all right."

Keeping his sleeves pulled firmly down, Terry locked his hands on the corner of Maxwell's desk. "There are always those who have no belief," he whispered, his eyes bright. "They will be punished. Punished in hell. And those who believe will take pleasure in their cries . . . and in the pain of their own blessed wounds!"

Maxwell could think of nothing to say. He found that he had unconsciously moved his chair away from Terry.

"Wounds . . ." Terry seemed to come to himself, to force himself to speak normally. "Wounds are blessed things. We must wound ourselves to know discipline, and we must know discipline to know God. That is the meaning of the stigmata."

"The . . . stigmata . . ."

"Yes." Terry nodded, clutching his hands together as though he had suddenly been handcuffed. "But there are . . . factions . . . at the hospital, just as there are . . . factions . . . at . . . Kingsley . . ."

Maxwell glanced at the manila folder, then quickly tore his eyes away for fear that Terry would notice. Terry was playing for Audrey. Terry was helping Audrey. If Terry should stop . . .

No. Unthinkable.

"I'll write your letter, Terry," said Maxwell. "I'll write it immediately." For an instant, he debated bringing up the questions that Jerusalem and Harris had raised in their troublesome letters . . . and in the documents they had sent to the curriculum committee. But he decided against it. Terry, after all, was helping Audrey; and Jerusalem, Harris, and the whole bloody curriculum committee could not deny that!

"Thank you," said Terry. He rose. "Thank you. I am very grateful. But we must be humble, and therefore . . ." His eyes had turned bright again. " . . . don't say anything in the letter about my work at First Friends' up until now. Hands of Grace musicians serve anonymously, and it's best to keep it that way."

"But they already—"

Terry looked troubled. Maxwell fell silent. "Anonymously," said Terry. "Thank you."

Terry left, and Maxwell was alone with himself and his memories of Audrey. Almost against his will, though, and trembling like a monkish novice who had suddenly discovered an obscene and blasphemous tome hidden away among the pious volumes of the library, he picked up the manila folder, opened it, and, haltingly, with a kind of horrified fascination, began to read.

Sandy came for her lesson that day, shuffling into the basement classroom, her gait shading into a lurching, downcast humility that always pleased Terry when he saw it. Humility and submission. Sandy, he thought, had something of both, and yet too little of either. It was up to him to teach her. The basis of the Hands of Grace was love—love of God, love of illness as a means of knowing God (Julian of Norwich had talked about that)—and love was a wounding, painful thing that would eventually bind Sandy, gash her heart with injuries that were all the sweeter for the arrows of divine passion that caused them, and bring her, submissive and helpless, to unsurpassable delight.

"Hello, Terry," she said.

Terry. It pleased him that she called him Terry, for it lessened the differences between them. They were friends, friends who had met on this lonely road of the world, friends who were here to help one another. And he would help her.

"Sandy." He smiled, seeing in her the reality and the potential both. "A very good morning to you."

She seemed distracted today. The sight of her eyes . . . eye, rather (for God had chosen to sacrifice one of those active extensions of her will so as to make her more receptive to His presence, just as He had caused her to be scarred so that she could concentrate more fully upon matters of the spirit) appeared to be turned inwards. But that, perhaps, was to be expected, for Sandy had visions. Sandy always had visions. And though Terry tried as best he could to stifle the jealousy he felt at the thought of one who had not known submission and who yet *saw,* still the jealousy was there. But he was not alone, and so there was nothing that he could do, for he needed privacy and secrecy in order to transfix with physical wounds a wayward soul that would not sufficiently submit to mutilations of the spirit.

"I have some good news for you, Sandy," he said as she dragged up a chair and uncased her harp. His words, though, did not produce the effect that he had anticipated. She simply looked at him with something much like resignation on her face.

"Good news?" she said as though she had finally realized that he expected a reply.

But this was indeed good news, and Terry knew that Sandy would appreciate it when she heard it. "The hospital that I've been working with has asked me if I have any students who are ready to play for the patients. There is a great demand, as you know, for this kind of musical-sacramental ministry. I told them that I had someone who was ready."

There. He had said it. And now Sandy would submit to him and, most important, confirm her status as his student, for he, a friend, was attempting to guide her into realms of such beauty and pain that her heart could not but be pierced by the terrible joy of mastery, and he could not do that without a program. And he could not have a program without a student.

Now she would stay. Now she would learn how to wait patiently to know his will, to lie passively while she was entered by wisdom.

Sandy, though, only looked at him. Again, that resignation. "Oh."

"Sandy, you're ready," he repeated, trying to make himself clear.

"Why?"

Terry stared. "Why? What do you mean?"

Sandy was staring as though seeing something besides the room. And he wondered again *how* she could see. How could one who would not submit presume to really *see*?

He found that he was almost angry with her.

"I'm not doing anything different with you now than I've been doing for the last nine months," she said. "How come I'm suddenly ready?"

Perhaps, he thought, he had misunderstood her. Perhaps

her strange attitude was a product not of willfulness but of real humility. After all, she had visions, visions so effortless that . . .

He cleared his throat, forced himself to smile. After all, he and Sandy were traveling the same road. "Your interior practice has grown," he said. "I've never met anyone with such a natural interior practice as you, Sandy."

Again, Sandy simply looked at him. Or, rather—as he suddenly realized with a sense of unease—through him.

"And it's . . . it's grown and developed immensely since you came to me." Terry made himself smile. She was his student. She was *his*.

Sandy said nothing.

Terry was growing increasingly uncomfortable. "It's time that you learned some of the real Hands of Grace material," he said. He looked around for his harp, discovered that he had, as usual, not brought it. "Ah, let me use your harp."

Sandy's hands tightened on her instrument. She shook her head. "No, Terry. I won't let you use my harp." She rose. "I'll come back tomorrow when you're ready to teach me," she said. But then her voice trailed off as though her attention had been caught by . . . something else. "Maybe . . ."

"I think," said Terry, "that we have to distinguish—"

"Between truth and lies," said Sandy. She blinked suddenly, as though shocked by her own words.

Terry said nothing. He was thinking of the manila folder on Maxwell's desk. Oh, he knew what it contained, for he had seen its counterpart elsewhere, and he had heard about the continuing efforts of Nora Jerusalem and her cohorts. But the Hands of Grace was too important, too much a product of living, growing Tradition: they could not derail it now with their spiritual adultery.

"Truth . . . and lies?" he said.

Troubled, Sandy bent her head, looked at the harp in her lap. "Sorry."

But Terry found himself asking, "What do you mean by truth and lies?" and was immediately sorry that he had uttered the words, for he suddenly became possessed by the terrible fear (a fear that would never give way, as in the case of divine vision, to a ravishment of peace, but only lead on to deeper fear) that she might reply. And then . . .

No. No.

He turned away quickly. "I think," he said, "that we are finished for today."

She was his student. She was, would continue to be, *his student.*

Silence from Sandy. Good. She would go home, and she would think, and then, as before, she would return.

But: "All right, Terry," she said.

He made sure that he did not look at her. "We are finished for today," he repeated.

"I don't know about that," said Sandy. "I think we may be finished forever."

He heard her case her harp, the zipper rasping up seductively: a little glissando that made him recall, against his will, the sound that his pants had made when he was a child, when Uncle Darryl had—

He heard her go toward the door, heard the turn of the knob.

And Nora Jerusalem, pagan and serpentine, asking about students! Classwork! Did she not know that—

The door closed behind Sandy. There was silence for the better part of a minute, and then there was the dull, thumping sound of a human arm smashing down repeatedly upon the edge of a desk.

"TK? This is Sandy."

"Sandy! Hey! How's Heather?"

Sandy sat slumped on her sofa, her harp lying across her lap. She felt at once empty and full, victorious and defeated. "About the same, TK," she said, and she dithered for a moment: compared with Heather's condition, her own predicament seemed absurdly trivial. "Listen, I'm sorry to bother you. I know it's late, but I really need to talk to someone." She choked. Would TK understand? But TK had understood before, and since she had been unable to reach Natil, she had turned to him once again.

"What you want, girl?"

She closed her eyes, saw stars. She had seen them constantly since the day her harping for Heather had taken her into places that she could not name, and their light had made the world both hazy and unspeakably clear. But she had not called TK about the stars: she had called him about Terry. The stars, she had decided, were too strange, were, perhaps, an emblem of madness, and she would not speak of them even to Natil.

"What is it, Sandy? C'mon. Tell Uncle TK about it."

She almost sobbed with relief at the sound of the rough sympathy in the big man's voice.

"What's going on, girl?"

"I . . ." The enormity of what she had done swelled the words until they caught in her throat, but she forced them out. "I told my teacher to go take a flying one."

"You told Natil—?"

"No, no, I told Terry."

"Terry? Who the hell's Terry?"

Indeed: she had come to wonder about that herself. "I came out to Denver for a program in . . . well, it's kind of like music therapy," she explained. "Only the guy who was in charge never taught me anything. So this afternoon I pretty much told him that it was all over." Pretty much? No, she had said *forever*. Now the Hands of Grace lay behind her, with all its frustrations, all its hopes, all its disappointments sitting in the middle of a now abandoned road like a heap of cast-off clothing.

TK responded with his usual directness. "So? What you whining about? If he was a buster, he was a buster, and you better off without him. You got Natil, Sandy. Shit, you got all of us."

She was almost afraid that he was angry at her. But no: TK was not angry, he was simply telling the truth.

Shit, you got all of us. The words made her feel warm with acceptance. "But . . . my fellowship. I'm afraid it's gone now."

"Your fellowship? Girl, people get along just fine without fellowships. Go get a job. We got a recession going, but they's always something you can find."

"But . . ." Sandy discovered that she was clutching her harp so tightly that her hand had cramped. Deliberately, she loosened her fingers.

"Hey, girl." TK's voice turned chocolate and soothing. "You got friends. You got Natil, and she teaching you harp. And if you want music therapy, you already playing in the hospital for Heather."

"A-and for some of the others, too."

"So you got it, Sandy. Say hey, there you are. Just what you want. You need a job, you head on up to Buckland Employment, let Ash and Marsh and Wheat take care of you."

"Well . . . uh . . . yeah . . . I could do that."

"See? You already there."

Sandy half smiled, half sobbed at TK's choice of words. Natil was already there. And Sandy, it appeared, was already there, too. Neither of them, however, seemed quite able to accept that fact.

For a moment, she tried to imagine what TK would say about her stars, decided not to risk finding out. "Okay . . . I guess." She wrinkled her nose: her tone did not even convince herself. "Uh . . . thanks."

"Don't mention it. You get some sleep, huh?"

"Yeah. You too."

A pause, and then a strange sound came from TK that might or might not have been a chuckle. There was something in it that sent a chill through Sandy, and before she knew what she had done, she had closed her eyes and was staring at her inward stars as though for security.

"I be all right, girl," said TK. "See you . . ." A pause. A terrible pause. Sandy kept her eyes closed, hoping that he would not repeat that mirthless, venomous sound. " . . . see you later."

She was still looking at her stars when she realized that he had hung up. That sound. It had been an expression of humor, and yet there had not been a shred of humor in it. Instead, it had been redolent of violence, of emotions that even she, with a life of abuse behind her, could not fathom.

She found herself punching in the number for Elvenhome, but she got no more answer than she had before. She tried Natil's office, but no, nothing. Doubtless, they had all stayed at the hospital right up until closing, and then they had gathered at the Home, turning off the telephone and linking together in that close community of spirit that she envied intensely but could understand no more than she could interpret TK's sudden, murderous expression.

Now, more than ever, Sandy needed to talk to someone. But not about herself: about TK. Somehow, out among the stars that now shone within her, she sensed a wrongness that was speedily growing into a certainty of danger.

She did not know how she knew that, but she knew. The starlight had told her a little about Terry, and now it was telling her too much about TK. Pacing up and down in her living room, then, caught between her grief for the loss of her carefully-planned life and her concern for TK, she stopped, turned suddenly, and impulsively dialed his number again.

Eight, nine, ten rings. No answer.

The stars were blazing within her, confirming her fears, prompting her to action. She grabbed her purse and headed down to the street.

CHAPTER 19

The front door of the crack house went down with a solid concussion that hit TK in the chest like a fist, fanned out across the street, and shattered the windows of the neighboring houses. But that was as nothing compared to the force that the charge had directed inward, and the door—no cheap, hollow core construction here, but a one and three quarter inch slab of oak—exploded into the entryway in a burst of splinters and metal fittings that reduced to an unrecognizable pile of shredded flesh and broken bone the gang member who had been standing guard.

Armed, angry, TK followed.

It was the past that had come to the crack house tonight, the past of cheap housing projects and lives thrown away for pittances. The past of the jungles and tunnels of Vietnam. The past of the brutal and limb-shattering match of reflex against explosive in an Iraqi bunker.

And it was the present, too. The present that had declared the life of a black child to be worth intrinsically less than that of a white woman. The present that had created this very crack house and the gang that dwelt in it. The present that at times seemed so hopeless that only the anesthetic effect of drugs—religious or chemical—could make it even briefly tolerable.

From the past, TK knew the use of the weapons he carried. From the present, he had learned a hatred so focused that it made the needle beam of a laser seem a vague and indistinct thing. And he entered through the gaping hole that his first demolition charge had created, sprayed a sudden movement down the hall with the Uzi, and drove forward.

He was going to destroy this house. He was going to bring it down just as he had brought down tunnel after tunnel in the heat drenched province of Cu Chi. He had, dangling from his web belt, three more charges with which to do it. But first he was going to find the man with the earring. He wanted to be sure of the man with the earring.

His prosthesis clicking faintly but precisely, his weapons—taped and tightened—all but silent, he went down the carpeted corridor that smelled of years and of mildew, of old drugs and new explosive. He saw a gleam as of metal in the darkness beyond the kitchen door and he dropped flat, his cheek scraping on tracked in pebbles and a scattering of stale corn chips. Slugs screamed over his head, and his stomach spasmed as it always spasmed at the sound of an AK-47.

But he was down, and the gunner's aim was high, and the slugs went out into the street, into, doubtless, the house across the way. Praying that no innocent was in their path, TK waited until he heard movement ahead, and then he let the Uzi do its work once more. A slither and a thump, and the AK-47 did not fire again.

Movement behind him. He had no time to turn before someone had leaped on his back, and he saw the flash of a knife. Or maybe it was a razor. It was too dark. He could not be sure.

Sounds from upstairs. Footsteps.

He swung the barrel of the Uzi, contacted something solid. The blade dropped to the floor with a clatter a moment before he shoved his weapon into something soft and squeezed off a burst. The weight on his back turned heavy, wet, inert.

Light suddenly. The lights were on, the footsteps were still coming down the stairs, and he was sprawled in the middle of a downstairs hallway with a body on top of him. Scrambling, then, almost losing his footing in the pool of blood that was fast growing on the floor, he threw off his burden, rose, and made for the kitchen. But, just for an instant, he looked down, and he saw that he had killed not a man but a boy.

And again, the sheer horror of the youth of those he had determined to murder struck him with a numbing weakness. So young. They were all so young. They had *always* been young. In the tunnels of Vietnam, in the bunkers of Iraq, in a crack house in Denver, they were all young. And where was all his helping and healing now? Did the blood that had saturated his shirt represent anything save the same arrogant and senseless violence that had put Heather in the hospital?

But Heather was one of *his*. And these . . .

What color was Heather? What color was that boy back there in the hall? Who best represented his people, his gang, his chosen friends?

Grimly, as though fleeing his own thoughts, he ran into the kitchen, vaulting, just within the doorway, a huddled, dead form that was still wrapped about its automatic rifle. He grabbed the edge of the stove and swung himself into shelter just as impacting lead powdered the walls of the hallway and cut a swath through the open kitchen door, shattering the jars on the far wall. Mayonnaise and ketchup sprayed TK in the face, and mustard stung his eyes, but he paid no attention, for feet were coming down the hall now, and there were shouts and curses as someone tripped over the body he had left there.

He aimed the Uzi and turned the fuse box on the wall into perforated and bent metal. With the vicious sparks of outraged 220 volt feed lines, the power went out and the house was in darkness.

The footsteps stopped. TK glided to the doorway to see heads and shoulders blocking the light from the street. Whispers. He leveled the Uzi, squeezed the trigger.

Nothing. The clip was empty. He did not have another.

The M16 was slung on his back, but behind him, the fuse box was still sputtering and crackling. TK suddenly realized that the intermittent light from the sparks was more than likely making him visible.

He threw the Uzi, heard it crack into someone's face and thump to the ground. Shots sped by him, and one grazed his arm like a burning coal as he ducked back into a kitchen that was beginning to fill with the smoke of smoldering plastic and rubber. He unslung the M16, thumbed off the safety, aimed it at the doorway. The smoke might strangle him, but it would also conceal him.

There were three of them, and they pounded into the kitchen as though they assumed that the empty weapon landing at their feet had marked the end of the armed assault. And, indeed, it almost had, for it had allowed them to draw close enough for TK to see how young they were.

But the tunnels had taken over now, and the smoke from the burning fuse box only added to his sense of the past, for the air had been bad in the tunnels of Cu Chi, and it had been smoky in the Iraqi bunker; and in both Vietnam and Iraq, though twenty years separated them, figures had loomed up out of the hazy darkness in just this way, and their faces had been young, and TK's need to kill them—quickly—had been urgent.

Just as it was now.

Traveling at nearly the speed of sound, impacting with a tumble that could rip steel drums from top to bottom, TK's bullets cut down the three who had entered, and the sparks flickered on their faces as they fell. Tinies. Tiny gangsters: boys who had found in the gangs a position and a status that their society had denied them. Perhaps it was only boys—children—who, innocent and fresh and open to experience as the hardened consciences of adults could never be, could discern so plainly the truth of the matter. There was no room for black men in this place, for the white men had bought the land and everything it contained. There was nothing for black men to do, therefore, but turn inward, turn toward themselves, turn, if necessary, upon themselves, acting out in internecine battle the very hatred that had been forced upon them, that was played out with quotidian regularity in the pageantry of social myth.

And so they turned to the gangs. Here were children who sold dope in order to buy hamburgers for lunch, who took an old woman's social security check so that a baby sister could have shoes or a new skirt, who killed because . . . because . . .

. . . because everyone killed. And how much difference was there, really, between splashing on a young man because he wore the wrong color bandanna in his back pocket and filling his BMP with incandescent shrapnel because he wore the wrong color uniform on his back? Killing was not such a big thing: after all, it happened from six in the evening to eleven at night every single day of the week, and all one had to do to see it was flip a switch and sit back. These children, dead now, had been exactingly schooled in the manner of their end, and one of them might well have held the gun that had put the slugs into Heather.

Jerking himself violently away from the abusive insight, trying to keep his mind only on that nightmarish memory of Heather collapsing on the seat of the truck with the back of her skull blown open, TK pulled one of the C-4 charges from his belt, armed the timed detonator, and placed it against what he knew—the tunnels had trained him well—was one of the main structural walls of the house. He had a few minutes. Time enough to place the other charges. Time enough to get out of the house. Maybe.

But first he was going to find the man with the earring.

With the fuse box still sputtering and smoldering and the M16 up and ready, he left the kitchen and crept down the corridor, silently glad that the darkness concealed what he had left lying on the floor ahead. In contrast to the shouting and footfalls of a minute before, the house had fallen abruptly silent, and TK judged that if there were anyone left in it—perhaps just off the entryway, in that living room he had passed by on the run—they were at present attempting to figure out what had happened and what best to do about it.

They did not know. Indeed, they could not know. In the light of the absolute primacy of profit in the drug trade, TK's actions were not only illogical, but insane. No one would expect that he was here not to rob but to destroy utterly. No one would think to look for bombs.

A doorway to the side. A closet. He ducked in, placed his second charge. As he armed the detonator, he realized that he should have taken the AK-47 from the dead grasp of the boy in the kitchen, but it was too late to go back now. The charges were ticking down the seconds, and he could not reset them. He had only minutes remaining. He had to make the best of them.

He left the closet, continued toward the front of the house. The stairs, he could see, would be a problem. They were the only way up to the second floor, and if he mounted them he would be vulnerable to attacks from both above and below.

But he wanted the man with the earring, and he suspected—sensing as though with a flicker of the radiance that had leaked out of his dreams and taken up residence in his mind—that the man with the earring was up there.

As TK passed the dark living room, though, he heard a stirring. With no time to reflect, he fired, and a high pitched scream slashed at his ears. A woman's scream. Somebody's girlfriend. But there were other stirrings, then, and he had to fire again. And again. The suppressor on the muzzle of the M16 dimmed the flashes to a faint glow, and so he had only a vague impression of soft flesh—too soft, he thought, ever to be in a gang, ever to know the seductive weightlessness of crack crystals or the metallic heft of lead, ever to count out bills in anything save singles, fives, or maybe tens—opening, falling.

And then a sound, and he turned, and at the top of the stairs, dull in the spill of street light from the gaping front door, TK saw *him*.

The automatic rifle upstairs fired and swept toward him. TK dived, cracked his head against the remains of the door, rolled as the bullets passed him by in a hot flicker of shock waves and plaster dust. Splinters scored his bare arms, nails and screws that his first charge had torn out of the wall gouged into his shoulder; but he had fallen like this in the tunnels, fallen and fired, and his counterattack fanned up along the banister, cutting through the uprights and leaving the railing supported by toothpick splinters.

"I want you, motherfucker!" TK screamed as he got to his feet, screamed as his finger clamped down on the trigger, screamed as he charged up the stairs. But he was squandering his ammunition, and although he could vent his frustration in a volley of copper-jacketed death, it was an expression as impotent as his repeated calls to the police and his attempt to shield Heather, and it left him swaying at the top of the stairs, his rifle empty.

The man with the earring had ducked the bullets, but he was rising now, and the muzzle of his weapon was rising, too. TK swung the M16 like a club and split his scalp just above one of the iron filled eyes; then, drawing his K-Bar, he threw himself forward.

It was dark here, not so dark as in the lightless tunnels where TK's only knowledge of the actions of his enemy had been the feel of the flesh and the flexing of the muscles beneath his hands, but dark enough. He could see shadows, gleams, the flicker of hate in narrowed eyes. The man with the earring was strong, just as strong as

TK, and clawing, swinging, lunging at one another with their teeth when their hands had been locked into mutual inaction, they rolled, tumbled, teetered on the edge of the landing that the M16 had denuded of its banister, slammed into walls covered with shabby and peeling paper.

And, downstairs, TK's charges ticked toward detonation.

They said nothing to one another, unless rumbles and grunts and harsh breaths could be counted as speech. This conflict had been coming for a long time, and it had, in the course of weeks and months, fermented into an acid brew of rage to which TK had added a generous helping of revenge. Revenge for the girl-child who had been no more than a shield, revenge for all the cluck heads and the junkies who had found willing and cooperative allies in their attempt at anesthetic self-destruction, revenge for all the non-white peoples of the world who had stumbled into the snares set by their own kind in the holy name of profit.

And added to all of this was his seething, irrational rage at the arrogant attack that had put Heather in the hospital, that had left her still hovering, even weeks later, between life and death. No one knew what would happen to Heather, but TK knew what he wanted to happen to the man who had touched her, and if life could be bought by death, he was going to make yet another payment upon the account.

The man's hands were on TK's face, tugging at his cheeks as though he would put his fingers through them, but TK's thumbs were pressing on clenched eyes, his entire weight bearing down on two square inches of flesh, bearing down until the straining grunts emanating from his opponent's throat began to shade toward screams, bearing down until the fingers that were raking at his face began to lose their will to clutch.

The man rolled, striving to break free. TK braced himself with his prosthesis and rammed his good knee into the man's briefly unguarded groin, feeling, even through the thickness of Levi's, the stale crunch of rupturing testicles.

The fingers on his face fell away, and the eyes beneath his thumbs opened along with a mouth that was suddenly screaming in pain. TK did not wait: his thumbs rammed home into warm jelly, and, with a wrench, he lifted the man's head, now slack and limp with shock, and battered it against the wall until he could not hold onto it for the blood.

Dripping, shaking, his eyes seeing nothing but the shades of the past, TK staggered to his feet, picked up his rifle, reached to his belt for the third charge. Unconscious of the pain, he rammed a hole in the lath and plaster wall with a bare fist, and he armed and thrust the explosive inside as though he were crouching on the dirt floor of a low tunnel, breathing air that reeked not only of the breath and bodies of other men but of a pungent, acrid scent that burned his sinuses and laid a scummy hand on the back of his throat: the unforgettable odor of panic.

Were there others still in the house? He did not know. The M16 was a stone in his hand, the faces of the children he had killed a swirling melange of memory that flowed together with the face of the young Iraqi officer, the pale, youthful faces of the Vietnamese in the tunnels, in the streets, in the bars . . .

He could not find the stairs. He could not find them. But was he looking for a way down, or a way up? He blundered into one of the bedrooms, stumbled over a supine form with another child's face and breath that smelled of refined cocaine. How old was this girl? How old were any of them? Who had he killed? Who had, finally, killed him?

Unthinking, or perhaps thinking too much, he slung her over his shoulder, staggered out of the bedroom, almost fell down the stairs. One step, two steps, repeat. Slowly he descended with his inert burden, wondering just how much time was left on the detonators, unable to know just how much time was passing.

He had reached the downstairs hall when the slugs came up from somewhere and churned the girl's head into a bloody paste. Mutely, he stared for a moment at the glistening travesty of a woman's features, understanding that her body had shielded his own, and then his instincts took over again. He dropped her as another burst of bullets spun her around in the air, and he ran for the open door, throwing himself out and down the steps.

He felt impacts, heard the splintering of plastic, tried to land running and found that his artificial leg had been cut away as though with a scythe. But as TK fell on his face on the sidewalk, skidded to a stop, and tried to scramble away, there was a gust of wind, a concussion, a shattering of glass, and with a shriek of rending timber and a crack of breaking joists and crumbling plaster, the house behind him folded and buckled.

Bricks were bouncing down the walk, tumbling from the outer walls, cascading from the upper story. A downspout, toppling, hit him on the back of the head and smashed his cheek down onto the curb. A sustained roaring was behind him, a roaring that seemed to stretch out too wide, as though it were attempting to snatch him up in a brutal paw. He had heard it before, and he knew what it meant. Soon, he would help haul out the bodies, laying them face up in the tropical sun. The officers would count the corpses and ship them away to wherever one shipped such things. And TK would be back in the tunnels tomorrow, killing more children . . .

The thought, the memory, brought him up, screaming: *"No! No! No! Dammit! No!"*

A piece of brick wall as big as a doghouse ran him down, and the world turned vague, hazy, the roaring of the collapsing house blurring into a dull rumble. He blinked at the darkness through eyes that were washed with starlight and blood both, and only an impelling instinct for self preservation goaded his arms and his one good leg into motions that might, perhaps, with much effort and time, take him back to his apartment.

Another crash from the house. Was he hearing sirens, now? And what would that particular uniform have to say to him? Oh, it was all just uniforms, was it not? Crip blue, Blood red, Police black, Marine drab . . .

And then out of a dazzle of headlights, he heard a car, a cry. Hands were on him. Small hands. Soft hands.

"TK!"

He was limp, unable to speak, unable to move. Someone rolled him onto his back, and another face—a living face—came into focus, took on detail. He saw dark hair. He saw brown eyes . . . and the obvious blindness of one of them. He saw a pale jaw made paler by caustic scars.

Dear Nora:

Sorry I've been missing you at school all this time. When I got into this business I thought that college life was sedate. Stupid me. It's nearly midnight, and I'm not about to call you at this hour, so I fired up the computer to write you this note.

Dave Dickens called me yesterday and suggested that we have a drink after work. We talked about the Hands of Grace problem. It appears that we've stuck our foot into a pretty delicate situation involving Maxwell's daughter, Audrey, who's in coma up at First Friends' Hospital.

Maxwell appears to be under the impression that Angel is doing something for Audrey under the auspices of the Hands of Grace program. But, of course, you've got those letters (I showed the copies to Dave) from every major hospital in the metro area, including First Friends', that they say they don't know anything about Terry Angel.

But Maxwell has been backing Angel's program because of what Angel has been supposedly doing for Audrey, and he's pretty vested in the whole affair. I can't blame him, and neither can Dave. But if Angel has been leading Maxwell around by the nose this long, it's going to be real difficult to change his mind about the program. We could go over his head, of course. Dave has a luncheon meeting with Chancellor Wickey next week, and he could bring it up. But Maxwell's been good to us all, and I don't want to stab him in the back this way. Or jerk the rug out from under him.

The problem is that there's no way of challenging Angel *without* hurting Maxwell. I don't know what we can do here.

And now for something completely different.

One of the reasons that I'm still up (it's one o'clock now) is that I disregarded your advice and read those Terry Angel articles that you sent me back in December. At night. (I know, I know. I said I'd read them immediately. *Mea maxima culpa.*)

You're absolutely right. Those bondage scenes he

put in "The Use of Plucked Stringed Instruments, etc." gave me the whim-whams. Tubes of fluid from wounds!?! The kids were trooping around in their pajamas while I was reading that one, and I felt positively unclean even having the thing in the house with them. I locked up all the articles in my desk drawer when I was done. No sense in having Nancy wondering what kind of a pervert she's married to.

But if Angel has been publishing stuff like this (thank God the real journals use peer review!), then I concur with your opinion that we've got a real loon here. The question is: how much of a loon? With this kind of stuff in his papers, is this guy dangerous? What about that student he's got? What's her name? Sara Joy? Is she crazy, too?

I don't know what to think, but I'm a little scared. Maybe it's just because it's so late, and I read those damned articles, and I can't sleep now. The whole world looks crazy sometimes.

Well, that's it. I'm starting to rave. I'll mail this in the morning, and you should have it by Tuesday. Give me a call then. Maybe we can escape Kingsley for an hour or two and figure out where to go from here.

Poor Maxwell!

God bless you,

Rick

———————————

CHAPTER 20

Having once been human, having too long experienced their lives as being circumscribed by the alternating cycles of a circadian existence to conceive of such endless consciousness as was now their birthright, the Elves of Denver had to bound their waking with some sense of oblivion; and therefore, gathered together in the Home they had built for themselves, with midnight having passed a little over an hour ago, they had fallen silent, lapsed into contemplative and starlit stillness.

Even in quiescence, though, their thoughts were bent toward Heather. They could do nothing directly for her, and since the unearthly powers of healing once wielded by those of their heritage had faded, they had turned to more homely methods. Now they held her as a constant presence in their minds, laving that presence in starlight, giving unstintingly of their willed energies in the hope that she might perhaps profit by such ephemeral help.

Hope. It was all a matter of hope. But Natil knew that, for the Elves of Colorado, hope had turned into a shabby and sere garment, fit, it seemed, only for mummery and cynical self-deception, no more effective than the quaint garb or exotic jewelry affected by some of Sandy's fellow witches in a pathetic attempt to garner some sense of belief and empowerment in a world seemingly bent upon crushing the life out of both.

Lauri had perhaps expressed it perfectly earlier that night. *"So what's it mean to be an Elf? Do we just do our little thing and smile and nod and try to help people who don't really want to get any better until someone offs us? Do we just go down one by one? That's a fucking stupid way to live!"*

Her language had been direct, even crude, but she had summed up everyone's thoughts with characteristically elven precision. Where before they had wondered what force, emotional or spiritual, might sustain them through their immortal lives, now they had all but come to the conclusion that they were on their own in a violent and irreparable universe . . . forever.

Yet, in that apparent desolation, Natil had found a spark of nurture. She could not share it, but she could believe in it, take heart from it, redouble her efforts because of it.

Kelly had seen *Elthia.*

But though there was more hope in that slender glimpse than Natil had felt in many years, still, she reminded herself, Kelly had only *seen* the Lady. There had been no direct contact, no speech, not even a meeting of glances across the abyss. And so she was, once again, left with questions . . . questions and a jumble of methods ranging from the elven to the human, methods which (she had tried them all again) did not work.

Drifting now among the stars along with her people, she wondered what stars Heather was seeing, wondered whether, if she shouted into the spaces between those incandescent points of light just a little louder, cast her will just a little farther, Heather might hear.

Or maybe Someone Else might hear . . . and answer.

Troubled, she rose, left the house, wandered among the pines and the aspens that stood upon the hills around Elvenhome. She ran her hand over bark, fingered needles, touched the dried canes of wild rose and the withered remains of yarrow that poked up through patches of snow. She tried to remember Malvern Forest, tried to remember all the brothers and sisters she had known in the past. How had it been then? Effortless. So effortless. One had only to go out among the stars, respond to the call, give oneself over to the light.

Had they so taken Her for granted then?

She covered her face with her hands. *"Elthia,"* she said, her voice heavy. "Goddess. Divine Mother, help me to find You. Not just for us. For all your children, mortal and immortal alike."

"Natil."

She jumped.

Lauri appeared to be as chagrined that she had surprised Natil as Natil was that she had been surprised.

"Hey," she said, "I must be getting the hang of this if I can sneak up on someone like you."

Natil considered herself, laughed softly. "Lauri, I have never doubted that you have the hang of it."

"Yeah . . . well . . ." Lauri shrugged. "You know, I've always kind of felt like the poor relation."

Natil stared. "Lauri!"

"You know: odd man out and all that."

Natil took her hand, linked arms with her, pulled her along. "Walk with me, Lauri," she said. "You are my kinswoman and my friend." For a moment, she tried again to think of Malvern . . . but no, this was not Malvern, this was not Adria. This was not any place but Colorado, and this Elf walking with her was not anything but an Elf. She had to remember that. The past was gone, swept away by the turning ages, but there were Elves again in the world, and in that there was hope. And now *Elthia*—

Elthia had appeared. What was going on?

Lauri was brooding. Had she been a human, she might well have been shuffling through the dry pine needles and the crusty snow, making crisp, brittle sounds in the winter cold. But she was an Elf, and so, despite her emotions, her steps remained utterly silent.

Natil squeezed her hand. "I thought that you and Wheat . . ." She lifted an eyebrow.

Lauri shrugged again. "Didn't happen."

"I am sorry."

"It all just kind of drifted away. You know how Wheat is. She works on her stained glass, puts on headphones and flies off with Judy Collins." Lauri plunged her hands into the pockets of her down vest. "Anyway, that's what she did after the October cookout. She's just . . . somewhere else right now."

Natil nodded. "We are all somewhere else right now."

"Yeah." An uncomfortable silence. Finally: "Listen, Natil. I got pretty carried away tonight. I followed you because I wanted to tell you that I'm sorry."

"For what, Lauri?"

"For that bit about getting offed, and about living stupid. I mean . . . what can I say? I've only been an Elf for a few years. I got no right to go shooting off my mouth about what's stupid and what's not."

Natil sighed. "You spoke the truth, my sister. Everyone knew that. I knew that. What you described was accurate, and your appraisal of it was accurate, too."

"I . . ." Lauri pressed her lips together, obviously having expected protest, denial . . . anything but total agreement. "Dammit, Natil, what kind of a thing to say is that? You're not being fair to yourself."

Natil shook her head. "The truth is often not fair. Indeed, this *world* is not fair at all, nor has it ever been."

Lauri stopped. The shimmer about her flesh was obvious, as was the trouble in her eye. "And you've . . . you've just been . . . living with that for . . ." She groped for words. "Since the beginning?"

There was no moon that night. They were in darkness. But Natil could see Lauri's expression, and Lauri, she knew, could see hers. And even had that not been the case, Elves lied very badly. And so: "I have not," said Natil.

"Then what have you got? What's been getting you through all this time?"

No one would understand, but perhaps understanding had to come later. Perhaps she simply had to say it first. "The witches call her the Goddess."

Lauri's lips acquired a twist that was both wry and sad. "Religion? That's all?"

As Natil had feared. "Not religion, Lauri. *Reality.*"

But Lauri had suddenly been distracted, and, following her gaze, Natil saw that headlights were flickering on the trees at the top of the surrounding hills. All the Elves of Denver save Heather were gathered at the Home. Who then, had come? Who had found the only refuge of the Immortals?

"What the hell's going on?" said Lauri. "No one's ever been able to find that turnoff except us."

But Natil, struck by a thought, was already running up the slope, and when she reached the crest, she caught her breath; for there, its exhaust smoking in the cold mountain air, was Sandy's little Celica.

Stars.

Sandy was seeing stars, and now they were brighter than ever, spilling over even into the matte, unconscious blackness of her blind eye, a presence at once frightening and reassuring. They had given her a glimpse of the emptiness that was Terry Angel and had made her proof against his manipulation. They had prompted her to go to TK and had brought her to his side in the middle of a street filled with flying glass and splintering wood.

And then, with TK sobbing and wounded in her passenger seat, they had brought her here, to the place called Elvenhome.

Natil reached her first, took one look at TK, and shouted for help. Lauri came then, the others arrived within another minute, and Sandy saw how gently they lifted TK out of the car, saw, too, their concern as they examined his wounds and bruises and the ruin of his prosthesis.

They bore him through the trees, into the house, up to a bedroom. Ash and Natil bent over him and laid their hands upon his head, and TK, of a sudden, fell into a deep repose as though he had suddenly shed the burden of continuing and fevered wakefulness. His breathing subsided from harsh gasps to something slow and easy, and the tightness went from his bruised face. Natil's gleaming eyes were inches from TK's lacerated chest, but she seemed to be looking through him, beyond the room, and she and Ash brought a soft power up out of themselves and put it into him as though they were ladling light.

Sandy felt the stars within her brighten even more, and she suddenly realized that what she was seeing was impossible, even by the standards of one who called herself a witch. The accumulated strain of what she had witnessed—the demolition of a house, a man wounded and bleeding and delirious, the continuing irrationality of the stars within her—struck then, and she sagged, almost toppled.

Lauri's strong arm caught her. "Come on," said the tall woman. "Come on downstairs. Let's get some food into you, and then you can go to bed."

"Oh ... Goddess ..." Overcome, feeling sick, Sandy started to turn away.

Lauri led her out of the room. "I'm going to have to ask you about that Goddess of yours someday." She flicked a starlit glance (Yes, Sandy realized, there was starlight there, too: she could *see* it) back over her shoulder at Natil, who was still intent on TK. "She seems to be in with all the right people."

Sandy nodded absently, her hand to her mouth as though to stop a scream of fear. She wanted her closet, wanted Little Sandy, wanted to hide.

Lauri took her down to the bright, friendly kitchen and began rattling about with pots and pans. "I don't know how you feel about things like this," she said as she brought water to a boil. "But oatmeal has always been my drug of choice. Gets me through everything." She paused thoughtfully. "Well, almost everything."

Sandy nodded at the prosaic familiarity of oatmeal. But when a steaming bowl was set before her along with milk, raisins, honey, and dried fruit, she could only stare at it. "I don't know what happened," she mumbled. "I just showed up, and TK was a mess, and that house . . ."

Lauri had taken a chair on the other side of the table. "You did the right thing."

"I should have taken him to an emergency room."

Lauri shook her head. "His wounds are the least of his problems."

"True." Natil had entered the room silently, was standing just within the door. And Sandy could see plainly the light in her eyes. Starlight. "The very least. The emergency room would have called the police, I am sure, and TK does not need the police at present. He needs us."

"Natil," said Sandy, "I'm sorry. I shouldn't have dragged you all into this. I've gotten you all out of bed . . ."

Natil and Lauri exchanged glances . . . and a soft smile.

". . . and I've made a mess of everything, and I don't even know what happened."

"I can guess," said Natil. "TK solved the problem of what to do about Heather. In his own way." Her face turned troubled. "And then he found that his way was actually no way at all."

"Does he have . . ." Lauri did not finish the sentence, but it did not appear that she had to, for Natil nodded.

"He does," she said. "And it has partly waked, and therefore what he did hurts him all the more."

"He's a good man."

"He is not a man, Lauri."

"Well . . . yeah . . ." Lauri looked even more troubled

than Natil. "Oh, God, what have we done now?" But she turned suddenly to face Natil. "Or should that be *Goddess*? You're messing with my head, lady."

Sandy was weeping softly by now, her face in her hands. Afraid, confused, she wondered whether she could find a place to hide in this strange house. "What's going on? No one's telling me what's going on. I want to go home."

She felt Natil's arms around her, soft as enfolding wings. "Beloved Sana, you *are* home."

Sandy's eyes were clenched tight, but she could not hide in the darkness, for there were stars burning within her, and she could see them clearly . . . with both eyes. "I want my closet. I want my doll. I want my harp."

"We shall go and get your harp and your doll," said Natil. "But I think that it would be best if you stayed with us for tonight. Perhaps for several nights." Sandy felt her friend lift her head. "Indeed, Lauri, TK will be staying with us, too. But he has little Rags, and I daresay the animal should not be left to shift for himself."

"Wheat's car gets the best mileage," said Lauri. "We can go into town with Sandy and pick up what needs to be picked up." A pause. "If Wheat's willing, I guess."

"She is willing," said Natil. "Give her time, Lauri." But then Sandy felt a head pressed to her own, felt something unclench within herself. "Be healed," whispered Natil.

"I don't know what happened." Sandy could barely get the words out. It was her father all over again: something had come up out of another place, out of the darkness, and had done . . . something . . . to her. But there the resemblance ended, for where Freddy Joy had used her and tormented her, this starlight was, she understood, trying to help her.

"What happened is not important," said Natil. "TK is here, and you are here. Everything that happens, happens as it should." A hug. Then: "How ever did you find the turnoff, though? I have always had to point it out to you."

"The . . . the stars told me."

Silence. Stunned silence. It lengthened. Sandy finally lifted her head. Natil and Lauri were both staring at her. Finally, Lauri mustered a tense laugh. "Hey, how about that? Two for the price of one."

Sandy was utterly without comprehension, but Natil suddenly smiled—smiled almost as though with relief—and placed a kiss on her forehead. "Welcome home, Sana," she said. "Welcome home doubly, trebly."

"It ..." Sandy looked back and forth between them, uncertain whether to be afraid or relieved. She was seeing stars. And these people actually appeared to *like* that. "It was ... like ... they guided me. And then there was this voice ..."

Natil's smile faded. "Voice?"

"Someone told me when to turn." Sandy waved her hands nervously, nearly upset the bowl of oatmeal. "Like she was sitting next to me. I'm ... just remembering that now ... I mean ..."

Natil looked at Lauri. Lauri spread her hands. "Don't look at me. I had my share of voices one night at TreeStar. Scared me to death." She leaned toward Sandy commiseratingly. "Do you get colors, too? Blue and silver?"

"Lauri!" cried Natil. "Blue and silver?"

Lauri sized Natil up as though she were a sparring partner. "That's something else you're going to have to explain, isn't it, Natil?"

"But ..." Sandy had never seen Natil so flustered. "But I cannot explain it." Natil appeared to look for words for a moment, then to give up. "I simply cannot."

"Yeah, sure," said Lauri. She shook her head, offered a hand to Sandy. "Come on. Let's go into town and pick up your stuff. We'll get Rags, too." Her mouth tightened for a moment. "We'll leave Ms. Enigma here with TK."

Sandy was confused, and she did not know what to think, what to say. But two hours later, riding back toward the mountains in Wheat's Honda Civic with Little Sandy on her lap, her harp at her side, and Rags sleeping contentedly in Lauri's arms, it occurred to her that, though she was still confused, she nonetheless felt safe. Very safe.

And as Wheat drove them all back to Elvenhome, Sandy fell asleep in the car, the stars shining within her, as bright and comforting as any childhood vision of paradise; and if there were traces of blue and silver in her dreams, and if, just for an instant, she caught a glimpse of a Woman's face, she remembered nothing of any of it in the morning.

Saturday morning was cloudy, overcast. Scattered flakes of snow drifted down as Maxwell Delmari pulled into the hospital parking lot.

The weather, he recalled, had been much like this on the day Greta had been killed and Audrey had been . . . sent away. Overcast, cool. There had been a snowstorm a few days before, and the roads were rich with melt by day, treacherous with ice by night. Greta, always a careful driver, had doubtless been taking the freeway slowly, picking her way along; and more than likely, she had been chatting with Audrey about college, about the scholarship, about—

Well, it did not matter any more. There had been no college. The scholarship had been transferred to somebody else. Not everyone was as careful as Greta, and when the Audi had crossed the center divider, she had probably not even had a chance to cry out.

Maxwell parked, sat in the silent car with his head pressed against the steering wheel. "See you in an hour," she had said on her way out, and Audrey had called "Toodles, Pop!" over her shoulder, and then they had left. But an hour had gone by, and then another hour, and another. It had been midnight when the black and white had stopped in front of the house.

He glanced at his watch. Nine o'clock. Now was the time that Terry came to play for Audrey, to try by means of ancient music and art to lead her back to consciousness and life. He had said that he came to her every day at this time, and Maxwell had taken him at his word, had himself gone to visit Audrey every evening, had seen in her face the improvements of which Terry spoke.

The sound of the car door slamming behind him sounded like the closing of a tomb. The cold air stung his cheeks, and the glass doors susurrated open at his approach, reminding him of the sucking of the respirator that had done all of Audrey's breathing for the last three years.

Inside: maroon carpets, mauve walls, efficiently maintained desks in white and steel. Maxwell knew it all. He knew where the elevators were, knew without looking the position of the button that would take him to the intensive care unit. He could have traversed the path from the elevator to Audrey's room in his sleep, and, in fact, he often did, his dreams taking him to the hospital almost nightly, leading him to a room in which a young woman—alive, alert, vibrant—looked up from her breakfast and said "Hi, Pop!"

"Dr. Delmari!" Phyllis, the head nurse, was on duty. "I haven't seen you in this early before."

"I thought ..." He had not planned on this. What was he supposed to say? That his hopes of the last two years had suddenly been dashed and he had come to inspect the pieces? That he was here to put the last few nails in the coffin of his hope? That he had been deceived?

No. He did not know that ... yet. He had to go and look.

"I was driving by on ... on an errand," he said. "I thought I'd drop in. Has ..." Should he ask? He had never asked before. He had taken it on faith. "Has Terry Angel been in?"

"Terry Angel?"

A sensation as of a cold hand about his throat. "Never mind," he said stiffly. "I'll just go and look."

He went down the corridor, but once he was out of sight of the nurses' station, he sagged against the wall, staring at the door that led to Audrey's room, wanting and not wanting to enter.

He was not hearing anything. Surely the sound of harpstrings would—

But the doors were thick here. And the sound of the heating system was loud. He might not hear.

Groping, wanting and not wanting to know, he stumbled across the hall, put his hand on the pull, swung the door wide.

Audrey lay with unclosed eyes, but he was used to that. She stirred and she trembled always, and there was a sense about her of imminent consciousness. The respirator attended to her breathing, and tubes dripped in food and took away urine, but Audrey murmured and shifted in her bed as though caught in the middle of uneasy dreams from which she would soon wake, from which she *had* to wake.

Hearing too loudly the silence in the room, the silence

unbroken by harpstrings, the silence made louder by the intermittent hissing of the respirator and the deep rumble of the heating blowers, Maxwell went to her, bent, kissed her on the forehead. "Hello, Sugar," he said.

Audrey moved, shifted, writhed. Her hands clenched and unclenched, her eyes flickered as though they would, in a moment, focus, recognize him.

Slowly, Maxwell turned around. There was no one else in the room.

He kissed Audrey again, went out to the desk. "Is there a doctor on duty, Phyllis?"

"Dr. Braun is here this morning."

"Could I . . ." He glanced back at the corridor. "Could I talk to him, please?"

"Certainly, Dr. Delmari."

Dr. Braun was a woman, and a tall one at that. Her blond hair seemed stuck on at random angles, but her eyes were clear. "Good morning, Dr. Delmari." She offered her hand.

He took it, hardly aware of the formality. "Ah . . ." How, then, to ask? How, then, to destroy it all? "Audrey . . . how is . . . ?"

"About the same."

"No change, then."

Braun shook her head.

"Even . . . I mean . . ." He looked back toward her room. The door was closed. "Even in the . . . uh . . . last six months . . . or so . . . ?" His voice trailed off on a rising note, like a child who had asked to keep a stray puppy, who had already read refusal in a parent's eye.

"There's been . . ." Braun appeared to be looking for a gentle way of putting it, but facts, abusive though they might be, were facts. ". . . no real change in her condition since she was brought in to us."

"None?"

"I'm sorry, Dr. Delmari. I've gone over Audrey's charts back to the very beginning. There's been no change, aside from some degeneration of her muscles and her lungs."

Maxwell stood, seeing nothing.

"Degeneration is natural under the circumstances. I'm very sorry."

"I've . . . had a lot of time to get used to it," he said. "Has Terry Angel been in here today?"

"Terry Angel?"

The cold hand about his throat. A weight above his heart. "You don't know him, do you?"

Braun looked genuinely puzzled. "Someone else asked about him once. I've never met him myself, and he's never come to First Friends'. Who is he?"

"He's a . . ." Maxwell bent his head to hide his tears. "Has anyone been harping for Audrey?" he blurted. The world filmed over.

"Dr. Delmari, I think you should sit down." Braun tried to guide him to a chair. "Phyllis, could you bring some water over here?"

But Maxwell shook her hand away from his shoulder. "Has anyone been playing music for her?"

Braun's face was concerned. "There's a woman who comes in every day to play for one of the other patients. She consented to play a little for Audrey and some of the others on the floor. I gave my permission."

Somewhere behind him, Phyllis sniffed derisively.

"I thought it might help," the doctor explained. "I didn't think it would hurt."

"That's . . . good . . ." said Maxwell. "That's . . . all right." His voice sounded distant, faint. "I'm glad . . . that someone's playing for her. For all of them."

Braun's voice was kind. "Why don't you sit down, Dr. Delmari? Here's some water. Would you like some coffee?"

He did not want to sit down. He did not want water or coffee. Stumbling, staggering, he found the elevator, rode it down to the lobby, and, groping like a blind man, made his way outside. The air was still cold, the snow was still falling. He got into his car and pressed his forehead against the steering wheel until he was sure that the skin had bruised.

A tomb—he knew it was a tomb now—forever. And there was not even an angel to keep watch.

PART THREE

Alba

CHAPTER 21

TK awoke, opened his eyes. Morning sunlight was streaming in through a window spattered with the tossing shadows of pine branches. Above his head, dark beams crossed a white ceiling.

He looked at the ceiling, he looked at the shadows. For the time, he formed no opinion or judgment, contenting himself instead with the simple, unthinking present of a half doze. What had brought him to this room he did not know. Why he was here, he did not know. He did not care. There would be time later to deal with such things as—

He started, cried out. The crack house. Children's blood slicking down his arms. That face, inches from his own . . .

A hand came down on his forehead. "Peace."

And at that touch, the sudden, violating memories faded to a soft undertone. They were there. He knew they were there. He would—would have to—deal with them. But for now, without a cry of pain or a grimace of suppressed horror, he could turn his head toward the woman who sat beside his bed.

She was dressed simply, in a white blouse and sweater and blue slacks, and her dark hair, unbound and streaked with much silver, fell to her waist. Her face was pale and calm, but there was a light in her eyes, and it echoed the light that had come to be an underlying presence in the back of his mind.

"Natil." His voice was hoarse, his throat raw with the screams of recent violence.

"Be at peace," she said. "You are safe here."

He understood where he was. "Elvenhome."

"It is so."

Outside, an optimistic meadowlark called, heedless of the fact that it was still winter. Somewhere below, someone was singing. The sounds, though, were almost painful: detonations and the abrupt and lethal reports of automatic weapons were infinitely more appropriate for someone like him. "Why . . . why'd you bring me here?"

"Sandy brought you," said Natil. "She brought you because you needed to come."

He shook his head. His presence in this place seemed to him a sacrilege, a defilement of what had once taken him in with gentle welcome and soft voices. "You know what happened?" he said. "You know what I did?"

Natil gave him a trace of a smile. A pained smile. "We know. It has been in the papers and on the radio. We do not have a television here, but I am sure that the visual media have also covered it adequately." She looked at him carefully, as though wondering just what sort of beast this was that had lain up in a bedroom in Elvenhome. "You are very . . . brave."

He saw the look, heard the hesitation. "I'm not brave. I'm just a killer. I killed kids."

Natil nodded, pained. "You did. And they would have killed you. And they had already killed others. And they were still killing." She sighed, passed a hand across her face: to Natil, the simple facts of life were as personal failings. "This place lives by killing, TK. I cannot condemn you for your actions."

She could not condemn him. But she could not approve, either. Surprised at how deeply her tacit censure stung him, he realized that it was no more than a faint echo of the inner condemnation he had directed at himself. Kids. Kids in Vietnam. Kids in Iraq. And what was all this shit about helping and healing?

Natil seemed to read his thoughts. "I cannot approve of hate. And revenge, I have learned many times, is a poor provision for a life's journey." She shook her head, dropped her eyes, seemed to be thinking of another time. "And yet . . ."

It was not a pardon, nor was it an excuse. There was no pardon or excuse for what he had done, just as there was no pardon or excuse for what had been done to Heather, or for what had been done to that little girl who had gone out to play in her yard on a summer afternoon and had died in the arms of a boy who thought of her as nothing more than a piece of meat he could hold up between himself and an automatic rifle.

No excuse. No excuse at all. Helping and healing? Fuck it all.

Pained by his thoughts, pained by his deeds, he glanced at the window. Gray sky. Morning sky. Winter sky. How long had he been out? What day was this? "The Man been here yet?"

Natil almost looked astonished. "Are you quite serious, TK? Do you really think that we would call the police?"

He felt it then, stronger than ever before. Colored. They were all colored. As much as any pack of welfare mothers might have banded together against the inquiries of Social Services, so these people of Elvenhome had closed ranks around him, protecting him even though they could not but be disgusted by his bloody actions. "You . . . you talk like a homie, Natil."

"In a sense, we *are* homies, TK." There was grief in her voice. Deep grief. "We have always been homies. We have never had anyone to turn to but ourselves."

For a moment, shocked, surprised at her emotion, TK saw only surfaces, was conscious only of the gulf of color and social opportunity that lay between himself and Natil's people. They did not know what it was like to live with a crack house just up the block. They did not know what it was like to grow up in a rat-infested project with an absent father and a gauntlet of rival gang territories to run every day between home and school.

No. They had grown up in suburbs, or in small towns with maybe a token minority family that lived safely across the way. Tow-headed kids with shiny tricycles and new clothes. Just like the fantastic and blatantly racist pictures on the Right-to-Life billboards: blond and blue-eyed and *Thank you for giving me life, mommy.*

He remembered the black girl he had tried to haul out of the house. Her head had been pulped, first by drugs, then by bullets. *Thank you for giving me life, mommy.* Yeah, sure.

"You ain't homies, Natil," he said. "You're white. All of you. Haven't you realized that? What's the matter with you?"

But Natil looked up, looked at him, and suddenly TK

was seeing below the surface of white skin and the commonplaces of middle-class clothing and inferred privilege. He had seen it before—in Heather's face instants before the bullets had entered her—and he was seeing it again now: a sense of difference that went beyond race, beyond social position, beyond anything external, that struck down to the very foundations of identity. He had seen starlight in Heather's eyes, and he had wondered whether she were human. And now he was seeing starlight in Natil's eyes, and he *knew* that she was not. Nor were any of them. Old blood, perhaps, but it was blood that had nothing to do with mortals, that—

No one to turn to but themselves, dwelling in the middle of a world hostile to every possible reason for their existence. Black. They were black, just like himself. They could not be anything *but* black.

"What the hell you trying to tell me?" he said. He was suddenly frightened as he had never been frightened before, whether in the projects, the tunnels, the bunker, or the crack house. Black. Blacker than black. Not even human . . .

The starlight in Natil's eyes was piercing, and she looked as though she were about to say something that TK found himself devoutly hoping she would not. But she paused, sighed, shook her head with a rustle of long hair . . . and the moment passed. "The police will not come," she said. "Fear not."

But it was not the police he was afraid of now, for he was suddenly confronted with the implications of everything that had happened since he had entered the offices of Buckland Employment and shaken the hand of a sweet young woman—woman!—named Wheat.

Who were these people?

"Sleep," said Natil. "Rest. It is Monday, if you were wondering. TreeStar will miss you, but your absence is excused. You can stay here as long as you like."

"What . . . what about the Man?" But his real question went unsaid.

"The authorities are apparently unable to decide whether to condemn you or laud you," said Natil as though she knew what he had not asked, as though she were determined to put him at ease by pretending that she did not know. "Fortunately, they do not know who you are, and therefore they do not have to make the choice. They found what was left of your prosthesis, though."

TK looked down involuntarily. The folds of the comforter told everything: one leg, one stump. "They'll trace me."

Natil shrugged. "I cannot say."

"I can't get a new leg. The VA'll report me."

"That is possible." Natil leaned forward suddenly, rested her hand atop his head, and peered into his face as though searching for an elusive fish at the bottom of a deep pool. After a moment, though, without any indication of whether she had found what she had sought, she released his head, sat back. "We have crutches for you," she said, nodding to the corner beside the bed. "They should serve you well for now."

He followed her glance. There was indeed a pair of crutches there. He managed a tight, nervous laugh. "You folks think of everything, don't you?"

Natil's gaze was suddenly on him again, and he had the sensation that he was being weighed, evaluated. There was kindness in her eyes, to be sure, but there was also a calm dispassion. Not human. Not human at all.

But that was just another layer—perhaps just another surface—of the woman he knew as Natil; and, looking beyond both the color of her skin and the dispassion she had put on, he could see how troubled she was. As troubled and as grieving as any human. And he discovered that, despite his unwillingness, his fear, and his despair, his urge to help and heal remained, and now it surged forward once again and with it, brought forward almost subliminal light in his mind.

Starlight, he thought with a flash of panic. But he rose up on one elbow and offered his hand to Natil. "Thanks," he said. "Thanks for everything. I'm sorry I . . ." But he was offering a hand that was stained with blood. He had no right to be here.

But as though she read his thoughts, Natil took his hand. He felt the smoothness of a woman's flesh, but there was more to it than that. It was, he knew now, immortal flesh. Odd: it was suddenly too real to be frightening.

Natil nodded. "Rest, TK. Rest as long as you like." A brief smile that was touched with sadness. "You are safe here. And you are welcome."

* * *

WHILE YOU WERE OUT

For: *N. Jerusalem*
Date: *Feb. 3*
Time: *9.40 am*
From: *Maxwell Delmari*
Phone: *Dean's office*
Fax:
Message: *call back ASAP. URGENT.*

Elvenhome was a big house, and it contained not only large, communal rooms that offered warmth and comfort and wide panoramas of trees and mountains, but also small alcoves, window seats, nooks: places where one could curl up with a book or a harp or simply with one's thoughts and the view.

It was in one of the latter that Sandy had seated herself with Little Sandy beside her and her harp in her lap. She was playing . . . and today she was making an effort to sing, too. Sandy had never thought of herself as having a particularly good voice, but somehow, with the warm, quiet house about her and the winter trees wreathed in gray cloud, it had seemed permissible to sing. Natil was in another part of the house, probably in TK's room, and the others had left in the early morning to go to work and to keep company with Heather: there was no one to be disturbed if she sounded bad.

But she admitted that today she did not think that she sounded bad. And the stars, she suspected, had something to do with that, just as they had something to do with the change in the inflections of her voice, the change that made her pronunciation of the ancient language of her song sound very like Natil's.

> *"Ele, asta a mirurore,*
> *Cira a ciraie,*
> *Elthia Calasiuove*
> *Marithae dia."*

Yes, very like Natil's, indeed. And she was also suspecting that the stars themselves, the stars that she was seeing, the stars that gleamed at her even out of her blindness, were also very like Natil's. Very like, in fact, the stars of all the people of Elvenhome.

She finished the hymn, repeated it, and then allowed her hands to find their way into a series of variations on the tune that took her away from the original mixolydian mode, through the dorian, and finally into a strong and joyful ionian in which (her modern origins betraying themselves) a trace of a back-beat became evident.

Easing into a conclusion, then, she let the spaces between her notes grow, until, finally, there was only the silence. And the stars.

"Lovely, Sana," said Natil, who had approached with absolutely silent footsteps. "You are a credit to harpers."

"I have a good teacher," said Sandy. "How is TK?"

"He is asleep," said Natil. "Sleep is the best thing for him at present."

"Sleep and ..." Sandy set her harp aside, considered. Her life had become very different. The stars had driven the barker away, muted the horror of her memories of her father, created within her a reservoir of peace from which she could, at any time, draw refreshment, confidence, and an inner sense of safety. Freddy Joy had been open and direct about what he had demanded of her, and she had had no choice but to surrender to him every particle of herself—body and will both. But here at Elvenhome, something else was happening. Subtle and mysterious, but carrying with it an inexplicable feeling of brightness for all that, it beckoned her on without explaining itself; and though it was within her power to refuse, to withdraw, she did not. She followed. Followed the deep compassion she saw in the faces here. Followed the healing. Followed the ...

"... starlight?" she asked Natil.

Natil hesitated, nodded. "It is so."

Sandy dropped her eyes. Starlight. Voices. Visions. She had swallowed them all willingly, as willingly as she had swallowed the Hands of Grace, tales of hospices and hospitals, stories about ancient plainchant and teams of Latinists. It was time to stop, no matter what the consequences. "I ... kind of feel like maybe you haven't been quite straight with me, Natil."

"In what way, beloved?"

Sandy kept her eyes on her harp, felt a thread of fright

tighten about her throat. Years ago, at the custody hearing, she had spoken, and for that speaking, her father had revenged himself upon her for most of a decade. And Terry Angel had tormented and manipulated her for the same reason: speaking, asking questions. But her father was dead, and Terry Angel lay in the past, and, in any case, this was Elvenhome. This was Natil. If there were consequences ahead, they were certainly nothing of which she had to be afraid. And so: "You've been going on about how you want to learn the Craft, and I've been doing my damndest to teach you, even though it seemed to me that you already knew everything worth knowing. And I told you that. But you kept at me, so I did my best."

A tremor of frightened nausea. Sandy thrust it aside, looked up. Natil had not moved.

"And now I'm finding out that it's not just you. You're *all* already there. You make all those boobs who call themselves witches—me included—look sick, every one of you. There's more Wicca in one of your fingernails than there is in all of us put together, because you all live it. You just live it. And then, the other night, I saw you and Ash do stuff with TK that I didn't think was possible. Oh, you didn't flash-bang heal him or anything like that, but you did . . . something. And something's been happening to me, too. And . . . and . . ."

"What do you wish to know, Sana?" Natil's voice was filled with compassion. "Ask."

Sandy felt cold. Her father had punished her. Terry Angel had tormented her. But here, in Elvenhome, it was all different. She could ask. She could ask for as much—or as little—as she wanted.

But she decided that, even had questions been forbidden, she would have asked, for her days of blind acceptance and fearful submission were over. "Tell me . . ." She hesitated, went on. "Tell me about the stars I'm seeing, Natil. Tell me why I'm seeing them. Tell me . . . as much as you think I can understand."

———

Rick—
　　Hit line 2 and pick it up—gently. Listen in. It's Maxwell. He's found out about T.A.
　　　　　　　　　　　　Nora

———

Bloody dreams drove TK up out of sleep and back to the comparative unreality of a simple bedroom. Tree shadows on the wall. Mountains through the window. Crutches in the corner. Natil, though, was gone. So was the singing. The house, Elvenhome, was silent.

He shoved himself up on his elbows, wincing at the pain from his bruises and cuts. A bandage about his left arm reminded him that a bullet had grazed him, and the bullet reminded him of the crack house and what he had done . . . and also of the friends who would not betray him to the police, who had, in fact, tried to ease his pain.

He could not understand it. It was as if they had accepted him as one of themselves instead of—

And then he remembered. They were not just colored. They were not even human. But though he instinctively looked about the room to see whether he was really alone, whether in actuality some preternatural being might have been perching on a lampshade somewhere, or sitting invisibly on the edge of the bed, he felt no fear. This room with its carpet and window, its soft bed, and its Sulamith Wülfing prints on the walls was too quiet and safe—he might even have said *holy*—to admit fear.

He sat up, put his foot on the floor, examined the stump of his left leg. Gone again. Bullets. The time before, it had been a grenade. And he certainly could not show up at the VA and ask for a new prosthesis, because if, as Natil had said, the demolition of the crack house was big news, then the police were going to be trying to score points, and that meant an investigation. Richard Kimball had been looking for a one-armed man. The cops were going to be keeping an eye out for someone with less than the standard allotment of legs.

He grabbed the crutches, tucked them under his arms, hoisted himself to his feet. He discovered, then, that someone had obviously gone to his apartment and picked up some of his clothes, for neatly draped over the back of a chair were a shirt, jeans, underwear, and socks, and on the floor was a pair of his sneakers.

Natil and her people thought of everything, provided for everything. And what had he himself done? Blown up a house and killed a bunch of kids? Was that all? And what had that accomplished? For whom had that provided?

It was a sour, bitter victory. There would always be crack

houses, just as there would always be enough despair in the world to support them. Oh, in the next century people would, doubtless, be plugging themselves into some diabolical machine that promised them nirvana while it emptied their pockets, and a hundred years after that, there would probably be an illegal operation that removed the brain and placed it in a warm bath of eternal orgasm, there to shudder with delight until it withered; but regardless of the mechanics involved, the essentials would be the same, and even if TK could somehow live forever, he would not be able to change that in the slightest.

He step-thumped over to the chair, sat down, dressed himself. Somewhere in here, he decided, he would have to get a shower . . . as though any amount of water would remove the slick tackiness of blood that had seemingly become an inseparable part of his fingers. The clothes, though, were good. Clean clothes, and maybe something to eat. For now, he could concentrate on clean clothes and something to eat.

But as though to drag his thoughts back to the wonder of this place and the people who had built it, a scrambling came from the hallway, and a moment later, a small dog burst in through the half-open door and threw himself into TK's lap.

It was Rags. Or, rather, it looked like Rags. But where the Rags that TK knew would have been snarling with outright venom and lunging with bared teeth at anything that resembled exposed skin, this dog was wiggling with obvious pleasure and licking TK's face, all the while whining frantically as though relieved that his master was well.

Once again, the magic of Elvenhome had worked a profound change on the yorkie.

"Hey, man," said TK, hugging him, "you OK? They get you and bring you up here? They been feeding you good?"

Rags licked. Of *course* they had brought him up. Of *course* they had been feeding him. It was just the sort of thing that they would do . . . effortlessly, unselfconsciously, without a thought about things like praise or merit. They had just *done* it.

Shutting his eyes, he hugged Rags until the dog stopped writhing and settled down with his furry muzzle up by TK's ear and his pink tongue going in and out, in and out. But in the darkness behind his closed eyes, TK was seeing stars:

the light that had for weeks surged and roiled in the back of his mind had at last manifested fully.

Stars. And Natil's eyes were full of starlight. As was the case with them all.

"Oh . . . sweet Jesus . . ."

He rocked Rags back and forth as though by doing so he could ease his own turmoil. But it was no use. He had come too far, done too much. Unconsciously, he had made his choices in such a way that he had effectively done away with any possibility of a return to anything that he might call normal or customary. Right now, he was in an impossible house that had been built by impossible people, and he was seeing, within himself, impossible stars. He had left the projects, his neighborhood . . . everything, in fact, behind.

Oh, he had said his brave words to Natil, had thought his bitter thoughts; but his hands had held the Uzi and the M16 when they had sprayed their death into the darkness, and he had not cared at all about the skin color of those he had killed. Worse, he had been thinking of Heather when he had killed them, and (yes, he had to admit it, even with Rags licking his ear and the stars burning within him) he had even been thinking of Heather as kin, as part of his gang, his set, his people.

Dressed, with Rags frisking with joy about his good foot, he stumped downstairs to the kitchen. There, he found a note in Natil's precise handwriting that told him that she had left for work, that Sandy had gone to the hospital to play for Heather and some of the other patients. There was food in the refrigerator, and she had even left him a bus schedule so that he could, if he wanted, return to Denver.

Many of us shall be back this evening, she closed. *We hope to see you then. Blessings.*

He crumpled the paper. Claimed. Claimed and jumped in without his even being aware of it.

He was not hungry.

"C'mon, Rags," he said. "Let's take a walk. Let's take a long walk."

It was cold, and he did not have a jacket, but he found a long gray cloak by the door, and, tolerably wrapped, with the crutches tucked beneath his arms and his wounds throbbing, he left Elvenhome and slowly climbed into the forested hills.

They were gone, all of them, and they trusted him with their home. And they looked forward to seeing him. He had become a friend, a comrade, someone they could count on. They asked nothing of him save that he accept them.

He remembered the unspoken plea he had seen in Hadden's eyes that day up at the Parker property. *Old blood,* Hadden had said. Well, perhaps it was, but it was obviously old blood that tried to do something for people, that accepted people regardless of color or idiocy. For Natil and Hadden and all the rest, all people seemed to be their people, and in whatever way they could, they rained compassion and grace upon everyone.

TK wanted to do that, too. It was the hospital and the janitor all over again. And yet, as before, the crushing weight of his impotence bore down on him, forced him to sit down beneath the branches of a tall pine and put his hands to his face. He, too, had tried to help, and all he had accomplished was the destruction of a house and the murder of a bunch of children who had long before forgotten what childhood meant.

What was left? What could he do? Wrapped in the warm cloak, staring at the trees, looking down at the house, he thought about it as Rags prowled and sniffed, as the sun descended slowly and lost itself among the clouds and the western ridges of the mountains.

It was February, and darkness fell early and brought the cold with it. But he had been remembered—he knew that he would be remembered—for the last light of sunset had just trickled out of the sky when he saw a flash of headlights off in the direction of the dirt road. The sound of an engine approaching, shutting off. A car door opening, closing. Silence for a moment, then: "TK?"

It was Natil, but he knew that the others would be coming, too. Coming for him. And he knew then who these people were. White or black, human or non-human, understandable or enigmatic, they were *his* people.

CHAPTER 22

That morning, while TK wondered, wandered, wrestled with himself, Sandy drove out to the hospital.

Natil had not told her everything, and she knew that. But Natil had told her enough. Enough for her to make some sense out of the starlight that appeared to be infusing more and more of her life with a crystalline radiance as sweet as spring water. Enough for her to feel that she had become a chalice of that radiance, pouring it out upon the earth as freely as her Goddess poured out unconditional love. Enough for her to be able to leave behind the horror and fright of the weekend and face Monday with a deep consciousness of the newness of the dawn and the rebirth and renewal it represented.

Old blood. Blood of another race. She pulled into a parking space, acutely conscious of the feel of her body, the look of her hands on the steering wheel, the glitter of the starlight within her. Rising beyond her memories of her father and her obsession (she saw it clearly now, wondered why she had not seen it before) with the fantasies and delusions of Terry Angel, she had, she realized, begun to heal herself. Learning from Natil and playing the music that rose freely and openly from her own heart, she had begun to heal others.

She looked up. The hospital gleamed in the winter sunlight, shades of pale beige and the dark sheen of windows. Healing herself, healing others: she could do both. There were secrets in the world, and they were lovely things indeed.

It had been that way when she had first come to the Craft, when she had first opened a second-hand copy of *The Spiral Dance* and had discovered beliefs that, like flowers in a hidden garden, had already been silently growing within her. Suddenly, the landscapes she had glimpsed in the backgrounds of childhood cartoons had turned from distant and inaccessible figments of celluloid imagination to attainable goals. True, her feet would never take her beneath those hazy forests or run on the even, perfect meadows that, in truth, existed only in pigments applied to transparent cels, but now there was a chance that her mind and imagination, properly nurtured, could take her to the realm of the Goddess, and though she could not actually be held in those divine Arms, she could be conscious of their presence, and could look into the depths of her soul and find there not the scummy residue of Freddy Joy's lusts, but rather the reflected image of the Deity she worshiped.

And now ... now something else had come to her—equally wonderful, equally layered with the plexed enfoldments of increasing joy—but this time it had come not from without, but from within, not from the pages of a book, but from her own interior wellsprings of creation and renewal. It was, in a way, Wicca made real, Wicca refined as though by spiritual alchemy into the essence of itself. The blood that had awakened within her had indeed grown like a flower—sinking down roots, lifting its leaves in starlight, forming buds that filled her with a deep sense of inner transformation and hope—and in comparison, the disciplines and rituals of Wicca seemed external things, mere mechanics, as lovely and yet as artificial as the cartoon lands of her girlhood.

She was a witch. She would never deny that. But she had in these last months become a little more than a witch. She had followed her Goddess along the paths of the Craft and had found herself beckoned down a less-trodden way. She did not look back. She did not want to look back. There was too much ahead, there were too many discoveries to make.

Feeling as though she were wandering through a waking dream, she got out of her car and, carrying her harp, crossed the parking lot, entered the hospital, rode the elevator up to the intensive care unit. Everything looked new today, new and almost luminous.

She closed her eyes. Stars.

The doors opened. She blinked at the nurses' station. Phyllis was witnessing to one of the orderlies:

"We're born dead," she was saying, her voice rising and falling just a little too much. *"Dead."*

Sandy stepped out of the elevator and stood, struck by the intended finality of the word. Dead. But death was a part of life: there could be no life without death. And, in any case, the stars were allowing her to hear the deep, almost erotic relish in the head nurse's voice as she expounded her doctrine.

"Dead," Phyllis repeated. "We have to suffer to live, we have to suffer to be saved. We have to *suffer.* God hurts us only because He loves us." She leaned toward the orderly, her hand clutching her Bible. "He *loves* us. So how can you say you don't want Jesus if you've never accepted him? How can you ever say that you reject God unless you've allowed Him to have His way with you?"

"Uh . . . good morning," said Sandy.

Phyllis looked up, startled. "Oh," she said, "it's you."

Sandy smiled, folded her arms across her harp, almost hugged it. "Good morning," she said again. "Blessings."

When, a moment later, she realized that she had used one of Natil's greetings, she blushed at the impertinence. Natil was ten times the witch that she herself could ever be, and, indeed, if there were any Wicca to be taught, it was most certainly Natil who should be teaching it.

And then she recalled that Candlemas had just passed. One of the holydays of her religion had gone by uncelebrated, the turmoil of the weekend having driven it from her mind. Well, that would be remedied. Tonight. Maybe next Saturday. *With* Natil. No more of this student-teacher foolishness: they would celebrate the season of purification and preparation for spring as two witches together.

Phyllis was staring at her. "Uh . . . yeah . . . good morning."

Sandy gave the nurse a smile. It was easy to smile this morning. "God bless you," she said.

Phyllis turned away, back to the orderly. "Dead," she said, as though she were expressing not a doctrine but a wish.

Heather's room was quiet, and the light that entered through the drawn blinds had a sense of stillness about it. There were flowers on the bedside table, flowers on the tray. Hyacinths. Heather's favorite. Quiet, half light, flowers: Sandy might well have entered a chapel but for the fact that, on the wall beside the bed, monitors traced their lines, displayed their graphs, occasionally hummed and whined as a computer-controlled servo made some adjustment.

Heather herself lay still, pale, her eyes closed, her chest rhythmically rising and falling. No stirring, not even the fluttering of an eyelid was present to say anything but that she was in deepest coma . . . and would likely remain so.

Sandy thought of Audrey, who, a few doors down, quivered and writhed in a state of undeath. Oh, she was gone, that was certain: everyone but her father admitted it. But Audrey's soul was, it seemed, chained to a body that would not yield to death, that sustained its existence by sucking nutriment from tubes of saline and glucose, by passively and periodically allowing its weakening heart to be dragged back to duty by implanted electrodes. Writhing and quivering and clenching her fists only by virtue of a limbic system gone mad, she possessed everything that pertained to life and consciousness save life and consciousness themselves.

And was Heather, sleeping so deeply, so quietly, destined for the same fate? The bullets had punctured her lungs, grazed her heart, and, more tellingly, entered her brain. By all rights, she should have died instantly, and yet something had preserved her. Unlike Audrey, Heather lived.

Sandy pulled up a chair, settled down by the bed, put her harp on her lap. Every day, she came to the hospital. Every day, she played for Heather first, then worked her way from room to room. That her life had been filled by her unpaid duties at the hospital instead of the Hands of Grace program had ceased to trouble her. She had come to Denver to harp for the sick, and it did not matter under what auspices she pursued that goal, for the importance of the work lay in the work itself. For now, she was playing. For now she still had the fellowship from Kingsley that supported her and paid her living expenses so that she could continue to play.

She gave Heather an encouraging smile. "Hi. I'm back."

Heather did not move.

"That's all right," said Sandy. "You just listen. That's

your job right now." She settled her harp, put her hands to the strings. "Natil told me a little about . . . what's been going on. You . . ." Her voice caught. No singing today: the grateful tears were too close to the surface. ". . . you've all been real good to me. Thanks. I'm glad I've got—"

She was going to say something more, to chat for another minute, but she stopped. Was there a radiance about Heather today? Was there a trace of a shimmer, as of starlight, playing across her pale skin?

Fascinated and unnerved both, Sandy leaned closer. She had seen something like this before, in Natil: a luminescence at the edge of sight, as though her skin had been dusted with diamonds. But though, in the past, Sandy had always been able to dismiss that vision as mere imagination, what she was seeing this morning was nothing so subtle. There was a solidity and a substance to it, an appearance of depth and three-dimensionality that Sandy could not explain away.

Who are these people? she wondered, and then she realized not only that she was seeing the light playing on Heather's flesh, but also that she was seeing it with *both eyes.*

She sat back, blinking, feeling cold. The room looked different. Images were sharper, textures clearer, and, moreover, the sense of solidity and substance and depth that she had seen in Heather's light persisted, carrying over to the hospital bed, to the sheets and tables and wire and tubing . . .

Unbelieving, she lifted a hand, covered first one eye, then the other. Though she believed in magic, she had given up believing in miracles a long time ago. And yet what she was discovering this morning seemed a palpable miracle indeed, one that neither evaporated nor dissipated under her increasingly frightened examination.

The sight had returned to her left eye.

"Oh, Goddess." She covered her right eye again. The room remained visible, clear. Heather and the light that surrounded her were—

Forgetting suddenly about her sight, Sandy dropped her hand, scared. Heather's eyes were open, focused, and as Sandy watched, her pale lips struggled, forming words that were hardly more than a trace of movement:

"Sandy ... get ... Natil. Have to ... talk."

Sandy—and the hospital, and the newspapers—called it a miracle, but Natil knew that it was not a miracle. By the transforming virtue of the ancient blood in her veins, Heather was made of such stuff as had survived since the beginning of the world. It would take more than a few bullets to kill her.

But though, despite physical damage, blood loss, and a chunk of lead that Edith Braun and the surgeons of First Friends' had spent eight and a half hours teasing out of her brain, she had regained consciousness, she was still very weak, and what few words she could bring forth entered the world as faint whispers, hardly audible save to those who leaned down to put an ear to her lips. The hospital, acting with prudence, restricted her visiting hours so that she would not tax herself. Even Sandy's harping was curtailed. Marsh and Kelly were the only individuals who had relatively free access to her.

But within a day—in the course of which she seemed to be dragging strength into herself by sheer effort of will—Heather began making her wishes known. Wishes? Demands, rather. She wanted to see Natil, and she wanted to see her alone. Immediately.

Dr. Braun argued, pleaded, implored, but Heather was adamant, and Marsh, sensing that she had reasons, good reasons, reasons that she could not explain, backed his wife. If Heather wanted Natil, then Heather was going to get Natil. He would take her to another hospital if First Friends' did not let her have her way.

Natil, with a vague sense of unease, remained very carefully neutral throughout these negotiations. For some time now, she had been possessed by the distinct (and, for an Elf, embarrassing) feeling that the world had changed, changed profoundly ... without her noticing. Sandy's blood had awakened. Lauri and Kelly had seen signs of the Lady. And now, Heather ...

She rode the elevator up to the intensive care unit on Thursday night, wondering why Heather wanted to see her so badly, suspecting that she knew. Yes, the world had changed, and Natil, who had been trying very hard to make it change for the last three years, had been caught off guard. Fully expecting to be caught off guard again tonight, she devoutly hoped that she would not be asked to make any sense of it.

Dr. Braun had arranged everything. Natil simply left the elevator, walked past the nurses' station, and went to Heather's room. No one stopped her, no one asked any questions. Natil noticed, though, that Braun was at the nurses' station, and though the physician did not look up, Natil saw the worried look on her face and knew that she was not seeing anything of the charts she appeared to be examining so earnestly.

Natil took hold of the pull of Heather's door, swung it open, entered. The hinges were silent, the pneumatic closer only hissed softly as it shut out the sounds of the corridor.

Heather had raised the head of her bed, but her eyes were closed, and she did not immediately acknowledge Natil's appearance. But though she appeared to be sleeping, she had in reality not slept since she had come out of her six-week coma. She would lie still, to be sure, and her eyes would at times be closed, but she did not sleep. Rather, she wandered among the stars like any Elf, drawing comfort and strength from their ineffable light as though she bathed in vivifying water.

Her face was pale. She had been an attractive woman, and the blood had refined her features and added an elfin slenderness to her physique. Even with a boyish two inches of hair—all that had been able to grow since her head had been shaved for surgery—she looked exquisite, a visitor from a delicate realm of leaf and starlight.

Natil watched her for a minute. This was all the elvenhood that the world would ever know now. This was a lass of the Secondborn, one in whom the blood once spread throughout humanity by the long ago love of Elf and mortal had reawakened. If anything of elven healing had managed to endure and hold true throughout the ages of loss, persecution, and fading, then surely this commingling of two races was its sole manifestation.

She remembered the Lady's words to Varden: *Not one of My Children shall be separated from me.*

Was this the hope, then? Was the blood so widespread that, eventually, all would change? It was not a question of the triumph of one race over another, it was, rather, a matter of life and growth, of humans finding, in elvishness, the roots of existence that stretched back to the foundations of the planet; of Elves, through a complete sharing of human condition, status, and struggle, relearning the limitless compassion that had once been theirs.

Not one . . .

"Not one," she murmured. "I am the Mother of all things, and My love is poured out upon the earth." It was a witch expression: human, but nonetheless perfectly in keeping with what the Elves had once known.

Natil passed a hand over her face. Had once known. But no more. And if it were not known again—soon—then the gift that the Elves had made of their own heritage and their own blood would turn awry like everything else, and all the hope would be stillborn.

"The hand of the Lady be upon you, Natil."

"Blessings," she replied without thinking. And then she stared, for it was Heather who had spoken. Heather, who did not know the Lady.

But was this really Heather? She looked like Heather, to be sure, and the slight tip of her head to one side as she smiled at Natil was a gesture that had certainly been characteristic of Heather. But there was something in her expression that was new: a simultaneous passion, dispassion, and inexpressible joy that reached far back beyond her human birth, back to the time when the Lady had, with Her own hand, shaped the Immortals who would call this planet home.

Natil might well have been looking into the face of one who, with her, had taken hands beneath the lowering sky of a world that was almost too new to know anything of solidity, who, with her, had looked ahead to a life of mixed healing, hope, sorrow, and endings. Who knew of no other possible termination to her existence than murder or fading. Who knew her Creatrix face to face.

And Natil realized that Heather did indeed know her Creatrix. Face to face.

"Come," said Heather. Her voice was soft, with a lingering weakness to it that sharpened its urgency and need. "Come sit down, Natil. You can't just stand at the door like a servant."

It had been a long time since Natil had spoken with one

of her own kind who knew both her origins and her future. "We are all servants," she managed.

"That's true," said Heather with a smile. "And so we're equals. Come sit down."

Feeling unaccountably as though she were holding a pistol to her head, Natil brought a chair to the side of the bed and sat. Heather offered her hand. Natil took it. Together, then, for several minutes, they remained in silence, Heather apparently enjoying the simple comfort that came from the touch of another immortal hand, Natil with conflicting emotions that ranged from joy to apprehension.

"I've seen Her," said Heather at last. She was husbanding her strength, pitching her voice just loud enough to carry, no more. "We talked. She helped me to heal, and then She sent me back." Another smile, broader. "Just like She sent you forward, Natil."

"You know, then."

"I know." A barely perceptible squeeze of Natil's hand. "Oh, Natil." Heather's blue eyes turned sad. "It's been so terrible for you. We just rattled on with our complaints and our whining, and you never told us anything."

"I could not."

"I understand . . . now . . ." Heather sighed, shifted. She was still hooked up to an IV, and for a moment she looked at it as though wondering how anything so clumsy and human had come to be in the veins of a Firstborn. But she made a small movement with her shoulders that Natil understood to be a weak shrug. "And I was such a . . ." Her weakness was telling on her already, but she tried to laugh it away. ". . . nice Catholic girl."

"Does it pain you greatly to have lost that?"

Heather shook her head. "I was lost. Completely lost. Even before I was shot I was lost. But after . . ." Her eyes closed as though in pain, and her voice turned even more distant. "I was wandering around . . . I don't know where. A long time. And I called to God for help, and I got nothing. And then I called . . . to things that mattered . . . to anyone who might care about me. And then She came, and She . . ." Words seemed to fail her for a moment, then: "She helped me . . . just like a friend." A slow shake of her close-cropped head. "You know, I'd wondered for a long time about who took care of Elves."

"Everyone has wondered." Natil's eyes were aching. A serene face. And dark hair. Robes of blue and silver. Strange how fleeting and insubstantial memories could be: she could, seemingly, hang on to no more than these. "And the lack of an answer has driven some close to despair." She had to fight with her words for a moment, for they insisted on rising as sobs. Close to despair. Closer than she had realized. "Can you go to Her?"

Heather shook her head. "She said that it isn't time yet."

Not time? It had to be time. If it were not time now, then when would it be time? "Did She say what I can do to bridge the abyss between Her and Her Children?"

Again, Heather shook her head. "She is the Dance. She doesn't create it. We do."

"I know," said Natil softly, but the hollowness had taken hold of her heart again, and she wept, her face in her hands. The stars within her burned clear and cold, but they seemed distant, terribly distant, for there was none among them that would call her, take her in, bring her to the arms of the Lady.

Heather shoved herself up, reached out to Natil, embraced her as best she could with the tubes and the monitor wires in the way. "It's not time yet," she whispered. "That's what She said. And, yes, it hurt to hear it; but I'll tell you, Natil, I believe Her, and even if I don't see Her again for a long time, just seeing Her that once is going to get me through a lot of awfulness." Her eyes were open, staring off as though she were even then reliving the vision. "And knowing that She's there, waiting . . ."

The bedside telephone rang. Heather gave a quiet giggle, released Natil, picked up the handset. "Yes, Dr. Braun." She met Natil's eyes, smiled. "Yes, I know my heart rate is up. I'll calm down. Thanks. No, it's not Natil's fault. Just let us talk, please."

She hung up, laughed weakly. "I'm setting off alarms."

"I am not surprised," said Natil. "Be at peace."

Heather shook her head. "I'm very much at peace, Natil. Please: try to take your own advice. Be patient."

"I do not know what to do, Heather."

"Keep on with what you're doing, then. It seems to be working. But remember this: I'm here, and maybe just that makes a difference. I mean ... there are two of us now. Maybe that'll help."

"Does Marsh know?"

"He's ..." Heather considered. She had paled a little: she was not anywhere near well as of yet, and the conversation was draining her. "He's guessed that something's going on. I wonder sometimes whether they haven't all guessed."

Natil recalled Ash's queries, Lauri's pointed questions. At least two suspected something. But why, she suddenly wondered, had she kept her mission so secret? Had there been a point to it all? Should she have just blurted out the whole story? Should she at least have given them a little *hope*?

But Heather was shaking her head. "I hear your thoughts a little, Natil. Be at peace yourself. You did the best you could, and I sure can't think of how I'd have done anything better. You can't talk about Her. You can't preach about Her. You can't explain. You simply have to see ... like a little kid. You just have to see." She shrugged. "Then it's all ... clear."

She had exhausted herself, and she was trembling. Natil caught her as she suddenly wavered, eased her back onto the pillows. Heather felt light, almost weightless. Natil thought of Little Sandy and smiled. "You are like a doll, Heather."

Heather mustered a faint, pale smile. "I'll get better."

"You will indeed."

"How ... is TK?"

Natil wondered whether Heather had heard about the crack house, decided to be circumspect. "He is still blaming himself."

Heather closed her eyes. "He shouldn't feel that way. Whatever happens, happens because that's the way it should happen." She pried an eye open, seemed unable to focus. "You've said that a hundred times, Natil. I finally understand it."

Natil kissed her brow. Heather had seen. Heather had confidence. Natil, though, had not seen for a long time. It was hard to have confidence when one had not seen for a long time. How terrible, then, to be human, and never see at all! "Rest, Heather."

"Yes ..." said Heather, drifting away into starlight. "Yes, I'll ... I'll rest."

———————

4 February 1992

Serena Kathryn Joy
5023 North Deborah Boulevard
Denver, Colorado 80221

Dear Ms. Joy:

I regret to inform you that the Hands of Grace program has been terminated. Any inquiries that you may have regarding its continuance at any other institution should be addressed directly to Mr. Terry Angel.

Your fellowship is herewith canceled. Your accumulated credits are of course applicable to other degree programs, but you will have to be accepted for a new major by the appropriate departmental head should you wish to pursue academic work at Kingsley College. Financial aid is available to qualified students through the Student Affairs office.

Sincerely yours,

David L. Dickens
Curriculum Committee

———————

CHAPTER 23

He could not stay at Elvenhome. He had to face reality eventually.

Natil, departing from her customary ecological behavior, had given TK rides to work all week in her battered old van, dropping him off at TreeStar and then continuing on to her duties at Kingsley, returning in the dusk of the early February evenings to pick him up and return him to the shelter of the mountain retreat. There he had slept, eaten, wandered with his crutches and his dog; and in the crystalline distance of those cold nights, he had heard Natil singing, had heard Sandy accompanying her, their melodies as fluid as Coltrane's, as perfectly fitted to the mountains as the unquestionably sylvan presence of Elvenhome itself.

But he had to go home again. Elvenhome was a retreat, a refuge, but it was not a permanent abode, even for the others, for their lives were in the city, among the very people who would without a doubt reject them if the truth of their existence were ever discovered. They lived in the city, they worked in the city, they helped and healed as best they could in the city.

Lauri drove him home after work Friday evening. Rags was curled up in his lap, dozing, but TK himself was looking out the window at the passing city as the freeway took them along through the far flung, landscaped suburbs of wealthy white people, then into stands of industry—warehouses, trucking depots, small struggling businesses that could not even afford signs to tell passers-by what they were—and finally among the older houses and ghetto neighborhoods that lay in the shadows of the chrome and glass towers of downtown.

He had spent all his life in cities, from the projects of Chicago to the poor neighborhoods of a score of American urban centers, but it was only now that he was discovering the terrible artifice that lay behind the buildings—the impotent defiance of nature, the determined ignorance of natural process—and it was a discovery that brought to him not only a sudden longing for the mountains and the forests that he could not have, but also the realization that an unbridgeable gulf of alienation had opened of a sudden between himself and these metropolitan hives. In returning to the city, then, TK found himself in exile, in diaspora, a captive of the necessity of the calling that had taken up residence in his blood had, perhaps *become* his blood. He was here to help. He was here to heal. He was here to do something, whether it bore fruit in his lifetime or not, whether it lay as pathetically unfinished at his death as it had at his birth.

It was quite dark by the time Lauri pulled up in front of his apartment house and helped him carry his things up the stairs. When TK, bracing himself on his crutches, fumbled the door open, Rags took one look at the shabby rooms and growled softly, but Lauri regarded everything with that curious sense of personal failure that so often manifested in her people. If this was where TK lived—run-down apartments, crack houses up the block, shakedowns on the corner—then it was simply yet another thing for which she was responsible, that she had to strive to change.

And so it was with TK. All that lay ahead of him now was striving. Success might be variable, strength might be variable, but the striving would remain the same.

"You going to be all right, big guy?" With characteristic concern, Lauri, butch but starlit, was looking through cupboards. His groceries, though, were depleted. In the last week before he had attacked the crack house, he had been too single-mindedly bent upon destruction to worry about such things as food. "You want me to run you over to the store?"

TK had settled himself on his bed and laid his crutches aside. Rags jumped up and settled onto his lap as though he owned it: the change in the dog's personality appeared to have become permanent. "I be OK, Lauri. I get me some stuff tomorrow. The store's on the way back from the bus stop."

"Yeah ... well ..." Lauri shoved her hands into the

pockets of her jacket, looked at him, shrugged. He saw it in her eyes: claimed. Claimed and jumped in. "I don't want to just abandon you."

TK leaned back on his elbows. Rags snuffled, curled up, and closed his eyes. "So what else should I be expecting, Lauri? What else's going to be happening?"

"Huh?"

"You say you don't want to be abandoning me. Well, so tell me what's coming. I been seeing stars. What's next?"

He had apparently caught her off guard: for a moment, she almost looked as though she wanted to flee. But the starlight set in then, and her troubled eyes regained their clarity. "It's . . ." she shoved her hands a little deeper into her pockets. Clarity or not, she obviously did not know what to say. "It's hard, TK . . ."

"You don't think I know that? Where you been all this time, girl?"

Lauri gave him a thin smile. TK recalled that she was gay, that she had experienced her own share of prejudice, lived in her own kind of projects. "I'll tell you this, guy: it's hard, and it's getting harder. But it's worth it."

"So what do I do?"

Her smile turned thinner. "What did that dude down in Texas say? Lie back and enjoy it?"

"You shittin' me."

"That's about all you can do. And grow your hair out a little. Or buy some of those knit watchman's caps."

It was TK's turn to be caught off guard. He shoved himself upright. "What?"

Lauri's dark eyes were pained and humorous both. "Hey, you asked me. So I'm telling you. Sure I can't do anything else for you?"

"Uh . . . nah," said TK, wondering what the hell she meant. Watchman's caps? He remembered with a sense of unease that most of the men of Elvenhome either wore their hair long—long enough, at least, to cover the tops of their ears—or else covered their heads with, yes, those knit watchman's caps.

Crazy. What did they have under there, anyway? Antennas? And what did all that have to do with him?

"I be OK," he said, wondering whether he actually believed himself.

"Okay," said Lauri. "See you on Monday."

"Yeah."

She left. He did not hear her retreating footfalls even on the perennially squeaky stairway.

For a few minutes, he thought about her words, considered the distance that had grown up between himself and this place. He was not the same. The apartment was not the same. Everything had changed. Even the M16 and the K-Bar were missing from their usual places, as though the part of his life that they represented—memories and violence both—had been left behind, amputated like a leg.

He clenched his eyes, shook his head. It had not even been a week.

"C'mon, Rags," he said suddenly. "Let's go see if you need to take a leak."

Rags did not use a leash, did not, in fact, tolerate a leash. TK simply step-thumped out into the corridor, and the little terrier followed him, waited while he closed and locked the door, and descended the stairs with him, running ahead and pausing on the landings while his master crutched his way down.

The night was cold, polluted. TK paused, zipped his jacket up to his throat. It was dark on the street— streetlights were a favorite for target practice—and the shadows were thick. They were thicker, though, just up the block, where the heaped remains of a house lay quarantined by yellow tape and signs that forbade entry save on police business. TK paused in front of them. There they were: shadowed ruins in the middle of a city.

But it was not just the house. It was not just the neighborhood. It was, he thought, the city itself: the city with its delusions of culture and civilization, the city that had nothing into which to put its roots save an animal lust for survival and the predilection of sentient monkeys for acquisition and power. If there had been nothing gentle in that house, there had, in fact, been nothing gentle in the city. There had been nothing gentle in the world.

He wondered whether all the dead had been found and buried.

"Hey, TK."

He stiffened, half expecting a shot. But it was one of his old neighbors.

TK almost smiled. He still lived here, would still, for

some time to come, spend his nights within the walls of
his little apartment. But this place would always be his
old neighborhood. This man approaching him, stocky and
hatted, with children in school who were no older than
the children that he had killed, would always be one of
his *old* neighbors. He had, it seemed, fallen in with out-
siders, and even as he greeted his acquaintance, he felt
the distance growing.

"Haven't seen you in a while, TK."

"I been . . . away."

"You miss the excitement?"

"This place?" TK kept his voice neutral. Had it been,
after all, someone else who had killed children and then
gutted their home? "Read about it," he said, the equivocation rank upon his lips.

"Cops've been all over the place this last week." The
man lit a cigarette, offered the pack to TK. TK declined.
"Whoever did it did a good job. Must've been a whole
gang."

"That what they saying?"

The man leaned on one of the sawhorses that held the
barrier tapes. "You know how it goes, TK. It's the usual.
Drug deal gone and went bad. Everybody shot up everybody else. But the whole set's gone now. The crack heads
went somewhere else. The neighborhood's safe."

TK stared into the night, into the ruins, into the past.
"They asking questions?"

"Who?"

"Cops." *Had* it been someone else?

" 'Bout what?"

" 'Bout who did it."

A dark smile. "You know how *that* goes, too, TK. They
don't tell us nothin', we don't tell them nothin'."

"Yeah. That's about the size of it, ain't it?"

The neighbor mused for a while. In the darkness of the
ruined house, something rustled, quieted. A rat, maybe.
Maybe just plaster settling. "You know, a lot of us on the
street think that it must'a been God's justice."

TK winced. How easily God came into it. Everything
from dropping bombs on air-raid shelters and bulldozing
men into premature burial to bullet-riddled fourteen-year-
olds.

"After all," the neighbor continued, "Sarah's little girl

got it back in June. Lot of people been prayin' for somethin' like this to happen."

TK nodded noncommittally.

"But, hey, it's done with."

"Yeah." Still noncommittally.

"But . . ." The neighbor drew on the cigarette until the cherry was a bright flare of distress. " . . . funny thing, though. They found a chunk o' artificial leg in the street afterwards."

TK's face did not change expression. He did not allow it to change expression. "How 'bout that."

"Yeah. How 'bout that." The neighbor inhaled again, exhaled through his nose. The smoke wreathed him for a moment as though he were a dark Buddha. "Personally, I think someone did us a favor." He dropped the cigarette, ground it out on the pavement. "A big favor."

TK looked down at his crutches. "Personally," he said, "I don't think it's any favor at all when someone gets killed."

They said good night, then—amiably—and the neighbor went one way, TK another. Rags, who had vanished with a snarl at the approach of a stranger, returned at a snap of his master's fingers.

Leaning heavily on his crutches, TK bent down and scratched the tiny head. It was a small, almost inconsequential gesture, but he guessed that if he wanted to help and heal tonight, it was about all that he could do.

Sandy was changing. Natil did not know whether she had noticed it herself, but in the half light of her candlelit apartment, wreathed in the smoke of incense that rose from the burner at the east point of the circle of small stones she had arranged in the middle of her living room, naked save for a necklace about her throat and a cord about her waist, Sandy was a sleek presence, her flesh glowing with the lambent sheen of immortality, her face, its scars fading as her blindness had already faded, beginning to take on the flashing beauty of the Elves.

Candlemas. Past Candlemas, actually, for the actual day, uncelebrated because of Sandy's distress and TK's violence, had come and gone a week ago. But Sandy was a witch, and Natil, as far as Sandy was concerned, was a witch, too, and so this feast of the first noticeable lengthening of daylight after the long darkness of the Winter Solstice, of the purification that went hand in hand with a preparation for the coming spring, had to be kept, even if it were kept a little late.

Sandy was casting Circle. In the old days, there had been groves, great rings of standing stones, grottoes and caves that had possessed a peculiar combination of beauty and grandeur. But the groves were gone, cut down out of Christian prejudice or a need for cardboard boxes, the standing stones were mere curiosities, the grottoes and caves were sources of tourist revenue. Now, those who followed the Old Ways had for a place of worship only a formally inscribed and consecrated Circle. But that was enough. The whole point of Wicca was to see what often went unseen, to reverence that which was usually taken for granted, to manifest in daily life the divinity that custom ignored.

And therefore, to Sandy who cast the Circle and to Natil who watched, the delineation of the sacred space and its subsequent consecration—acts of will, acts of reified imagination—were as real as if they had, together, erected monoliths, planted trees, hewn caverns out of living rock. Here, as ephemeral as starlight, as immediate as the ponderous processes of the natural world, was the place of the witches, the temple of the Goddess.

Moving gracefully (Did she notice, did she feel the alteration in her steps, see the slenderness of her hands as they grasped the ritual knife, of her arms as they lifted in invocation?), Sandy traced the boundary of the Circle, purified it with incense and salt and water, stood at each cardinal point and asked for the presence, help, and protection of the elemental powers of Earth, Air, Fire, and Water. And in her mind, Natil saw the Circle take shape, glowing softly, the pentagrams that Sandy had traced in unison with her invocations gleaming. It was real. Sandy had made it so.

And it was because of that ability to make the inert substance of reality bend to the force of imagination that Natil had turned to Sandy for aid, for teaching. The Circle was real. The Goddess, she knew, was real, too.

Goddess? Sandy herself was the Goddess now, standing, slender and shining, among the candles and the smoke, and at her nod, Natil rose, her hair, unbound, cascading over her bare skin, falling to her waist as she stepped to the threshold of the holy place.

"Welcome, Natil," said the witch. "People usually have to go through initiation to get this far, but . . ." She smiled softly, and Natil saw the starlight growing within her. " . . . like I said: you're already here."

Already? And not even a glimpse of *Elthia*? Natil took Sandy's hands. "Are you certain, Sandy?"

"Oh, I'm certain." Sandy stood aside, gestured into the candlelit Circle. "Come in. Be welcome. You'll always be welcome in my Circles."

Natil, who had known Roxanne and Charity, knew the passwords. She spoke them even though Sandy had not asked. "Perfect love and perfect trust."

Sandy's smile broadened. "See? I told you."

Neither Natil nor Sandy were inclined toward elaborate rituals. Indeed, the closeness and trust that came from their being in Circle together was, in many ways, the rite itself. While some might have processed with water and candles, or made a show with elaborate costumes and speeches, here, in Sandy's small apartment, Elf and witch simply embraced, kissed, sprinkled one another with salt water, anointed one another with oil, shared a chalice of wine. The love that existed between them was their purification; the filled cup their promise of the future.

But Natil, staring down into the darkness of the chalice, could not but think of the future, could not but wonder about its promise. *Elthia* had appeared . . . to others. But the Elves of Colorado were still, with but two exceptions, ignorant of Her. Heather had seen and understood. Kelly had seen, wondered . . . and instinctively loved. Natil had not seen at all.

"My Mother made me," she murmured, "and I am She."

Sandy was watching her. "That's a nice way of putting it, Natil."

The Elf nodded, but her smile was thin and pained. "It is true."

"Sometimes . . ." Sandy looked at the ritual knife that lay on the flat stone she used for an altar, at the incense burner that was still sputtering faintly with the resins she had spooned into it. " . . . sometimes it's hard to remember that when you're out in the world. Sometimes you have to be in Circle to really feel it. But ... " She held up a hand, examined it. It was, like the rest of her, shimmering faintly. " ... I'm feeling it a lot better these days, I think."

"You see, then," said Natil.

"Yeah. I've been seeing for a while." Sandy covered first one eye, then the other. "In stereo. It's ..." Her voice almost choked. " ... incredible."

"The blood is healing."

"Yeah ..."

Natil fingered the chalice. There was one swallow left. "I noticed ... that you did not invoke the Goddess tonight."

"I don't always invoke Her," said Sandy. She shrugged, her face unlined, relaxed. She felt safe here. In Circle, with a trusted friend, she was as she could be, as she should have been all along. "Sometimes it just doesn't seem like it's really necessary. Just being in Circle ... it's like ... well ... She's here. I can feel Her. I haven't got any doubts about it."

And Natil nodded, though she had not felt what Sandy was describing for a long time. "She is really present for you, then."

"Yeah. Like, if I knew how to look, I could really see Her." Sandy was smiling, and it was not just the starlight. "Don't you feel it?"

Natil considered lying, but: "I do not," she said after a time.

Sandy looked concerned, embarrassed, a little shocked. "Oh, Natil, I'm sorry. I didn't realize ..."

"As I said, I have ... deficiencies." Natil tried to take the edge off the admission with a shrug. "I need ... to learn how to invoke Her. I need to learn how to make Her real. It is essential that I learn. I cannot tell you how essential."

But Sandy, though still concerned, was nodding. "You're trying too hard, Natil."

"I ...?"

"Way too hard." Sandy gestured at the floor, made Natil sit. "Relax. You're coming at it like you're trying to climb a mountain. You've just got to relax. You say the Goddess is your Mother. Well, be her kid. Kids don't have to try to have a mother. She's just there for them."

And if there was a trace of a haunted, hollow look about Sandy's eyes—a look that told of a mother who, by court order, had not been there for her—it was as nothing to the emptiness that Natil felt.

The Elf bent her head. She felt old. Incomparably old. Four and a half billion years old. It was hard to think of oneself as a child when one was so old. But Sandy was only repeating what Heather had already said. *You simply have to see . . . like a little kid.* It was true. Perfectly true. But infinitely hard to accomplish.

"When I was a kid," Sandy was saying, "I saw Her in cartoons. She was, like, the soft stuff behind the action. People would be beating one another up in the foreground, but back there, there would be trees and flowers and . . . and . . ." She closed her eyes, sighed. "Now it's like all those things are inside me. These stars . . ."

Natil nodded. The chalice was still in her hand. She looked again into its dark cup. One swallow left. A real witch would have made that last mouthful of wine a symbol, would have first infused it with a personal desire for future success, and then, ceremonially, drained it. Natil had, in fact, already participated in that symbolism, for that was the meaning of Candlemas. And yet, she could have done more, could have made that last swallow of wine . . . everything.

She lifted the chalice. She could have done many things. She could have faded. She could have vigilantly avoided the despair that had claimed her in the summer of 1500. She could have held tighter to the vision of Elthia, not allowing it, even for an instant, to slip away. Maybes. Might-have-beens. She wished that Mirya were still with her: she had some questions to ask her about maybes and about might-have-beens.

Sandy sighed again. "What do the stars mean, Natil?"

Natil paused with the chalice suspended before her face.

"They're . . . doing something to me, aren't they?"

"They are. You know that. I told you."

"They're going to do more, aren't they?"

"They are."

Sandy licked her lips as though they had suddenly turned dry. "I'm a little scared, Natil. I've always just been me, for better or worse."

Natil examined her as, she fancied, Terrill had once examined a young woman named Miriam who was trying to accustom herself to a new body and a new face. Sandy was getting something of both, and, like Terrill, Natil was now faced with the question of how to reveal the true meaning and depth of a transformation that had, in many ways, already taken place. "It is for the better, Sana."

"I know." Sandy smiled through her fear. "I like that name. I really do. It feels like me. I wish that everyone would call me that."

"No more Sandy? No more Serena?"

"No. Just Sana." Sandy blushed. "I'm being idiotic, I know."

"Not at all." Natil leaned forward, put an arm about Sandy's neck, and kissed her. "I name you Sana. May it be so in all the worlds, for all time, in accordance with your own free will and choice."

Sana caught her breath, stared as though she had been struck. "Dear Goddess . . . that . . ."

"Sana?"

" . . . really makes a . . . difference . . ." She sat back, rubbed at her eyes. "Damn. If you've got deficiencies, Natil, I'm scared to think of what you'd be like without them."

"It was time for you." Natil eyed the last of the wine, shrugged, swallowed it with a simple prayer. Was it a child's prayer? Maybe. She hoped so. "Whatever happens, happens as it should."

Sana still looked a little dazed. "Yeah. Jeez . . ."

"Let us break Circle, then. It has been a difficult week. You should think about going to bed."

"I'm kind of tired, I guess," Sana admitted. "But, you know, I haven't been sleeping as long as I used to. I keep waking up earlier and earlier."

Natil was nodding. Yet more changes. "Perhaps you simply need less sleep."

"Yeah . . . maybe . . ."

In another minute or two, Sana had regained her composure enough to rise, take up her knife, and dismantle the Circle. Grounding the mental energies she had raised, dismissing the powers she had invoked, she was soon standing once again in a living room that was no more than a living room.

And then the telephone rang.

Sana gasped, whirled on it as though it were a serpent. Hesitantly, almost unwillingly, she went into the kitchen to answer it, and Natil saw that her hand was shaking as she picked up the handset. "Hello?" She stood for a few moments, then hung up. She was now shaking all over, and she sagged into a kitchen chair.

Natil was bewildered by the magnitude of her reaction to a wrong number. "Who was it?"

"No one. At least ... well ... I pick it up, and there's no one there. I mean, no one answers. It's been like that all week."

It had not been a wrong number, then. "This has been happening ..."

Sana was pale, sweating. Her hands were covering her face, "Since Tuesday."

Natil rubbed Sana's shoulders until they loosened, then got her a glass of water. "Sit back. Drink. Breathe. Breathe the starlight."

Sana nodded, shut her eyes, sucked in air as though it were indeed light, let it out slowly. She drank a little water, and the liquid took some of the tightness from her voice. "It's ... it's Terry," she said. "He never says anything, but I know it's him. I just know."

Natil glanced at the telephone. "But why would he be doing such a thing?"

"I dunno ... I just ... I just know it's him. And it keeps happening."

"What does he want?"

Sana, fresh out of the warmth and trust of the Circle, had been badly shaken. "I don't know."

The telephone rang again. Biting back a surge of anger, Natil grabbed it. "What is it that you want?" she said into the handset, and both elven accent and elven starlight were clear and cold in her voice.

"Whoa!" came Lauri's voice. "Who pissed in your Wheaties, Natil?"

Natil gasped, blushed. "Ah ... my apologies, Lauri. We have been receiving some harassing calls here."

"Well, I hope you get the bastard that's doing it next time, 'cause you sure scared the hell out of me. Talk about a deep freeze! I'll have to see if I've got an ear left."

"I am sorry."

"That's OK. Hey, is Sandy there?"

Natil smiled in spite of her embarrassment. "Sana is here."

"Sana?"

"She used to be Sandy."

Lauri understood. "Oh, gosh, we'll all have to get used to it now, but it was coming, wasn't it? How's she taking it? Does she know? I mean ... everything?"

Natil looked at Sana. It was indeed coming. Soon Sana would be asking even more questions. "She is well. Not ... quite everything."

"Okay. Well, let me talk to Sana."

Natil handed the phone to Sana, who listened for a few minutes, nodded, said yes several times, and hung up as though dazed for the second time that night. "I guess I don't have to worry about what to do about the fellowship money being withdrawn," she said, shaking her head. "Hadden's offered me a job at TreeStar. Bright just got her certification, and she's going into the field on Monday. They need a receptionist at the office. They want me. Hadden is even springing for front office clothes."

Everything that happens ... Natil smiled. "You are loved, Sana."

Sana was staring. "Yeah," she said. "It's so weird. It's never been like this before."

But she looked up, and her eye apparently fell on the telephone again, for she turned away quickly, much like a child who had seen something unpleasant, something frightening, something that had reminded her too much of how it had been before.

February 10, 1992

Dear Dr. Jerusalem:

First off, I want to congratulate you all on a splendid job of closing the book on a potentially very embarrassing situation for Kingsley College. As you all know, we're planning to upgrade our status to that of university later this year, and an academic scandal of this sort couldn't do anything but hurt the future vision thing.

That said, I need to make a few things perfectly clear.

1) The parts of the general budget freed up by the end of HOG are certainly not going to be reallocated this late in the fiscal year, and they certainly won't accrue to the budgets of your departments. I'll admit that there is talk among the trustees of a fund for refurbishing Aylesberg, my office included, but this is only talk. Repeat: talk.

2) The trustees are unaware of the magnitude of the charade that Mr. Angel and his "student" have pulled off. They will not be made aware. I trust I am understood.

3) The reputation of this school as an elite, private college (soon to be university) is a delicate thing. I'm sure you all know this. Therefore, I would *strongly suggest* that all further discussion of Terry Angel, Serena Joy, or HOG be curtailed.

4) Just a reminder. While I don't expect anything to change all that much, there are potential shakeups involved in the university upgrade thing. You all have nothing to worry about, of course.

Very sincerely yours,

Ronald M. Wickey
Chancellor

cc: Dr. Rick Harris, Dr. David Dickens

CHAPTER 24

"Yes, sir," said Sana Joy. "Mr. Winters is in. May I tell him who's calling, please?"

Three weeks into her job at TreeStar, and she was finally beginning to relax. The delay, though, had been her own doing, for no one at the surveying offices had ever given her reason to feel anything but perfectly comfortable, accepted, safe. Even her occasional bunglings with an unfamiliar computer and a word processing program that at times bore an uncanny resemblance to a data-encryption utility were met not with irritation, but rather with genial assistance.

The assistance, in fact, had started even before she had taken up her new duties, for Hadden had followed through on his promise about the front-office clothing, and Allesandro, who ran a beauty salon when he was not planting trees, had sat her down in his chair, looked intently into her face with dark, starlit eyes, and then had recut her hair into a simple but elegant coif that she had never thought possible for her lank and mousy locks.

"Oh, Goddess," she had said, touching it gingerly. "What did you do to me?"

"What did I do? What did I do, she asks?" Allesandro gave her a mock frown. "I gave you a decent haircut. The first decent haircut you've ever had, unless I miss my guess."

Sana stared at the stranger in the mirror. Her jaw had lightened, turned almost delicate, there was some kind of alteration to her cheekbones, and there was an openness about her eyes that seemed to make the starlight—yes, it was starlight, she knew it was starlight—all the brighter.

"And that's *your* color, and *your* texture," said Allesandro. "Wash it, comb it back, and give it a shake when it's dry. Scrunch it if you want to be entirely devastating, but I warn you: you'll have to beat the men off with a stick."

"But . . . how . . ."

Allesandro turned her chair around so that she was facing him. "I only cut hair, Sana," he said gently. "Everything else you see is you. Cutting your hair just let you see it."

"But . . . this isn't me!"

"It certainly is." Allesandro wiped styling gel from his hands. "That's the way it is with a lot of women. They get so used to looking at themselves—and usually not liking what they see—that they stop seeing what's there until something happens to make them look again. I cut your hair and made you finally take another look." He shrugged. "You're just beautiful, Sana. That's all."

"But I can't be!" Lighter, more delicate . . . and yet undeniably her. "I mean . . . I never was before!"

He plunked his comb into a jar or sanitizer. "So I'm supposed to waste my time on potatoes? Hasn't Natil told you anything?"

"Uh . . ." There was a quaver in her voice, and she thought back to Candlemas. Natil had, in fact, told her a great deal. But not everything. And Sana knew well that she herself had deliberately held off from grasping all the implications of what was happening. "About what?"

He harrumphed. "She didn't tell you. Of *course* she didn't tell you. She's too cautious. I've been trying to get her to cut that mop of hers for three years, and she won't do it. Looks like an old hippie. An absolutely gorgeous lass who has all the style of a carp. Doesn't wear makeup. Doesn't wear heels. Frets and stews about everything she does. Too cautious." He sighed. "Oh, well. So *I'll* tell you. You're one of us, Sana. You're changing. The old blood changes you."

Sana looked again into the mirror, noticed now that the scars on her jaw were fainter.

"But you knew that already, didn't you?"

"I . . . I guess so . . . yeah . . ." she admitted, staring—with two good eyes—at the fading scars. Changing. "But I never expected . . ."

"A pretty face and good hair," he said, running a hand appreciatively through his work. "Two of the perks you get." But when he smiled at her, it was with a hint of sadness. "I suppose it makes up for some things." He took her hand, then, brought her up out of the chair. "Go now. Go and have some fun. Try not to break too many hearts."

And Sana, acutely aware of the unfamiliarity of her appearance, but nonetheless certain both of the reality of it and of its inherent rightness, had left the salon immersed in a kind of waking dream, not even noticing that Allesandro (who *had* scrunched her hair) was absolutely right about being devastating.

And the dream had continued. TreeStar was, in many ways, just a deeper layer. This morning, though, something was happening that jarred, that was at odds with the sanctity of the office. The caller was polite, but Sana caught the hard edge of authority in his tone. "I need to speak to Mr. Winters," he said. "Now."

And she heard the accents of her father. *You come here, now. You spread your legs, now. You open your mouth, now.* But where before she would have wilted and hastened to do as she had been told, now she felt an upwelling of strength that her inner starlight channeled into her voice.

"I understand that, sir," she said. "If you'll please tell me who you are, I'll put you through directly."

Silence.

Sana cleared her throat. "Please," she said, and her tone turned what would normally have been a request into an unequivocal demand.

"This is Lieutenant Brown of the Denver Police," came the reluctant response.

She was a little shaken. A police officer? She had used that tone of voice with a *police officer*? But her fear, she realized, lay in her memories of her father, and so she shook it off. "One moment, Lieutenant."

She put him on hold, punched in TK's extension. "TK, Lieutenant Brown from the Denver Police on line one."

A long pause. She heard TK sigh. "Well, I guess this was coming," he said. "Okay. Thanks."

Sana set down the receiver, saw the light on line one turn from flashing to steady. The office was quiet—there was no one in it at present save herself and TK—and she heard, faintly, the dark murmur of his voice.

She tried to go back to the report that she was typing,

but she could not keep her mind on it, for she knew what the call meant. Although it had become apparent that the police were not looking very hard for the person or persons responsible for the demolition of the crack house, they were, nonetheless, looking, and some of the evidence—the ruined prosthesis, the M16, the explosives—had begun to point toward TK.

All of which awakened her memories of the thorough search her father had initiated when her mother had taken her and fled the horrors of an incest-ridden household. Freddy Joy had been comparatively wealthy, and his story of his wife's irrationality, coming as it did from a pleasant, professional man in a three piece suit, had been perfectly believable, whether in the course of a search that covered three states, at her mother's arrest at a bus stop in Bakersfield, or in the courtroom.

Closing in. Sana recalled the furtive, nocturnal flight, the sense of creeping presence at her back. And then she suddenly remembered Terry's continuing telephone calls. Ring. Hang up. Was that it? Was he closing in, too?

She started as the computer screen went black. She had been lost in thought and memory for so long that the screen saver had activated. But line one was dark now, and she rose and went to TK's office, seeing her faint reflection in the glass that covered the watercolor—one of Wheat's—hanging by his door. Sana Joy looked very much the perfect receptionist. No one would have guessed her past. But, then, there were many women in the world whose outward beauty masked souls so deeply scarred that an eternity of healing would not make them whole, and no one ever guessed their secrets, either.

Wondering a little at the sight of her own hand, manicured and slender, that had once been forced around the shaft of a father's penis, she pushed open TK's door and tried to leave the past in the past. Like Elvenhome, TreeStar was safe.

But the police had called. TreeStar was not quite so safe anymore.

"TK?"

He looked up from his monitor. "Hey, Sana."

"What did Brown want?"

"You guessing already, girl." He shoved his chair back, swiveled to face her. "Old Uncle TK made such a big fuss about that crack house that his name's on the short list. And that leg they found . . ." He looked at his empty trouser leg, rolled up neatly and pinned. " . . . well . . ."

"What did he say?"

TK shrugged. "Asked me a few questions. Asked me if I wore a fake leg. Said no to that one." He grimaced.

She felt his thoughts. "It's the truth, TK. You can't wear what you haven't got."

"Yeah . . ." But he frowned, shook his head. "I don't like to lie. It was too much of a lie."

Sana nodded. She did not like to lie either, and it was strange to look back on her life and see how much of it had been made up of lies. Lies to her mother about her father. Lies to her teachers about the bruises on her arms and face. Lies to the doctor about her persistent vaginal abrasions and infections.

Lies to herself about Terry Angel.

She had absently put a hand to her face, and the touch of her skin reminded her again of her altered appearance. And then she noticed that TK's features had softened, that though he was still a big man, there was a sense of grace and litheness about him that, she was certain, had not been present before. "You see stars, too, don't you?" she said impulsively.

He nodded.

"What . . ." It was a dream. She was greatly afraid that it was only a dream. Would questions cause it to evaporate in the harsh light of consciousness? ". . . what do you think it means?"

"What's it mean?" TK shook his head. "Ever see *Saturday Night Fever*?"

"Yeah."

"That guy who wasn't a priest anymore?"

"Yeah."

"Well, it looks like I'm not black anymore."

You're one of us, Sana, Allesandro had said. *You're changing.*

"Oh," TK went on, "I might look black. I might act black. I might get jumped by a bunch of skinheads who *think* I'm black . . ." He sighed, his jaw tightening for a moment. " . . . and I might break their necks, too. But I'm not black. I'm something else."

"What?"

He lifted his eyes, looked at her. "I'm open for suggestions, Sana. And, anyway, that's a question you best be asking yourself, too."

She licked lips that had gone dry despite their coating of color. "What . . . what's going to happen? With the police, I mean?"

TK shrugged. "Oh, he told me to stay in town, thanked me for my cooperation, and then hung up. I suppose he'll be calling back." .

Closing in. "TK, what are they going to do?"

"Hard to say," he said. "They might shoot me." He dispensed a carefully-measured smile. "Then again, they might give me a medal. War on drugs and all that. Hard to say."

He went back to work after that, slogging through data entry and map generation as though to take his mind off Brown's call. Sana returned to her front desk and her report. Hadden and Lauri both phoned in later that afternoon to say that they would not be returning to the office that day, and Sana told them about TK. Hadden listened gravely to the news, and in her mind's eye, Sana could see him standing at a pay phone somewhere, nodding, his gray eyes calm, their starlight flickering with the responsibility he seemed to feel for everything that happened . . . anywhere.

Lauri, on the other hand, exploded.

"Those bastards!" she said. "Don't they think he's gone through enough already?"

Sana thought back to her own experiences with the police, with the kind of justice that was dispensed in the courtrooms of America. "No, Lauri. They don't. They're just doing their jobs."

"Doing their jobs! I'll tell them about jobs!" But then Lauri fell silent, and Sana heard the familiar impotence settling in. Oh, they were all trying. Whether their efforts lay in playing harp, cutting hair, or planting trees, they were all trying. And they all knew about impotence.

"Well, listen," said Lauri after the silence had lengthened uncomfortably. "Give TK my love, and tell him that we're all behind him. Hundred and ten percent and all that stuff. No matter what happens. I'll call him tonight." Another pause. "Damn."

"Lauri . . ."

"How are *you* doing, Sana?"

"Me?"

"You hanging in there?"

"Uh ..." Sana did not know what Lauri meant, but, then again, maybe she knew more than she was willing to admit. "I'm all right."

"Good. Don't worry: we'll get you through." A shrill beeping. "Oops! My pager. God has spoken: I gotta go."

She hung up, and Sana was left holding the phone to her ear. "Get me through what?" she said to the dull emptiness of the broken connection, and she was still thinking about it as she and TK closed down the office, as she took her little harp out from behind her desk, as she loaded it into her car and drove to the hospital.

Giving. Giving and giving and giving. That seemed to be all that these people did. She had no doubt that TK would be supplied with whatever he needed to see him through any ordeal the law might have in store for him, just as she herself would be supported throughout ... well, whatever she had to be supported throughout. But with her face altering, her sight returning, her scars fading (she risked a look in the rear-view mirror: yes, they were now almost invisible), she could not help but wonder whether her future was going to be anything but wonderful.

"A pretty face and good hair," she murmured, turning into the hospital parking lot. "Oh, Goddess. And I don't have the faintest idea what to do with either of them."

But when she reached the intensive care unit, she was surprised to find, instead of the whispered conversations of technicians and nurses, shouting and loud arguments. A group of men were gathered at the nurses' station, some in suits, some in sheriff's uniforms, and among them she recognized Maxwell Delmari, who was screaming into the face of a short, thin man:

"She's dead! She's dead! Your damned papers aren't going to change that one iota!"

The thin man held his ground. "I have been hired to represent the interests of Audrey Delmari."

"Audrey is my daughter!"

"Yes," drawled the thin man, examining Maxwell, "and you want to murder her."

Dr. Braun was running up now, wayward hair and white coat flying. "What is this?" she gasped.

The thin man handed her the papers. "I represent the interests of Audrey Delmari, one of your patients. I have here an injunction forbidding any interruption in her life support systems." He glanced at Maxwell. "Pending a judicial review."

"Dear God," said Maxwell, "just let her go, will you? She's . . . she's . . ." Despite his previous outburst, he could not utter the word, and he gasped, grimaced, and finally wrenched the conversation away from Audrey. "Who hired you?"

"God hired him," said one of the other men. He had a broad, red face, and he wore a clerical collar. "Audrey is a human being, with an innate right to life that supersedes any concern you might have about hospital costs."

"Costs have nothing to do with it! She's d—" But Maxwell's voice caught.

"See?" said the minister, stabbing an index finger at him. "You can't say it, can you? You don't really believe it, do you?"

Braun was reading the injunction. "I'm afraid this is valid as far as I can tell, Dr. Delmari. I'll have the hospital lawyers go over it in the morning, and the administration will have to take it up, then. But for now . . ." She looked at Maxwell, shook her head. "There's nothing I can do."

"It's the will of God," said the minister. "Praise the Lord."

Maxwell flushed. "Was it the will of God that put Audrey in that car wreck? Was it the will of God that's kept her in that bed for the last three years? Was it—"

Dr. Braun lifted a hand, but the minister ignored her. "God does whatever it pleases Him to do," he said. "Audrey is here because He willed her to be here, and it's His will that she stay here."

"Was it his will that—?"

"His will! Everything is His will! We have no choice but to submit!"

"Damn you! My God doesn't throw people into comas for three years!"

"You'd kill your own baby! How can you look at her,

struggling to wake up like that, and kill her in cold blood!"

Despite Braun's efforts, they were shouting again. But a voice, soft but oddly compelling, stilled their voices in midword.

"I will remind you gentlemen that this is a hospital."

And, standing at the entrance to the corridor, clad in nightgown and robe, one hand outstretched to steady herself against the wall, was Heather Blues.

She looked thin and frail, and her face was white with strain, but what held Sana's gaze was the look in her eyes. For a moment, she seemed taller, and Sana caught a brief flicker of a nimbus about her, an aura as of blue and silver that seemed to wrap her in wings at once protective and imperious.

She tottered forward, but her steps might have had the surety of a queen's as she approached the minister. "Go," she said. "You've done enough here."

"Heather . . ." started Dr. Braun. "You really should—"

"You have the law," Heather said to the minister. "We have life and natural process. All you can do is prolong the pain, but I'm certain that you will do just that. Go, then."

She started to turn away disdainfully, but she caught sight of the confused and frightened harper standing just outside the elevator doors. "Sana!" she said. "Hello! Come help me back to my room, please."

Sana saw the tears in Maxwell's eyes, saw the flustered look of doubtful victory on the minister's face. But, heels clicking sharply and precisely on the linoleum tile, she ran to Heather and caught her arm just as she seemed ready to collapse.

Heather smiled. "They're letting me wander around now. They actually took me off my leash. Can you believe it?"

"I don't think going *mano a mano* with religious fanatics is exactly what they had in mind." Sana guided her back to her room. "I don't want you dropping dead in the corridor after all these weeks."

Heather shook her head. "I won't drop dead, Sana. It is very difficult to kill an Elf."

"But it's not—" Heather's words suddenly sunk in, and

Sana choked because she knew that she was neither joking nor speaking figuratively. An Elf?

She drew up short, turned, stared into Heather's face. Suddenly, despite her best, rational efforts, it made a kind of bizarre sense. All of it. Everything from the starlight that had, seemingly, entrenched itself in her life to the set of Heather's cheekbones, the grip of her hand.

Heather regarded her sympathetically. "It's time for you to know, Sana."

"Know? Know what?"

"Child, you're one of us."

Allesandro's words came back with a chill. *One of us.* But Elves? "I'm . . . I'm not any such thing!"

"Are you certain?"

Very deliberately, Sana took Heather's arm once more and guided her down the corridor. "Just . . . let me get you back into bed, will you?"

Footsteps. Dr. Braun. "I'm so sorry, Heather," she said even before she had quite reached them. "This is completely unacceptable. I was down the hall when the locusts descended. I'm very, very sorry."

"That's all right," said Heather, squeezing Sana's hand. "I was supposed to handle it."

Braun blinked. "Supposed to?"

Heather shrugged. "Everything that happens, happens as it should."

"To bed," said Braun. She took Heather's other arm. "You're far from well."

Heather tolerated the order with an amused shrug. "I thought you said yesterday that I could go home in a week."

"Not if you keep trying to be hospital policeman."

"I think she did very well," said Sana.

Braun blinked at her voice. "Sandy! My God, is that you? I go on vacation for a couple weeks, and when I get back, Heather's uppity and Sandy looks like a model."

"Her name is Sana," said Heather.

"Sana?" Braun looked puzzled.

"I . . . uh . . . changed my name," said Sana quickly, feeling another chill. Her name, her face, everything. Changing.

Heather was smiling.

"Well, good for you." Braun put Heather back into bed

and then gave her a quick exam. "You're still healing," she reminded Heather. "I had to take a bullet out of your brain. Give yourself time."

"I want to go home," said Heather, still with that sense of toleration and amusement. "It's time for me to go home."

"Give yourself another week, okay? We'll see then." Braun turned to Sana. "I've got rounds to finish up," she said. "Keep her in bed, Sand . . . ah . . . Sana. Sit on her if you have to."

"Marsh and Kelly will be along in a bit," Heather offered. "I'm sure they'll be glad to help."

Seemingly a little unnerved, Braun left, and Sana was alone with Heather. With what Heather had said. With what she sensed was the truth of what Heather had said.

Slowly, she set her harp down, took a chair. "Elves," she murmured, looking at her hands. Slender, perfect. That was it. Perfect. Blindness, scars, memories: everything rough and hurtful in her life was being smoothed and healed. Everything was being washed in starlight. Everything . . .

"Elves, Sana." Heather's voice was quiet but firm. "Natil told you about the old blood. It's elven blood. It's been around from the beginning. Many people have it, and sometimes it wakes up. When it wakes up, it transforms you."

Dream . . . or nightmare? Sana was suddenly not sure. She wondered whether it could perhaps be both.

"I'm sorry it's such a shock, Sana. It was time. You just couldn't go on in ignorance anymore. Natil was worrying about it, but I don't think she quite knew how to tell you."

"She's cautious," said Sana absently, caught between fear, longing . . . even a little anger. "She . . . doesn't take risks." Then, flaring: "Why the fuck didn't anyone tell me before this?"

"It wasn't time."

"The hell it wasn't!"

"Consider," said Heather. "Would you have believed it?"

Sana could not answer. Or, rather, she could not answer as she wanted. TK had found out that he was not black. She had found out that she was—

"Heather," she said, "this is crazy."

"It's not crazy," said Heather calmly. "It's true. You know that."

Twisting, turning, wrestling with knowledge that she did not want. "I didn't ask for this."

"Didn't you?" Heather folded her pale hands on the white sheets. "Didn't you want to help and heal?"

Sana glared at her through starlight. "Helping and healing has nothing to do with this."

"It has everything to do with it," Heather insisted. "Haven't you noticed? Helping and healing are the reasons for Elves. They're what Elves do."

Heather was speaking the absolute truth again, and Sana knew it, felt it. No, nothing had closed in on her, crept up behind her, laid a sweaty hand on her shoulder, dragged her off into an incestuous bedroom. Rather, the blossom she had watched so earnestly, into which she had put so much of her hope, had at last fully opened. "And Natil . . . and all the others . . .?" But she knew the answer already.

"Yes, Sana. All of us."

"TK?"

"As much as you. He will have to be told soon."

Silence. Lengthening silence.

"Sana?"

Sana's eyes were on her harp, for that slender instrument seemed for her now to be an anchor for her psyche, something to keep it planted firmly in what she had freely and passionately claimed as the bedrock of her existence: helping and healing. But that meant . . .

"Sana?"

. . . that meant that she had fallen in perfectly with the purpose of the ancient blood—elven blood—in her veins. And that meant . . .

"Sana," said Heather gently. "Would you play for me?"

Sana was still staring at her harp. Anchor. Icon. And she herself was the blossom. "Will it help?"

Heather nodded softly, sympathetically, lovingly. "Yes. Greatly. Both of us."

. . . that meant . . . everything. And so, lifting onto her lap that fragile symbol of her health, her dreams, her longings, Sana put her fingers to the strings and began to play softly, the music floating through the room. She played the melodies that Natil had taught her, that had become a part of the inner melodies that rose from her own heart. Elven melodies, she did not doubt. Elven melodies, elven blood. And she was one of them.

She played for Heather, and then, making a conscious choice, a conscious acceptance, she went to every one of the other rooms on the floor and played. She played for Michael, who, racked with herpes and pneumonia, was dying of AIDS. She played for Therese, who was so wasted that she could no longer move. She played for Thomas, who drifted in a drug overdose coma but might yet awaken.

And when she came to Audrey's room, she played twice: first for the memory of the dead woman whose body lay writhing and gasping in the grip of respirators, legal injunctions, and religious beliefs, and then for Maxwell, who sat, unmoving, at the side of the bed, his eyes brimming with tears for the daughter he could not recover, the daughter he could not release. Sana played, and she helped, and she healed. She could not do otherwise. Those were, after all, the reasons for her existence.

CHAPTER 25

"You *what*?" said Natil.

Even compressed into the two-octave compass of a telephone, Heather's voice was blithe. "I told Sana what she was. I thought she should know. I thought you should know, too."

"Oh, dear Lady! How is she taking it?"

"Fine."

"Heather!"

"All right, she was a little shaky at first, but she pulled out of it."

Natil, sitting at her desk at Elvenhome, put a hand to her face. Shaky? Heather, having told Sana that she was not human, was now characterizing her resultant emotional condition as merely *shaky*? "Heather, how much do you know about Sana?"

"I know enough, Natil. Remember that she's been playing for me for weeks now."

"Are you not worried—?"

"No, I'm not," said Heather, and Natil heard the elven accent coming through clearly. "Sana is strong. Incredibly so. She wouldn't have survived her childhood if she weren't."

"You know about that, too, then."

"I know. She didn't tell me, but I know." Behind Heather's words, shadowed as though by the eternal sorrows of the Elves, Natil heard a more immediate grief over what had been done to a defenseless human child. "You just have to look into the stars, and you know."

Natil sighed. Matters had, she thought, gotten a little out of hand. Well, matters had gotten out of hand before. But it bothered her greatly that, in this case, it was someone else's matters that had gotten out of hand. Sana was her student, her teacher, and, most more important, her friend. She should not have to deal alone with this kind of knowledge. "Very well. Where is she now?"

"She went home to her apartment. She played for everyone on the floor, and then she stopped in, said goodbye, and left."

Natil was already standing up, reaching for her purse, her car keys. "I had best go to her—"

"Natil, we need to talk."

There was an edge in Heather's words that put Natil back into her chair. It was not judgmental, it was not capricious: it was, rather, an indication of a calm evaluation of the patterns of the universe, of as much of the Dance as any Firstborn could now perceive.

It was happening. Heather had seen. The old blood was truly coming alive, coming into its powers. *Firstborn ...*

"About what, Heather?" Natil tried to keep the tremor of mixed hope and apprehension out of her voice. She was not sure that she succeeded.

"About ..." Heather hesitated, as though she too had realized that her relations with Natil—with all the Elves—had forever changed. "... about what you've told us."

"Speak."

"Natil, love ..." Heather almost giggled nervously at the familiarity. "... you never told us about the Lady. You never really told us about *you*. You've kind of ... well ... been treating us like children. Not telling us what you didn't think was good for us and all that."

"Would you have believed me? Would you have comprehended?" Natil's voice sounded a little hollow even to her own ears. "You said yourself that—"

"You don't understand, do you?"

"Understand ...?"

Heather sounded very patient. "Natil, if you told us that the sky was chartreuse, we'd believe you. And, you know, we'd go outside, and the sky would be chartreuse, too, just because you said it was. Haven't you realized that yet?"

Natil sat, stared through the window at the cold night. There was frost on the glass. "I ..."

"We used to be human," said Heather. "Used to be. But we're not anymore. We can take it. Oh, some things will upset us, but we all made it from human to Elf without exploding, so I'm sure we all can deal with whatever we have to deal with. But ... but that's not quite it, either ..." She broke off, considering. "I guess what I'm trying to say is this: you've spent the last three years wandering around with the whole world on your shoulders, and you were doing the same thing for a long time before you showed up in Colorado. It's time you started to share the burden. Not for our sakes. Not for the Lady's sake. For yours."

Natil bent her head. "Healing and helping, beloved?"

"We have to heal and help one another as much as we heal and help the rest of the world. We're all in this together, Natil. We're all Her children. Stop trying to act like a kindergarten teacher in the middle of a nuclear war. You can't handle it all yourself. You can't be the only adult." Heather caught herself. "Listen to me, will you? Telling you that you're a kid. Dear Lady!"

But, really, Heather was right. And Natil recalled again Sana's words—and Heather's, too—about children and the Lady. One had to be a child, approach Her as a child. Simply. Trustingly. Unassumingly. She suddenly began to wonder whether Sana were actually the one who held the key to reestablishing contact with *Elthia*. Sana with her primitive religion. Sana with all her fears and her correspondingly intense longing for a childish land of cartoon sunlight, softness, and warmth. Sana with her ability to invoke ... and make real.

She looked up, stared at the night without seeing it. Candlemas had passed. Waxing light. And Sana was changing, becoming elven.

"Natil?"

"You are ... wise, Heather."

"I'm just trying to take care of someone I love. Someone we *all* love. Remember that. But, please, *start talking to us*. You've got to. You just can't go on like this."

"I hear you." Natil's voice was husky with tears, with gratitude, with sudden, renewed, tangible *hope*.

"Don't cry. Please don't cry. I didn't mean ..."

"I weep for happiness, Heather." Natil was still staring out at the night. She had forgotten so much. Forgotten how to be a child. Forgotten what it was like to be loved. Forgotten the compassion—one for another—of the Firstborn. And now maybe Sana . . . "It has been a long time since I could speak openly to anyone."

"I'll help," said Heather, "any way that I can. Kelly, I think, already understands. I'm working on Marsh. I think maybe Ash suspects. Hadden . . . some of the others, too. Like I said: you can't just talk about Her. But if you don't know She's there, you can't even *talk*. You can't even . . . well . . . you know . . ."

Natil suddenly laughed. "I do know, Heather. And my thanks. Give my love to Marsh and Kelly . . ." She let the sentence hang for a moment. ". . . who, I assume, are with you, listening?"

"Uh . . . yes."

Natil shook her head slowly. Indeed, completely out of hand.

"Natil? Are you mad at me?"

"Elves," said Natil, "are known for being ingenious. Peace. I am going to call Sana." She heard the question in Heather's silence. "For my sake."

She said good-bye then, but when she dialed Sana's number, she heard nothing but ringing . . . and no answer. Disquieted, she fretted for a while, tried again, and got the same result.

It was a dream, it had to be a dream, but having, with a harp in her hands and music welling up from within her, evaluated it with as much objectivity as her longings and wishes allowed, Sana was determined not to wake up. Too much of her life had consisted of undeniable reality, too many of her waking hours had found her pinned against an adamantine wall of inescapable, physical existence for her to want to leave this ineffable realm of starlight and love. Did she have to forsake her humanity? She would. Did she have to dismiss all her fond hopes for a simple, workaday existence of mundane normality? She would.

She drove home from the hospital plunged into a kind of bewildered acceptance of everything. Sana Joy had found her calling, found herself, found her people: the world could not but be right. And if, in the back of her mind, a qualm of experience insisted that the cartoon always had to end, that the gentle landscapes of dream consisted, after all, only of pigments upon celluloid that were, in turn, projected as insubstantial shadows into the vacuum of a cathode ray tube—ghosts of ghosts—she allowed the starlight to rise up in a wave and drown it.

She parked outside her apartment building, climbed the stairs to the second floor. It was a shabby set of rooms she occupied, but though she saw the shabbiness tonight just as she always did, she saw also the potential. The apartment was bare and dirty (she had not yet even cleaned the oven: the canister of cleanser—unused, unopened—still resided in the cabinet beneath the sink), but all that could be remedied, *would* be remedied. And, as with her apartment, so with the . . .

Standing in the doorway, harp in hand, she blushed at the thought.

. . . so with the world. It could change. It *would* change. All the children who hid in closets, trembled in their beds, stifled screams as ungentle and uncaring parental words and fingers penetrated them—all of them would be helped. It would take time. It might take forever. But it would be done.

"Goddess . . ." she murmured. "I can help. I *can* help."

The telephone rang. For an instant, she shivered, but after closing the door and laying aside her coat and her harp, she picked up the receiver. The connection was broken almost instantly. That did not surprise her, but for the first time it did not bother her, either. Maybe . . . maybe she could help there, too.

She changed clothes and washed the makeup from her face, wondering as she did whether her features had altered a little more. Something about her cheekbones, as though—

On an impulse, she shoved her hair back . . . back behind her ears. She looked at herself for a long time, then, her heart beating furiously, but, gradually, under the influence of the starlight, slowing down, quieting. She had almost expected it. Now her face was all of a piece. Everything fit. And she noticed, too, that the scars along her jaw had faded completely.

With a soft shake of her head, she settled her hair once again, and Allesandro's cut fell into place as though it had been designed not only to flatter . . . but also to hide. He had known. Of course he had known. They all had known. Natil had hinted, and Heather had finally told her.

As she pondered, as she wondered, a knock came to the door. For a moment, Sana was puzzled, but then she decided that it was probably Natil. Doubtless, Heather had talked to her, and Natil—who was cautious, who did not take chances—had come to answer questions and offer help.

With a laugh, she ran to answer, her feet noiseless on the threadbare carpet. But when she turned the deadbolt and opened the door, she found Terry Angel waiting for her.

"Uh . . . Terry . . ."

Terry's face was radiant, his smile winning. "Sandy!" he said. "I'm so delighted to see you again. It's been so long!"

"Uh . . ." In truth, she wanted to slam and bolt the door. But had she not, a few minutes ago, thought that she might be able to bring healing even to Terry? And, if not, then at least compassion? "Uh . . . come in, Terry."

"Thank you. Thank you."

She helped him off with his coat and hung it up for him. He was, as usual, dressed simply and neatly: the long sleeves of his pressed shirt pulled down to his wrists, his slacks unobtrusive, his shoes polished. There was yet about him a sense of the monastic, as though, without much trouble, he could have exchanged his modern garb for a habit and called himself satisfied.

Hands clasped loosely, he gazed about, nodding and smiling. "Very nice, Sandy. Very nice. I'm glad you have such a lovely place to live. Ah!" And he seemed to stare beyond the walls, beyond her. ". . . that interior practice of yours, so expressive in everything that you do!"

"Um . . . yeah." Although she wanted to help, Sana found that she was acutely uncomfortable. "What's going on, Terry?"

"May I sit?"

"Yeah. Of . . . of course." She cleared the newspapers off the sofa and he settled himself, perching like a delicate, alert bird. Feeling a little uncertain, she sat down beside him.

"I infinitely regret not having answered your telephone calls," he said, his eyes bright. "But I was involved in . . . some work." He smiled at her.

Sana nodded. "Okay."

"There were some . . . funding problems at Kingsley. Maxwell Delmari—the dean, you know—told me how sorry he was that the facilities he could offer were inadequate. There was just not enough money."

He was smiling. Sana made herself nod. "Okay," she managed.

"And Dr. Delmari was very helpful," Terry continued. "He put me in touch with a team of physicians and philosophers in Montana. At the university in Billings. They had heard about the Hands of Grace, and they jumped at the chance to have the program relocate to their Institute of Medicine and the Humanities."

Terry was enthusiastic, winsome, sweet . . . and insane. Sana knew that now. All his conviction, all his ability to sway, to make believers out of even the most determined skeptics—everything was a product of a mind adrift upon oceans of pathological fantasy.

"Okay," she said.

"They want to have contemplative musicians on their staff right away."

"Okay." Sana nodded, numb.

"The Institute is a unique medical model in the United States," Terry went on, "a group of philosophers, liturgists, and linguists all working together in an extended dialog." Bright smile! "We're in a situation, Sandy, in which we can form our own program. Isn't it wonderful!"

Sana licked dry lips. "Terry," she said, trying to keep her voice gentle, "that's what you said about Kingsley."

He stared at her.

"That's what you said we had here in Denver." Helping and healing. But how? How to help such mammoth self-delusion? How to heal a mind? "You told me all about the hospitals. You told me all about the hospice and the facilities that the college had given us."

Terry was nodding. "It was all true. It was simply unfortunate that—"

"Terry, it wasn't true." She kept her voice kind, her thoughts on compassion. "There weren't any hospitals, there weren't any hospices."

Terry stared at her. For an instant, his face lost some of its pale sweetness, and a flush crept up his cheeks. But he was back to normal in a moment. "But of course there were. Their administrations asked to be anonymous because of the revolutionary nature of our work, and we were anonymous, of course, because of the intrinsic loss of self necessary for our ministry."

He sounded perfectly convincing, perfectly believable. Terry Angel always sounded that way. Whether he was telling Maxwell Delmari that Audrey was hearing music every day, or writing to Sandy Joy about the Hands of Grace program, his words inevitably held the accents of unalloyed reality.

And so, reluctantly, Sandy admitted to herself that it was useless. She could not help Terry. She recalled the old Alcoholics Anonymous prayer and shrugged inwardly: maybe Natil could tell her how the Elves dealt with things that they could not change; or maybe she would just have to learn what would get her through the inevitable disappointments that came from trying to help human beings.

"Okay, Terry," she said. "That's okay. I'm glad to hear that you've got another program up in Billings. I'm sure they'll be very proud of what you'll do up there. But I'm not following you to Montana."

He stared at her, and the flush came again, rising, darkening. "Don't you understand, Sandy? This is what we've been waiting for! You'll finally be able to play for the sick and the dying!"

Sana found that she was shaking. Maybe it was that Terry had come to assume many of the characteristics of her dead father, albeit on a more rarefied and pernicious plane, or maybe it was simply hard to maintain one's equilibrium in the face of such an absolutely diseased reality. Regardless, she felt suddenly weak, dizzy, as though she had lost control. Healing and helping? How could she heal and help anything as fundamentally deranged as Terry Angel!

"I'm not going to Montana," she said, keeping her voice even. "I've got my work here."

"There is work of the flesh and work of the spirit," said Terry, suddenly bland, pale, and smiling again. "You have to choose which of them you want to devote your life to."

Again, this was nothing that she had not heard before. "I . . . I don't think that I need to choose," she said, consciously struggling against the upwelling of weakness.

"I'm doing both, Terry. I'm playing at First Friends' Hospital. I've been playing there for weeks."

Fighting for equilibrium, fighting to speak the truth, she hardly noticed that Terry was not looking at her, that he was instead looking down at the floor, that his jaw was clenched, that his flush had returned, had deepened into crimson.

"I play for a friend who was shot," she continued. She felt distant, vague, unsure of her words and therefore all the more determined to say them. "I play for Audrey Delmari. They like me at First Friends'. And I'm doing what I've always wanted to do."

Terry was silent for a long time. Sana finally gathered her wits enough to look at him and was shocked to see how dark he had become. His forehead was damp, his eyes almost glazed. He was trembling as though he held within himself urges and angers of which she knew nothing. "Sandy," he said slowly, "I've always told you that it was very important for you to learn submission in order to really be free in your musical expression. The soul of the musician—"

"Thanks, Terry. Thanks. I . . . I appreciate your advice, but I'm really happy . . . with what I've got."

Terry suddenly lifted his head, and his gaze focused upon her with a strange light. "God is in you, Sandy. God is in you. You must submit to Him. You must give yourself over to Him. You must allow Him to penetrate every particle of your being until you are helpless, bound by His will, sensible only to His omnipotence and His desire that you continue with the Hands of Grace."

"Terry . . ."

"The saints gave themselves over that way. The saints truly manifested God by their helplessness. He laid them down, and He entered them, and He pierced their hands and their feet with the sweet arrows of His divine love."

Despite his flush, despite his fixed and almost glazed expression, he was speaking calmly, almost sweetly. And then, with a slack and willing mouth, he reached, caught Sana's shirt, and dragged her toward him. With horror, she realized that he had an erection . . .

. . . and suddenly Freddy Joy had her.

"You're mine," he said softly. "You're my student. You're my program. You must submit to me." His grip tightened, his voice hardened. His lips were flaccid, moist, glistening. "You must submit *now!*"

"No!" She pulled away, but he clung to her, and she succeeded only in falling back with Terry on top of her. She felt his weight, his breath on her face. Her father had pinned her down that way, pinned her so that she could not move, groped for the fastenings of her skirt with thick fingers.

Terry was pleading with her, almost weeping with emotion. "You have to submit! You have to suck the sweet blood from the side of Jesus ... through the golden tube of His resurrected flesh!"

But she was not a child anymore. She was not Sandy: she was Sana, and with a cry, she struck, shoved him off to the side. He rolled off the sofa, onto the floor, but as she tried to scramble away from him, he caught her by the foot, his nails raking her skin. She kicked, lunged away again, felt something slip around her ankle. She looked down to see that he had jerked the telephone cord out of the wall and was starting to tie her ...

... and Freddy Joy tightened the clothes line around her legs, around her wrists, pinched her cheeks against her teeth until she opened her mouth to keep him from drawing blood ...

"You have to learn ... you have to be bound ..."

Something broke within her, something gave way, and she screamed, a long rising howl that summed up all the unvocalized torment that had been pumped through her child's body, all her frustrated efforts at escape, all the desperate but impotent flight that had led nowhere but back to Freddy Joy's bed. He had her now. She could not escape. She had to submit. Now and forever.

But the starlight surged, flashed—and she hit him. For a moment, Terry looked drained and uncertain, but then the color came back into him along with the madness, and he seized the telephone and threw it into her face. Sana's vision went fuzzy, distorted.

Terry was shouting something, now, imploring her, tearing at her clothes. She kicked out weakly, shoved him back once again, half ran and half crawled ... somewhere. She did not know where she was going, only that she was trying to get away.

But he had found her before—in her bedroom, in

Bakersfield, in her apartment—and now he found her again. Her vision cleared enough to see that she was in the kitchen, lying face up on the dirty linoleum with her head inches from the oven. Terry was on top of her, and he was holding a paring knife that she had left on the counter.

She stared up at him, and then she felt a pain in her right palm that grew into a hot fire as though she had plunged her hand into molten metal. She tried to pull away, but the pain only spread. With a shriek, she brought her knee up and knocked Terry over her head. He fell, but was immediately crawling back toward her. "Mine!" he said. "Please. Yes. You'll come. You're absolutely necessary. I'll sign you with the stigmata, to show that you belong to the program. Such opportunities! We can make the program together! And you'll play for the dead . . ."

She lifted her hand and managed to focus on it enough to see that Terry had put the blade of the knife straight through her palm, that her attempt to free herself had jerked it through tendon and muscle. Instinctively, she tried to move her fingers, but they only writhed uselessly.

She felt another touch of the knife, and she screamed again, but Terry was swarming over her, his face pale, his lips curled into a vague, distant smile. Abruptly, he grabbed her other hand, stabbed the palm.

Sana felt her grip going. "Leave me alone! Leave me alone! Leave me alone!" She was crawling across the kitchen floor now, slipping in old grease and fresh blood, but Terry was following. With an effort, she turned, struck him with an elbow. He gasped and fell, his head thudding against the cabinet beneath the sink. The doors rebounded, popped open, and the overfull trash basket toppled, scattering its contents, knocking the cleansers and the can of oven cleaner onto the floor with a clatter.

"I want you. *God* wants you."

She had no hands with which to push him away. "Leave me alone, Daddy! I don't want you! I want the starlight!"

"I'll teach you to submit! Jesus—"

Her eyes fastened suddenly upon the oven cleaner. Freddy Joy had known how to use oven cleaner. He had taught her how to use oven cleaner. *I'll make sure no one but me ever wants you,* he had said. And he had sprayed it—

Wedging the can between her forearms, she battered it on the floor until the childproof cap came off, and then she rolled it into the crook of her elbow. Terry was crawling up her body, his eyes wide, the knife in his hand gleaming. "Five wounds," he said calmly. "The stigmata replicates the five wounds of Christ." And then he smiled.

Sana saw only Freddy Joy as she brought the mangled remains of her right hand down on the spray button of the canister, and Terry's features suddenly turned white with foam, then crimson with the bright rawness of caustic burns. She saw his eyes—now wide with surprise—turn pale and featureless as the eager corrosive ate through the tissues and turned transparency to blank.

And then Terry was screaming. And Sana was screaming. And she did not stop screaming until she saw uniforms and people, saw the flashing of squad car lights on the curtains of the front windows. They asked her questions, then, and she was not sure what she said in reply, for she was not sure whether they had arrested her mother yet, whether they would send her immediately back to her father, whether her vagina would have a chance to stop bleeding before Terry . . .

She did not know what Terry told them. But by the time the paramedics arrived, she had been handcuffed and read her rights.

CHAPTER 26

DENVER SAINT SCARRED IN SATANIC ATTACK

The newspaper lay face up in a puddle of pale sunshine that had found its way in through the windows of Elvenhome to fall upon a kitchen table laden with pitchers of milk and plates of pancakes and fruit—all uneaten, all untouched this morning—and the headline said it all.

It was, Natil thought, the old story, come back now to haunt them. Prejudice. Ignorance. Hate. Harbingers of the future, echoes of the past. But as though these were not enough, today the Elves were confronted with something even more insidious, more damaging, perhaps more enduring: an appetite for self-delusion that seemed at times to be so innately human that Natil half wondered why it was not listed in the current textbooks as one of the attributes of psychological health.

Though now both blind and scarred, Terry Angel was holding to his saintly, winning, lucid persona, and his story, interspersed with heartfelt protestations that he pardoned Sana with all his heart, was damning. He had, according to his statement, come to visit his student for the purpose of offering her a position at his new program at the University of Montana. Instead of appreciating the opportunity, though, she had attacked him out of what he could only assume was either jealousy gone rank with disappointment, or, given the books and tools that the police had found after they had searched her apartment, a derangement brought on by the practice of some bizarre and pathological cult.

Lies. If no one else knew Sana, if she were, to the rest of Denver, now only a diabolized assailant come up out of the darkness of the societal unconscious to rend all that was intellectually pure and spiritually sanitary, the Elves knew her, and they knew lies when they heard them.

But Sana was under arrest and inaccessible, and the Elves—as was so often the case, as had been so often the case—were helpless. All their gathering together, all their helping and healing, all their concern and passion and power was as nothing.

"Listen, Clarice, I *know* it's the weekend. But you know how to do all that legal shit, and you've just *gotta* know some judge who'll come down to the courthouse and set bail on a Saturday."

Lauri was on the telephone, the receiver pressed to one ear, her free hand covering the other as though to shut out extraneous sounds. But there were no extraneous sounds, for though the kitchen of Elvenhome was full today, it was, in fact, silent save for Lauri's voice and the tinny, unintelligible whisper of Clarice's replies.

"You get it set, we'll raise it," said Lauri. "Just get it set, for crissakes, will you? We've got to spring this lady." A pause. "Don't give me any shit about Satanism, Clarice! You're a lawyer!"

She hung up after another minute, looked at the floor for several seconds before she spoke. "Clarice says she'll do what she can."

"And what does that mean?" asked Raven.

"She's good. She goes after those wife beating cases and really tears them up. She'll do something."

Lauri was trying to sound confident, but as she spoke, she was looking at Natil, and Natil knew that she was recalling the words that had passed between them a few weeks ago, words that had been interrupted by the sudden arrival of a Celica and its burden of violence and grief, words that had continued shortly thereafter, words that had resolved nothing. Words. Questions. Questions that remained unanswered.

She looked at those who were gathered about the big kitchen table—Hadden, Ash, Fox, Raven, Tristan, Wheat . . . all of them—and she read their faces. Behind their concern for Sana, submerged in their grief like a lumbering and deadly behemoth floating in the depths of an ocean, were the same inevitable questions.

First Heather. Now Sana. Lauri had, in fact, summed it up perfectly weeks ago: *Do we just do our little thing and smile and nod and try to help people who don't really*

*want to get any better until someone offs us? Do we just
go down one by one? That's a fucking stupid way to live!*

And Natil had agreed. And she still agreed. But she
still had no answer, nothing with which to counter the
eternal futility, for neither Heather's entreaties nor her
own resolve could supply her with the means to explain
what could only be experienced, to give what she herself
did not have, to bring to manifestation what seemed to be
withdrawing even farther into stellar and spiritual distances now that yet another Elf had fallen.

Lauri was still standing by the phone. "I want to kick
his teeth down his goddam throat."

"I'll help," said Raven.

Natil shook her head. "Peace. TK found out what violence accomplishes."

Wheat looked up. "What about TK? Is anyone taking care
of him?"

"Kelly and I are going into town to see Heather," said
Marsh. "We'll check in on him then." He turned to Kelly,
put an arm about her tiny shoulders. "Come on, honey,"
he said gently. "Eat your pancakes."

Kelly shook her head slowly. Her eyes were downcast,
shadowed. "I'm not hungry, Papa."

He bent, kissed the top of her head. "I know, Elfling."

"I want Mommy and Sana home."

Lauri folded her arms. "We'll do our best, Kelly. And
Marsh: bring TK back with you. If he'll come. He be-
longs here. He's one of us."

A murmur of assent from the others, and Natil nodded.
TK would have to be told soon about what was happening
to him. But Lauri's thoughts, filtered through other faces,
other eyes, still hung in the air. Was this the best that the
Elves could do? Smile and nod until someone offed them?

"You know," said the tall lesbian, "if they make this
stick, they could put Sana away for a long time. And all
that Satanism stuff is going to make it that much worse
for her. She doesn't have a snowball's chance in hell of
getting a fair trial."

"You don't think we know that, Lauri?" Raven's breakfast, like everyone else's, remained untouched. Even the
blueberry muffins on her plate lay unsplit, uneaten.

But Lauri's eyes were on Natil. "Natil . . ."

Natil did not look at her.

"C'mon, 'fess up. Tell us something. You've been around for a long time. You've seen shit like this before. You've seen worse. What do we do?"

"We're not going to go down," said Raven. "We're not going to just take it."

Natil knew that. Not one of them was willing to go down, not one was willing to just take it. They would fight the law, fight their natures, fight, with increasing viciousness, the weakness and desires that chained them to the world. But, yes, if the past were any indication, they would indeed go down . . . one by one.

Lauri was still looking at her. "So what do we do, Natil? What did we do before?"

"The time was wrong," murmured Natil. "The world was wrong. We had no place in it."

"Well, we've obviously got some kind of place in it now, or we wouldn't be here."

"That is so." Natil could not deny it. She had come to Colorado. She had been *sent* to Colorado. Could she really say that the Lady's action—a direct intervention into the physical reality that was consubstantial with Her own being—had been for naught? Fruitless?

Impossible.

"So . . . ?" Lauri had not moved from her place by the phone. She was a casual sort of dyke: a mop of black hair, jeans, a t-shirt, a down vest. Lambda symbols in her ears. Starlight in her eyes.

Direct, straightforward. And with a hollowness that had nothing to do with Sana or with her own repeated failures to contact *Elthia*, Natil knew that she herself had been anything but direct and straightforward.

Hadden glanced at Ash, sighed. "I think it's time, Natil. I think we've all talked about this privately at one time or another, and we've all decided that you'd tell us what we needed to know when we needed to know it."

"Sorry to put you on the spot," said Lauri, "but we need to know it now."

Natil nodded. It was true. And had she possessed any hope that she could, with any kind of clarity, tell them, she would have spoken. But as much as she knew that they would not understand what she said, she knew that her own lack of cognizance of the patterns of the Dance would turn her every word into a lie as heinous as that which had been uttered—continued to be uttered—by Terry Angel.

Religion? That's all? Lauri had said once, and, indeed, it would sound precisely like that was all.

Silence. A long silence. Finally, Ash rose and stood like a girl at Sunday school. "Natil, there doesn't seem to be much that we can do for Sana right now. I'd really like to go and pray."

Natil looked at the newspaper. For the second time in her life, Sana had been trapped by a madman. Indeed, prayer seemed the only course of action left open at present.

Ash's eyes were needy. "Can you tell me who I should pray to?"

Marsh, Natil noted, looked away. He knew. Heather had told him. In a way, though, they all knew. They all knew that Natil had not told them ... something. And regardless of what that something was, they all wanted it, and they all would fight to comprehend it. Just as their elven natures impelled them to help the very beings who had killed them in the past, were attempting to kill them in the present, would, probably, kill them in the future, so those same natures struggled to fill a gap in their elven spirits, a gap they instinctively knew should not exist.

Ash was still standing, her very presence a plea.

Natil struggled unsuccessfully with words. Finally, she stood up. "Please," she said. "Pardon me. I must think."

She turned away from the table, toward the door. But as she laid her hand on the knob, Lauri spoke:

"Hey, Natil," she said. "Don't forget, huh?"

"Lauri?"

"We love you." Lauri's eyes were grim, but kind. "We'd do anything for you."

The world was blurry with both starlight and tears as Natil went out into the chill day. Long ago, she would have had a gray cloak to keep her warm, but cloaks, like swords and magic and garb of green and gray, were gone, and today in Colorado she had only a sweater, slacks, and a scarf. But, in any case, what was the cold of a Rocky Mountain morning to one who had known the earth when it breathed methane and hydrogen, when oxygen was a poison and the green of summer forests and soft meadows a nightmare rather than a dream?

It was all so different now! She thought back to the tortured landscapes of the Precambrian, felt in her mind the jut and crag of rock that had, but a week before, flowed and frothed with all the violence of a planetary birth. Here, though, were soft needles and the crunch of old snow, and here also were pines whose drooping branches were patched with clumps of white, the flutter of dry and stubborn aspen leaves, the crisp scent of mountain air, and—oh!—the blueness of the sky.

Even Malvern had not been like this, for the old forest had been at once both gentler and wilder than this place of steep slopes, tall conifers, upthrusting strata . . . and a paved highway not twenty minutes away. To all this, civilized and savage, the Elves had come, taking upon themselves in this latter age the ways of simple humanity, offering their hands to their mortal brothers and sisters not as preternatural visitors from realms of magic and wonder, but as equals, offering skills and help that, as often as not, would go unrecognized and unloved.

But Heather still lay in a hospital bed, and Sana also was separated from her people . . . by concrete walls and bars of steel. To this also the Elves had come. And there would be more.

Natil had climbed the slopes, and below her lay the white neatness of Elvenhome, a blue plume of smoke rising from its chimney like a cock on the shoulder of morning. To this place she had been sent. To teach. To speak. To tell the story and the meaning of the Elves to those so new to immortality that they still measured their lives in mere decades. And yet she had remained silent, had taught nothing, had said nothing.

Standing on a snowy slope in Colorado, dressed in the garb of a woman of the late twentieth century of the Christian dominion, Natil wondered what had become of her, wondered whether she could, in fact, claim anything that she saw as home or as refuge. She was a wanderer from the past who had come into a world so strange that it did not even have words to describe someone like herself. And yet she had to find those words, for to describe herself truly, without reservation, inadvertent omission, or concealment, would have been to describe *Elthia*, and it was to describe Her that Natil had come to this place.

And, indeed, it was to claim this place as home that she had come, too, for if the world had changed once, it had

certainly changed again. Here was the old blood, awakening, blooming in starlight. Here were Elves, living, helping, and healing . . .

. . . and shot, and unjustly jailed . . .

. . . and asking, pleading, for knowledge.

Shaking now, she turned and went down the slope to
Elvenhome, opened the kitchen door. The odor of pancakes and syrup and muffins was warm in the air, and
warm also was the presence of the Elves . . . the only
Elves the world now knew.

They were all still there. They were all still waiting.

Natil took her chair again. The newspaper lay before
her, and for a moment she regarded it as though it were
an embodiment of everything that once had caused the
Elves to fade, that now threatened their struggling renaissance. But then she sighed, lifted her head. "Her name,"
she said, "is *Elthia*. She made us. She *is* us."

They were listening. Natil licked dry lips and went on.
She talked for a long time.

Sunday was cloudy. Rain started to fall by noon, turning shortly thereafter to snow. It snowed all night. On
Monday, it was still snowing.

Sana blinked at the flakes that fluttered down past the
plate glass doors while Natil, at the counter, signed papers that she could not sign herself. She had thought that
she would not see snow again for a long time. She had
thought that she would not see much of anything. But,
still, she knew, it would all eventually be taken away
from her. It had been eighteen years before. It might well
be eighteen years again. Freddy Joy's incarnations, it
seemed, were legion, and she had been a fool to think that
she could ever get away from him.

Her hands throbbed, but, in truth, they did not feel
much like hands anymore. The paring knife had been
sharp, Terry's grip had been strong, her own struggles had
been fierce: the blade had slid through tendon, blood vessel, muscle, even bone, and it had turned her hands into
things that, really, were no more hands than she was a
free woman. Beneath their layers of bandages, they
seemed shapeless lumps of flesh: throbbing, racked with
sharp splinters of pain, but essentially inert.

"Summerson," Natil was saying to the uniformed clerk. "Natil Summerson."

"What kind of a name is that?" The clerk was both laconic and hostile. He believed the stories about the Satanism. For him, Sana Joy had ceased to be a human being.

"It is my name, sir," said Natil calmly. Her tone was carefully neutral.

"Yeah, and I suppose you're one of *them*."

The remark warranted no reply, and Natil offered none.

Sana thought back to those last few minutes before Terry had arrived . . . before her life had ended. Now, that brief flush of joy she had experienced was as nothing. Oh, to be sure, she looked the same, she saw, dimly and distantly, the starlight that had transformed her, but she was numb. She had nothing. She was nothing. And what good, she thought, was helping and healing when those she had come to serve looked at her with hate, put their fingers into her in the course of repeated strip searches, regarded her with covetous eyes that bespoke as much lust and violence as she had ever experienced at the hands of her father?

But now Natil was taking her arm, steering her toward the door. "Come, Sana. Let us go home."

She saw her apartment, saw the oven cleaner hit Terry's eyes with a splash of foam and dissolving corneas. "I can't go back there. Please don't make me go back there."

Natil tightened her grip, and Sana saw tears in her eyes. "Your apartment is still sealed, Sana. I am taking you to Elvenhome. Your home."

Outside, the snowflakes spun down like falling angels. Sana's face was beaded with melt. "Is it, Natil? Is anyplace my home? Is there anyplace I can go where they can't come and take me away?" She wanted her closet, wanted the safety of the warm, close darkness; but the closet with its futon and its tumble of blankets was in her apartment, as were Little Sandy and her harp, and that containment, perhaps, summed up the salient characteristics of a life in which safety was inevitably bounded by destruction, security kept forever out of reach by the violence of the past.

Natil had lifted her head. She was looking off into the snow. "There is," she said.

"Not Elvenhome, though."

"That is so," said Natil.

Sana leaned heavily on her arm as they went down the

slick steps to the waiting van. Natil had taken the day off work in order to come down and post bail, but Sana's feelings were mixed, for an anesthetic lassitude had enveloped her, turned her days into a numb elongation of a threadbare present.

She had not asked for a lawyer, she had not even asked to make a telephone call. She had sat in her cell until she had been taken out for questioning as she had sat in her bedroom until Freddy Joy had taken her out for sex. She had answered the officers' questions as she had spread her legs for her father. She had given what was asked for, no more. And when they had finished with her, when they had returned her to her cell, she had looked at the floor. She had not looked at the bars. In much the same way, in fact, she had once looked at cartoons instead of windows, for windows could open, and therefore they had been too much a reminder of her powerlessness, her inability to escape. Perhaps that was why she had, long ago, taken for her hope the soft but nonexistent realm of animated television.

What was left of her hands throbbed. The harp had been a hope, too. Once. Now ...

She bent her head quickly, teeth clenched against the wail that surged up out of her throat. Natil, understanding, put her inside the van, got behind the wheel, and held her. In comparative privacy, then, Sana screamed, cried, shuddered with all the despair of the captive recaptured, of the freed slave reduced once again to bondage, of the abused child returned to her abuser.

Natil rocked her, murmured to her softly in a language that seemed as cool and liquid as a river, that seemed to speak by its very nature of safety and comfort, of azure sky and blue water; but Sana knew that although it seemed at times that Natil must surely have come from one of those same cartoons in which she had found her childhood escapes, that she had surely climbed out of the realm of phosphor image and streaming electrons so as to offer to her a release from her world of bondage and violation, such a release was, nonetheless, a matter of fantasy, as illusory as the display of color and light in an old RCA picture tube.

And yet here was Natil, as real as Freddy Joy, as concrete and determined as the jail that had, with reluctance, yielded her up this morning after putting a brand on her soul that marked her as one of its own. Scars, brands: it was all the same. But Natil . . .

"Let us go to Elvenhome, Sana. Everyone is there, waiting for you."

Yes, and they would look at her, and they would *see*. "Please . . . no . . . I don't want them to . . ."

"They will not look upon you if you do not wish it. But they love you, and they wish you well. And they want you to feel loved and safe."

"You're all . . ." The sobs were still choking her, and she could not believe that her lips could still utter words that expressed anything save loss and grief. " . . . wonderful. You've all been good to me."

"That is what we are here for, Sana. We are your people."

The reminder, coming in Natil's gentle voice, touched with her unmistakable accent, made Sana open her swollen eyes. "My people," she said. "Elves."

Natil nodded. "Elves."

Sana put her bandaged hands to her face. "And what good is it all? You can't help me. Nobody can help me." The numbness was failing her. In strange surroundings, frightening circumstances, it had kept the brunt of the horror away, but now, in Natil's van, surrounded by the commonplace and the ordinary, it was receding, allowing her to see the grotesque helplessness of her condition. "You can hire all the lawyers you want, but Terry's got his story down, and everyone's already made up their minds, and . . . and . . ."

"Peace."

Sana's hands were still pressed to her face, and she felt the lumps of flesh swaddled in the bandages. "*I don't even have my hands anymore!*"

"Sana . . ."

Panicking, the white rawness of the world forcing itself upon her, Sana shook her useless hands. "They don't work! They don't do anything! The paramedics just wrapped them up, and the city just let them rot! No one wanted to pay for a doctor!"

The wave of despair sucked at her with a vicious undertow. No hands, no harp, no escape . . . no hope: the summation of her life.

She felt hands on her shoulders, felt the touch of Natil's head to hers. "Find the stars, Sana. Find the stars."

"The nerves are gone!"

"Sana. Elf."

The title made her gasp in a lungful of air. Though Terry and madness and the blind course of senseless events had dragged her out of her dream and mired her once again in the abuse of the world, she had, for those fleeting minutes in her apartment, seen the truth of her trans formation. She was an Elf. Regardless of what might be done to her, that fundamental identity could not be taken away.

"The stars, Sana."

And she saw them, then, burning unquenchably within her, and though she knew from astronomy books that they were no more than chance collections of incandescent gas with lifespans that, though immense, were nonetheless finite, still, as she watched, they turned from futile, scientific abstractions into a new icon. They were spirit. They were the soul of her people, and she was of that selfsame stuff that, from microsecond to microsecond, fired light into the universe, sustained it, drove it on and on through the unending cycles of life, death, and rebirth that she had celebrated in the Circle of the Witches.

"But I can't . . ." She stared at the stars. " . . . go on."

"You can," said Natil, "and you will."

"But there isn't any hope."

"There is."

"No one can save me."

Natil did not reply, and when Sana opened her eyes again to fill her sight with that gentle and compassionate face, something about Natil's expression—solemn, but touched as though with a memory of joy—made her recall all the landscapes into which she had wanted to escape, all the soft grass and sunlit meadows for which she had reached . . . only to find her hands stopped by impenetrable glass.

Stopped. Always stopped. Even now, here, with starlight flowing like a luminous mist through her mind, she had been stopped. She had reached for what she had thought was a living embodiment of her childhood dreams of safety, and she had been stopped, her hands mutilated as though to preclude forever any more reachings.

And yet Natil's expression told Sana that the elven harper had seen those sunlit dreams, that, somehow, miraculously, the barriers and the abuse had fallen before her slender hands. And, though her own hands were destroyed, her hopes crushed, still that expression kindled in Sana a kind of sickly optimism, for though hope had become painful—as painful as the aching wounds in her hands—it seemed that at least Natil believed that someone could save her.

———————

Date: March 13, 1992

TO: Ronald M. Wickey, Chancellor
FROM: Nora Jerusalem, Rick Harris, David Dickens

Re: HOG, Terence Angel, Serena Joy

We have been abiding by your injunction regarding any discussion of HOG. We are aware of the fact that even a completely internal document such as this letter *de facto* breaks that injunction, but as scholars and teachers of the humanities, we believe that both our positions at Kingsley College and the reputation of the college itself are of little importance when compared with the potential destruction of a young woman's life.

For some time, two of us (Jerusalem and Harris) were engaged in research that attempted to confirm or deny Mr. Angel's manifold claims regarding his so-called academic pursuits. The research, ultimately, proved his claims false. However, it also demonstrated, in our opinion, a capacity for violence and an almost pathological fascination with torture, bondage, and sadism.

You have, we are sure, been reading the newspapers, and therefore we assume that you are acquainted with the Serena Joy case. It is our considered belief that Ms. Joy, who has now been indicted for first degree assault, is in fact innocent. She is a victim of Mr. Angel's continuing delusions, which as we all can testify, are both compelling and very convincing.

We dislike the prospect of being forced to choose between the truth and our loyalty to an institution we have served for many years. Rather than immediately approaching the police investigators with our findings, therefore, we wish to consult with you first.

We would appreciate your immediate attention to this matter.

———————

CHAPTER 27

The TreeStar offices were closed, and TK knew what was happening. They were all up at Elvenhome, were all trying to help Sana deal with something that essentially could not be dealt with.

Sana had been caught, and though TK no more believed that she was guilty of the charges brought against her than he believed that he could grow a new left leg, he had seen what justice was and how it worked against those who from birth had been deemed powerless. And so, while Hadden and the others deserted the office for the isolation and sanctuary of Elvenhome, TK did not join them, for he knew that isolation was an illusion, sanctuary a sham. When the Man wanted Sana, the Man would come for Sana. And, for that matter, when the Man wanted TK, the Man would come for TK.

He had to admit it, though: there was anger behind his thoughts. Oh, everyone had some anger, and black people, perhaps, had considerably more than minimal rights to a reservoir of that emotion that must by now have grown peatdark with the accumulated residue of centuries. But TK had stars floating in his mind, too, and they made it very difficult for him to dissemble with himself, forced him, in fact, to acknowledge his anger for what it was.

He was, in fact, angry with the people who had taken him in and accepted him, who had caused him, in turn, to accept them. He was angry at their slow but steady untying of the knots that had held him to his race and his heritage. He was angry at their having given him a glimpse of a world in which skin color did not matter, in which hands were offered in faith and honesty, in which nothing was hidden, nothing was held back, nothing was waiting in that dark, starlit ship anchored off the coast but smiles, friendship, and a passage not to a land of auction blocks and lingering death, but to a realm of azure skies, blue water, and service that was, in truth, perfect freedom.

Marsh had asked him to come up to the Home on Saturday, but he had refused. Yes, they were his people. No, he would not come. Now that the innate bigotry and futility of human endeavor had touched even Sana, TK needed time to deal with his anger at the world for being the way it was, at Elvenhome for so steadfastly insisting that it did not have to be that way at all.

TreeStar was closed, but TK went to work anyway, digitizing maps, entering figures, clicking and dragging nodes from place to place in the network of control points that Lauri or Raven had laid down on a patch of earth somewhere. He traveled to and from the office not in the placid uniform of the white business world, but in t-shirts and fatigue pants that allowed him to work in comfort, and he listened to the surreptitious click of automobile door locks with a head full of stars that allowed him to shrug inwardly with the thought that, yes, things like that happened in this place. And he was angry about that, too.

He went in early. He worked late. He did not seem to need much sleep these days: an hour or two at most served him, and if he needed anything more, the want appeared to be well filled by a quiet pondering of the stars within him. And if his instincts—engendered by a janitor in Georgia and, seemingly, made permanent by starlight—prompted him to help and heal, why, come evenings, he had his neighborhood; and with conflicting emotions he guided drug addicts to rehabilitation centers run by nice white people whose smiles held not one tenth of the sincerity of the folk of Elvenhome, gave money away to those who would doubtless squander it on Night Train or Thunderbird or Mad Dog 20-20, gave up his sofa to someone who needed a place to sleep for a night . . . and who, come morning, turned out to have obviously needed his portable television, too.

It was futile. It was useless. But he had to try. And, well, he had to die sometime: it was not as though he would be saddled with the job forever.

In truth, though, there was every chance that he would not be saddled with the job for much more than a few weeks, for as he read the paper every morning in an effort to keep abreast of Sana's predicament, he was aware of stories that had, with time, dropped into the relative obscurity of the center pages. The police were still looking for the man (and they knew now that it was only one man) who, in the space of fifteen or twenty minutes, had singlehandedly destroyed a well-armed crack house, the man who, as far as they could tell, was now hobbling around on one leg because his prosthesis had been shattered in a final burst of gunfire.

They were saying little about suspects, but that was nothing unusual, and TK knew what was happening. Reluctant though the city was to prosecute someone who had made away with both a palpable nuisance and an imminent danger, it also had to contend with questions of credibility and equal enforcement of the law that apparently had not arisen when a little girl had been shot to death in her front yard. TK could only conclude that, like Satanism, gangs and drugs were trendy. Little black girls were not.

He fell asleep Thursday night wondering when they were going to come for him. A simple check of the records at the VA would tell them who had been issued such-and-such a prosthesis of such-and-such a manufacture and such-and-such a serial number, and with the stink he had been making about the crack house for months before the demolition, it would not take them long to add two and two together and arrive at a reasonable approximation of four. Proof, to be sure, was another matter: proof could get interesting. But, given time, they could get proof, and then they would come for him. Oh, they would come.

He slept for a long time. The sun, in fact, had risen well into the sky by the time he awoke, and even then his thoughts were so fuzzy that, for several minutes, he did not comprehend the dim apartment with the light filtering in through its makeshift drapes, hardly understood the Yorkshire terrier sleeping on his chest, was outright bewildered by the distant squawk of a police radio . . .

It was all wrong. There were supposed to be . . . trees about him. And mountains wrapping around the horizon. And lakes blue enough to pigment a worldful of skies with their deep color. And there was supposed to be birdsong, and animals, and . . . and—

A knock at the door, and Rags was suddenly on his feet, growling and snarling, as feral as ever. TK blinked stupidly at the cracked ceiling, wondering why he could not see the sun. Where was he? What—

Another knock, louder.

Comprehension forced itself upon him, then, and in spite of his dreams, he finally remembered where—and who—he was. There were mountains and lakes and trees like that somewhere, he supposed, but not here. This was his apartment. This was the city. He was TK Winters.

Yet another knock. Pounding, rather.

Rags snarled and snapped at the air. Still fuzzy, TK threw back the covers, swung his feet over the edge of the bed, and padded across the floor in his boxers, blinking at the unreality that had suddenly descended upon his world. His bare feet were almost soundless on the linoleum as he approached the door, but he paused with his hand on the knob, thinking back to a boy with an Uzi, a boy he had first spared, then killed.

Rags snarled, twining himself between TK's feet like a cat, making little, vicious leaps at the door as though to frighten away what lay on the other side of the wood.

"Who is it?" said TK, wondering why his voice sounded odd.

"Denver Police."

"Shit." He looked at Rags. "Man, I going to have to call Natil or someone and have them feed you."

Rags simply redoubled his efforts, seemingly bent upon clawing his way through the door.

TK grabbed him by the scruff, dragged him away, tossed him back into the room. "Now you stay there, man," he said. "Don't go biting no one and getting Uncle TK into more trouble than he already got."

With a growl, Rags retreated, but he stood, poised, as though readying himself for an attack.

TK, resigned to what was coming, turned the deadbolt, flicked off the chain, opened the door. There were two officers in the hallway, one black, one white. Well, TK reflected, having the nigger dragged off by two white boys would look bad to the press. He assumed that the press was somewhere. He assumed that there were other officers somewhere . . . maybe, for that matter, a whole fucking SWAT team.

TK glanced at the brother in uniform, received in return as stony a glance as he had ever gotten from the OG in charge of the crack house. He wondered why that did not bother him, why his thoughts about the SWAT team,

accurate though he suspected they were, made him feel
sad rather than angry, disloyal rather than persecuted.

"Theodore Karlington Winters?" said the white officer.

"That's me."

Rags chose that moment to charge, turning instantane-
ously into a small, furry projectile. Instinctively, TK
stuck out his left foot, and the dog, too fixed upon his target to stop, ran directly into his master's leg. TK felt the
impact of teeth, and when he looked down, his calf was
bleeding from a ragged set of puncture wounds.

"Rags! Damn your fucking hide!" He reached down and
scooped the offending terrier into his arms. Rags did not
struggle: he seemed rather dazed by his miscalculation.
"Sorry, officers," said TK. "He's . . . uh . . . kind of protective."

But neither of the officers were looking at Rags. They
were, instead, looking down. At the floor. Maybe, TK
thought with an odd sensation, at his wounded leg.

"It's all right," he said. "Shit, he bit me worse than that
dozens of times. He was a stray, you know. Street fighter.
But he's had all his shots."

The officers were still looking down.

"Really. No problem. What can I do for you guys?"

He knew what he could do for them, though. He could
answer a few questions, listen to his rights being read to
him, hold out his hands for the cuffs, and go without a
struggle. Well, if that was what they wanted, he supposed
that he could give it to them.

But the officers were still looking at his left leg, and
TK, growing more puzzled, saw their gaze shift to his
right leg, then back to his left. Straightening suddenly,
they exchanged glances. One shrugged. The other
shrugged. Almost embarrassed, then: "You . . . uh . . .
wear an artificial leg, Mr. Winters?"

He allowed himself the tacit lie again. "Nope."

"Do you . . ." Another exchange of glances. Another
pair of shrugs. ". . . have some form of ID?"

TK nodded, went to his jeans, took out his wallet. Returning to the door, he handed the white officer his driver's license. "It's not a very good picture."

"They never are, are they?" It was a sort of a joke, but
there was not a bit of humor in it. The officer looked at
the license, then at TK. He stared for a moment, shook

his head. "It's you all right." He handed the license back. "Uh ... stay in town, Mr. Winters. We'll probably want to talk to you again. Later." Another glance at TK's leg. "I ... I guess."

And with that, they turned and left.

Holding Rags, TK looked after them as they descended the stairs. Feeling uneasy, feeling as though the morning had first taken one odd turn and then yet another, maybe several others, he went to the window and gingerly shoved back an edge of the improvised drape.

Three squad cars at the curb. A fourth at the corner. Doubtless one or two in the alley. Reporters? Hard to tell. Probably. But why then had they just asked him a few inane questions and then left?

With the departure of the police, though, Rags' good humor had returned, and he wriggled in TK's arms and strained up to lick his face. "That's enough, Rags," said TK, wiping away the wet. Odd, his fingers told him that he would not have to shave today, even though that was patently ridiculous: his whiskers had been, as usual, something akin to barbed wire the night before. But all he felt now was smooth skin.

He padded into the bathroom, examined his face. No beard. And his face looked a little different, too. Something about his cheekbones, and—

He stared then. He had looked into tunnels this way. He had looked into the dark mouth of an Iraqi bunker this way. Now he was looking at his own face, and he was re-membering Lauri's comments about hair and knit caps.

With a wrench, he left the bathroom, slammed the door behind him. He turned on all the lights in the apartment, jerked open the drapes. Light—sunlight—was what he needed now, for he was sure that he was still dreaming, that shreds of his unconscious and nocturnal wanderings were still clinging to him, mocking his waking life. Oh, he had noticed some changes in himself before this, but now ...

No. No, it was crazy. Just crazy. Elvenhome ... he wondered why they called it Elvenhome ... wondered why he had not figured it out before ...

Shaking, he grabbed a paper towel from the kitchen and sat down on the edge of his bed to clean and bandage the bite in his calf. It was, fortunately, not deep—for all his vi-ciousness, Rags was, after all, just a toy terrier—but the blood had run down and dried, and TK had to scrub for the better part of a minute before he could get it all off.

And then he realized that he was tending a wound in his left leg. The one he had lost in Iraq.

Something vital had gone out of Sana. It was as though the uselessness of her hands had infected her entire life, for there had come to be a sense of damage and ineffectuality about her. She believed that she could no more shape the world to her desired ends than she could hold a fork.

Natil took her to see a hand specialist within twenty-four hours, but the doctor could recommend nothing more than a lengthy series of operations that might restore partial use to a few of her muscles. Or might not. It was, he said, doubtful.

"If you'd gotten in here right away, we might have been able to do something," he said. "As it is . . ."

Natil noticed that he had made sure that his desk was interposed between himself and Sana. Despite his casually professional tone, his hands were clenched tightly together. He had obviously read the papers.

"Maybe some therapy," he continued, fishing in a drawer. "I can put you in touch with—"

"Therapy to accomplish what, my good doctor?" said Natil.

"Well, she's got partial use of her left thumb and index finger." He was not looking at her. He did not want to look at her. "Therapy might firm that up."

Sana drooped. Natil thought of delays. The city had not helped to heal the hands of a suspected felon because it did not want to spend the money. This doctor did not want to heal because he was afraid.

A touch of anger in her voice: "So she can perhaps learn to feed herself. Is that what you mean?"

"There's nothing I can do." He was suddenly defensive. "Conservative treatment is probably best. There's no sense in wasting money."

They left, and Sana stared out at the pale light of a Denver morning as it was shuttered and unshuttered first by the passing buildings, then by the trees that lined the road to Elvenhome. Natil knew her thoughts. Useless. Completely useless. Others might hope, believe, and be saved, but not Sana.

Sana stayed at the Home, hiding among the pines that

stood like dark guardians, among the aspens that were beginning to leaf out with an unusually early spring. There, the reporters could not find her, and so she was spared their constant intrusions and harassment. The law, however, was another matter, and as, years ago, she had been dragged out of the safety of her bedroom, so now she would be dragged away from the safety of Elvenhome. A trial was coming, and there were lawyers to consider and defenses to be mapped out; but Natil could tell that Sana, despite the starlight, despite all the support that the Elves could offer, had given up.

Natil could not blame her. Terry was angelic, sweet, and very convincing, and the press had been diligent in exploiting not only Sana's religion, but also her past: the long ago accusations of incest made against her father, his subsequent complete vindication. Sana, it appeared, was a chronic and habitual liar who had carried the most bizarre and perverse of her childhood fantasies into her adult life.

The lawyer that Clarice recommended was expensive, and he demanded twelve thousand dollars for a retainer. Cash. Up front. The Elves raised the money and paid without even blinking.

"But I'm not worth it," said Sana as she and Natil drove away from his office. Bob Sentry had at least been honest: proving Sana's innocence was a doubtful proposition. At the very least, it would be a lengthy one. He would try, though. And, yes, he might well use up every scrap of the twelve thousand dollars before he was through.

"You are a kinswoman," Natil replied. "You are worth kingdoms."

"They'll just . . ." Sana clenched what was left of her hands. ". . . they'll just fry me. That's what they want, that's what they'll get. They'll put Terry on the stand, all bandaged up and blind like that, just like they put my father on the stand, and he'll sound just wonderful . . . just like my father. And no one'll even ask how I managed to put that paring knife right through both of my own palms, just like no one ever asked me about . . . about . . ." She covered her face as though to keep the memories away.

"He . . ." Natil could not blame Sana. No harp, no future, nothing. Her life had fallen into dust. Even winning her case would make no difference: the damage to her

soul had already been done. "He fantasizes about the stigmata, does he not?"

"Yeah." Sana dropped her bandaged hands, looked at
the passing cars and the buildings as though she were in
her own mind, already a prisoner. "The five wounds of
Christ. The miraculous sign of abject submission to
God." She shuddered. "What kind of a God would do that
to people, anyway?" she demanded suddenly. "There's
stuff in the paper every day about people knifing up their
kids, or sticking hot irons on their backs, or chaining
them up and starving them. Isn't that just like the stigmata? Is their God just an abusive son of a bitch?"

Natil kept her eyes on the road. "He is for some of them."

But as though her outburst had drained her, Sana fell
suddenly silent. "I could sure use some kind of miracle,
though," she murmured after a time. "I could sure use
some real magic."

"Is magic not real?"

"It doesn't work in the courtroom. No more than
wishes worked back . . . back then." Sana shook her head,
regarded her hands as though reading in them the truth of
her life. With careful bandaging and as much of the old
powers as they could gather, Natil and Ash had restored
the use of her left thumb and index finger, and of her
right ring and little fingers. She could, with effort, feed
and dress herself, but she would always be crippled, and
she would never harp again.

But Natil was thinking. Miracles. Magic. The old powers.
Could she still hope? So much had happened: so much tragedy, so much damage . . . Could she even hope to hope?

"The Goddess *is* the universe," Sana went on, "but you
can't just expect Her to change Herself around for your
benefit."

"Have you . . . have you ever seen Her?" said Natil.

"Seen her?" Sana looked up. "Well, in the world. In the
trees. In you. In me. I feel Her when I invoke Her."

There it was. The key. Quivering, floating as though a
harpstring were trembling in a sunbeam. "As though She
were . . . right there . . ."

"Yeah. Like that."

"But not directly. Not face to face."

"No." Sana had, unconsciously, slipped back into the
role of teacher of Wicca. The press could talk provoca-

tively about knives and Books of Shadows, occult shops could buy and sell belief and empowerment, fundamentalist ministers could fulminate about the rise of Satanism and rock and roll, but the Craft—the real Craft, the worship of the Mother Goddess—went on, unsullied, in the hearts and loves of people like Sana. "That's not something you can do except . . . like . . . maybe in dreams or visions or something. The Goddess is a symbol, don't forget. The universe is too big to relate to, so we make a symbol and call it the Goddess and relate to that."

Natil nodded. "I recall you saying that many times."

"It's important. Lots of people forget that."

"But what if . . ." Natil looked for words, found none. What she wanted to ask, what she *had* to ask, defied words. Indeed, it was arrogant, even cruel, to ask it of someone as damaged as Sana.

The silence lengthened, and its gravity penetrated even Sana's sorrow. "Natil?"

"What if . . . what if that . . . is not true?" A horrible choice of words, but for all her age and power and blood and experience, Natil could think of nothing better.

"What if what isn't true?"

Natil prayed, went on. "That She is just a symbol. Or, rather, what if She actively enters into that symbol? What if She makes it real? What if the . . . universe . . . makes the symbol real?"

Horrible. Utterly horrible. She sounded as uselessly scholastic as Aquinas.

Sana sat for a time. Her brow was furrowed, her mouth twisted. "Hey look, Natil. I said that I'd teach you about the Goddess. But I can only teach what I know. This is beyond me."

Natil spoke slowly, carefully. "When I asked if you would teach me, I had . . . other motives."

Sana stared. Natil had been less than honest? "What?"

Natil pointed the blunt nose of the van straight down the highway, straight toward the mountains. The mountains. Almost everything that was left of Elves, of immortal helping and healing, lay up in those mountains. But in the van with her was perhaps the most precious remnant of all. "I am . . ." Her voice faltered for a moment, but she prayed, and perhaps she was answered, for she found words. " . . . four and one half billion years old, Sana. The Lady, *Elthia,* made me at the beginning of all things, and I looked into Her face when She had given me eyes to see, and I took Her hands when She had given me hands with which to take them."

Almost unconsciously, Sana had dropped her eyes. Her own hands could take little, and the immensity of Natil's admission defied immediate comprehension. Natil pushed on.

"I have seen Her, Sana. Face to face. I have been held in Her arms. In time of trial I have spoken to Her, and She has offered counsel and love."

Sana's hands were clenched, her head was bent. Natil saw tears. Understanding had come.

Her own eyes were misting as she continued. "That vision sustained the Elves throughout all the ages of the earth. But when the Firstborn faded, so did it also, and it took with it all the power and magic that had once been theirs."

"I'm sorry." Sana's voice was a hoarse whisper. Natil saw the yearning in her eyes. Sana was a witch. Sana loved the Goddess. Sana had always wanted to be held.

Natil swallowed. Another prayer. Maybe. Maybe Sana could indeed be held. "When I asked you about invoking the Goddess . . . about making Her real . . . I was speaking literally."

"Natil?"

Natil did not look at Sana, for she was sure that if she looked, she would lose her nerve. The most precious remnant of the Old Ways on the face of the planet, and yet— crippled, persecuted, despairing—how fragile a thing it was! "I was sent here to bring the vision back. I was sent to bring the magic back. I . . ." She had to look. She looked. Sana was staring, half frightened, half wondering. ". . . I think I was sent here to find you."

The nurseries had been forcing lilies for Easter, and even now, five weeks before the feast, the stores were full of them. Audrey's room was full of them. Audrey had liked lilies. She had liked all sorts of flowers, but she had liked lilies most of all, and she had liked them best when they had been budding, trembling on the verge of opening. Betweens. Audrey had liked betweens.

The room was quiet save for the hissing of the respirator, and Maxwell Delmari sat beside the bed, holding his daughter's hand. Audrey, dead, writhed and stirred, quivered as though fighting her way toward wakefulness, but there was no wakefulness. This was a room of the dead. There were no betweens here, only finality. Despite the lilies, there would be no resurrection for Audrey, and nothing, medical or musical, would ever change that.

Outside, Maxwell knew, his attorney, Dr. Braun, and several of the orderlies and sympathetic nurses were standing guard, ready to obstruct and interfere if anyone attempted to interrupt what he was going to do this March morning. And he expected that someone would indeed try to interrupt, to counter with yet another legal document the writ that lay now, freshly signed, on the table by Audrey's bed. He, in fact, did not have much time to act, and he knew that. But still he wanted to sit for a few minutes at the side of this bed, just as he had sat beside it every evening for the last three years. In a little while, though, he would rise, and he would leave, and he would never come back.

He heard an automobile squeal to a halt outside. A door slammed.

Dr. Braun had told him which switch to throw. It was plainly marked. It was even taped and sealed. But the seal was thin, and the tape was brittle with the dryness of hospital air. A flick of a finger would break it. And so Maxwell Delmari broke it, removed the seal.

He heard Dr. Braun close the door of the room. That was good. He did not want to hear anything but Audrey's last breaths.

There was shouting in the corridor. Something about Jesus. Something about an injunction. But it was distant shouting, very faint, and his attorney and Braun and her people were, doubtless, doing their jobs, because it drew no closer.

Maxwell leaned forward. "Good-bye, sugar," he said.

And then he threw the switch, and with his eyes clenched tightly shut, he put his lips to the flushed, bloated cheek of his daughter and held them there until she writhed no more, until she quivered and fought for illusory wakefulness no more, until, maybe, she really did awake—to a world of freedom, to a world in which all betweens came to a kind of fulfillment so unbearably bright and lovely that no flesh and blood, but only spirit, could look upon it with sufficient joy.

CHAPTER 28

God was light. God was beauty. God was the inbreaking of luminous bondage into the abject darkness of His submissive creature. God was the fire of love kindled in the burning soul that, thusly transpierced with the dart of the assailing Seraphim, thereupon felt the wound with unsurpassable delight, was made radiant by it, was allowed by God at times to manifest that divine sore outwardly.

But Terry could not see beauty. He could not see light. He could not see anything. His blind eyes ached with chemical burns, his face was scarred deeply enough to be perceptible even to his blistered fingers. He could not perceive light, he was not beautiful. How could God love him?

The city's assistance program provided some initial treatment, but it did not have sufficient resources for a complete cure, even if a cure were possible. And it was not possible: the lye had eaten his eyes. He did not have anything that could be cured. For a time, then, he would have help, money, and aid. After that, though, he would be on his own, and whether Sandy were imprisoned for her actions or not, he would still be blind, and scarred . . .

. . . and God would not love him.

He spent his days in the little house that he had rented near the campus, passing gropingly from bed to chair and back again. His devotions, his mortifications, went all unperformed, for as someone from the city came in twice a day to fix his meals and to make sure he was well, he could no longer be sure that his worship would be uninterrupted and unperceived. Unable, therefore, to count upon having extended periods of sacred time in which he might (if he were good, if he mortified himself sufficiently) catch, with his mind's eye, a fleeting glimpse of Jesus' hands, or of a saint's face, or to see (again, with the inner sight that was all that had been left to him), hanging in the air before him as though upon sharp hooks, a beating, shuddering heart that thrust gouts of blood at him out of countless wounds as though inviting him to come forward, drink, partake of a communion of ecstasy reserved only for the most humble, the most submissive, he could only sit—idle, sinful, scarred, blind, ugly—longing for the touch of divine shackles upon his senses, helpless to invite them.

And God could not possibly love him.

Oh, he was bound now, suspended between life and death, his blindness an outward sign of perfect submission. But as when, months ago, his ears and his spirit had been seduced by the music of a simple gardener, so his present condition represented once again a submission not to God, but rather to physical reality, to the realm of the Serpent. He could not see because of his body, and that failure, coupled as it was with the rage he felt at so being mastered by what he had thought he had reduced to bondage, demanded penance. But he could not perform his penance, because he could not see, because he had no privacy, because he was afraid that those who entered his house every day might (as had happened once before) see what he did, misunderstand, think him, perhaps, mad.

Bound and helpless, therefore, unable to atone for his evil, he existed in his little house, smiled and nodded into his personal darkness as the volunteers came and went, listened to their sympathetic words, expressed his complete forgiveness for the woman—herself submissive to nothing and no one—who had blinded him in the midst of the most important lesson of her life. But Terry was determined that if he achieved nothing else through his blindness and scars, if he himself was made forever a stranger to God, he would at least teach one who should have known better, who should have embraced helplessness willingly, who should have matched her immense talents with an equal measure of sanctity. He would teach her the value of enthusiastic, unalterable submission to divine will. And if not to divine will, then to its earthly representatives.

Sandy would learn. He would not waste everything.

But her lesson would not help him. He was blind, he would be blind forever, he had no hope that he would ever see, in this life or the next, any wondrous light kindling before him, whether in the mysterious apparition of a burning bush or the miraculous showing of a Face—a Face he would know, a Face that would fix him with an eternal stare and so rive him to the core, burst his heart, open him, body and soul, to the ineffable ecstasy of the thrusting, heaving Godhead.

———————

Dear Nora:

It's been a week now, and I haven't heard from Wickey. I'm afraid that he's just going to let us hang on this one.

Dave is still on our side. He doesn't know anything about Serena Joy, but he saw enough of Angel's articles to make him a convert. And the stunt that bastard pulled with Maxwell!

Well, Audrey's gone now, God bless her. I saw you at the funeral, but didn't get a chance to talk. It seems like we've got even less time now than we did when we were involved with the whole HOG mess.

Anyway, what I'm trying to say is that I'm still on our side, too. I guess the question now is whether we go through channels, good or bad, and make things so hot for Wickey that he'll have to back down, or go the polite route, submit our resignations, and get the hell out of here. Part of me keeps thinking about my folks' apple farm. It would sure beat all the crap that comes down at this school, though I have a feeling Nancy and the kids wouldn't like it one bit.

Let me know what you think. I'll be in my office all next week, although the way things have been working out, I'm sure that means you'll be out of town. As it is, we've got time. Joy's trial isn't slated to start until May. It'll be messy, though. The DA's office has bought Angel's story, but Joy's got Bob Sentry for a lawyer. You remember what he did with that police rape case a few years back, don't you? I hear that Kiowa will never be the same.

Love,

Rick

———————

Cartoons.

Sana had always thought that cartoons had contained her salvation, that, paradoxically or, perhaps, appropriately, the salvation they had offered had been imaginary, fictitious, the wish-fulfillment fantasies of a battered child. But in the course of the drive back to Elvenhome that morning, Natil told her about the Lady, about the spiritual relationship that the Elves, by their nature, shared with Her, and suddenly the world of the real and the concrete—the world she had always assumed would never offer her anything more than indefatigable hostility and persecution—held within it a potential for peace and wholeness that she had before only perceived in animated paint.

It was not a cartoon. It was not an illusion. Natil had said it: it was true. It was real.

As a witch, Sana believed in the Goddess, connected with Her, felt herself to be one with Her; but as an Elf, she had access to a closer intimacy that, though lost (and it had indeed been lost: Natil made that clear), could be found again.

To be held in Her arms . . .

Sana wanted to be held. She wanted to feel, for the first time in her life, safe, beyond the grasp of those who manipulated, those who persecuted, those who, through the simple, countless, and unconscious actions of living, abused and battered their way through their lives with unutterable and oblivious cruelty.

"But . . . but . . . what can I do?"

Natil guided the rattling van along the mountain road. "You are a witch, Sana. You invoke the Goddess into yourself. And you are an Elf, and therefore you instinctively yearn for *Elthia*. The connection between the Lady and Her children has been broken, but you stand with one foot on either side of it: wiccan and elven both, you wield powers and emotions that might be able to remake it."

Sana stared, momentarily forgetting her mutilated hands. The Lady and Her children . . . and she so desperately wanted to be held. "But . . . how?"

The road had been roughened by snow and spring rains. Natil kept the van from lurching to one side, swerved its wheels straight again. "Can you invoke

Elthia? As a witch? As an Elf? As a child calling for her mother to return?"

Sana felt the bitter tears well up with an ache that reached far back. Years ago, she had wept for her mother, had, with bruised wrists and a raw, swollen vulva, called out for her to return. But her mother had not come, her mother was not there, and the warm, California darkness of her bedroom had been close, confining, her father's snoring a constant reminder of what could happen again, what undoubtedly *would* happen again. "I . . ."

There was a plea in Natil's voice. "Can you?"

A child calling for her mother? Sana tried to dry her cheeks with a sleeve, but the ache of tears deepened. For years now, she had been holding Little Sandy, trying to make up for all the emptiness and the loss. "Will . . . will She come?"

And Natil must have heard in her question the failures, the desolation, for Sana saw that the harper's eyes were damp, the light in her eyes shadowed, troubled. It seemed that she, too, had called, called for a long time, and had received no answer.

"I . . . cannot say," said Natil. "You are my last hope, Sana. You are an Elf who remembers humanity. And you are a child of Elthia who knows the Craft of the witches. There is no other like you among us."

Sana clenched her hands within their bandages, felt the pain. Vulva, palms: it was always pain. Turning away as much as her seatbelt allowed, she pressed her forehead against the window, stared at the sunlight and the trees. Another wall? Another glass wall? "Goddess, just . . . just hold me . . ."

Natil did not speak for a time. Then: "She can, Sana."

The trees were blurred, fleeting. They might well have been phosphor images. "I want to believe that."

"Can you believe it?"

Sana shut her eyes. Wicca, she realized, was a religion solely of the mind. She could summon the Goddess, but only in her imagination did the Goddess come. Perhaps that was why she had become a witch: it was easy to imagine all sorts of things that were not—and would never be—real.

She shook her head, felt the glass against her forehead. "I don't know. It hurts too much."

Natil nodded slowly, tiredly. Once again, she had received no answer. "I understand."

The van crested a rise, then descended to the little clearing of packed earth that the Elves used as a parking lot. It was empty this morning: everyone had gone into town to see Heather, to attend to businesses and lives that had been left idle since Monday. They would, come nightfall, be back. For Sana. For themselves.

But when Natil and Sana came within sight of the house, they saw someone waiting by the front door. Tall, dark, dressed in jeans and a flannel shirt, he wore a knit cap pulled down low—over the tops of his ears.

"It's TK," said Sana.

"It is."

"How . . . ?"

Natil sighed as though already exhausted, she had left one task incomplete only to turn to another that would doubtless prove even more daunting. "It appears . . . that it is his time, Sana."

His time. As they approached, he seemed half inclined to come forward to meet them, half to flee. And so, compromising, he stood his ground.

"Blessings," said Natil when they had joined him.

Sana swallowed the tightness in her throat. "Hi, TK."

He nodded. His face was as serious as ever, but there was a softness about it that she had not seen before. He seemed, in fact, to have been touched with a hint of the womanly, and she noticed that there was not a trace of beard on his cheeks. "How're the hands, Sana?" he said slowly. His voice was firm, definite, but there was a catch in it.

She glanced at Natil. "About the same, TK. Natil and Ash have got me fixed up so that I can use a few fingers. We're going to see another doctor next week." She did not say that she had lost hope in doctors, that she could no longer have brought herself to touch her harp, even had it been with her, even had it not still been sealed within her apartment—along with Little Sandy, along with everything else—as the police continued to gather evidence. Her dream about Little Sandy and Terry had been prophetic: like the doll, she had been effectively dismembered, sundered from herself, from her wishes, from her aspirations.

And now Natil was asking her to make whole what she had come to believe was, by nature, permanently sundered. Helping and healing? Natil was asking her to take care of the entire universe, and she could not even take care of herself!

TK, though, was nodding. "That's good."

They stood there, all three of them, shifting uneasily because of what had not been uttered, because of what had to be uttered eventually. Hands went into pockets, came out again. Feet shuffled. Starlight flickered uneasily.

Natil began. "You found the Home, TK."

He nodded. "It ain't too hard, once you know what to look for."

His knit cap was an anomaly. Sana guessed what it meant. "Are . . . are you okay?"

"Depends on your point of view."

"How did you get here?"

"Took the bus up as far as the last stop," he said. A pause. "And then walked." Another pause. "On two legs."

Natil bowed low.

TK's face, soft though it had become, contained all the emotion of a block of granite. "All right. What's going on?" His words fell like hammers. "You tell me what's going on. I don't want no more shit. I got handed a line about old blood and all that. I don't want no more lines. I want to know what's going on."

Sana realized, then, that it was not that TK's face was without emotion. Rather, it was that so much emotion had arisen within him, so many conflicting desires and angers and rejections, that one face could not contain them all. Roiling and turbulent, they had frozen his features into a tumultuous stasis in which not one could gain ascendancy long enough to manifest. And as TK's face, so, she knew, his soul.

Without thinking, she offered her bandaged hands. Helping and healing. For one another. For the world. Maybe . . . maybe indeed for the universe. And whether her hands were whole or not, whether she were afraid or not, whether the police or Freddy Joy or anyone else would come for her or not, the helping and the healing had to start. It simply had to. She could not harp, would, in fact, probably never harp again, and so she had to find other ways. And with a sense of wonder, she discovered that she was determined to find other ways. "TK," she said, "you've got the blood. It's . . . waked up. When it wakes up, it takes over."

His face did not change. "So what the fuck's it done to me?"

"It's . . ." Sana looked at Natil. The harper was unseeing, stricken, and Sana suddenly understood what she had been going through for the last week, for the last month, for the last eon. Sana had lost her mother. Natil had lost her Goddess, her Creatrix, her sustenance . . . and had as yet no hope that she would ever find Her again. "It's transformed you."

TK's eyes were dark, an obsidian abyss.

"You're . . ." Sana faltered, striving to put aside the thoughts about her hands, about her mother, about her Goddess, about what Natil had asked her to do, striving to concentrate instead simply upon the welfare of another. That was what Elves did. That was the reason for Elves.

But how did one say it? How had Natil said it to her? As she recalled, the knowledge had been given to her as she had been ready to accept it, parceled out slowly until Heather had abruptly put an end to the foolishness by telling her everything. Coming, though, from a life of continuous desperation and tragedy, she had, perhaps, been less concerned than most about the cataclysmic nature of the changes that had welled up from within her. She had become used to trauma: a little more was as nothing, particularly when it offered an escape into such a starlit world of solace.

But she did not know TK. She had worked with him, eaten with him, even played with him. But she realized that he was still as a stranger to her. And though there was starlight in his eyes just as there was in her own, it seemed to be coming from great distances, other places.

She felt the cold of a March morning. She had, once, tried to speak fragments of truth to her father. His reply had been a fist, and so she had not tried anymore. But her elven blood had awakened, and she had been transformed, and now it seemed to her that her entire life was going to consist of trying. Trying to help. Trying to heal. Trying to give. Trying, yes, to speak the truth. And if she received a fist in reply, she was simply going to have to keep trying.

It would be a harsh life. Only an Elf would think of enduring it. And then she thought again of what Natil had asked.

Could it then be made, perhaps, less harsh?

She was afraid of the answer, was more afraid of the potential for failure that lay at the heart of it. But at the same time she met the starlight of TK's eyes with her own, and, since he had not responded to her offered hands, she reached and took one of his in her fingers.

"You're not human anymore, TK," she said. "I'm not either. The blood transformed you. You're an Elf . . . just like the rest of us."

Slowly, very slowly, TK shut his eyes, sagged against the white wall of the Home. "And that's it?"

"That's it."

"Just: *You're an Elf, TK?* And that's it?" His eyes snapped open. "What the hell I supposed to do now? Go out and dance on flowers or something?"

Natil finally spoke. The accents of despair and disappointment were plain in her tone. "You are . . . supposed to do exactly what you have already been doing, exactly what you have always wanted to do."

TK pulled away from Sana's hands. His fists were clenched when he put them to his forehead. "Set-up city." His breath smoked in the mountain air.

Natil shook her head. "You chose your path long ago, TK."

"Sure I did." TK would not look at either of them: he was hiding behind his fists.

"Are you with us, TK?"

"With you? Who the hell are you? You're not my people."

Again the tired shake of the head. "But we are."

His eyes were hard when he dropped his hands, but it was a shallow, brittle hardness. "Don't give me that crap. What gives you the idea you know anything about what it's like to be—?"

"TK." Natil's voice—and her tone—brought his protest to a halt. "I was not born white, TK. I was made when the world was made. I am Firstborn. And therefore I am most assuredly not white."

Some of the hardness went from TK's eyes. "When . . . when the world . . . ?"

Natil was not angry: she was, as always, simply speaking the truth. But Sana heard in her voice the many fists that she had received in return for so speaking. Too many fists. For too long. "Your people were enslaved, TK. Mine were exterminated. I was the last. But beyond all hope this grace has been given to me . . . to *us*: to be here. Now. To help. To heal. Now." She hung her head, and Sana felt the weariness that hung about her, the product of deathlessness, the product of an innate longing that had been—was still—unfulfilled. "I am but passing, TK. I wish that I did not have to pass."

"We're . . . we're all passing, then," said Sana. "You, me, Heather . . . everyone."

Natil's eyes were downcast, but she nodded. "We will have to do so for a long time."

But TK's eyes were no longer hard. "Natil?" he said softly. "How long you say it's been for you?"

"From the beginning." Natil seemed as sere and transparent as an autumn leaf. "Four and one half billion years."

It was an amount of time that would have been, for a human, incomprehensible. But, like Sana, TK was no longer human, and like Sana, he comprehended it. "That's . . . that's a long time, lady."

Natil nodded slowly. "It is so," she whispered.

"I'm . . . I'm sorry," he said and Sana heard compassion growing in his voice. "That's a hell of a long time to go and then have someone like me ragging on you."

"It happens." Fatigue. Resignation.

"No. No." TK shoved himself away from the wall, stood upon two legs. "I mean it. I'm sorry."

Natil nodded. "Blessings, TK."

"That's a hell of a way to have to live. Can I . . . can I do anything for you? Anything to help?"

It was an honest question, honestly asked, springing straight from an honest heart. And when Sana saw him extend a big hand to Natil—palm up, offering he knew not what, offering whatever he had to offer—she knew that it was an elven heart.

Natil looked up, looked at his hand, his offering, but she did not take. Instead, she gave him hers. "There is

nothing, TK. You have . . ." She smiled. The fatigue was
still there, but she smiled nonetheless. ". . . already done
much for me."

But it *was* a long time to go, and there were, Sana
knew, longer times ahead. And though TK could do nothing for Natil—nothing to ease the burden, nothing to
help, nothing to heal—maybe. . . .

"Natil," she said quickly, before memory and fear
choked her words, "TK might not be able to do anything,
but I can."

Natil looked at her, hope kindling.

Sana grappled with panic, reached for the stars with
damaged hands. "I'll do it." She clenched her fingers, ignored the pain. "In the name of the Goddess, by my oath
as a witch, I'll do it. I'll do it."

CHAPTER 29

The last part of winter was mild, very mild, and spring came on early. By mid-March, gardeners who were either brave or foolhardy (depending upon one's point of view) were beginning to think about transplanting.

Lauri and Wheat drove up into the mountains that weekend. The all-terrain tires on Lauri's Bronco would not have been disturbed in the slightest had there been a few remnants of snow on the road, or even some stubborn traces of black ice in the lanes left shaded by the low sun, but, in fact, the pavement was mostly dry, and where it was not, it only glistened with the low steam of evaporating melt. The air was surprisingly warm, with just a hint of a snap to it, and it fluttered the leaves of the aspen tree that lay, balled and burlapped, on the truck's cargo deck, upper branches protruding from the open rear window like a green flag.

And that green fluttering, Lauri thought, could well have been the emblem of the Elves. Long ago, human beings, driven by a desire for civilization, coveting doubtful achievements like honor and sin, had forsaken the forests for the cities, even going so far as to hew down mile upon mile of trees in order to make room for their houses and their industry. And with that forsaking had begun the fading of the Elves. At first, the Immortals had withdrawn into the green wilderness; then, with the loss of the wilderness, they had withdrawn from the physical world.

But now they were back, and where once the forests had been pirated and stripped, now trees were being returned to the trees, aspen and pine, reared in the urban deserts, taken back to their rightful homes. And if humans could not see the need for such giving, the Elves could. It was not even a matter of giving *back*. It was simply a matter of giving. Because it was good to give. Because it was time to give.

With branches waving and leaves fluttering out the back of her Bronco, then, Lauri drove up into the mountains to plant a tree with Wheat. To give as the Elves had always given.

"It's up here a little farther," said Wheat, pointing ahead.

"We gotta do any fourwheeling?"

"Of course not. There's a road."

"This time of year, you can't count on anything."

"There's a road."

They both laughed a little nervously at their non-argument. They were driving into the mountains together, but they were still closed to one another.

Closed. Yes. Just as the Lady was closed to them. Or as they were closed to Her. Lauri was not exactly sure which way it worked, or whether either was a valid way of expressing it at all. Even Natil, though, was unsure of what had happened, so Lauri assumed that she would be forgiven if she got it wrong.

Still, with so much starlight in her present and in her past—and, she hoped, in her future—she found it strange to drive today into the mountains she had seen, loved, and reverenced for years and know that she had not yet seen, loved, or reverenced them completely. There was more, much more, that she had not seen, that she had neither loved nor reverenced. And yet, desirous as she was of doing all those things completely and without either conscious or unconscious reservation, she was also acutely aware of what she was leaving behind.

Oh, Lauri had thought occasionally about feminine divinity. It was impossible to be involved in lesbian issues and not come into contact with some self-proclaimed priestess, a political witch or two, or even the more grounded but at the same time hazier currents of rebellion against patriarchal Christianity embodied by Women-Church. But though Lauri had never been able to accept any of it as anything more than an opportunity to demonstrate intellectual tolerance, what Natil had said about the Lady had stirred a pool of regret within her, as, she was sure, it had stirred it in everyone else. Yes, the past—humanity and religion both—was really gone. Elves really did stand apart. Jehovah and Buddha and Allah and all the rest of the Gods and the teachers and the prophets of mortality and transience had nothing to offer them. The Elves had Someone Else. Someone Who cared. Someone Who got them through.

Someone Who had, centuries ago, been lost.

"Here," said Wheat.

Lauri came out of her thoughts and turned onto a dirt road. Steep, rocky, washboarded by rain and melting snow, it shook the Bronco like a terrier might shake a rat. Lauri's foot found the brake. "Fourwheeling, Wheat?"

"It's not that bad." Wheat's cornflower blue eyes were wide as a lurch threw her against her shoulder belt. "Is it?" she added in a small voice.

Lauri laughed, dropped into low, let the truck crawl forward. "As long as I don't have to lock in the hubs," she said, "it's not that bad."

They drove for a long time. It was Wheat's practice to scatter her trees, planting as unobtrusively as possible amid older growth, planning ahead not just for the next year or two, but for the coming decades and centuries— decades and centuries that she would see—and the road took them to higher ground, up above the valleys that, alpine and shadowed by the surrounding peaks, were beginning to green in earnest with the warmth of the season. When they stopped at a widening in the road, the sun was high in the sky.

"It's a good place for planting trees," said Wheat.

"Uh . . . yeah . . ." Lauri examined the steep slopes, the narrow path. She did not see any trees at all, only patches of scrub and grass. "You and Allesandro got through this?"

Wheat nodded. "All by ourselves. We didn't even need a Bronco." But her face turned shadowed then, her eyes pained. "We came to check in December. That's when we found . . ." She sighed, shook her head. "It was so stupid. Why do they do that?"

Lauri shrugged. She did not know. "They're humans."

"But we're going to be doing this forever! Is it ever going to get any better?"

"You're starting to sound like me, Wheat."

Wheat nodded. "Well . . . I've been thinking a lot about you."

Lauri kept her eyes very carefully away from her passenger. "I've been thinking a lot about you, too."

Silence. Wheat shifted uncomfortably. "Let's go plant a tree, Lauri."

Lauri touched the brim of an imaginary cap. "My pleasure, ma'am."

They dropped the tailgate and eased the tree out onto the ground. It was a good, sturdy sapling, about twelve feet high, its trunk almost two inches in diameter. New leaves caught the wind and the sunlight when Lauri swung it upright. Again, she thought of the green flag. And of the Lady. And of Wheat.

Blinking back the ache that welled up in her eyes, she pulled out two folding shovels and slung their straps over her shoulder, then, taking hold of the heavy, burlap-covered root ball, she tipped the tree back until Wheat caught the middle of the trunk. With Wheat calling directions, they carried the sapling down a steep trail that seemed, at first, to lead into nothing but bare rock. After about ten minutes, though, Lauri smelled water, and a turn abruptly brought them into view of a tiny lake with a stand of aspen and pine lapping about it on three sides.

The trail dwindled and turned indistinct as they went down a shallow slope to the trees; but here by the open water in this sheltered valley, mixed in with the beginnings of spring flowers and the hardy presence of kinni-kinnick, Lauri saw papers, scraps of cardboard, a bent aluminum beer can.

She set down the root ball. They would plant, and then they would clean up.

"I don't think *too* many people come up here," said Wheat. She was not breathing heavily, and she dragged a sleeve across her forehead more from old habit than from need. "But a few come. That's what happened to . . ." She pointed.

Lauri followed her finger. Over near the water lay a dead aspen sapling, its roots bare and withered. Beside it was the hole from which it had been pulled and the stake to which it had been tethered to keep it straight for its first year.

"There wasn't any reason to pull it up," said Wheat. "There just wasn't any reason."

Lauri shook her head. The dead sapling lay across the

ground, its branches trailing like the hair of a young girl.
"I'm not sure they need a reason, Wheat."

"But they had to go out of their way to do it!"

"Yeah. They did. They had to go out of their way to
shoot Heather. They had to go out of their way to get
Sana."

Wheat shoved her hands into her jacket pockets, looked
at the trees, dead and living. "It's going to be a long time,
Lauri."

Lauri sighed. Wheat, along with Hadden, had been the
first. The first to change. The first to intuit just how long
the Elves were going to have their work before them. It
seemed strange that even someone like Wheat was still,
in many ways, dismayed at the prospect.

But Natil had finally said what she had come to
Denver—to Colorado, to the 1990s—to say. And Lauri,
like the other Elves, believed her. There was no question
about it. Still . . .

"We'll have help, I guess." She wished she could
sound more certain than she did.

"Did Natil say what she's going to do?" Blue eyes,
dark hair: Wheat stood at the edge of the water like a
slender columbine. Lauri marveled. She was beautiful.
Beautiful . . . and uncertain, and confused, and . . .

. . . in love? Lauri directed an inward laugh at herself.
She had apparently become an optimist.

"No," she said. "She didn't."

"Is she going to do something?"

Lauri shrugged. "She said she would. So I imagine she
will. But she's been spending most of her time with Sana.
I can't blame her: Sana needs it."

Wheat pressed her lips together as though considering,
thrust her hands deeper into her pockets. "Do you ever
think about God, Lauri?" she said after a time.

Silence. A breeze. The papers fluttered. The beer can
rocked back and forth.

"Yeah," said Lauri. "I didn't for a long time, but ever
since Natil told us about *Elthia* . . . well . . ."

"We're . . ." Wheat seemed uncertain of her words. Finally: "We're going to have to say good-bye to Him."

Lauri understood. "Yeah."

"So that we can . . ." Wheat shivered. "Maybe we just
need to think about *Elthia* more. Maybe that'll do it."

"Yeah. Maybe." Lauri looked at the ground. Thinking about something, she had learned, did not help very much to bring it about.

But Wheat suddenly lifted her head. "Lauri," she said, "let's plant this tree for God. Let's give it to Him. Let's make it a thank-you gift. We're Elves. We've got to find the Lady. But ... let's tell God that we're still friends, and that we're grateful for what He gave to us when we were human."

Lauri was silent.

"And then we can leave ... and not have to look back."

"You ..." Lauri examined the sapling. It was slender, almost feminine. She had always thought that only big, patriarchal oaks would be suitable for Someone who, according to one story, was willing to incinerate a city because of its inhabitants' sexual preferences. "You think a tree's enough?"

Wheat spread her hands. "He's God. Would anything be enough?"

And so they planted the aspen tree, redigging the hole for it, slashing its burlap wrappings to give its quickening roots a way out, lowering it in, backfilling and tamping the earth about it. And when they were done, they stood on either side of the tiny trunk and took hands, encircling it.

Lauri bent her head. Stars. Stars and stars and stars. When she had left California, she had never thought that she would find the stars, that she would become something other than human, that she would stand someday in the cool isolation of the springtime Rockies and say good-bye to God.

Wheat's hands were small, slender. The perfect Elf. "Thanks, God," she said softly. "Thanks. But we have to go now."

Lauri looked up. She stared past Wheat, stared at the mountains that rose, crag and tree and lake and stream, about them. And behind the mountains, living through them, sharing their being just as She shared the being of Her two Children who clasped hands about the tiny trunk of their parting gift to a Deity in whose Providence they could not be included, immanent but, for now, still terribly, terribly distant, was Someone Else.

Instinct, elven instinct, tore at her heart. Lauri wanted the Lady. She wanted to see, to speak with the Woman who had made her, who *was* her. But all that would have to come later. For now, she turned a last thought to the past, mentally offering her hand as Elves had always offered their hands: in friendship, in giving, in an effort to help and heal . . . everybody. Even God. "Good-bye," she said. "Blessings."

For perhaps the twentieth time in the course of the last two weeks, Edith Braun dialed Sana Joy's number. Before, there had been no answer: the telephone had only rung and rung. This time, though, she got a recording. The number was disconnected, no longer in service.

Braun hung up, tapped her fingers impatiently on the desk. Who was Sana's lawyer? Bob Sentry? Maybe she could try him.

"I think . . . I think we should aim for Spring Equinox," said Sana.

Sunday evening. I-70. Natil behind the wheel of her van. Ahead, the lights of Denver shimmering in the inversion layer. *"Arae a Miriea."* She nodded. "Day of Beginnings. It would be fitting. It is rather close, though. This Friday, or am I mistaken?"

Sana looked at her. Fitting. Close. Yes, it was both. It had to be both. "I don't think I'll be able to hold out much longer, Natil."

Natil touched Sana's bandaged left hand. "Peace, beloved."

Sana shook her head. "I'm scared, Natil. I'm really scared. Everyone's helping, and the starlight keeps me going . . . kind of . . . but underneath it all . . ." The tears forced themselves out. She was surprised that, after crying so much, she could still cry. ". . . I'm just scared. I'm just a scared little kid."

Natil nodded. She too, as Sana well understood, had known fear, doubt, despair. Indeed, she still knew them. "I understand," she said, and those two words, spoken in the harper's soft voice, told not only of past pain, but also of transcendence, transformation . . . and endurance. Natil had endured. Sana, too, could endure.

They pulled up in front of Sana's old apartment. The

police had finally finished their work, gathered their evidence: Sana had received word from her lawyer that she could at last return. But, aside from this brief visit tonight, she would not be returning. Instead, she would gather together a few of her things and take them back to Elvenhome. For now, the mountains were her home, her sanctuary, her refuge.

Sana blinked at the building. It looked as mundane and as normal as the façade of Freddy Joy's house.

She did not want to go in.

She heard a stirring, felt lips touch her damp cheek. "Do you want some company?" said Natil.

Sana brushed aside her tears, nodded. Together, they got out of the van, entered the courtyard, climbed the stairs. Sana took her old key from her purse, unlocked the door, swung it open, switched on the light . . .

. . . stood, unbelieving.

The walls had been painted. The carpets had been shampooed . . . no, replaced. The furniture was gone. It took her a moment to comprehend, to double check the number on the door to make sure that she had, in fact, come to the right apartment; but then she did indeed comprehend.

Everything was gone.

With Natil at her side, she entered and went from room to room. Books, clothing, blow-drier, makeup, futon: all were missing. Nothing remained. The apartment had been emptied, cleaned, repainted, recarpeted. New linoleum had been put down on the kitchen floor, the stove had been replaced, the cabinets and sink had been scrubbed free of every trace of the caustic foam that had taken Terry's sight and her own future.

Sana swayed, dazed, unable to focus on anything. "Everything," she managed. But then the realization struck her. *"My harp! Natil! My harp! Where's my harp? Where's Little Sandy?"*

Sobbing with fear, she ran from room to room, but she found only white walls, bare expanses of carpet, sterile linoleum. There was not even a broom or a mop.

"My harp . . . my harp . . ." Sana sat down in the middle of the living room, her bandaged hands to her face. She had no hands with which to harp, and now she had no harp. And Little Sandy . . . well, perhaps that loss was appropriate in a way that only her father would have understood. She had not been able to protect herself: what business did she have attempting to protect a child?

Natil had knelt beside her. "Sana ... Sana, beloved ..."

The door of the apartment slammed open. "What the hell are you doing here? You get the hell out right now!"

Sana looked up. The manager was shuffling into the apartment. His eyes still peered out from behind their hard little shields of glass, his undershirt was still stained, his canvas cap was still planted firmly on his head.

"You god-damn kids," he said. "You go running out on me and expect to just waltz back in like you owned the place." He was scuffing forward, fists balled, arms waving, and Natil put her arms protectively about Sana. "You owe rent, you don't pay, I give the rooms to someone else. I told you that when you moved in. God-damn kids."

Sana was crying. Terry had taken her new life, and this man had, seemingly, taken what was left of her old. "My harp," she said. "My ... my doll ... Where are they?"

He bent down, glared at her. "You owe me rent. You don't pay, you get out. You left this place a mess, and I had to put money into it to make it right. My money! I ought to charge you for that!" He pointed at the new carpet. "What the hell do you think that costs?" He pointed at the new stove. "What the hell do you think that costs? God-damn kids take money out of my pocket! My pocket!"

Natil stood up, and Sana saw her hands clench. "Sir," she said. "This young lady asked you a question."

He was unfazed by starlight, unfazed by anything. "Tossed it. Garbage. Junk. All you kids have is junk, and I'm not going to keep it. Costs money to keep it. Didn't pay your rent, didn't keep the place up. Expect me to do everything. You owe me rent, but I'll keep the deposit and that's that." He glared down once again at Sana, who, hands pressed to her mouth, saw another figure leaning down, berating, threatening, ordering: *Come here. Now. Go away. Spread. Little cunt.*

Little Sandy, her harp ... everything.

"You and your god-damn Satanism. Dirt. Dirt and

filth. Had to clean everything. I read the papers. I'm not stupid. You get the hell out of here."

Everything. Everything she had kept hidden, sacred, private, unsullied. Gone. "M-my harp!" She could hardly form the words. "My doll!"

"Go on. Get out, or I'll call the cops, and you can tell them about this, just like you'll tell them about all the other things you did!"

Sana felt Natil's arms about her, felt herself lifted, guided to the door, helped down the outside stairs. "My ... my harp ..." she mumbled, hardly aware that she was saying anything at all. "My harp ..."

"We will find your harp."

"It's gone ... it's gone ... it's all gone ..." Sana hardly saw anything. Her tears blurred into her stars, and her stars blurred into her tears. Which was bringing more pain now: the newness of her life, the loss of the past, or the future that promised to make a mockery of both?

Natil got her out to the street, bundled her into the van. "Sana," she said, "find the stars."

Sana had doubled over, wrapped her arms about her head. She had spent many nights like this, trying to eke some sense of safety out of her own body. Then as now, though, safety was illusory. "They hurt. I want my harp."

"Let me see what I can do." A long pause, lengthening into silence. Sana finally looked up. Natil was still standing on the asphalt outside the passenger side door. "When is the trash picked up here?"

Sana closed her eyes, doubled over again. Trash. Her harp was just trash. The manager had summed it up perfectly. Junk: junk to be taken away, thrown out.

The elven accent was strong in Natil's voice. "Sana. Please. I will help you, but only if you allow me to help. When is the trash picked up here?"

Sana thought, dredged up old, painful memories now doubly painful. "Monday," she managed. "It always used to wake me up. The truck, I mean."

Natil nodded, got behind the wheel of the van, switched on, and pulled around the block. "Then we will look," she said as she turned into the alley. "I daresay he had the furniture hauled away, but if money is of such concern to him, he more than likely took care of your belongings himself."

Sana's head was bowed as Natil parked next to the dumpster behind the building. Her clothes could be replaced. Her books—those that had not wound up, along with her tools, in an evidence drawer—likewise. Everything could be replaced, even, to be sure, her harp. Even Little Sandy.

But it was not the loss of her harp that pained her as much as the destruction of the symbol and the salvation that it embodied. Likewise Little Sandy: that the doll had been so casually and brutally thrown away was just another echo of what was happening to Sana herself. Thrown away. Thrown away into prison.

Natil was undeterred. She slipped out of the van and, after eying the dumpster for a moment, climbed in among the rubbish and the bones and the grease.

"Natil . . ." Sana found herself protesting numbly. Four and a half billion years—and now Natil was crawling around in a trash bin. It was not right. ". . . you can't do that."

"Do not tell me what I can and cannot do, Sana," came the calm reply. Then, with vexation: "So much waste here! He could at least have recycled some of this, or given it to those in need. But—ah! Books! I believe that I have found your books!"

Rustles from the dumpster. Clanks. Sana put her face in her bandaged hands. *Find the stars,* Natil had said. In truth, they were always with her, but they seemed at present comfortless, unconcerned with such earthly, material matters as the loss of a harp and a doll.

Minutes went by. Sana hardly noticed. But then her door swung open, the dome light came on, and when she looked up, Natil was standing there. Dust and cottony fibers were matted in her long hair, her blouse was smeared with mustard and the indefinite leavings of fast food wrappers, and mottlings (was that charcoal?) streaked her face. But under one of her arms was tucked a battered canvas case, and under the other was a shapeless mass of colored cloth.

"Sana," she said, "I found them. I am sorry . . ."

Clumsily, Sana reached out and gathered the case and the doll into her arms. Even through the canvas, she could tell that the harp was broken, probably crushed when

something large and heavy had been dumped on top of it
Little Sandy, though . . .

Sana was reminded again of the dream that had come
to her months ago, when she had first begun to suspect
that there was more to Terry Angel than smiles and winning words. Dismembered, her face mashed and filthy,
her clothes ripped and stained, Little Sandy was now
hardly anything more than cloth and stuffing. Certainly
she was not anything that could be called a doll. And yet,
pressing the eyeless face against her cheek, Sana was surprised that she did not feel once again the despair and
hopelessness with which she had clawed her way out of
the dream. She felt, instead, oddly distant, removed.

And then she understood why. Broken harp, broken
hands. She herself was Little Sandy.

CHAPTER 30

TK caught the phone on the second ring, and it took him only a moment to recognize the dark, female voice on the other end of the connection. It was Bess. She was asking for TK. He wondered suddenly whether his voice had altered along with everything else. Probably. Why should his voice be exempt?

"It's me, Bess," he said.

"It don't sound like you."

"It's been a while. I've ... changed a little."

"Yeah. Yeah, I heard about your leg."

"Oh ... don't you worry about my leg. I'm OK."

He had already guessed why she had called, but he decided that she had to be the one to say it. He would not help her, would not contribute to the perpetration of such a useless and unprofitable stereotype. Of course black people did not have good family lives. It was just that way, was it not? Something about race, right? Something about the gene pool? Or maybe, just maybe, about culture and discrimination and a welfare system that made it more profitable to break families apart than to put them together.

He put a hand to his face. So many things to do. He had forever in which to do them, but there were just so many things. And what would some white Goddess want with a black man like himself? The thought made him sad. Not angry. Not anymore. Just sad.

"The lawyer tell me we can do this easy, or we can do it hard," said Bess, saying what she meant to say without actually saying it. "I got to know which you want."

"You better tell me what *you* want, Bess."

"Divorce."

"That's what I thought."

Silence. Then: "You mad? You gonna fight it?"

"Naw . . . I'm not mad. I seen it coming." In truth, ha
he been able to think or form words at the time, he migh
have seen it coming when he was but newborn, when h
could first lift his head up enough to take a good look a
the color of his skin.

"I don't want no child support, either. I don't wan
none of your money. My momma gonna help me take
care of the kid."

Her momma. Yes, and Bess had a father, too. Some
where. How neatly everything followed from a few addi
tional molecules of melanin . . . even across generations
"How's the kid?"

"Fine. Just fine. I want custody. Full custody."

"You sure that's what you want?"

"That's what I said. What you mean?" Bess sounded
frightened, as though a game she had been playing had
suddenly turned from lighthearted to serious. Here she
was now, a single mother with a baby, and she was asking
for a divorce. Maybe she had someone else lined up to be
a father to the little girl. Maybe she was simply trying to
play the game right, to make sure the stereotype ran true
to form. Regardless, she was unsure, scared: the world—
race and privilege, welfare and machine guns—was hard
on little girls and little boys alike.

TK hung his head, ran his hand through his hair. He
would be seeing a lot of little girls and little boys. Generations of them. Millennia full of them. "I mean, is tha
what you want? A divorce. Custody. All that. Is it?"

"I can do it by myself."

Single motherhood. Just another part of the game. "I
know you can, Bess. I ain't got no doubts."

"So, you willin' to give her up?"

"You willing . . ."

His daughter. His only daughter. And the thought was
occurring to him now that there was immortal blood in
the world, and that if he himself had it, then the chances
were good that his daughter had it, too.

He would be there for her. Custody or not, he would
know, and he would be there.

". . . to take care of her?"

"What the hell you mean, nigger? Take care of my
daughter? Of course I'm gonna take care of my daughter."

TK was unfazed. "Make sure she gets to school, stays way from those gangs, has someone to look after her—meone good, mind you—while you at work? Can you o all that?"

Bess turned hesitant. "Well ... yeah ... my momma ..."

"I got nothing against your momma, Bess, but that's my daughter you talking about. That's our daughter. I'm ot trying to make trouble." Of course he was not trying o make trouble, he thought. Elves did not abuse: they rovided. "I just want to help."

"I can do it." Defiant now. Determined.

"I won't fight it, Bess. I'll do what you want. But I vant you to know that if you need me, I be there. For ou. For the kid. I be there."

"How come ..." She was mustering her anger now, rying to build up what she had been given no cause to eel. "... you keep callin' her *the kid*?"

TK sighed. Sad. Like the clicking of car door locks, ike the echo of machine guns in the night, like the glazed yes of adolescent boys staring up at a sky they did not ee. Sad. "I don't know her name, Bess. I was overseas vhen she was born, remember? You never told me her ame."

A long pause. Then: "It's Star."

He smiled. "Star, eh? That's a good name for a little ,irl."

"I thought so."

"Well, I be there for you. And if you need money, you ust ask. Whatever Star needs, you just say the word.)kay?"

"Uh ..." The conversation had not gone at all as Bess aad expected. She had been looking for something to ight against, had found instead only a hand offered in riendship. It was obviously disconcerting to her, upsetting. But, then, she was human. "Okay. I'll call you when he papers are done."

"Good," he said. "But don't you forget: I be there for ou and Star." He said good-bye then, hung up. Yes, he vould be there. For Bess. For Star. For everybody.

Forever.

* * *

"I'm sorry. Mr. Sentry is not in the office today. know that, Dr. Braun, but I'm sure you understand tha he's a very busy man. He *does* have other clients beside Ms. Joy. Yes, I'll tell him about your offer. You're ver kind. I'm sure Ms. Joy will be appreciative. Yes, I' leave him the message. I don't know. I can't say. I'll b sure he gets the message. Yes, of course. Certainly."

Sana was failing.

Besides the harp and Little Sandy, Natil managed t salvage many of Sana's books and much of her clothing and she put everything into the van and took it up to th Home. But though books could be repaired and reshelve and clothes could be laundered, hearts and hands were no so easily attended to: Sana continued to apply herself t the task of finishing a rite that would both keep the Equi nox and summon *Elthia* back from long separation, bu there was an emptiness behind her eyes and a hollownes to her voice that told Natil that she had essentially give up hope.

Perhaps, with time, Sana might have been able to re new herself. But there was no time. Constrained as th Elves were by the physical limitations of human beings they were subject also to the bonds of temporal existence and time in this case would lead Sana not to an opportu nity for calm, strength, and wholeness, but to further pai and, perhaps, incarceration, for her trial had been sched uled for May, and Terry Angel's story, combining as i did spirituality and pathos in proportions that moved eve the skeptical, was still convincing.

That Thursday night, then, though Natil and Sana wen out into the forests about Elvenhome to celebrate th Equinox, to try to bring back the vision of the Lady, Nati was already anticipating failure, for Sana, clad in th black robe of a witch, all but shuffled along the sof paths. Her head was bent, and her face, fair now as only an elvish face could be, held within its expression seeming negation of anything that starlight could offer, a hearkening back to an all too human past.

Had they lost then? Had simple fact defeated them, the new persecutions of a new age taking hold so quickly tha they had blighted the ground even before the sowing Natil did not want to admit that, but Sana herself—

abused, trampled—was an answer proof to her most stubborn optimism.

Near midnight, they came to the small clearing that they had picked out the day before. Natil sat her friend down on a fallen tree and herself set about cleaning the ground in the old manner of the witches, sweeping burrs and pine cones and needles away with a stiff broom while keeping in mind the purpose of the rite which lay ahead.

For You, Lady. All for You. Please come back. On this day of all days, this day of beginnings, Arae a Miriea, come back to us, give us Your Hand.

And when she was finished, when the earth was bare and smooth, she took dead, fallen wood and built a fire in the middle of the clearing, striking the first spark with flint and steel that she had brought with her from Adria, from the days of friendship and openness in Malvern Forest. The tinder caught, the flames flickered uneasily, stirring like restless hopes, then finally settled, grew, burned brightly. As the fire threw light in all directions, turning her robed movements into a wavering shadow that flitted among the surrounding trees, Natil placed candles at the four cardinal points, lit incense in an earthenware bowl. This was but a forest clearing, but it was slowly becoming a temple of the Goddess, the only temple that the witches now knew.

Would the Lady of the Elves come to a place so redolent of the stinks and gritty practices of humanity? Natil fought to believe that She would. She knelt before the hissing incense for a moment, understanding at last how mortals could see in the white ascent of smoke the mounting of their prayers to the Old Gods, and then, after adding her own appeal to the massed entreaties of the past, she got to her feet, crossed to the fallen tree, and stood before Sana, her teacher. She bowed. "All is ready."

But Sana shook her head. "You go ahead and cast, Natil."

Natil looked at Sana for a long time. All the hopes of the Elves, all the potentials for the future. And the vessel that contained them, broken. "It must be you, Sana."

"Me?" Sana half laughed, half sobbed. "I've got no tools: the police took them all. And I don't have any hands to hold a knife with even if I had one."

"You told me once, my teacher, that all that was necessary to cast a Circle was a willing heart."

Sana looked at the bandaged hands that lay uselessly in her lap.

"Are you willing, Sana?"

A long silence. A night bird called in the distance. A tree, yielding up some of the warmth of the day, creaked. It was very still.

Sana nodded at last. "Yeah. I'll try."

I'll try. The words were a weight in Natil's heart. Trying implied nothing of confidence or success. Trying but implied attempt.

But Sana rose and went into the space that Natil had marked with fire, candles, and incense. Her eyes half closed, she traced the Circle with a mangled hand. But her steps were uncertain, her concentration seemingly elsewhere, and when she was done, she stood for a long time before the central fire, looking into the flames as though they alone offered a release from the subtle stake to which she had been bound.

After a time, though, she stirred herself, went to each quarter in turn and, asking softly, almost plaintively, for help and protection, invoked the spirits of the directions. Natil looked away, biting her lip: where had help and protection been when Terry Angel was putting a knife through Sana's hands?

Sana stumbled back to the central fire. Hands at her sides, she stood before it. Her face was expressionless, drained, her eyes blank. "Natil?"

"Here, Sana."

"I can't do this."

"Beloved, you must. I cannot."

"I don't think I can stand to fail again."

"Teacher," said Natil, forcing the words out through her growing fear, "you are the Goddess. You know that. Be Her. Simply be Her."

"I'm shot."

"I know."

"I haven't even got my hands."

"I know."

"They'll put me in jail. You know what goes on in those places. You know what they'll do to me. They've already done a lot of them."

Natil fought back tears. She did not want Sana to see her cry. "I know."

Sana's eyes turned from blank to focused, fixed themselves on the fire. "It's like the Burning Times all over again. I'm a Satanist. I'm a devil worshiper. I throw lye in the faces of nice Christian men. I suppose they'll be saying next that I hid his penis in a bird's nest."

Natil was silent. Then: "You survived the Burning Times," she whispered.

"Yeah . . . so now we wear fake eagle feathers and talk about divine energy like it's a nine-volt battery. Sure we survived."

"You survived. The Elves did not."

Sana put her hands to her face. "Oh, Goddess. And it's all down to me."

"Bring it back, Sana. Call Her. She is close, very close. Heather has seen Her. You and Lauri and Kelly have felt Her presence. Call."

Sana was hiding in her hands. The firelight was ruddy on the white bandages. "Can't you do it? Please?"

Natil shook her head. "I do not know the calling of another. I know only how to be called. I do not know the growth from separation into oneness. I know only unity. I cannot do what you can do. I do not know the way."

"Oh, Goddess . . ."

Natil went to her. "Try, Sana. I ask only that you try. If we fail, then so be it. We have an eternity in which to keep trying—"

"No." Her face still muffled in her wrapped hands, Sana shook her head. "No, we don't. We all need Her. We can't just keep on going like we have. We're running down. It's got to be tonight."

Shrugging herself away from Natil's arms, then, Sana stepped back from the fire, lifted her arms, lifted her shaking voice in the invocation she had written for this night:

> *"I am the Star of Light,*
> *And I am the Abyss of Darkness.*
> *By My hands are you made.*
> *By My breath are you sustained.*
> *By My will are you empowered.*
> *By My love are you nourished—"*

She faltered, stopped. More than any other Elf right now, Sana needed sustenance, needed empowering, needed nourishment. But there was nothing for her. Her strength, even eked out as it was by the undying fires of the stars, was nearly exhausted.

But Sana went on, pushing the words out as though she were shoving panicked children out of a burning building:

> *"My names are many, My manifestations infinite.*
> *Know this: here am I called Elthia Calasiuove,*
> *Here do I manifest ... manifest ... mani ..."*

Her voice caught, and the final words trailed off into a sob. Still, though, she stood, arms uplifted, waiting.

The fire crackled, snapped. The smoke of incense rose fragrant. Natil, though, was intent upon Sana. Her awareness of the surrounding trees, of the stars above, of the light that streamed down from a moon two days past full had faded. All she saw was Sana, all she saw was a solitary witch who waited with mixed devotion, sincerity, and despair for what she no longer believed was possible.

What *had* to be possible.

Minutes went by, and Natil could see that Sana was struggling, trying to forget the persecutions, the wounded hands, the futile attempts she had made to escape her paternally-ordained fate. She was striving for the Goddess, for the memory and support of all the quiet and safe Circles that she, with Little Sandy on her lap and her harp at her side, had ever experienced. But Little Sandy was no more than rags now, and her harp was broken, crushed. Sana was alone, and memories, no matter how good, were not enough. Slowly, then, she sank to her knees, put her bandaged hands on the ground, hung her head. "Momma," she said, her voice dry, hoarse. "I want my momma."

Gloria Joy was dead by her own hand. The Goddess had not come. Who would comfort this child?

Natil went to her. "Sana, dear Sana. I love you."

"Momma." Sana had nothing left. No witchcraft, no stars, no hope, immortal or transient. Stripped, bare, raw, she had turned to the last, most primal of calls, the original cry, the prayer that was at once the most trusting and the most often betrayed.

Natil knelt beside her, wrapped her arms about her. "Sana."

Sana's voice was muffled, indistinct. "I want . . ." She choked. "I want my momma."

Feeling the ache of unfulfillment, cursing herself for having used friendship and loyalty to drive one who was so dear to her to this precipice of hopelessness, Natil pressed her head against Sana's. She herself had struggled and failed. She had tried everything without success. And now she had involved in her failures one who had already failed too much, who could withstand the pain of loss no more.

Hopeless. Yes, it was hopeless. Fleeting glimpses of the Lady were all the Elves would have now, and the limitations of their human cousins would become, with time, a familiar if painful part of immortality. The Elves would have to get themselves through, it appeared, for there was no one to do it for them.

Natil kissed her friend, touching her lips to a cheek glistening with firelight and starlight and tears. "It is all right, Sana. Let us open the Circle and go home."

"Momma."

"It is so, darling. We are Her children. She will take care of us whether we see Her or not." And so Natil struggled to find hope in the nightmare, in the prospect that the vision was gone, that it would never be found again.

But Sana's head suddenly snapped up, and for an instant, her eyes—hot, feral, blazing with starlight—met the flames of the fire. But then her features twisted, her eyes clenched again, and the truth of her grief wrung her tongue, wrung her voice until her cries turned to screams and her words—hoarse, almost unintelligible—echoed off the trees and the distant mountains.

"Momma! Momma! Momma! MOMMA!"

"Darling . . ."

"MOMMA! MOMMA!" Desperation sending a thread of spittle from her lips, Sana was, for now, one concentrated plea, one focus, seemingly, of all the sorrow that the Elves had ever known: all the loss, all the futile helping, all the healing that had turned with time and human perversity to hurt. Finding in her desperation open pas-

sage, the pain flooded into the world in a new invocation, an invocation of desolation.

"MOMMA! MOMMA! MOMMA!"

And Natil, feeling in herself a growing echo of Sana's cry, held her as she shrieked, tried to keep her from battering her already damaged hands on the ground. Sana's mother had been torn from her by law and power. Natil's Mother had been taken by history and hatred. Together, vocally and silently, they uttered their abandonment.

"MOMMA!" Sana struggled and fought in Natil's arms, the cries racking her, tossing her, beating her from side to side like fists. *"MOMMA!"*

She was blubbering now, incoherent, her words fragmenting, faltering and lurching, thick-tongued, to a halt. Sweat and saliva and dust had mingled with her tears, and her dark hair was matted with the mud they had made. Elf she was, but like all the Elves—like all the Elves, it seemed now, forever—she was touched and bound by the mortality that surrounded her.

Bent, gasping, spent, Sana let her forehead rest on the earth. Finally: "I . . . want Her, Natil."

Natil, having held her friend through the deep shaking of her sorrow, held her still, her head pressed against the dirty hair and her eyes clenched shut as though the sight of the stars within her could somehow make up for the vision that was no more. "I know, dearest sister."

"I want Her."

"She knows that."

"Goddess . . ." Sana shook as she dragged the whispered names forth. *"Elthia . . ."*

Drained, broken by the sight of one who was herself so broken, Natil nodded slowly, haltingly, silently. Words, even screams, were inadequate: they could not convey even a trivial part of her emotion.

Sana mumbled, coughed, sobbed once more. "I want Her." But then, lifting her head as though preparing to confront her failure, she caught her breath with a hoarse, abrupt sound, as though she were dragging in a soul along with the air.

Natil looked up, looked beyond the Circle.

Sana was staring fixedly. "Natil . . ."

Unbelieving, wanting to believe, Natil stared, too. "I see, Sana."

"What. . . ?"

"Stars, beloved."

Stars, yes. Where once had stood the dark trunks of pine and the soft glimmer of aspens, now there was only a black darkness spangled with stars. Gemlike, glistening, brilliant, they surrounded the two Elves, hung above their heads, shone from below.

The forest was gone. The clearing was gone. The stars were everywhere.

"What . . ." Sana was clinging to Natil. ". . . what does it mean? What's happening?"

"It means . . ." Natil drew Sana closer both for Sana's reassurance and for her own. Beyond the Circle, the stars drifted, gleamed. "It means that . . . I mean, I think it means that . . ."

Ahead, one star began to shine more brightly than the others. A nova might have kindled suddenly amid the quiet, stellar depths.

Natil fell silent. She remembered.

"It's calling us," said Sana. "Natil . . ."

"Let us go to it, then."

"Natil . . ."

The star brightened, grew, approached. In a moment, it was a perceptible disk, its radiance pounding at them, forcing them to lift their hands to shield their eyes. A sound like a wind arose, hissing through the darkness and the unnamed constellations, and as the star filled their sight, harrowed their minds with light so great that there seemed to be nothing else in the universe but light, eternal light, living light, their robes billowed in a roaring rush of Spirit. Sana clung to Natil, Natil to Sana, and the star drew ever closer.

Natil shut her eyes, but the light bore on, engulfing her, smothering her. Heat then, one terrible instant of unbelievable heat . . .

. . . and then the wind faded, the light faded, the heat diminished to mere warmth.

Dazzled, dazed, hoping, afraid to hope, Natil opened her eyes, discovered that she was on her hands and knees. Discovered that she was looking down. Discovered that she was looking at grass.

Unable for the moment to think, she touched it, plucked at a tender blade. Grass? Such lush, springtime grass in the middle of a forest clearing at the tail end of winter?

But it was not just grass. It was sunlit grass. Warm, yellow light was all about her, and Natil lifted her head to see a green land, sparkling and clear, soft as a child's dream of paradise. Distant mountains were clad in the feathery presence of trees, streams glittered like cascades of crystal, and fresh meads rolled away and down the slope on which she knelt with a hazy immediacy that seemed equal parts reality and wish. The sky was blue, shading from paleness at the horizon to ultramarine at the zenith, the air was scented with flowers and the clean odor of water; and all of it, all of it was bathed in radiance from the disk of solar brilliance that was rising into the eastern heavens as though determined to knit together every particle with warm and shimmering strands of sunlight.

She did not recognize this place. Here was no grassy plain, no dark sky full of untwinkling stars, no gleaming moon shining at the edge of the world like the polished ring of a Queen. Here instead was a spring that might have bloomed out of the fond, nimbus-wrought borders of the sweetest of fairy tales: a gentle land, a place of safety and light. There were no shadows here, not even a thought of pain, certainly not a shred of abuse.

And then she remembered Sana's cartoons, Sana's escape, Sana's—

Sana? Where was Sana?

She rose quickly, looking around. But Sana had already understood, had already risen; and, robes fluttering, hair flying, hands—healed and whole—waving wildly, she was racing down the slopes of her infant fantasy toward a lake that filled the valley below with the presence of deepest sapphire, toward the solitary figure of a Woman who, robed in blue and silver, stood at the meeting of light and water and earth and air, who, at Sana's approach, opened Her arms, caught her, and held her closely while she sobbed out the last leavings of her sorrow and her grief and her fear in the sheltering, nurturing, everlasting embrace of her Goddess, her Creatrix, *Elthia*.

EPILOGUE

Planh

CHAPTER 1

Sana Joy drove north from the TreeStar offices, taking the back streets so as to avoid the rush hour traffic. Kingsley College lay up near 50th Avenue, but in these warming days of spring, with the trees needing attention as they struggled out of another taxing winter, the flower beds waiting impatiently for tilling, and the lawns crying out for fertilizer, Natil was working late as a matter of course. There was time for a slow journey.

There was time, in fact, for everything.

Sana picked her way through the winding streets of the Bow Mar enclave, then struck directly across Lakewood. It was Friday, the end of her first week back at work. She had typed, made phone calls, taken letters ... and, yes, she had smiled, for there had been a brightness to the world, a kind of simple joy that had welled up from seemingly inconsequential things: the lie of light on a puddle of melt water, the flight of a sparrow as it fluttered to her open hand, the color of a freshly sharpened pencil, the precise click of the switch on an SVGA monitor. And there had been also a quietude that had lapped about the TreeStar offices, just as it had lapped about Buckland Employment and Style-On Salon and North Oaks Tree Service and the Colorado Department of Vital Records—anywhere, in fact, that there had been Elves—a quietude that would (she knew without the slightest doubt) continue indefinitely, continue forever.

In the passenger seat, wearing a knit cap that just covered the tips of his ears, TK rolled down the window to let in the crisp air. He was looking ahead, and he was musing as though he were seeing much more than the budding maple trees and the Siberian elms that lined the streets.

Sana smiled. Silence. Elven silence. There was not much to say, really. But: "How was your day, TK?"

"Oh ... all right." His voice was soft, quiet, pitched just loud enough to carry, no more. And there was an inflection in it, as there was now in the voices of all the Elves, that indicated an innate knowledge of another language, of words of wonder that had first been uttered at the kindling of a new sun. "Pretty much the same." He glanced at her, smiled. "Same shit, different day."

They laughed, and even TK's dark bass was touched with an edge as of silver. There would be many days, much shit. But they would get through, just as they had gotten through all the days of the past. They were Elves. They were Firstborn. They had seen the world created, and they would see it end.

And Sana had memories. Of Cambrian seas teeming with new life. Of the rain and muggy days that nourished the alternately placid and violent life among the skyscraper ferns of the Paleozoic. Of quiet love and the sound of Natil's harp beneath the trees of primitive forests. Of meadowflowers and butterflies, and of hands offered to hominid cousins who had not then hesitated to take them. And, true, along with those memories came others: burnings, and sorrow, and the slow encroachment of hate.

She did not remember her father. Freddy Joy belonged to the life of ... someone else. She was Sana. She had always been Sana. And as her memories stretched back into a past so profound that it swallowed up anything so paltry as a mere twenty-five years of human existence, so her vision stretched forward into a future of help and healing: the fulfilling of her elven heritage, the realization of her elven desires.

She had no doubts. Doubt had been erased forever when she had stood face to face with *Elthia Calasiuove,* when all the Elves, wherever they had been, had turned inward, found themselves called to their Lady, and come gladly, eagerly.

She flexed her slender hands on the steering wheel. Healed. Healed in body and in soul. Even the trial—

"Yeah." TK eased down into his seat. He seemed to be looking ahead, but the shadow in his eyes spoke of the past. "Didn't get shot at. Didn't have to kill nobody." His calmness remained, but there was a flicker of deep sorrow. "A pretty good week all 'round."

Sana freed a hand from the steering wheel, laid it on his.

They stopped at TK's apartment to pick up Rags, then continued north. Dusk still came early this time of year, and Sana had to flick on her headlights before they finally reached Kingsley College. Natil was waiting for them just outside the door of the groundskeeper's shed. One hand in her pocket, the other wrapped about the forepillar of her little harp, she was inspecting the oak trees that stood on the other side of the lot. She waved when she saw the Celica.

TK got out, hugged her, and shifted to the back seat, folding his long legs and turning crosswise in order to fit. Natil climbed in, settled her harp carefully on her lap. She gave Sana a kiss and Rags a pat on the head. *"Alanae a Elthia yai oulisi."*

"Manea," replied Sana, the language coming to her, as did many things now, effortlessly.

TK nodded thoughtfully. "You know," he said as Sana put the Celica into gear. "I still ain't sure what to make of all this."

Natil nodded. "Everyone was taken by surprise." She looked fondly at Sana. "Myself included."

TK sighed. "Damn near scared me to death when She showed up." Rags jumped into his lap, turned around twice, plopped down and went to sleep. TK folded his hands, worked the fingers back and forth as though kneading thoughts along with his knuckles. "All I can say is that it's a good thing She's black, or I just might've told you all to fuck off."

Sana pulled across the lot, but she stopped at the driveway and considered his words. "Of course She's black, TK," she said. "We're all black. What other color would She be?"

"Yeah. That's about the size of it, ain't it?"

Sana looked at Natil's harp. Natil did not usually take her harp to work. "Straight up to the Home? Or did you need to stop somewhere?" She could, she knew, have gone out among the stars within her, examined the flow of patterns and events that made up the day, learned without asking what Natil needed. But the homeliness of the simple, warm question felt good, as did the pleasure of the respect and privacy that they could offer one another.

"I ..." Natil looked down at the harp, then at Sana. "I had something in mind. I do not think that it can wait any longer." She ran her fingers along the smooth wood. "Do you know where Terry Angel lives?"

Sana suddenly wished that she had looked at the patterns after all. "Uh ... yes."

"Can you take me there?"

Sana instinctively turned to her stars. But not to look. To breathe the light, rather, to seek strength from the Woman whose presence, for now unseen, upheld and informed her inner firmament as the background of comforting darkness upheld and informed the stars themselves. "Yes. I can."

Her eyes were closed, but she sensed that Natil was nodding.

"But I need to tell you both something," Sana continued. "I was going to save it until we got up to the Home, but ... well, I think I'd better say it now. I don't think we're going to have to worry about Terry Angel, even if there's a trial. And there might not be a trial."

Silence. Traffic went by on the street. Sana let the Celica idle in the driveway.

"I got a call from Bob Sentry this afternoon," she said. "He'd just heard from some professors at Kingsley. They're willing to testify that Terry defrauded the college. And then ..." She caught herself and shrugged, a little embarrassed. "Well ... that's the story on Terry."

"What's the rest, Sana?" said TK.

"Bob ..." Sana wondered whether Elves could be embarrassed. Well, obviously, the answer was yes. "Bob got a letter from Edith Braun. You know, the surgeon at First Friends'. She offered to work on my hands. Free. The hospital is willing to donate the operating room, and she's convinced a hand specialist to help."

TK blinked. "What ... ?"

Sana was even more embarrassed. "They liked my harping. They think it helped. They want me to come back if I ever can. They might even be able to swing a paid position."

Natil and TK, she knew, were both looking at her hands, and she squirmed a little. Braun's offer, though generous, was now entirely superfluous, for since Sana had risen to her feet in the sunlit land of the Lady, her hands had been healed.

"Oh," said Natil, "I do not think that surgery will be required." She met Sana's eyes, smiled. "But you can definitely go back and harp."

"No Satanism bullshit?" said TK.

"No," said Sana. "Nothing." She thought of Phyllis, stifled a delighted laugh. "Braun apparently convinced them . . ." But she fell silent, suddenly wondering. Braun. Was it possible? And since the blood could be triggered off by interaction and empathy, then . . .

TK grumbled. "You leaving TreeStar? I don't think I like that very much."

Sana dragged herself out of her thoughts. She had gotten through. She would, if necessary, get Edith Braun through, too. "Not . . . not at first. I want to get this trial out of the way. And then I'll need a harp." She remembered her little gothic instrument, tried to forget the cracked wood, the smashed soundbox, the curling spirals of broken strings.

"I will help." Natil's voice was reassuring. "I have built a few harps in my life, and it would be best if you had one from elven hands." A shadow, then. "But for now it is necessary that I see Terry."

Sana winced. "Natil, you don't have to do that. Really. Bob can handle it. I can get through the trial. I've got the Lady to take care of me, and . . . well . . ." In truth, she admitted to herself, she simply did not want to go. Her memories had faded, and she had access to the strength and nurture that could only come from a direct vision of divinity; but she did not want to see Terry, his house, or anything that had to do with him.

But Natil shook her head. "Helping and healing, Sana. That is what we are here for. And now we can heal not only by word and by touch, but also by magic. If Terry is healed, then he benefits, and the case against you collapses. Let us defend you, then, not through conflict, but through healing." She passed her hands over her face, sighed. "I, for one, am tired of fighting. And I have already killed too much."

TK looked up. "Natil! You?"

Natil nodded. "Me. Take me to Terry's house, Sana."

She dropped one hand to the forepillar of her harp, gripped the wood. "I have healing to do."

Sana bent her head. The past was gone. Or was it? Later, perhaps, she could go to the Lady, speak with Her, sort out the feelings and the disappointments that had followed her even into immortality. For now, though, she clicked on her turn signal, pulled out into the street, and drove toward the house of Terry Angel.

Lauri was in her apartment, loading a few things into a shopping bag for the trip up to Elvenhome. Nothing much, really. Fruit juice, packages of hot dogs, rolls, a bottle of pickles . . .

Everybody was back now. Everybody was whole. Heather was as strong as ever. Sana's hands were sound, better than new. TK's legs were perfect. Once again, they could gather together without painful absences, and they could be Elves among Elves. No hiding. No words carefully chosen so as not to frighten the human beings. No concerns and sorrows that had to go unmentioned because no one who was not immortal would ever understand them. Just Elves. Elves and, now, their Lady.

Lauri finished up, rested her hands on the counter, stood for a moment with her eyes closed. *Elthia* was out there among the limitless stars. She was there for Elves. Lauri had seen Her, spoken with Her: such was the privilege of the Firstborn.

"And She's real," she murmured to herself. "She's . . . real. She's, like, regular." And she both laughed and wept because her choice of words was at once woefully incongruous and strangely fitting.

The patterns of starlight drifted and flowed, beckoning, but she shook her head. No. No patterns right now. "I'll get my head good and messed up if I start doing *that* all the time," she said, but there was a tremor in her voice, because there was something about which she did indeed want to consult the patterns.

She opened her eyes quickly, before the temptation proved too great. Wiping away the tears, she checked the shopping bag, nodded. Time to go. And if there was any sense of unfulfillment or pain in the prospect of seeing one particular face tonight (nothing much, really, just a little something that still hurt), she did her best to ignore it.

The doorbell rang.

"Oh, man, it's probably Jehovah's Witnesses or something. That's all I need." She wiped her hands, strode to the door, opened it.

Wheat was standing there. She was dressed for the office, and in addition to her purse, she carried a large tote bag. "Hi."

"Uh ..." Lauri felt the lump in her throat. Just a little something. The Lady could not fix everything, and it was idiotic to expect Her to. "... hi."

Cornflower blue eyes. Starlight. "Can I come in?"

"Sure." Uncertain, suddenly clumsy, Lauri stood aside. Wheat entered. Lauri shut the door. They both stood there, fidgeting, nervous.

"Did you ... uh ... want to ride up to the Home together?" said Lauri. "I was ... uh ... just leaving."

"I ..." Wheat dropped her eyes. "I wasn't going up to the Home tonight. Tomorrow, I think. But ... not tonight. At least ... I mean ... I don't *think* so."

"Oh." Lauri had the feeling that there was some meaning in Wheat's words that she was supposed to intuit. She was not intuiting it. "OK."

Wheat shifted her tote from one hand to the other, fidgeted some more.

"What can I do for you, Wheat? You ... uh ... need something?"

Wheat shifted the tote back. "Well ... well, yes." She shrugged, blushed. "Would you mind ... not going up until tomorrow?"

"Whatever you want." Lauri was puzzled. "How come?"

"Well ..." Wheat shrugged again. "I wasn't going ... until tomorrow."

Worse and worse. This made no sense at all. Lauri nodded. "OK." They stood, speechless, for several eternities. Lauri found that she did not know what to do with her hands. "I guess I thought that you'd be going up ... uh ... tonight. I mean ... with the tote and all that."

"Oh ... the tote. That's just some clothes and things." Wheat swallowed, looked up, looked Lauri in the eye. "For tomorrow morning."

"Tomorrow morning?"

Wheat blushed again, but the starlight in her eyes was bright, determined. "Lauri," she said, "I'll need some clothes for the morning . . ."

Lauri stared.

". . . if I spend the night with you."

It was a small house that was set between big cottonwood trees that had filled its gutters with leaves and twigs, a run down example of the postwar housing that had been troweled into the Denver suburbs like so much gray cement and then left to fall into a state of uniform decay.

Natil, though, saw beyond the house, beyond the neglect, beyond the implied history of what had come, with such complacent ease, to be called the modern age. As she, harp in hand, stood facing a porch that had needed paint for the last decade, she saw a vision of despair etched deeply into the webs of being that drifted and wove among her inner stars.

Oh, she could have allowed Bob Sentry to destroy Terry's story in the courtroom. Even from Sana's sketchy description of the aid that had suddenly been offered, Natil could tell that, blind or not, smiling or not, Terry could very quickly be reduced to a mass of contradictions. But Natil had seen the vagaries of human justice for a long time, and she knew firsthand the power of prejudice, and in any case, she was an Elf. They were all Elves: they had not put their hands on the smoking earth four and a half billion years ago in order to indulge in questions of winning and losing, they had not endured persecution, faded, and then returned in order to play zero-sum games. They were here to help and to heal. They were here for everyone. Even Terry Angel.

But the despair . . . She saw it among the stars as though it were a roiling nebula of sullen reds and blacks, a fist closing in upon itself until the nails dug deep into the palm and brought forth the blood. How much healing would it take to cure Terry? To cure him completely? She was afraid to consider it.

Sana and TK were waiting in the Celica parked at the curb, and she could have turned, gotten back into the car, and left. But she did not turn, she did not go back. She went up the walk, climbed the creaking steps, knocked on the door.

A long silence. A slow, tentative shuffling. "Who is it?"

"My name is Natil Summerson," she said. "I am the groundskeeper at Kingsley."

"What . . . what do you want?"

In shades of blue and lavender, Natil could see the shape of a face beyond the sheer curtains. Bandages. Dark glasses. The livid remains of caustic wounds.

She shuddered. She saw other wounds, too, less visible, perhaps, but no less caustic. Terry was alone and frightened. He had been alone and frightened for many years. "Your welfare," she said, and she let the elven accent come through plainly in her voice, hoping that some faint, instinctive recognition might reassure Terry that she was someone who wished him no harm.

Terry fumbled clumsily at the latch. "Natil? I remember you. You . . . you play the harp."

"I do," she said softly.

He hesitated. Even through the curtains, she saw fear on his face. "What . . . ?"

"I am here to help, Terry."

Hesitantly, almost unwillingly, he swung the door open for her. "Come in," he said. And then his smile went up, hoisted into place like the backdrop of an amateur play. "God bless you. God bless you. You're too kind."

Natil entered the house, knowing that, as had been the case since the beginning of the world, she was, in reality, not half kind enough. Even with all their ancient powers now returned, Elves nonetheless labored under limitations of which humans could not conceive. "Thank you."

Terry was nodding, beaming, but Natil knew what lay behind his expression. "Come sit down," he said. "It's so nice to have visitors. I can't do much by way of refreshments . . . I can't see, you know . . ."

Natil nodded. "I know, beloved."

". . . but you're welcome to anything you find in the kitchen. The city has been sending housekeepers for me. They keep everything quite well stocked." He lifted his head. A smile. "I think." And then his smile turned a shade too disingenuous, as though he were inviting her to consider the reason that he was sightless and scarred.

"Thank you," said Natil, "but I need nothing. I have, in fact, come not to take, but to give."

He stood, hunched as though with the burden of blindness, in the middle of the living room, his hands floating before him like pale antennae. "To . . . give . . ."

"I have come to heal you."

The shift in the patterns was like a blow to Natil's face. Hope, hate, fear, eagerness, lust—all cascaded through the webs of being in the space of a caught breath. But: "That's impossible," he said. "I have no eyes. Sandy took my eyes. Not to say that . . . that I don't forgive her. We must forgive one another—"

"And put one another in jail, Terry?" Natil felt the starlight within her turn to steel. "I think not."

His smile turned brittle. "God will judge us. I can't judge anyone. I can only fulfill my small part of the divine plan, make manifest in my own little way God's will—"

"I have come to heal you."

He stopped short. A long silence. The room was dark, very dark, but Natil did not need light in order to see, and light of any sort would have been wasted on Terry.

"Can you?" Again the cataract of emotions.

"I can. But if I do, you must, in return, do something for me."

Terry stood in the middle of the room, white hands drifting as though to sense the furniture, the walls, the movements of air, Natil's hidden meanings. "What?"

"You must tell the district attorney and the police the truth of what happened between you and Sandy."

"But—"

Natil fought for compassion. "Terry, beloved, I *know* what happened. I am offering you this grace." Grace? In return for payment? Was this, then, the first act of the reborn Elves? Natil's heart ached at the thought. "I will heal you. I will restore your sight. Will you tell the truth? Will you clear Sandy?"

He was shaking now, and Natil knew that behind those dark glasses, his useless eyes were widening with eagerness and damaged hope. His hands clenched, unclenched, his fingers curved into frantic claws. "I . . . don't believe you," he said, jerking the words out. "You can't do that."

"I can and I will," she said.

His mouth worked, and he half turned away from her. "God ..." His voice dropped to a whisper. "God ... would You love me then? Would You love me?"

Natil looked away quickly, but she could not so easily escape the sight of the patterns. The others, new to the vision, were still learning how to see. Natil, though, remembered. And she saw too well.

But she waited for Terry's answer, knew what it would be.

"You can ... ?"

"Heal you," she said. "Now. If you are willing."

With a burst of spasmodic effort, he clawed his way over to a chair, knocking over a lamp, sending a dish of religious cards clattering to the floor. His feet slipped and slid on the tiny paper pictures: the Sacred Heart, the Virgin, Saint Francis ...

He sat, his hands clenched together on his lap. "Please," he said, his face straining toward her. "Please."

"Will you clear Sandy's name?"

"I'll do it," he said quickly. "Please."

She examined him for a moment, contemplating her next words. "There ... will be consequences if you do not keep your word," she said at last. "We do not forget. Ever."

"I'll do it. Please ... oh, please ... oh, do it to me ..."

There was horror in the patterns, horror on both sides of Natil's harp as she sat down and set her instrument on her lap. As though unwilling to be forced into complicity with such sacrilege, her fingers felt reluctant and stiff when she put them to the strings. But over the last week, she had examined this action from a thousand different angles and had seen no other way.

And so Natil played. She remembered now. She had forgotten, in the course of the long years of fading, how much it hurt to find one's healing turned to harm, how futile it was at times to try to do anything. The setbacks and disappointments that the Colorado Elves had experienced, deep and real though they had been, were as nothing compared to the eternal futility that lay hugely behind the movements and the patterns of the Dance.

She played, weaving the strands of cause and effect as she wove the melodies of her harp. She did not look at Terry. She did not think that she could endure the sight of so much healing mixed with so much that was wrong, that could be nothing else but wrong.

For there was no healing, however profound, that could fill the gaping abyss of sickness that was Terry Angel. Long ago, perhaps, an Elf named Mirya might have been able to do something for him, for she had been able to heal minds as well as bodies. But Natil suspected that even Mirya would have found herself daunted by Terry Angel, would have been able to cure him only by transforming him, leaving him without a scrap of soul he could recognize.

Natil played, and Natil healed. And as she healed, she saw the futures altering. She saw already that Terry would keep his word, that he, in fact, would call a press conference the next day to proclaim his untruth with a vengeance that seemed to Natil to be one with the mutilations he inflicted upon himself with his teeth and his ropes and his lengths of barbed wire. And he would tell the police that he had lied. And he would call the office of the district attorney on Monday. Sana would be vindicated, cleared. Perhaps a few shreds of the ignorant and popular misconceptions about witchcraft might cling to her, but nothing that would last. Certainly nothing that would ever touch her in the safety of TreeStar Surveying, or that would affect her standing at First Friends' Hospital.

But Natil, deep in her music and healing, saw farther, too, and with a growing sense of futility and sorrow she faced the inevitable futures that fanned out from this act of compassionate healing like the lethal and undulating spines of a scorpion fish.

She saw the images, one after another, running their course and then repeating as the flickering and shifting potentials called them up before her: Terry pointing his automobile at the edge of a steep embankment out along I-70, holding his course steady until the wall of rock came up to meet him and sent his face through the splintering windshield. Terry taking up a razor blade and drawing long, deep gashes along the length of his forearm as the blood, hot and red, geysered up from the opened arteries and spread across the kitchen table in a viscous flood. Terry with a knife, hacking at his groin. Terry with pills, his face bloated and gasping. Terry with gasoline. Terry with a noose of barbed wire.

Was there, then, ever any real healing? Perhaps Mirya, long ago, had seen the truth of the matter when she had stood above the healed body and violated soul of Roger of Aurverelle: that only eternity afforded sufficient time in which to contemplate or attain renewal, that only the Immortal who had reached the end of immortality could find forgiveness.

Natil finished, dropped her hands, sat in darkness. She heard Terry breathing hoarsely, heard his dark glasses fall to the floor. Feeling the weariness then, feeling the fatigue, she rose slowly and flicked on the lamp. Terry flinched away from the light. His eyes were sound, his face unscarred.

Natil bowed to the dead man. "Remember," she said.

And then she left the room, left the house, returned to the waiting car.

She opened the door. Sana's face was pale. "Did you . . . ?"

Natil nodded, got in, slammed the door shut. "That," she said. "And worse."

And she did not speak again during the drive up to Elvenhome. She did not speak even after they had arrived. Instead, after nodding her greetings, she went up to her room and put her harp away. She changed clothes, donning for what she knew to be the last time her old garb of green and gray, and then she descended the back stairs and slipped out into the forest.

She was missed. Of course she was missed. And, late that night, when she still had not returned, Sana, searching for her friend, her teacher, her sister, went out among the stars, passed through the incandescence of solar fire, and entered the lands of the Lady. She went down the green slopes among the flowers and the soft breezes and the songs of birds, went down to the shore of a lake that glittered in the light of the sun that was always rising; and there, wrapped in the embrace of the Woman who was all, the Woman who loved without question, condition, or limit, she found Natil, crying.